First Thrills

High-Octane Stories from the Hottest Thriller Authors

D1051909

FIRST THRILLS

HIGH-OCTANE STORIES FROM THE HOTTEST THRILLER AUTHORS

*

Edited by
LEE CHILD

*

FORGE®

York

FIRST THRILLS: HIGH-OCTANE STORIES FROM THE HOTTEST THRILLER AUTHORS

Copyright © 2010 by International Thriller Writers, Inc.

All rights reserved.

A Forge Book
Published by Tom Doherty Associates
175 Fifth Avenue
New York, NY 10010

www.tor-forge.com

Forge® is a registered trademark of Macmillan Publishing Group, LLC.

ISBN 978-0-7653-9822-2

Our books may be purchased in bulk for promotional, educational, or business use. Please contact your local bookseller or the Macmillan Corporate and Premium Sales Department at 1-800-221-7945, extension 5442, or by e-mail at MacmillanSpecialMarkets@macmillan.com.

First Edition: June 2010
First Premium Mass Market Edition: August 2017

Printed in the United States of America

0 9 8 7 6 5 4 3 2 1

Copyright Acknowledgments

We dedicate this collection to
our friends and families for their unending support
and to our readers: you are the reason we do what we do.
Because of all of you, we can write what we love.
Thanks for reading!

Contents

Acknowledgments

A lot of people work very hard behind the scenes to bring a book to life. A collection like this involves even more work because of the number of authors involved. We would like to thank these unsung heroes:

Scott Miller and everyone at Trident Media Group, for their unending enthusiasm and hard work in bringing this project to life.

Our editor, Eric Raab, his assistant, Whitney Ross, and everyone at Tor/Forge, for taking our words and giving them a home.

International Thriller Writers' board of directors, for their inspiration and guidance. The ITW staff who work tirelessly to keep everything in working order. ITW's Debut Author Program, which provides new authors with support, encouragement, and camaraderie.

And, finally, our guardian angels: Lee Child, Steve Berry, Liz Berry, Jon Land, Kim Howe, and Eileen Hutton.

Thanks, guys! We couldn't have done any of this without you!

Introduction

LEE CHILD

As of this writing, the International Thriller Writers, Inc., organization—ITW—is a little more than five years old. It grew quickly and strongly and in short order became very good at what such organizations are supposed to be good at, but what was fascinating was the way it ebbed and flowed and tested uncharted areas and developed skills and interests that were new. Its annual conventions—ThrillerFests—were immediately distinctive. Its internal disciplines were immediately professional. But I believe its support of new members will be most remembered.

New authors face a tough challenge. Publishing was never an easy field to break into, and it gets harder all the time. Sometimes lightning strikes, but for most of us, a career is built slowly and painstakingly, year on year. The first couple of years are crucial. Early buzz means survival. Established ITW members know that—indeed, how could they not? By definition, they all survived that test, and they all remember it well. So, early and organically, the organization felt its way into a situation where sending the elevator back down became a major priority.

Not that it wasn't a two-way street. Our first debut generation organized itself into Killer Year 2007, and ITW recognized a great idea and ran with it. Some members of that class are now three or four books into stellar careers and are well on their way to becoming household names. The obvious quality of their emerging talent reinforced ITW's commitment, and the organization stepped up its efforts and developed a solid program of support. Inside the organization, debut authors get access to advice and mentoring, and they mix with the biggest names on an equal footing.

And outside the organization, they get exposure, in the kind of volume you're holding right now. This is a short-story anthology, and it's intended to function as a sampler, as a shop window. Read these stories, and you'll sense the talent the same way we did, and you'll be excited to pick up the participants' full-length novels, and buzz will build, and the participants will survive the crucial first year or two, and careers will be started, and the next generation of household names will be forged.

But publishing is a tough business, especially right now, and we were realistic enough to know that readers would be a little reluctant to buy a book by people they had—by definition—never heard of. So the call went out for big names to help. The idea was to sprinkle some major attractions in the shop window, to draw your eye. And the response was overwhelming. Eleven big bestsellers immediately offered to join in. Alphabetically, Ken Bruen, Stephen Coonts, Jeffery Deaver, Heather

Graham, Gregg Hurwitz, Alex Kava, John Lescroart, John Lutz, Michael and Daniel Palmer, Karin Slaughter, and Wendy Corsi Staub all contributed stories—free, gratis, and for nothing, simply because they remembered their debut years and didn't want to stand by idle. Among them they sell many millions of books a year, and we think they brighten up the shop window enormously. Their enthusiasm was so infectious, even I was moved to contribute a story.

But don't let the established names' glitter and glamour distract from the thirteen new names here. Again alphabetically, we are proud to present Sean Michael Bailey, Ryan Brown, Bill Cameron, Rebecca Cantrell, Karen Dionne, J. T. Ellison, Theo Gangi, Rip Gerber, CJ Lyons, Grant McKenzie, Marc Paoletti, Cynthia Robinson, and Kelli Stanley. Read them, and I think you'll agree that the only real difference between the big names and the new names is chronology. Fifteen years from now the new names will be the big names. Their talent is amazing.

Which actually explains why the eleven big names—plus me—agreed to help. Of course there's an element of altruism involved—unsurprisingly, since thriller writers are the nicest people you could hope to meet—but there's a little self-interest, too, because writers are first and foremost readers, and like any other readers, we want a constant stream of great new stuff to consume. This is our way of making sure we get it. So join us—you won't regret it.

First Thrills

High-Octane Stories from
the Hottest Thriller Authors

The Thief

GREGG HURWITZ

Momma came into the living room and asked where I got the Power Rangers pencil case and I didn't say anything. I just scrunched my eyes shut tight and pretended I'd gone away.

She said, "Tommy, you're a teenager. You can't keep stealing stuff from the kindergarten kids. If I call Mrs. Connelly and she says something went missing, you'll be in big trouble and you'll skip dinner."

The last part about skipping dinner floated in through my scrunched eyes and settled in my stomach and made it hurt. "I'm sorry," I said.

She sighed and pressed her hands to her curly brown hair. "I can't trust you, Tommy. And that's an awful thing."

When her mouth got like that it meant I should get out of her way for a while, so I went back to my room and sat on my bed. My dad left after I was born. I don't have a picture of him in my head. Just the picture on my bookshelf next to my comics. My favorite is Wolverine. No one knows how strong he is inside. He's got a skeleton made of adamantium. You never see it, really, just bits and parts, except one time he got in this plane crash and he burned down to his skeleton and I didn't like that at all. He looks like a normal guy, but I like that he's stronger than he looks, way stronger, beneath his soft skin. I'm fat. Momma says the proper term is "heavy," but I know what it's really called from the kids outside Mrs. Connelly's classroom at school. They aren't special, those kids, but I'd trade not being fat for not being special.

I could smell the pot roast from the kitchen and it made my stomach hurt some more thinking about not getting any because of a tin pencil case that you can see your reflection in even if it's wavery.

Momma says she can't trust me when it comes to stealing things. But that's not true, at least not always. Like I know that she keeps a shoebox full of money in her closet and I've never stolen that. And she has this pearl necklace and a CD of Frank Sinatra and I don't want those either. It's just some things I have to have. Like the long, shiny shoehorn I took from the Foot Locker. Or glowy green bubble gum people leave on sidewalks. We have a problem with the salt and pepper shakers from Momma's work, and she searches me before we leave just like the cops do black people on TV. And the cook at the diner just laughs and says, "Let him take 'em," and she says, "You have no idea what I put up with, Frank."

There was a knock at my door and she came in and

sat next to me on the bed and I closed my eyes again, tight. She said, "It's okay. I forgive you."

So I said, "Can I keep the Power Rangers pencil case?"

Momma said, "No."

I opened my eyes. I said, "I thought you forgive me."

She sighed again and said, "Help me, Jesus."

So I said, "Okay. You can give back the pencil case," because I don't like when she brings Jesus into it.

The doorbell rang, and she said, "Oh, that'll be Janice."

Ms. P works with Momma at the diner and they go to movies sometimes and do each other's hair and drink pink wine out of the skinny glasses. I followed Momma out to the front door. Ms. P said, "Who's that handsome fellow there?" like she always does even though she knows it's just me. Ms. P wears pretty magenta lipstick like in the sunset I drew in Mrs. Connelly's class. I like sunsets.

I didn't say anything about not eating pot roast and Momma must've forgotten because I took two servings and even had grape juice. I liked the sound of Ms. P's voice in our kitchen. We don't have people come over to our house much. Usually, Momma goes out and leaves a TV dinner in the microwave and the numbers already put in so I just have to push the green button. I watched Ms. P's magenta lips all through dinner. They crinkled and smiled. Magenta is my favorite color.

After, Momma said, "Why don't you go read your comic books?"

And I said, "I don't read them. I look at the pictures."

And Momma said, "Well, whatever, same difference."

I never know what she means by "same difference" since the two words don't really go together and they sort of cancel each other out if you ask me, but no one ever asks me. So I went to my room. But I didn't really go to my room. I opened and closed my door and then I tippy-toed down the hall again so I could listen to Momma and Ms. P. That wasn't very nice of me, but I'm home alone most nights so when I can hear other people talking in the house, it's a treat.

I hid behind the little half table at the end of the hall. Ms. P's purse was there, right by my head, and her keys, which had more key chains than keys, which made no sense.

Momma kept saying, "It's so hard, Janice."

And Janice kept saying, "I know, honey. I know. But he's a sweet kid."

And Momma said, "I feel so alone," which made me feel weird because Momma's not alone, since I live with her.

Momma said, "Sometimes I just miss grown-up company, you know?"

And Ms. P said, in a different kind of voice, "I know." Then she said, "There was that salesman I fixed you up with last year."

Momma said, "He was nice and owned a house, unlike the jerks I used to date. Maybe that's why it didn't work. He wasn't enough of a loser to interest me."

They laughed about that. Then Ms. P said, "I heard he met someone, moved to Cleveland."

"Maybe I blew it," Momma said. "He was very nice. Plus he wasn't hard on the eyes."

Then Ms. P said something in a low voice and they both laughed.

My shin itched so I reached to scratch it and I hit the table and Ms. P's keys jangled and I said, "Oops."

Momma said, real pointy-like, "Tommy!"

And I said, "Uh-oh."

And Momma said, "Come out here, Tommy."

And I didn't say anything. I just hugged my knees and squeezed my eyes shut but then I heard some rustling and opened my eyes and Momma was standing right there.

I said, "I'm sorry."

She said, "Remember the guest rule when I'm in the living room?"

And I said, "Oh yeah," like I'd just remembered it, but I don't think she believed me.

As I went down the hall, I heard Ms. P say, "You're too buttoned up in all this. You deserve something for *you*. A warm little something on the side."

But Momma just gave a giggle and said, "I can barely remember."

I went into my room and closed the door, which made me sad because I couldn't have their voices keep me company, but a closed door was part of the guest rule. So I played for a while and then read *Batman* until I got to the Joker, who always scares me too much because he smiles all the time but he's not happy. And someone like that you can't trust. And that's an awful thing.

After a while, I heard the front door close and then I heard Ms. P's car drive off and then Momma came in my room and stared at me and said, "You look ridiculous. Where'd you get that lipstick?"

The next night I walked home after school alone. The fourth graders followed a few blocks like they sometimes do and threw rocks, but they didn't mean anything because they threw little pebbles not like the real bullies. The fourth graders were just jealous because they weren't in the special class. At least that's what Mrs. Connelly says. And they never throw real rocks because they know if they do I'll sit on them and they don't like that very much at all.

I got home and ran into the kitchen and checked the microwave, like I always do first thing. But it was bad news. There were numbers punched in already, which meant that Momma was working a night shift and she wouldn't be home until after dinner. That made my stomach go all achy, but not big achy like when I ate all those hot dogs and threw up in the back of Ms. P's Mustang named Coop.

The doorbell rang and I ran over, excited, and opened the front door even though Momma always tells me not to. A guy stood there. He wore overalls with stains on them and he had big shiny arms and black tangly hair down over his eyes. A silver pen stuck up out of the bibby part of his overalls. In front of our house was a beat-up brown truck.

He said, "Is your dad home?"

And I said, "I don't have a dad. I live with Momma."

And he smiled a real toothy smile like in the soap operas and said, "I fix driveway cracks. I finished the house up the street a bit early today and I noticed you had some in your driveway. Cracks."

I said, "I didn't do it."

He stared at me sort of funny, then said, "Is your mom home?"

I said, "No."

He ducked his head a little to look past me into the house and said, "It's just you and your mom living here?"

I said, "Can I have your pen?"

He pulled the shiny silver pen from his overalls and turned it so it caught the light. It sparkled a bit. He said, "This pen?"

I said, "Yeah."

He said, "This one right here?"

I said, "Yeah."

He said, "You won't tell your momma I gave you this pen?"

"Oh, no," I said. "No sir."

He handed me the pen and walked back to his truck. After a few tries, his truck started and he drove off.

I went into Momma's room and played in her closet. She's got this one shirt that I like to pet that's all shimmery like snakeskin. I took it a few times but she always notices right away so I don't take it anymore. I wasn't supposed to touch it neither but Momma wasn't home and what was I supposed to do? Next I took the lid off the shoebox and looked at the rows of green bills. Momma gets paid a lot in cash—her tips, she calls it, but the tips of what?—and if she keeps it in the shoebox instead of a bank then she gets to keep more of it instead of the damn government stealing it, which is weird because I thought it was harder to steal from a bank. It's the only time Momma says "damn" except when she's talking about her damn life insurance which she has so she'll know I'll be taken care of if something ever happens to her. The damn life insurance costs her an arm and a leg and I don't even know where to start with how many ways that doesn't make sense. If something happened to Momma she'd go to heaven and I'd go to the home where some of the other kids in Mrs. Connelly's class live and they get movie nights and chocolate ice cream if they earn points by behaving well. If I behave well I don't get any points. But every Wednesday Momma buys me a comic book so I guess that's something.

A couple nights later, Momma came in my room. She was wearing her shimmery snake shirt, and makeup, which was weird since it was her day off work.

She said, "Tommy, listen. I have someone coming over for dinner, and I'd really like it if you could behave."

"Is she a waitress, too?"

"It's a *he,* actually."

"I don't want him to touch my comics."

"He won't touch your comics."

"Can we have pizza?"

"Sure. We can have pizza." She stopped in the doorway and her eyes looked a bit tired, even with the makeup. She said, "This is important to me, Tommy," and I wasn't sure what that meant so I didn't say anything.

I read *Batman* again, but still couldn't get past page eleven where the Joker comes in smiling that smile. So then I read one of my *Wolverines* and that calmed me down so much I didn't even notice Momma was at my door until she said, in a stiff voice, "Tommy, I'd like you to come meet someone."

So I got up and followed her down the hall. Who do you think was there but the guy in the overalls who'd given me the pen! Except he wasn't in overalls now. He was wearing jeans and a flannel shirt and a leather jacket and he smelled like cologne.

Momma said, "Tommy, I'd like you to meet Bo."

I remembered about the pen and about how Momma wasn't supposed to know, so I said, "Nice to meet you, Bo."

And he shook my hand and said, "Good to meet you, Tommy."

He came in and was all nice to me, slapping my knee and asking if I like football (no) or baseball (no) and saying he betted the girls were just crazy about me at school (no). Momma watched and smiled except when I said, "no," then she stood behind him and gave me that angry scowl, which was weird because Momma always taught me not to lie. But she also taught me not to talk to strangers and now here she was wanting me to lie to a stranger. It was very confusing.

The doorbell finally rang and Momma said, "Oh, that must be the pizza," and got up.

Bo said, "No, please, let me," and he pulled a cool wallet out of the inside pocket of his jacket. The wallet was leather with pretty Indian-looking stitching on the back that showed a sunset, the sun all yellow and wobbly going down into the ocean. Bo took out a twenty-dollar bill and handed it to Momma and she bit her lip and smiled at him then went in the other room.

I said, "I can eat eight slices."

Bo said, "I bet you can, chief," and then Momma came back in with the pizza.

Momma put the pizza on the kitchen table and said, "Thank you." Then she looked at me and said, "Say 'thank you.'"

I said, "Say thank you."

Momma hates when I do that but I pretend I don't know any better. She smiled at him and said, "He doesn't know any better."

He said, "I completely understand."

We ate. I ate a lot. Momma excused herself to the bathroom. Bo got up and looked around a little, peering through the door to the garage and into the closet door and the little den, checking out the rooms like he was gonna buy the place. When the toilet flushed, he sat back down in a hurry.

Momma came back in. She said, "I just need to clean up and read Tommy his story before bed. Unless . . ."

And Bo said, "What?"

Momma said, "Unless you want to read him his story. Then we could be done quicker and, you know, alone."

Bo smiled extra-wide and said, "I'd love to."

I went back and got in my jammies and he watched me while I changed, and smiled but it wasn't a nice smile. It was like the Joker's smile.

The water was running down the hall in the kitchen and Momma was humming to herself.

I climbed into bed and I said, "I want *The Hardy Boys*. The one about the missing gold. Momma and I are on chapter three."

Bo said, "Tough luck, retard. I'll read you *Goodnight Moon*."

I think he picked that one because it's the skinniest.

I said, "*Goodnight Moon*? You think I'm a baby?"

And he said, "No, I think you're a retard."

I told him he was jealous, but he just laughed.

He read it real fast, not even turning it so I could see the pictures. Then he put the book down on his knee. I could hear Momma putting the dishes away in the cupboards. He said, "This is a nice house. A real nice house."

I said, "Uh-huh."

He said, "I could get used to living in a house like this."

Then Momma walked down the hall and leaned against the door and said, "How *sweet*."

And he said, "It was nothing at all."

He walked out and she stayed behind and whispered, "Remember the guest rule." And then she closed my door.

But I didn't want to sneak down the hall and listen to them. I didn't like listening to him the way I liked listening to Ms. P.

The next day at breakfast, Momma said, "Do you like Bo?"

I said, "He's mean."

She said, "He's not mean. He read you a story, didn't he?"

And I said, "He's mean."

She said, "You're just jealous."

I said, "*He*'s jealous."

She looked at her coffee cup for a while, maybe checking for cracks. Then she said, "Sometimes grown-ups keep company for different reasons."

"Than if someone's nice?"

"Yeah. You know when you get lonely?"

"No."

"How lovely," she said, and got up to go to work.

That night when I walked home from school I saw Bo's truck outside. But when I went in, the numbers were punched into the microwave anyway, so that meant they were going out to dinner. They were sitting on the couch together and Momma's hair was wet, which was weird since she only showers in the morning. They were all smiley and their faces were red. Bo pretended to be nice to me but I went back to my room to read comics.

I heard Momma say, "Let him go."

They went out. Momma came in to give me a kiss first and she held my head and said, "You know I love you, right?"

And I said, "Me, too."

I ate alone. They got home late. I was watching TV. Momma opened a bottle of her pink wine so I hid in my room because when Momma drinks her pink wine she gets louder and her voice sounds different. She never gets mean, but I don't like her voice getting different. It's sort of like this one time when Wolverine was in the plane crash and it burned away all his skin and, well, you get the idea. I went to bed and got up later to pee and I heard them kind of grunting in Momma's room and I thought they were moving the bed because Momma likes to redecorate sometimes.

At Mrs. Connelly's the next day I drew a big pumpkin head with a mean, fake smile like the Joker's. Or like Bo's.

Momma was supposed to work because it was Tuesday, but there weren't any numbers on the microwave when I got home. I stood there for a long time, staring at the blank microwave, getting that hurt feeling in my stomach when I think there's no food. A toilet flushed. And then Bo came out.

He held out his arms like a scarecrow. "I'm your babysitter tonight," he said. "Your mom's working the night shift. Ain't I a nice guy?" And then he laughed but it wasn't like he thought something was funny. It was a Joker-smile kind of laugh.

I stayed in my room until I got too hungry and then I came out and said, "Will you make me a sandwich?"

He was watching a football game and he didn't look over at me. He just said, "No."

So I got the Salisbury steak TV dinner from the freezer and said, "Will you punch the numbers into the microwave?"

He said, "What numbers?"

And I said, "I don't know."

He said, "Retard," then he got up with a groan and shoved the box in the microwave and hit some buttons and after the ding went off the steak was all rubbery. I ate it anyways.

I didn't see Momma that night, but I saw her the next morning, dressed for work again. Bo was there, too. I think they had a sleepover. Momma's mouth got the way it did when I was supposed to leave the room, but I think

Bo got it that way, not me, and besides, I wasn't done with my Corn Flakes.

They kept talking in quiet voices like I couldn't hear but I was sitting right there.

Momma would say, "It's too soon."

And then he'd say, "It could save you some money, too, having me help out."

And she'd say, "Not in front of him." Or, "He doesn't do well with change." When she said, "Plus, we're still getting to know each other," he frowned and Momma looked like her stomach hurt.

Then he said, "Maybe that's how *you* feel."

She said, "I'm off at two. He doesn't get home until three. We'll discuss it then." And she went to put her hand on his shoulder, but he shrugged it off.

When I got home from school, the lamp by the couch was knocked over and that made me stop inside the door and scrunch my eyes shut. I was pretty sure I didn't do it, but you never know when you're gonna get blamed. In the dark, I said, "Momma?" but she didn't answer me.

When I opened my eyes, I saw that Bo's leather jacket was hung on the back of the kitchen chair. I went over and looked at it. It felt smooth and had lots of neat hidden pockets and stuff.

I said, "Momma?" again, but no one answered me. That almost made me forget how hungry I was.

I walked down the hall past my room and checked the bathroom. No Momma. I went in her room.

Momma lay on the floor with her mouth open. I thought she might be dead.

I said, "I want a sandwich."

But she didn't say anything back. Then I held out my toe and shoved her shoulder and she moved a little, but stiff, all at once. It was like the hamster babies in Mrs. Connelly's class, who also went to heaven.

When I turned around, Bo was standing in the doorway behind me. He looked at Momma, then at me. He said, "What'd you do?"

And I didn't answer because I didn't know what I did.

He shook his head and made a tut-tutting sound. He had a book in his hand. He said, "You like stories, right?"

I nodded.

He said, "Come on, let's get out of here. Away from what you've done."

And we went in my room. He pushed me onto the bed and sat in the chair like he did last time when he read me *Goodnight Moon*. He took out this skinny book and said, "Here's a book about a guy like you, retard. He's a stone-cold killer."

He read some then skipped a bunch of sections because there were no pictures and he probably got bored, too. There were these two guys who talked funny and one was tall and then there was a huge imaginary talking rabbit and someone died in a barn. That's all I figured out. I would have rather watched *Pokémon*.

He closed the book when he was done. "Did you get it?" he asked.

And I nodded because people get mad at me when I don't get it. And he said, "Every story has a moral. And the moral of this story is that people like you can't be trusted."

He walked out into the other room. After a while, I followed. He was wiping off doorknobs and the glasses in the sink with a rag.

He said, "People tell you you think different, right?"

I nodded.

Now he was wiping off the kitchen chairs. "I'm not really here, retard. I'm in your imagination, you hear? You ever seen *Pinocchio*?"

I said, "I want to be a real boy."

"That's right. I'm like Jiminy Cricket. Or like that big rabbit in that book. I don't exist. I'm a voice in your head. Got it?" He put on his leather jacket and walked out, using the rag to open the front door and close it behind him.

I stood there for a while. I went back into Momma's room and looked at Momma. There was blue around her eye. Then I went in my room and read *Batman* again, up to page eleven. I checked the microwave but there were no numbers and I wasn't sure how I would eat so I called 911.

The cops came in and looked in Momma's room. Then they patted me down like Momma does at the diner after her shift when she's looking for salt and pepper shakers. They sat me down on Momma's bed and asked me some stupid questions. Then another guy showed up who I knew was a cop from the shiny badge on his belt even though he was too lazy to wear a uniform.

He came into Momma's room, looked up, and said, "Holy Christ."

I said, "You'd better not say that in front of Mrs. Connelly."

He said, "Who's Mrs. Connelly?"

And I said, "She's Irish."

He said, "Let's get him out of here, Eddie."

Eddie said, "Okay, detective."

He and Eddie took me into the living room and I sat on the couch. Other cops were putting dust all over the glasses and the doorknobs and using makeup brushes to wipe it off, which didn't make sense because why put it there in the first place? They kept shaking their heads. I didn't blame them.

Eddie said, "Why'd you kill her?"

I said, "I don't know."

And the detective said, "What were you feeling?"

I said, "I wanted a sandwich."

Eddie said, "There's our headline."

I said, "I don't know why I would've killed Momma because I love her and she makes me sandwiches and I'm real hungry."

The detective said, "Aren't you sad?"

I said, "She's in heaven now."

And he said, "Well, there's that."

Eddie said, "You're gonna go away. To a different place."

I said, "I'm in a different place now. I ride a van to school and sit in a different classroom."

Eddie frowned and said, "Not like that, exactly."

One of the other cops stopped in my doorway and said, "You never know with these types."

The detective said, "I guess not."

The other cop said, "Hit her pretty good first. The black eye. Maybe it was accidental."

Eddie said, "Naw, the bruising needed some time to come up before he twisted her neck."

The other cop said, "He's got the weight for it," and then he walked off.

I said, "I must be stronger than I think. Like Wolverine."

The detective said, "What do you mean?"

I said, "He heals fast." I held up my hand. "No owies."

The detective took my hand in his, then my other, and

looked at my fingers. His hands were warm and they felt nice.

I said, "I punched Sammy White once when he tried to put Jenny Little's head in the toilet and it hurt my knuckles and the skin came up and Mrs. Connelly had to tape up my hands and put orange stuff on it that smelled funny and I cried. But not as loud as Sammy White."

The detective said, "I'll bet."

He let go of my hands and said, "Not a mark, Eddie."

I said, "Momma said she couldn't trust me. But she *could* trust me. I never took her Frank Sinatra CD or the shimmery snake shirt or the shoebox in the closet."

The detective said, "Shoebox? What's in the shoebox?"

"Momma's tips."

"How many tips?"

I held up my hands, like showing how big the fish was I caught. "About that many."

Eddie walked out. He came back a few minutes later and shook his head.

"There's no shoebox," the detective said.

"I guess I took that, too," I said. "I can't be trusted."

"Is that true?" the detective asked. "That you can't be trusted?"

"I think so. That's what the voice in my head told me."

"A voice in your head told you to do this?"

"Yeah. He's like Jiminy Cricket. He doesn't exist."

They looked at each other like when people say, "There you go."

I said, "But know what's weird about it?"

The detective was watching me closely now, with wrinkles in his forehead and his mouth a little open like

I sometimes keep mine before Momma reminds me to close it. "What?" he said.

"I have a picture of him, even though he's just in my head."

The detective said, "You do?"

"Uh-huh." I stood up and they followed me down the hall. I went into my room and dug beneath my pillow and took out the wallet with the pretty Indian stitching on it and opened it up and there was a little driving card with Bo's picture on it.

I said, "I stole it from his jacket and I'm sorry."

The detective smiled and said, "That's okay. You did just fine."

I said, "Can I have a sandwich?"

*

GREGG HURWITZ is the critically acclaimed, internationally bestselling author of ten thrillers, most recently *They're Watching*. His books have been short-listed for best novel of the year by International Thriller Writers, nominated for the British Crime Writers' Association's Ian Fleming Steel Dagger, chosen as feature selections for all four major literary book clubs, honored as Book Sense Picks, and translated into seventeen languages.

He has written screenplays for Jerry Bruckheimer Films, Paramount Studios, MGM, and ESPN, developed TV series for Warner Bros. and Lakeshore, acted as consulting producer on ABC's *V*, written issues of the Wolverine, Punisher, and Foolkiller series for Marvel, and published numerous academic articles on Shakespeare. He has taught fiction writing in the USC English Department, and guest lectured for UCLA, and for Harvard in the United States and around the world. In the course of researching his thrillers, he has sneaked onto demolition ranges with Navy SEALs, swam with sharks in the Galápagos, and gone undercover into mind-control cults. For more information, visit www.gregghurwitz.net.

Scutwork

CJ LYONS

The dead guy was a skinny old fart who didn't have the good sense to have a Do Not Resuscitate on file. He'd spend his last few years at a nursing home, decaying from a plethora of old-timers diseases. Diabetes, hypertension, strokes, kidney disease, cataracts, pneumonia, broken hip. After surviving all that, Mr. "I'll live to be a hundred and don't need a DNR" finally succumbed to food poisoning from the nursing home's egg salad.

What a way to go—covered in shit and no family left to give a damn. But the dead guy's bad luck was just the break Andy needed.

As an emergency medicine intern, Andy was usually assigned the most boring cases: peri-rectal abscesses, drunks who needed to detox, screaming babies with earaches. He was expected to perform all those piddling tasks that the nurses and techs were too busy for, like art gases and IV sticks and blood draws—scutwork.

Andy was destined for greater things. Scutwork was for fools, not future chief residents.

Yet, here he was, performing the ultimate in degrading scutwork: pushing a "death box"—the gurney equipped with a sealed steel box containing the fresh remains of a deceased patient—down to the morgue. And loving it.

Andy had been waiting for this opportunity all night long. Thanks to the kinky Goth chick he'd met last night at Diggers, the bar across from Angels of Mercy's cemetery.

Syrene was her name. "Think gy-rene," she'd told him while bending forward to rack the pool balls, giving him a glimpse of come-to-papa cleavage. "But instead of *gy*, you sigh."

Yeah, no points for intellect, but when she tilted her head to give him a full wattage glimpse of her baby blues highlighted with contact lenses to an impossibly brilliant shade, he'd found himself sighing.

Her hair was dyed jet black except for one sapphire streak that matched her eyes. Her eyebrows, ears, nose, and tongue were pierced. Celtic knots and intertwined flowers were tattooed on her lower back, a glimpse of one thorny rose peeked up from the black lace edge of her camisole, and an intricate Hindu pattern extended from her left ring finger across the back of her hand and up under the black leather biker jacket she wore over the peek-a-boo lace camisole. Completing her outfit were a pair of skinny jeans form fitted to her curves along with some heavy-duty shit-kicking Doc Martens.

And she was all his for the asking. Only he hadn't had to ask—all he had to do was hint at his profession and suddenly her tongue was in his ear, her hand down his pants, and she was whispering things he'd only dreamed of.

The rest of the night was spent at her place, time fractured by sweaty groans and moans and shrieks. He hadn't slept at all; she'd kept at him all night and most of the day until he reported for his shift at seven P.M.

Now at three A.M., he was wrecked, barely functioning. But it was worth it. The heavy gurney squeaked to a stop as he paused, sighing so hard it emerged as a whistle echoing from the steam pipes overhead. Man oh man, was it worth it.

He couldn't wait to see what she'd do for him after tonight. After he brought her the corpse.

All she'd asked for last night, her black lipsticked mouth pursing into the cutest pout this side of Hollywood, was a glimpse at a "real live dead guy."

She'd do anything for that, she'd said, rubbing her body along his. "Anything you want, baby."

Andy pushed the gurney faster, its squeaky wheel emitting a soprano wail.

Oh yeah, this was going to be *soooo* damn good.

He turned the final corner leading to the morgue. He'd seen no one the entire journey through the tunnels—no surprise, at three A.M., security would be busy in the ER with the after-hours bar crowd. Besides, there was nothing of value to bring anyone down here.

He punched in the code to unlock the main door to the morgue and the lights came on. Behind him, Syrene stepped forward from the shadows, wrapping her arms around his waist, her fingers greedily kneading the flesh below his bellybutton. He'd called her before he left the ER and told her how to get to the morgue. She'd made good time.

"Is that what I think it is?" she asked, her breath hot against his neck.

He shoved the flat-topped gurney into the cavernous room with a single push that sent it ricocheting off an empty autopsy table. Then he turned to Syrene.

She was all in black again, except for white eye shadow that made her look more like a corpse than the dead guy. Before he could say anything, she wrapped one leg around him and snagged his hair in her black-taloned fingers, pulling him into a kiss. The smooth roundness of her tongue stud danced along the inside of his mouth, in and out, mimicking the motion of her hips pulsing against his.

Syrene rocked back and forth, pushing him into the room and spinning him until he had his back against the wall behind the open door. She released his hair, her fingernails biting into his flesh as they scraped down his body, until she finally untied his scrub pants and slipped her hand inside to tease him.

She tightened her grip. Andy closed his eyes, his head banging against the door as he arched back. Just as he was about to come, right there in her palm, he smelled a curious mix of stale beer and cigars. Cold steel nudged the side of his neck.

"Time to get to work, bi-itch," a man's voice sang out, accompanied by a cackle of laughter from Syrene.

"Who the hell are you?" Andy grabbed his pants, fumbling them closed. "You can't be down here."

"Oh no?" The stranger smiled, revealing gold-capped teeth with skulls chiseled into the metal. "You gonna tell me what I can and can't do?"

He stood a head taller than Andy's five-ten, with muscles that screamed steroids, and was either a light-skinned black man or a dark-skinned Hispanic, Andy wasn't sure. What he was sure about was the big, black gun in the man's hand. Pointed at him.

Syrene stood on her tiptoes and gave the man a languorous kiss. The man locked eyes with Andy over her head, one hand caressing her butt, his aim never wavering. Andy was trapped in the corner behind the door, nowhere to go, no choice but to watch.

"What's going on here?" he demanded, using the sharp tone that usually worked on nurses in the ER. "I have to get back to work."

Syrene broke away from the man, melding her body into his side and watching with a Cheshire grin, one black-taloned finger tapping her lips. The man shoved the gun under Andy's chin, leveraging his head up, the gun barrel pressing against his larynx with bruising force.

"You ain't going nowhere, honeybear." The man's dark eyes dilated as he watched Andy squirm, trying to relieve the pressure on his throat.

"Don't hurt him, Dutch," Syrene crooned. "We need him."

Dutch? The guy sure as hell didn't look Dutch, but who was Andy to argue. Hell, Andy could only hope it wasn't the guy's real name—he didn't want anyone worried about him remembering little details like that. Worrying about the gun jabbed into his throat was more than enough.

Dutch released the pressure a microfraction. Enough for Andy to breathe and find his voice. "What do you want?"

"Nothing you'll miss. Just a body."

Andy yanked the drawstring on his scrub pants tighter and tied it into a knot. Christ, he was going to get killed by a couple of freaks who wanted to screw a corpse. "So take one, what do I care? I'm going back to work."

He stepped forward, trying to brush Dutch's hand aside. No go. The arm was as rigid as a steel I-beam, not going anywhere. Just like Andy.

"Did you bring my stuff?" Syrene asked, ignoring the standoff between the men. Ignoring Andy like he wasn't even there, like they hadn't spent the night and most of the day together. Guess since he wasn't cold and dead, he hadn't really turned her on.

Dutch shrugged his shoulder, releasing a black messenger bag. Syrene hauled it to an autopsy table and dumped the contents. Large colorful dart shaped objects spilled out. Then she removed something shiny and dangerous looking with ribbons of steel glistening in the overhead fluorescent lights. She slid it onto her hand. It looked like a medieval gauntlet turned into a torture device.

"I'll need juice." She dangled an electrical cord from her fingers.

"Let's get the body first." Dutch grabbed onto Andy's lab coat lapels and dragged him out of the corner. Andy didn't even try to resist; it was obvious the other man could easily out-muscle him. Better to wait for an opening to escape. "Check the one he brought us."

Syrene laid her steel torture implement onto the table and trotted over to the gurney Andy had transported down from the ER. She seemed giddy. Probably high on something. Like this was a fricking party. Whisking the sheet off as if she was Vanna White, she tried to unlatch the body box. "I can't open it."

Dutch shoved Andy forward. "You do it, Goldilocks."

Andy straightened and turned to face Dutch. "Stop calling me those names."

"I'll call you whatever I damn well please, bitch." Dutch didn't bother to use the gun to bolster his menacing tone. The scowl on his face and gleam of the gold skulls flashing from his teeth were enough. That and the ripples of muscle extending down from his hunched shoulders.

Andy didn't answer, but instead moved to the gurney housing the corpse, wheeled it alongside an autopsy table, and undid the latch that held the top shut. Opening the lid, he swung the side of the metal box against the tabletop, where it acted as a ramp.

Before he could reach for the body, Syrene leaned over the table and yanked the old man wrapped in sheets across to her. As she eagerly tore at the swaddled corpse, Andy swung the side of the box back into place, leaving the top of the gurney open, the large hollow box waiting its next occupant.

Which would be him if he wasn't careful. He glanced around the room. All the instruments that could help him, like scalpels and shears and the like, were neatly tucked away in glass-fronted cabinets on the other side of the room. The only thing useful near him was the walk in refrigerator that held the bodies awaiting examination. Maybe he could lock them inside?

"Damn, it's just an old fart," Syrene said. "The cops would never buy him as you, even after we torch him."

"Where are the others?" Dutch asked. "Don't you have those metal drawers like in the movies?"

"No." Andy walked over to the refrigerator and swung the heavy door open. A light came on automatically. "We keep them in here."

Dutch and Syrene joined him. Inside the refrigerator were several gurneys, each containing a body wrapped in clear plastic.

Dutch held back, obviously not happy about being

surrounded by so many dead people. But Syrene practically danced into the cooler, rummaging through the corpses like she was selecting the perfect side of beef. The expression on her face resembled the expression she'd had last night in bed with Andy, supposedly in the throes of passion.

God, how could he have been so stupid?

"Look, man," he tried to reason with Dutch. "You don't need me. Do what you want, I won't tell. It'd mean my job if I did."

Dutch slanted his eyes at Andy. He thought he might have a chance, began to edge toward the exit, taking a deep breath, ready to run.

"Found one!" Syrene chimed out, her voice bouncing off the steel walls like a rock skidding across an icy pond. "He's a big one. I need a hand."

Dutch jerked his chin at Andy. Shivering not only from the cold but also from the gun muzzle at his back, Andy entered the refrigerator and helped Syrene steer a gurney out the door. The corpse was large, over six feet, and dark skinned. Dutch glanced down. "Yeah, he'll do." He nodded. "Strip him, sugarloo."

Andy scowled at the name, but began to unravel the plastic enshrouding the dead man. To his surprise, as he worked, Dutch shrugged free of his jacket and stripped his shirt off, revealing a cobra tattoo encircling his waist and chest, the snake's head coming to rest over his left shoulder, staring back at Andy with glistening emerald green eyes. Syrene skittered around, humming an eerie cadence, plugging in her steel torture device and inserting one of the colorful darts into it.

"It needs to look old," Dutch said. "Can't look fresh."

Syrene frowned at him, rolling her eyes. "I know what I'm doing."

She plunged the needle end of the machine into the corpse.

It didn't take a genius to figure out the scam. Syrene was meticulously copying Dutch's tattoo onto the corpse. Andy was certain that dismemberment of the hands and head were soon to follow. Add a fire and the easiest way to identify the corpse would be through the ink trapped beneath the skin—ink soon to look identical to Dutch's.

What he wasn't certain of was why they kept him alive—or how long that would last.

"Why here?" he asked. "Just take him with you, do what you have to."

"Cops looking for me will never look here. Besides, if she messes up, we'll need to get another—the cops have pictures of my art."

"I won't mess up," Syrene grumbled, now wearing a pair of magnifying glasses as the machine on her hand hummed.

Cops looking for Dutch—Andy didn't dare ask what he was wanted for. Whatever it was, the man was desperate enough to add tonight's fun and games to his list of felonies. Hopefully homicide wasn't soon to follow.

"You don't need me," Andy tried again. "And someone will come looking for me soon."

"That's what's keeping you alive. Anyone comes looking, you're our fall guy—giving kinky sex tours of the morgue."

Andy didn't care for the chuckle Syrene and Dutch shared at that. Or the fact that as soon as Syrene was done, so was he. He considered his options. The refrigerator was his best bet—he could lock them inside. There was an alarm button, but they wouldn't use it—wouldn't want security to come get them out. The day shift would find them in the morning, cold but no worse for the wear—they might even talk their way past the day shift. As long as it wasn't his job on the line, he couldn't care less.

Okay, he had a plan. Now how to put it in motion?

Dutch did half the work for him. Syrene had him turn away and lift his arm over his head. That put him directly in line with the empty body box on the gurney.

"Stand up on that stool so I can see better," she ordered, peering over the tops of her glasses, wielding the tattoo gun like it was Michelangelo's brush. Dutch complied. Andy saw his chance.

"Need more light?" He reached up to adjust the overhead operating light that was extended on a swivel.

Dutch had his back to them and never saw the blow coming. Andy smashed the heavy, metal-rimmed light into the back of Dutch's head. He followed through with a tackle to the waist, toppling the larger man facedown into the gaping steel box. The gun flew free, sliding across the floor and under a cabinet.

Dutch shouted a curse, but it was muffled as Andy slammed the lid shut and latched it.

"You bastard!" Syrene lunged at Andy with her tattoo gun. She brought it overhead and plunged it down, aiming at Andy's face. Andy raised his arm and was instead impaled in the meaty part of his forearm. The machine whipped free of the outlet, its cord snapping through the air.

Syrene was on him, their weight hurtling against the gurney with Dutch inside, banging on the lid and shouting. They skidded across the room, crashing against the wall. She landed a knee on Andy's inner thigh, missing vital organs but still painful, and scratched his neck and arm. Andy tried to grab her but it was like wrestling a rabid squirrel, all claws and writhing limbs.

Finally, he grabbed the electric cord and wrapped it around her neck—not tight enough to strangle her but it got her attention. He doubled over, heaving in a breath, then yanked the tattoo gun out of his arm.

"Let him out," she whimpered, trying to lunge past him to reach the latch on the box. He hauled her back. "He's afraid of the dark."

"And I'm afraid of dying. You can let him out yourself—once you two are in the meat locker." He twisted the cord in his good hand, making her yelp but not cutting off her air. He shoved his weight against the gurney and rolled it into the refrigerator, then pushed her inside as well, flinging the tattoo gun in after her.

As soon as the door was secured, he collapsed against its cold steel and slid to the floor.

"Hey, man, where you've been all night?" Blake Crider, one of Andy's fellow interns, asked him when seven A.M. finally rolled around. "You hear about the popsicle people they found in the morgue?"

Andy had kept himself busy in the suture room—once he'd finished cleaning and dressing his own wounds. Wounds he hid under a long-sleeved T-shirt and his lab coat.

"What happened?" A sense of dread roiled in his gut. Had the day shift let them out? Were Syrene and Dutch going to come after him now?

"Some chick and dude were messing around, got themselves locked in the meat locker," Blake said. "The dude suffocated—couldn't get out of a death box."

Dead? No one was supposed to die. Andy swallowed hard, his arm throbbing in time with his pounding pulse, and tried to ignore the trickle of guilt that chilled him from the inside out. He had no doubt Dutch would have killed him, but still, he should have called the police, should have confessed everything, should have . . .

"What about the girl?" Had Syrene told the cops he was the one who let her in? If so, he could kiss his future good-bye.

"That's where it gets even freakier," Blake continued. "The chick must have been locked in there for hours—long enough that she tattooed a note on herself."

Andy could barely swallow past the fist-sized lump in his throat. "A note?"

"A confession. Don't know what it said, but apparently the cops are pretty interested."

Andy found himself nodding as if agreeing to his guilt even as he backed up a step.

"Then the chick hung herself with an electrical cord. Freaky-deaky," Blake said, wagging his eyebrows as if any of this was funny.

It wasn't. The two men in suits who entered the ER and were talking to the charge nurse didn't look like they thought it was funny either. They looked dead serious as the nurse pointed to Andy. He licked his suddenly parched lips, jerked his head, searching for an escape. Shuffling his feet, he finally sighed and gave up, slouching against an empty gurney.

Blake didn't notice the men approaching Andy, their hands reaching under their suit coats, splitting up so that he was trapped between them. No, Blake just kept on talking. "You have to admit, it was convenient as hell.

I mean, they're already right there in the morgue. Saved someone some scutwork."

*

As a pediatric ER doctor, **CJ LYONS** has lived the life she writes about. In addition to being an award-winning medical suspense author, CJ is a nationally known presenter and keynote speaker.

Her first novel, *Lifelines* (Berkley Books, March 2008), received praise as a "breathtakingly fast-paced medical thriller" from *Publishers Weekly*, was reviewed favorably by the *Baltimore Sun* and *Newsday*, named a Top Pick by *RT Book Review*, and became a national bestseller. Her second novel, *Warning Signs*, was released January 2009, and the third, *Urgent Care*, followed in October 2009. To learn more about CJ and her work, go to www.cjlyons.net.

The Bodyguard

LEE CHILD

Like everything else, the world of bodyguarding is split between the real and the phony. Phony bodyguards are just glorified drivers, fashion accessories, big men in suits chosen for their size and shape and appearance, not usually paid very much, not usually very skilled. Real bodyguards are technicians, thinkers, trained men with experience. They can be small, as long as they can think and endure. As long as they can be useful, when the time comes.

I am a real bodyguard.

Or at least, I was.

I was trained in one of those secret army units where close personal protection is part of the curriculum. I plied that trade among many others for a long time, all over the world. I am a medium-sized man, lean, fast, full of stamina. Not quite a marathon runner, but nothing like a weightlifter. I left the army after fifteen years of service and took jobs through an agency run by a friend. Most of the work was in South America. Most of the engagements were short.

I got into it right when the business was going crazy.

Kidnapping for ransom was becoming a national sport in most of South America. If you were rich or politically connected, you were automatically a target. I worked for American corporate clients. They had managers and executives in places like Panama and Brazil and Colombia. Those people were considered infinitely rich and infinitely connected. Rich, because their employers were likely to bail them out, and those corporations were capitalized in the hundreds of billions. Connected, because ultimately the government would get involved. There was no greater sense of connection than a bad guy knowing he could talk in a jungle clearing somewhere and be heard in the White House.

But I never lost a client. I was a good technician, and I had good clients. All of them knew the stakes. They worked with me. They were biddable and obedient. They wanted to do their two years in the heat and get back alive to their head offices and their promotions. They kept their heads down, didn't go out at night, didn't really go anywhere except their offices and their job sites. All transport was at high speed in protected vehicles, by varied routes, and at unpredictable times. My clients never complained. Because they were working, they tended to accept a rough equivalent of military discipline. It was all relatively easy, for a while.

Then I left my friend's agency and went into business for myself.

The money was better. The work was worse. The first year, I traveled the world, learning. I learned to stay away from people who wanted a bodyguard purely as a status symbol. There were plenty of those. They made me miserable, because ultimately there wasn't much for me to do. Too many times I ended up running errands while my skills eroded. I learned to stay away from people who weren't in genuine need, too. London is a dangerous town and New York is worse, but nobody truly needs a bodyguard in either place. Again, not much to do. Boring, and corrosive. I freely admit that my own risk addiction drove my decisions.

Including my decision to work for Anna.

I'm still not allowed to mention her second name. It was in my contract, and my contract binds me until I die. I heard about the opening through a friend of a friend. I was flown to Paris for the interview. Anna turned out to be twenty-two years old, unbelievably pretty, dark, slender, mysterious. First surprise, she conducted the interview herself. Mostly in a situation like that the father handles things. Like hiring a bodyguard is the same kind of undertaking as buying a Mercedes convertible for a birthday present. Or arranging riding lessons.

But Anna was different.

She was rich in her own right. She had an inheritance from a separate branch of the family. I think she was actually richer than her old man, who was plenty rich to start with. The mother was rich, too. Separate money again. They were Brazilian. The father was a businessman and a politician. The mother was a TV star. It was a triple whammy. Oceans of cash, connections, Brazil.

I should have walked away.

But I didn't. I suppose I wanted the challenge. And Anna was captivating. Not that a personal relationship would have been appropriate. She was a client and I was close to twice her age. But from the first moment I knew she would be fun to be around. The interview went well. She took my formal qualifications for granted. I have scars and medals and commendations. I had never lost a client. Anything else, she wouldn't have been talking to me, of course. She asked about my worldview, my opinions, my tastes, my preferences. She was interested in compatibility issues. Clearly she had employed bodyguards before.

She asked how much freedom I would give her.

She said she did charity work in Brazil. Human rights, poverty relief, the usual kind of thing. Hours and days of travel in the slums and the outlying jungle. I told her about my previous South American clients. The corporate guys, the oil men, the minerals people. I told her that the less they did, the safer they got. I described their normal day. Home, car, office, car, home.

She said no to that.

She said, "We need to find a balance."

Her native language was Portuguese, and her English was good but lightly accented. She sounded even better than she looked, which was spectacular. She wasn't one of those rich girls who dresses down. No ripped jeans for her. For the interview she was wearing a pair of plain black pants and a white shirt. Both garments looked new, and I was sure both came from an exclusive Paris boutique.

I said, "Pick a number. I can keep you a hundred percent safe by keeping you here in your apartment twenty-four/seven, or you can be a hundred percent unsafe by walking around Rio on your own all day."

"Seventy-five percent safe," she said. Then she shook her head. "No, eighty."

I knew what she was saying. She was scared, but she wanted a life. She was unrealistic.

I said, "Eighty percent means you live Monday through Thursday and die on Friday."

She went quiet.

"You're a prime target," I said. "You're rich, your mom is rich, your dad is rich, and he's a politician. You'll be the best target in Brazil. And kidnapping is a messy business. It usually fails. It's usually the same thing as murder, just delayed by a little. Sometimes delayed by not very much."

She said nothing.

"And it's sometimes very unpleasant," I said. "Panic, stress, desperation. You wouldn't be kept in a gilded cage. You'd be in a jungle hut with a bunch of thugs."

"I don't want a gilded cage," she said. "And you'll be there."

I knew what she was saying. She was twenty-two years old.

"We'll do our best," I said.

She hired me there and then. Paid me an advance on a very generous salary and asked me to make a list of what I needed. Guns, clothes, cars. I didn't ask for anything. I thought I had what I needed.

I thought I knew what I was doing.

A week later we were in Brazil. We flew first class all the way, Paris to London, London to Miami, Miami to Rio. My choice of route. Indirect and unpredictable. Thirteen hours in the air, five in airport lounges. She was a pleasant companion, and a cooperative client. I had a friend pick us up in Rio. Anna had budget to spare, so I decided to use a separate driver at all times. That way, I would get more chance to concentrate. I used a Russian guy I had met in Mexico. He was the finest defensive driver I had ever seen. Russians are great with cars. They have to be.

Moscow was the only place worse than Rio for mayhem.

Anna had her own apartment. I had been expecting a gated place in the suburbs, but she lived right in town. A good thing, in a way. One street entrance, a doorman, a concierge, plenty of eyes on visitors even before the elevator bank. The apartment door was steel and it had three locks and a TV entryphone. I like TV entryphones a lot better than peepholes. Peepholes are very bad ideas. A guy can wait in the corridor and as soon as the lens goes dark he can fire a large caliber handgun right through it, into your eye, into your brain, out the back of your skull, into your client if she happens to be standing behind you.

So, a good situation. My Russian friend parked in the garage under the building and we took the elevator straight up and got inside and locked all three locks and settled in. I had a room between Anna's and the door. I'm a light sleeper. All was well.

All stayed well for less than twenty-four hours.

Jet lag going west wakes you up early. We were both up at seven. Anna wanted breakfast out. Then she planned to go shopping. I hesitated. The first decision sets the tone. But I was her bodyguard, not her jailer. So I agreed. Breakfast, and shopping.

Breakfast was OK. We went to a hotel, for a long slow meal in the dining room. The place was full of bodyguards. Some were real, some were phony. Some were at separate tables; some were eating with their clients. I ate with Anna. Fruit, coffee, croissants. She ate more than I did. She was full of energy and raring to go.

It all went wrong with the shopping.

Later I realized my Russian friend had sold me out. Because usually the first day is the easiest. Who even knows you're in town? But my guy must have made a well-timed phone call. Anna and I came out of a store and our car wasn't on the curb. Anna was carrying her own packages. I had made clear that she would from the start. I'm a bodyguard, not a porter, and I needed my hands free. I glanced left, and saw nothing. I glanced right, and saw four guys with guns.

The guys were close to us and the guns were small automatics, black, new, still dewy with oil. The guys were small, fast, wiry. The street was busy. Crowds behind me, crowds behind the four guys. Traffic on my left, the store doorway on my right. Certain collateral damage if I pulled out my own gun and started firing. Protracted handgun engagements always produce a lot of stray bullets. Innocent casualties would have been high.

And I would have lost, anyway. Winning four-on-one gun battles is strictly for the movies. My job was to keep Anna alive, even if it was just for another day. Or another hour. The guys moved in and took my gun and stripped Anna of her packages and pinned her arms. A white car pulled up on cue and we were forced inside. Anna first, then me. We were sandwiched on the backseat between two guys who shoved guns in our ribs. Another guy in the front seat twisted around and pointed another gun at us. The driver took off fast. Within a minute we were deep into a tangle of side streets.

I had been wrong about the jungle hut. We were taken to an abandoned office building inside the city limits. It was built of brick and painted a dusty white. I had been right about the thugs. The building teemed with them. There was a whole gang. At least forty of them. They were dirty and uncouth and most of them were leering openly at Anna. I hoped they weren't going to separate us.

They separated us immediately. I was thrown in a cell that had once been an office. There was a heavy iron grille over the window and a big lock on the door. A bed, and a bucket. That was all. The bed was a hospital cot made of metal tubes. The bucket was empty, but it hadn't been empty for long. It smelled. I was put in handcuffs with my arms pinned behind my back. My ankles were shackled and I was dumped on the floor. I was left alone for three hours.

Then the nightmare started.

The lock rattled and the door opened and a guy came in. He looked like the boss. Tall, dark, a wide unsmiling mouth full of gold teeth. He kicked me twice in the ribs and explained that this was a political kidnapping. Some financial gain was expected as a bonus, but the real aim was to use Anna as leverage against her politician father to get a government inquiry stopped. She was the ace up their sleeve. I was expendable. I would be killed within a few hours. Nothing personal, the guy said. Then he said I would be killed in a way that his men would find entertaining. They were bored, and he owed them a diversion. He was planning to let them decide the exact manner of my demise.

Then I was left alone again.

Much later I learned that Anna was locked in a similar room two floors away. She was not in handcuffs or ankle shackles. She was free to move around, as befitted her elevated status. She had an iron hospital bed, the same as mine, but no bucket. She had a proper bathroom. And a table, and a chair. She was going to be fed. She was valuable to them.

And she was brave.

As soon as the door locked she started looking for a

weapon. The chair was a possibility. Or she could smash the bathroom sink and use a jagged shard of porcelain as a knife. But she wanted something better. She looked at the bed. It was bolted together with iron tubes, flattened and flanged at the ends. The mattress was a thin thing covered with striped ticking. She hauled it off and dumped it on the floor. The bed had a base of metal mesh suspended between two long tubes. The long tubes had a single bolt through each end. If she could get a tube free she would have a spear six-feet six-inches long. But the bed frame was painted and the bolts were jammed solid. She tried to turn them with her fingers, but it was hopeless. The room was hot and she had a sheen of sweat on her skin and her fingers just slipped. She put the mattress back and turned her attention to the table.

The table had four legs and a veneered top about three feet square. Surrounding it was a short bracing skirt. Upside down it would have looked like a very shallow box. The legs were bolted onto small angled metal braces that were fixed to the skirt. The bolts were cheap steel, a little brassy in color. The nuts were wing nuts. They could be turned easily by hand. She unfastened one leg and hid the nut and the bolt. Left the leg where it was, propped up and vertical.

Then she sat on the bed and waited.

After an hour she heard footsteps in the corridor. Heard the lock turn. A man stepped into the room, carrying a tray of food. He was young. Presumably low man on the totem pole, confined to kitchen duties. He had a gun on his hip. A black automatic pistol, big and boxy and brand new.

Anna stood up and said, "Put the tray on the bed. I think there's something wrong with the table."

The boy lowered the tray onto the mattress.

Anna asked, "Where's my friend?"

"What friend?"

"My bodyguard."

"Downstairs," the boy said.

Anna said nothing.

The boy said, "What's wrong with the table?"

"One of the legs is loose."

"Which one?"

"This one," Anna said, and whipped the leg out. She swung it like a baseball bat and caught the guy square in the face with it. The edge of the corner hit him on the bridge of the nose and punched a shard of bone backwards into his brain pan. He was dead before he hit the floor. Anna took the gun off his hip and stepped over his body and walked to the door.

The gun said *Glock* on the side. There was no safety mechanism on it. Anna hooked her finger around the trigger and stepped out to the corridor. "Downstairs," the boy had said. She found a staircase and went down and kept on going.

By that point they had dragged me to a large ground floor room. A conference hall, maybe, once upon a time. There were thirty-nine people in it. There was a small raised stage with two chairs on it. The boss man was in one of them. They put me in the other. Then they all started discussing something in Portuguese. How to kill me, I presumed. How to maximize their entertainment. Halfway through a door opened in the back of the room. Anna stepped in, swinging a large handgun from side to side in front of her. Reaction was immediate. Thirty-eight men pulled out weapons of their own and pointed them at her.

But the boss man didn't. Instead he yelled an urgent

warning. I didn't speak his language, but I knew what he was saying. He was saying, *Don't shoot her! We need her alive! She's valuable to us!* The thirty-eight guys lowered their guns and watched as Anna moved through them. She reached the stage. The boss man smiled.

"You've got seventeen shells in that gun," he said. "There are thirty-nine of us here. You can't shoot us all."

Anna nodded.

"I know," she said. Then she turned the gun on herself and pressed it into her chest. "But I can shoot myself."

After that, it was easy. She made them unlock my cuffs and my chains. I took a gun from the nearest guy and we backed out of the room. And we got away with it. Not by threatening to shoot our pursuers, but by Anna threatening to shoot herself. Five minutes later we were in a taxi. Thirty minutes later we were home.

A day later I quit the bodyguarding business. Because I took it as a sign. A guy who needs to be rescued by his client has no future, except as a phony.

*

LEE CHILD is the number-one internationally bestselling author of thirteen Reacher thrillers, including the *New York Times* bestsellers *The Enemy, One Shot, The Hard Way*, and the number-one bestselling novels *Bad Luck and Trouble* and *Nothing to Lose*. His debut, *Killing Floor*, won both the Anthony and the Barry Awards for Best First Mystery, and *The Enemy* won both the Barry and the Nero Awards for Best Novel. Child, a native of England and a former television director, lives in New York City. His fourteenth Reacher thriller, *61 Hours*, was published in September 2010.

Last Supper

RIP GERBER

Apertivo

C **hris,** I'm pregnant."

Everything about that dinner is vivid, crystallized in my mind: the smell of garlic-roasted cauliflower on the stove, the honeyed taste of her lips, the toasty softness of her body . . . such a delicious sensory hash does not fade with time, it grows stronger, more complex, like a Chateau Mouton Rothschild or Italian Caciocavallo Podolico cheese. Delectably unforgettable.

Like murder.

Nine o'clock, Monday night, seems like a million years ago. Mary and I were cooking together for the first time in months. That evening she had planned a surprise, even left work early to pick up provisions at the farmer's market.

"Tell me," I teased.

"Get back to work. Chop those onions," she replied.

"Not even a hint?"

My pleas fell on wooden ears. I would sneak behind her as she worked, pushing myself into her, kissing the back of her neck, slipping my hands under her brown chef's apron, sucking in the smell of her sweet blonde hair. And she'd bark at me like a mess sergeant: Trim the meat! Fire up the grill! Pour yourself some Chardonnay!

"No wine for love bug?" I asked.

"Uh-uh."

"Not even a sip?"

That's when I knew. I rested my chin on her shoulder, grabbed her belly from behind. "Can't feel anything."

"You're in there baking, trust me," she whispered, then we kissed.

"So much for joining the clergy."

She laughed. On our first date back in New York I had been wearing black pants, a black turtleneck, and a black sports jacket. She had called me The Priest. Ever since, whenever I wore black like I had that night, she'd joke that I would have made one hot reverend, a priest with benefits, a pope that poked. The clergy jokes were endless, she couldn't get enough. The curse of a Catholic upbringing.

While she chopped and steamed and grated, I took my wine into the living room, my head spinning. What else could I do? I was going to be a dad. I flipped channels between commercials and the news and the Cowboys Monday night game.

"Damn, I forgot mushrooms for the oysters," she shouted, her voice muffled under the stove exhaust fan. "Honey, can you go around the corner and get some buttons?"

"What are those?"

"It doesn't matter. Porcinis, shiitakes . . . whatever they have."

"Hey, Peter Radin's on TV!" I said, sitting up. Ten years ago Peter and I joined the Guardsmen together, a Houston charity that raised money for inner-city youth. While I stayed in software, he moved up in state politics; now he was running for the board of supes. "God, Peter looks great."

"Are you getting those mushrooms for me?" Mary shouted.

"In a few minutes? I can never tell those damn things apart."

"That's OK, I could use the walk. Just keep stirring my soup."

"Thanks, honey." Then she left.

Just keep stirring my soup.

The last words I would ever hear my wife say.

Insalate e Zuppa

It was dead cold that night in Houston. The Prince Market at the corner of King and Jensen glowed yellow like a beacon, drawing the killer out of the shadows. The streets were empty, dark. All clear. His stomach gurgled, but tonight he would feast on vengeance. Tonight, at last, he would kill the Turk.

"I've been patient," he muttered to himself. "Now it's Puffer time."

He entered the quaint grocery. All quiet except for the trumpets blaring from the television that hung from the ceiling. Puff was hungry; he hadn't eaten all day. Part of the plan. When the Turk bastard shot his son in this very store two years ago, his boy had been starving, too. His boy wasn't some gangbanger, he was just hungry; all he wanted was the ninety bucks in the register and a stupid box of cereal, but the Turk wasted him.

Now it was Puff's turn to feed.

Puff strolled up to the market, his 250 pounds gliding with grace and purpose. He flashed a yellow crocodile grin at the Turk, but the Turk did not look up. Puff shoved a box of Cap'n Crunch in his jacket, same cereal his son had grabbed that night. For poetry.

Time to say grace. Puff pulled the shank from his back pocket. Holding it tightly to his side, he approached the counter.

"Empty it." He flashed the switchblade so the Turk could see. The Turk kept a gun back there, probably the same one he used to kill his son, but it was stashed on the other side of the coffee maker, well out of reach. Puff had been watching, paying attention. Revenge demanded sweet, sweet patience. Now he had the Turk cold, at knifepoint. All according to plan.

"Are these buttons or meadows?" a voice behind him asked.

Instinct took over; Puff turned like a panther, blade swinging wildly. The knife slid through the woman's brown apron and into her chest like turkey meat. She screamed. Puff's eyes met hers and she staggered into him.

"I'm sorry—Puff didn't mean to—"

A gunshot sounded. Puff felt the bullet pierce his back and rip through his gut, clean through. They fell together in a herringbone pattern of blood-splattered limbs. The bastard Turk was screaming behind him. Trumpets blared.

Black blood seeped across the linoleum floor, his blood and the woman's blood mixing as one, the syrupy mess souping around the spilled white mushrooms.

Strangely, as death approached, the hole in his kidney did not alleviate the pain of Puff's hunger.

Primo

"Father, could you pass the juice?"

Seven years have come and gone. I push myself away from the table with a satisfied grunt, pleasantly stuffed with lamb and spring vegetables and red potatoes drizzled in olive butter. Passover, and I've never felt so stuffed, so content. My dining room is buzzing with conversation, laughter, the clinking of forks and knives on antique china. When Mary's mother brought over those boxes right after the funeral, I assumed it was part of her own therapy, not mine. When was I going to use twenty-four place settings of yellowed, chipped Dresden?

After a year the answer became clear.

Every Monday.

I reach for the porringer. "It's au jus, not juice, and don't soak it." I pass Peter Radin the warm bowl. "You don't want the rosemary infusion to overpower the lamb."

Peter pours it on, then taps his fork on the gravy boat. "A toast, everyone." Glasses rise. "God is great and God is good, but thank the Lord for Chris and this goddamn great food. To the best chef on heaven and earth."

I scowl, a rousing cheer ensues, the eating continues.

Mary would have been thirty-five this year, and I would have been her minister that mambos, her rector that rides. Since the stabbing my hair has turned from sleek black to snow bank, I've put on a few pounds, and I wear thick glasses that make me look like Martin Scorsese, not *The Last Temptation of Christ* Scorsese but *The Departed* Scorsese. And Peter has lost weight, damn him; he runs two triathlons a year and as the new Texas state attorney general, he's the closest I now get to the devil.

And we're still best friends.

But I never told him about how I held Mary that night in that common store, how the mushrooms I should have fetched hovered over her blood like sourdough croutons on roasted tomato soup. I never mentioned how the cutlery in my kitchen included a perfect match to the 9-inch Switchblade Stilleto CarbonFiber that slit open my wife's belly and our unnamed fetus, a cut made by a killer with three priors, a cut which prompted a .38 caliber bullet to explode out of the cashier's Smith & Wesson Model 60 Double Action revolver and into her heart, the same gun I bought on eBay for $423 six weeks after my wife was pronounced dead on arrival at 9:11 that October night. I never told anyone about those things.

At first, the only way I knew to avenge her senseless death was eye-for-an-eye. I bought the knife, I bought the gun. I drained my savings for lawyers and fought like hell to get the death penalty for that monster. Cook the bastard, let his foul Puff ass burn in hell.

The jury agreed. Puff received the death penalty and a dank sixty-square-foot pen at Polunsky Unit in Huntsville.

And I started a new path.

It began with the parish priest, then the diocese's vocations director, then the retreats, then five years in seminary. After I passed the psychological examination, barely, I was called to the Holy Order and ordained a transitional deacon. I took a vow of celibacy and obedience. Never again would I be Mary's fornicating friar, her bishop that boinks.

Oh, Mary, why didn't I leave you safe and warm in that kitchen?

Becoming a man of the cloth is supposed to cure the nightmares. It doesn't. Sure, all the activities and services and confessions and consultations help pass the time, and I don't pull that Smith & Wesson Model 60 out from under the bed as much anymore, but I still feel empty inside.

Except when I cook.

The weekly dinners started when I was in seminary, on a Monday night, the night he took Mary away from me. Every Monday I cooked that same dinner: French onion soup, cauliflower with oyster sauce, grilled Tuscan chops, stir-fry vegetables. Same portions, same ingredients, same order.

And for months I just threw it all out.

Then I invited a few members of the laity over, parishioners suffering from grief and loss. They invited others. It became a weekly ritual, I had to accept reservations. I was featured in the *Dallas Morning News*. People started driving in from all over Texas.

I never realized just how much victims enjoy a home-cooked meal.

"Just keep stirring my soup."

It was Bishop Michael Neal who recommended that I take my meals on the road. "Your guests aren't the only victims in need of spiritual nourishment," he told me. "Those who commit crimes are victims, too. And they are in no less favor before the eyes of God."

Sure, but where to start? Texas is a crime-infested state, and one of the biggest states at that. Like victims, there were evildoers everywhere. So I cut straight to the heart of darkness, where even angels don't tread. At 400 and growing, Huntsville boasts the largest Death Row population in the country. What better place to start my capital nourishment than in the belly of capital punishment?

Contorno

Judd's face is so swollen that he can barely breathe in the feces-infused stench of his concrete cell. He's doubled-over, holding his gut. The guards always smacked their clubs right there, right where the bullet went clean through his kidney, right where they knew it hurt bad.

"Get up, Judd-Ass."

Judd K. Perkins, a.k.a Puff, was counting the days: in exactly one year he would have his shot, his last hurrah, his gurney nap, his meal card punched.

Dead man walking, the Texas Death Row Shuffle.

Nobody cared; no relatives, no friends, certainly none of the inmates in Polunsky Unit who complained that the overweight old man always smelled like shit. It was a fair criticism. The south end of the 12 Building, Puff's end, was often flooded and musty. Puff had molded several bricks using his feces and food scraps and stacked them in a damp corner of his cell, and every couple of weeks he harvested the ashen mushrooms that magically appeared.

Then the guards found dried spores in his pocket. Convinced he was carrying Mary Jane—marijuana hash—they beat him. Real bad.

"I told you to get up, Judd-Ass."

As Puff held onto the bars, a lone Texas Department of Criminal Justice guard watched him, making sure the fat old man didn't choke and check out before his time.

"The Lord forgives you," Puff coughed, spitting up a chunk of blood.

"Shut up," the guard said, "and gimme two."

"Please, not my cookers!"

"Rules. Pass 'em through."

Puff stood up. "I don't jack the tray never and I don't throw my shit at you like Ritchie and—"

"Should I make it three?"

Puff's coughs melted to a whimper. He pushed two books through the tray slot.

"'*Martha Stewart Living Cookbook: the Original Classics*,'" the guard read. "And what's this? '*Without Reservations: How to Make Bold, Creative, and Flavorful Food at Home*, by Joey Altman'? You're one twisted fork, Judd-Ass."

Puff just smiled. "No fried drumsticks for my last supper, no sir. I'm starting off with a duck pâte followed by a lobster risotto and then—"

The guard let out a hearty laugh. "And for dessert, a menagerie of sodium thiopental, pancuronium, and potassium chloride, right? 'Night, Judd-Ass."

Secondo

The locals call it Prison City, a small Baptist town in east Texas, a company town where the company is the penal system. I took a furlough from my weekly feasts and spent Mondays at 12 Building and "the Walls." Each visit I brought four-dozen homemade chocolate chip cookies for the guards; I brought the inmates pastries and took their confessions: long, teary-eyed confessions. My how the predead talked and talked and talked, and always about the same old things: the past, the Lord, the shame, and the pending trip to see Joe Bryd, the name of the prison cemetery.

Except for inmate TDCJ #1962.

All he wanted to talk about was cooking.

"Guard says you a chef."

"Of sorts," I answer. I'm in the visitor's booth and we're separated by thick glass. It gives me little comfort.

"Preacher, can you use an immersion hydrothermal circulator to prepare a two-hour egg?"

"Sure, but why would you, when you can just boil it?"

"Georges Pralus says you can, but you gotta watch out for botulism poisoning at 'dem low temperatures. You ever make carrot caviar?"

"Once."

"Did you use sodium alginate? It's a damn good emulsifier, ain't it?"

I listen in awe as TDCJ #1962 debates the benefits of hydrocolloid gums—obscure starches relegated to the bowels of food labels on Ring Dings and Twix. He wants to know if it's possible to make a condiment that you could wrap around a hot dog like a string using an emulsified puree of mustard seed and xantham gum. When our time is up, I ask how he knows of such things.

"My cookers. That's all I read. I like the ones with pictures best. I know they wash 'em in detergent and paint 'em with food coloring and all that, but still the food in 'em pictures looks mighty fine."

"You know a lot about cooking."

"Spent eight years planning my last supper. I deserve to die, no question about that, but I also deserve a good home-cooked meal before I go."

"Might be tough to pull off something fancy in the kitchen here."

"But you could cook it for me, Preacher."

"Me?"

"Sure. Please?"

"No, Preacher can't," is all I say. I want to add: "Especially not for the bastard who murdered my wife," but the good Lord holds my tongue in place.

It's almost dawn. I can't sleep. The Puff monster didn't recognize me; guess I had changed a lot in eight years. How easy it is for some people to forget the taste of murder. I pull the Smith & Wesson Model 60 out from under the bed, stumble down to the kitchen, and place it on the counter next to the 9-inch Switchblade Stiletto CarbonFiber. The gun is dull, chunky, and awkward, but the silver blade dances smooth and fit under the kitchen lights. Yin and yang, male and female.

I sell the Double Action .38 caliber for $495 on eBay; the auction takes seven minutes.

I'm not going to shoot Puff, not now, not after how much I've grown, evolved. Mary wouldn't want that; the man she married is a priest, not some common thug.

That day I beg Peter Radin to do everything he can to grant Judd Perkins a clemency. I pull the Bishop Neal card, too. My campaign begins: an eye-for-an-eye makes the world go blind.

And I decide to cook Puff's last supper.

The most delicious meal of his entire wretched life.

Formaggi

Two weeks left for Puff.

I'm in the visitor's booth at Huntsville, working through the menu. "I researched deadmaneating.com," I report. "You're right, not one death row inmate ever asked for mushroom pâte."

"So you'll do it?" he asks.

I pull out a pad and a pen. "I was thinking we'd start off with puffball soup, you know, given your nickname and all that."

"No, no. I wrote it all out for you already."

"So you knew I would agree to cook for you?"

Puff grins a yellow smile. "Make sure you get only the freshest ingredients, local and organic, like Martha says."

"Like Martha says," I repeat, now relegated to a sous chef to Death Row's very own Julia Child. A guard passes me the slip of paper filled with perfect handwriting:

Country Duck and Hen of the Woods Pâte
Lobster and Wild Mushroom Risotto with
  Basil Mascarpone Crème
Porcini-crusted Lamb Loin with
  Sautéed Chanterelles and Fava Beans
Candy Cap Mushrooms Pots de Crème
Six bottles of Yoo-hoo

The Yoo-hoo I was expecting, the rest of the dishes I was not.

"Sure have a thing for mushrooms," I say.

"Eight years I've been planning. I can imagine every one of 'em dishes too . . . the textures, the smells, the complexity . . ." Puff closes his eyes and moves toward the visitor booth glass, his mouth dangerously close to where the previous inmate had cow-licked or spat. "It was the last thing I saw before they locked me up."

"What last thing?"

"Mushrooms, I saw mushrooms. Last thing I saw on the outside."

I want to scream that, no, it was my beautiful wife gored and dying beneath him, that was the last thing he saw. But all I say is:

"Mushroom it is."

Frutta

The shopping takes more time than the cooking, but I don't mind; Mary would have wanted me to do right by Puff. I'm at the farmer's market on the Rice University campus, inspecting fava beans and asparagus, when Peter calls.

"Texas Board of Pardons is almost sewn up," he reports. "Cost me a ton of markers. Your letters helped a lot; nobody's gonna make a fuss on this one if you don't. You sure about this?"

"Mary and my unborn child would have wanted it this way."

As I'm thumping an organic cantaloupe, Bill Reater, owner of Texas Mushroom Farms, presents a bag full of fresh Morchella esculenta as if holding out a newborn.

"Dug 'em up thirty miles east of Austin; going back this afternoon to find me some more," Reater says. "Mighty healthy walk out by the Pedernales River. God's country. Helps work stuff out."

Somehow he knows I need stuff worked out in the worst way. Maybe the old farmer sees the sin whirling in my brain, smells the most wicked fantasy I'm baking. It was impossible, but yet I cannot let go of the puzzle:

How do I get my beautifully efficient switchblade on the table for Puff's last supper?

I agree to go mushroom hunting with Reater.

We spend the afternoon drudging through an elm forest, noses down, eyes glued to the undergrowth. Reater talks in a low whisper, as if he might spook the mushrooms and they would fold up their caps and slurp themselves back into the soil. He peppers our hunt with juicy morsels: "mushrooms are like people; some good, some bad, some downright poison" and "all you need for shiitakes is olive oil, salt, and pepper."

Puff may have been obsessed with mushrooms, but Reater was in love with them.

"There, a fungus among us!" he shouts at one point.

"What are those?" I ask, ever the obedient student.

"Highly caespitose," Reater reports, pulling fresh specimens from under a juniper bush. "Those gray ones are forest mushrooms, and these are clamshells."

"Look the same to me. I can never tell them apart."

The afternoon ages and soon my basket is stuffed with strange, twisted, alien fungi: morels and meadow mushrooms and what not. An owl hoots above in the elms. I sit on a fallen tree and bury my face in my hands.

"Told you," Reater says, giving me space. " 'Shroom hunting works stuff out."

The old farmer is dead right. The tears are there but the revenge is gone, the hate is gone, the emptiness, gone. For the first time since Mary passed, I feel whole, I feel alive. I look up into the sun streaming through the forest canopy, clasping my hands in prayer.

"Took me eight years, Mary," I mutter, eyes wet. "But I finally got those mushrooms you asked for."

The old man of the woods shouts from a clearing: "D'you know one Portabella mushroom has more potassium than a banana?"

I stand up, a great weight lifted off my shoulders.

It was time to cook.

Dolce

Puff's last day.

Peter calls three times that morning, apologizing profusely, the Board of Pardons hasn't gotten around to the appeal. I tell him that he did all that he could do.

I pass through security and into 12 Building at Huntsville at dusk pushing a luggage dolly loaded with two thermally insulated plastic bins. The guards follow me, anxious to inspect the chef priest's meal. I pass them a grocery bag filled with cookies.

"Two dozen with cinnamon and walnut, two dozen plain," I announce.

"Will go nice for our party," the shift captain says. The guards always threw a party the night before an execution.

"There'll be plenty of leftovers, too," I say. "I made twelve servings of everything."

As the guards inspect my bins, I encourage them to sample the cookies. My distraction fails. One of the guards hands the captain my 9-inch Switchblade CarbonFiber knife.

"Can't take this in, Reverend."

"How's he supposed to cut the lamb?"

"We'll give you a plastic knife."

"Plastic? That will just shred the meat and make a mess. Can't I just cut it for him?"

"Nope. State reg."

"It's not like I'm gonna try to kill him or anything."

The captain shrugs. "But he might try."

At last I'm allowed into the dining cell. Puff is wearing all white, smiling like an angel. "I could smell it cooking all week," he says, pining over the warm bins. He catches himself, embarrassed, then shuts his eyes and prays. While he recites obscure scriptures even I can't recall, I cover the table with plastic utensils and paper plates and a rainbow assortment of Tupperware bowls.

I join Puff in grace. We bow our heads together, for a moment, brothers.

"First, an aperitif," I begin when he is ready. I pass him a plastic shot glass filled with brown liquid. "Kombucha, a mushroom-infused tea to cleanse your palette, best served cold. Compliments of the chef."

"Yum. Tastes like apple cider."

I take the empty cup and slide Puff a small plate.

"Next, a wild duck and mushroom pâté served on a fresh bed of baby greens and arugula . . ."

One by one I present each course. Puff eats like a horse, bare-toothed. His appetite is unstoppable. Between bites he chants: "Puff in heaven. Puff in heaven." I worry that there won't be leftovers for the guards' party.

At last maple sweetness fills the air and he's shoveling his way through the candy cap mushroom dessert. That's when I make my confession: "Mr. Perkins, I tried to stay your execution. I have friends in Austin and I thought they could get a clemency granted. But they couldn't. I'm sorry."

Puff drops his spoon. "Why the hell you do that?"

"So you wouldn't die, of course."

"But I wanna die! Been waiting eight years to see Joe Bryd! And this is exactly how I want to go, too, with a belly full of the best food ever cooked!"

I don't know what to say. I ask Puff if he wants to join me in prayer.

He says no.

"Preacher, you don't make no sense. I don't know why you wanted to cook for me like this, and I don't know why you'd stop my injection after what I did to you. All I can figure is that the good Lord is deep inside you."

"What you did to me?" I ask.

"Well, not you. Your woman."

"You know who I am?"

Puff wipes a dab of pots de crème from his charcoal lips. "Won't never forget. I'm sorry about your Mary. I pray for that woman every night. Heard she was with child, too. Damn shame. I could never be the man you are, Preacher . . . a forgiving man, a man that don't take revenge. I had to kill that Turk bastard for taking my son from me, but you, you're strong. I'm twice your size, but I could never be as strong as you."

The silence that follows isn't awkward, it's music. As I stack the discarded plates and Tupperware back in the bins, Puff rubs his belly, grinning and burping like a sleepy child.

"Good-bye, Puff. God be with you."

Digestivo

I'm not hungry after watching a man eat like that. I drive home, exhausted. Five messages are waiting for me on my answering machine, all from Peter.

"Where the hell have you been?" Peter shouts when I call him back.

"At Huntsville, had my phone off. What's up?"

"I got your clemency, that's what's up! Two parts expert politicking and one part Miracle of God but the governor signed it. Your boy Judd Perkins is off Death Row. State won't be killing that one."

"Thank you, Peter. Can't tell you how grateful I am."

I go straight to bed. Funny thing about that night: I don't recall sleeping that well in years. Slept right through dawn, right through breakfast. If the phone hadn't rung, I might have slept all the way through lunch.

"Reverend? You coming in today?"

It was the warden at Huntsville calling.

"Thought I'd take a day off after last night," I reply, my voice all gravel.

"Damn bizarre night, I agree. We got your dishes all cleaned up. Your fancy knife, too."

"I'll pick it all up next week, thanks."

"You got a minute? Dr. Klausner needs to ask you a couple of questions."

I heard the warden whisper, place his hand over the receiver. Dr. Klausner was the medical examiner for Huntsville. I sat up in bed.

"Morning, Reverend. This is John Klausner, the ME over here. Need to ask you a couple things, procedural stuff."

"Fire away."

"I'm trying to nail down the cause of death of one Judd Perkins. From what I can gather—"

"Puff is dead?"

"That's right."

"That's not possible," I interject. "The attorney general called me last night, the governor granted clemency."

"That's right, he did. Perkins never went to the gurney; he didn't die from injection. He just, well, near as I can figure, he just up and died in his cell last night."

"Died? How?"

"Not sure. I'm thinking it was the stress of the execution, that and maybe some overeating—"

"You're not suggesting that my dinner caused him to—"

"No, not at all. The guards ate your leftovers and not one had so much as a bellyache. There was nothing wrong with your food. I heard what you did, pulling strings to try to get the governor to stay the execution."

"So what happened?"

"Reverend, this inmate had a history of kidney problems. He was a diabetic. I'm just wondering if I should pull a full autopsy and order extra blood work."

"Maybe you should."

"Was Perkins complaining of any stomach pains last night?"

"No, nothing. He ate like there was no tomorrow."

A pause. "For him, there wasn't."

"So you gonna run a full autopsy?"

"Not if it's just kidney failure, which I suspect it is. It's the warden's call. It's his budget."

I clear my throat. "Doctor, for what it's worth, Perkins was looking forward to the execution. Speaking strictly as a spiritual counselor, I knew he was prepared, even willing, to die."

"Thank you, reverend. Can I call you if I have more questions?"

"Sure."

I hang up the phone and roll back to bed. The sun fills my bedroom with light. I imagine Mary lying next to me, the honeyed taste of her lips, the toasty softness of her body, the smell of her sweet blond hair.

And I can't help smiling.

Dr. Klausner would never perform a full autopsy.

Would cost too much, and nobody cared about old Puff. Even if he ordered advanced blood work, he wouldn't dream of testing for alpha-amatoxin, not for someone with a preexisting kidney condition.

So he would never conclude that Puff died from mycetism.

That's what Amanita bisporigera did to you. The destroying angel mushroom was such a gorgeous fungus: plump, round volva for a base, pure white gills, a smooth porcelain cap . . . truly angelic, sent down from heaven.

Just one bite and within hours came the cramps, then the nausea and delirium, and then death by kidney failure. Not even a bite was required: the destroying angel could easily kill as an emulsified blend in Kombucha mushroom tea.

The empty plastic shot glass is still in my black jacket pocket. I need to dispose of that.

Honey, the soup is ready.

I can picture Mary inventing her quirky phrases . . . a cleric who kills . . . a monk who murders. Now I have one, too.

An angel that assassinates.

Doesn't have the same alliteration, but I know she'll love it. Funny how angel mushrooms look just like meadows, just like buttons.

I could never tell those damn things apart.

*

RIP GERBER'S first thriller, *Pharma* (Random House), was a bestseller in Germany in 2007. His second thriller featuring the Food and Drug Administration was released by Random House in October 2010. Rip received his biochemical degree from the University of Virginia and his master's from Harvard Business School. Rip lives in San Francisco, California, and does make a run to the market when asked. More than forty varieties of mushrooms and one hundred cooking terms are mentioned in his story. Happy Hunting!

After Dark

ALEX KAVA and DEB CARLIN

Madeline Kramer slammed on the brakes inches from the Lexus bumper in front of her.

"Calm down, Maty," she scolded herself and watched the Lexus driver give her the finger from out his window. She balled up her fist, disappointed that she wasn't able to return the gesture. She could have avoided rush hour traffic if she hadn't stopped by the office. Her first day of vacation was wasted, and for what? Gilstadt wouldn't even look at her marketing proposal the entire time she was gone. And now she'd never make it to the cabin before dark.

She glanced in the rearview mirror. Why did she let the job take so much out of her? The lines under her eyes were becoming permanent. She raked her fingers through her hair, trying to remember the last time she had it trimmed. Were lines beginning to form at the corners of her mouth? How did she ever let herself get to this point?

A honking horn made her jump. She sat up and grasped the steering wheel in attention.

God, how she hated rush-hour traffic.

They were stopped again with no promise of movement. She glanced at her copy of the marketing proposal sitting in the seat beside her. Forty-two pages of research, staring up at her, mocking her. This was the hard copy, the stats and Arbitron ratings. What she left with Gilstadt included a five-minute video presentation. Six long days' worth of research and preparation, and Gilstadt had barely glanced at it, simply nodding for her to add it to one of the stacks on his desk. By the end of the day all her hard work would probably be buried under another stack.

Story of her life. Or at least, that's how it had been lately. Nothing seemed to be going right. One of the reasons she needed this vacation before she simply went mad.

Her cell phone blasted her back to reality. God, her nerves were shot. She let the phone ring three more times. Why hadn't she shut the damn thing off? Finally she ripped it from its holder.

"Madeline Kramer."

"Maty, hi, I'm glad I caught you."

Her entire body stiffened on impulse. "William, is everything okay? Where are you?"

"Everything's fine. Relax. I'm at home."

"I thought you left for Kansas City early this morning? Your conference."

"My presentation's not until later this week. Where are you? You're not at the cabin or you wouldn't have a cell phone connection."

"I stopped at the office."

"Jesus, Maty. It's your first day off. Are you *still* at the office?"

She clenched her fist around the steering wheel and tried to ignore the sudden tightness in the back of her neck.

"I'm almost at the cabin," she lied. "If fact, I may lose you soon. What is it that you need?"

"Need?"

"You called me," she reminded him. He was already distracted. She could hear something in the background. It sounded like a train whistle. Their home was nowhere close to train tracks. "You were glad you caught me," she tried again.

Why did he do this to her? He was checking up on her, again. She had come to resent his constant worry, his psychoanalysis, his treating her like one of his patients. Did he think he could try to talk her out of this one last time with more concerns that it might not be safe for her being out there all alone? No, she wasn't a camper. This wasn't about camping. This was about going someplace to be completely away from everything and yes, everyone. Besides, she had listened to him enough to bring along her father's old Colt revolver. William didn't even know she had kept it from the estate sale. He hated guns. Hated the very idea of them being in the house.

"I just wanted to tell you I love you," he said.

Maty closed her eyes. Took a deep breath and moved the phone so he couldn't hear her releasing a long sigh. He did worry about her. He loved her. That was it. That was all. Her nerves were wound so tight she couldn't even see what she was doing to her marriage.

"I'm sorry, William. I love you, too."

"There might be thunderstorms tonight. I just wanted

to tell you that. Oh, and Maty, remember not to mix your meds with too much wine. Okay? I don't mean to be a nag but I saw that you packed several bottles."

Her face flushed. Embarrassment. A bit of anger. Calm. She needed to stay calm. He was concerned about her. That's all. Don't shove everyone out of your life, she told herself.

"Maty?"

"I'll remember."

"Promise?"

More and more of their conversations sounded like doctor and patient. No, that wasn't true. They sounded like parent and child.

"I promise, William."

"Good girl. Now you go out to your cabin retreat and get some rest. Relax, take it easy. I'll see you in three days."

Now if that didn't sound like a prescription. And patronizing.

Stop it!

She needed to stop sabotaging everything with her paranoia and her negative attitude. "You get what you sow." That's what her mother always said. "If you think good thoughts good things will come to you." The power of positive thinking. What a bunch of crap. Maty Kramer knew that everything she had gotten in life was because she had fought for it, not because she focused on positive thinking. Okay, so she hadn't been much of a fighter lately. Deep down the instinct must still exist, didn't it?

She found a hole in the traffic and gunned the engine. Traffic was moving again. She could relax, and yet a familiar throbbing began at the base of her neck and tightened the tension in her shoulders. It would take more than some peace and quiet to get rid of all this.

She took her exit off the interstate and drove onto the two-lane highway that would take her far away from the city. She needed this vacation. She glanced at the marketing proposal. The shoulder pain eased its way down into her chest, following its regular path.

"God," she thought out loud, "I'm only thirty-five. A thirty-five-year-old woman shouldn't be having chest pains."

She pressed the button, rolling the window down and grabbed a handful of pages. She stretched her arm out the window and listened to the pages flapping in the wind, slapping each other and licking her wrist. She held her breath and told herself to let go. Just let go. Suddenly, she jerked her arm back into the car, holding the papers tightly in her lap.

"Am I going completely mad?"

She shook her head and placed the pages safely back on the seat, before she had time to reconsider.

It was after seven when she pulled up to the park office. The sun disappeared behind the massive cottonwoods and river maples. Maty had spoken to a woman in the park's office earlier in the day. She had assured Maty her late arrival wouldn't be a problem.

"I'll just leave your cabin key in an envelope and tape it to the door. You're in Owen, number two, dear. Remember that, because the key doesn't have any markings on it."

It sounded odd at the time, to leave something as valuable as a key on an office door for anyone to grab, but now looking at the place Maty understood. The small brick building sat in the middle of the woods, in the middle of nowhere. Shadows had already started to swallow what sunlight was left. One lonely lamppost glowed at the edge of the parking lot. There was a bare lightbulb above the office door. There were no other cars in the lot and no sign of anyone.

The woman had warned her. "It's the off-season, dear. You'll be the only one here. The park superintendent has a conference in the Omaha. And I'm only here Friday through Monday. Are you sure you'll be okay, dear?"

"I'll be fine," she told the woman. It seemed even strangers didn't believe she could handle being on her own.

Now as she got out of the car she realized how good it felt to stretch and breath in the crisp, fresh air. Then she closed the car door and its thud echoed. There was something unsettling about the silence. A knot twisted inside her stomach. Was she prepared for all this quiet?

Of course she was. It was late. She was hungry. She'd get to her cabin, slice some of the expensive cheeses she had splurged on, pour a glass of wine, and before she knew it she would be relaxed and enjoying the beauty— and the quiet.

It really was quite lovely here. The trees had just begun to turn yellow and orange with some fiery red bushes in-between. Hidden in the treetops, locusts whined and a whip-poor-will called. A breeze sent fallen leaves skittering across the sidewalk in front of her. As a kid she loved going to her grandfather's cabin in the woods. She used to go every year before, what her mother called, "grandpa's madness." The entire family would make a holiday of it, swimming in the lake, hiking in the woods, and at night gathering around an open fire. Those were some of the best, happiest times of her life. If she could capture just a fraction of those feelings, this vacation would be a success.

But as she reached the office door Maty knew something wasn't right. She felt it almost as if someone had sneaked up behind her and tapped her on the shoulder. There was nothing on the door. The envelope with her cabin key was missing.

The woman simply forgot, Maty convinced herself. No one would take it. There was no reason to take an envelope with an unmarked cabin key. She told herself this as she hurried back to her car.

She could simply drive back to the city. Go home. But what would she tell William? It was exactly the kind of thing he would expect of her. And that was enough reason to not consider it.

Up the road and between the trees she noticed a light. What would it hurt to check it out? A sign at the end of a long driveway read *Park Superintendent*. The front door of the ranch-style house had been left open. Before Maty decided to stay or go a tall lanky man in a brown uniform appeared alongside her car. She jumped and accidentally tapped the car horn.

"You lost?"

Maty saw a patch on his sleeve that identified him as the park superintendent. He looked too young to be in charge of anything.

"No, I'm not lost," she said, rolling down her window, but only half way. "I've rented one of your cabins for the week. I called the office earlier to let them know I'd be late. I'm afraid they forgot to leave my key for me."

"Helen never forgets. Maybe it just fell off the door."

Maty met him back at the office. They searched everywhere—in the bushes, under the bushes, in the grass. Darkness replaced shadows and Maty was getting impatient.

"Maybe Helen just forgot to put it on the door." He still wouldn't relinquish the fact that Helen just plain forgot.

"Or someone got to it before I did," Maty joked as she followed his tall shadow into the dark office.

"No, no that wouldn't be possible," he said in his deadpan tone, oblivious to her attempt at humor. "There's no one else here," he explained. "I'm getting ready to leave, too. Even the grounds men aren't due back until next week."

He flipped on the light switch in the office and both of them searched the peg board that held two keys for each cabin. Her eyes found Owen number two. Only one key was left.

Maty watched Ranger Rick, or whatever his name was, reach for the remaining key. "See, I knew Helen must have gotten your key for you. It probably went home with her." She didn't care anymore. She simply wanted to get to the cabin and get to bed.

"Sure, that's probably what happened."

By now it was dark despite a sky full of stars and a moon that was almost full. The park's trees grew thicker as she drove. Her car's headlights sliced through the darkness. She wondered, again, if this was a bad idea. Perhaps the lost key was a bad omen. She laughed out loud. Not even to her cabin, and already she was sabotaging her vacation.

The cabins were tucked back in the woods, only patches of rooftop visible from the parking area. Small wooden signs and arrows indicated what path to follow for which cabin. She found the sign for Owen number two, slung her backpack over her shoulder, and with a flashlight in one hand and grocery bag in the other, she followed the narrow trail. As she got closer she discovered the lake.

Maty stood paralyzed by the beauty of the moonlight on the water. A chill slid down her back. She shook her head and hugged the bag to her chest. It was a lake in the woods in the dark, and it was chilly. Did she really believe she'd be like Thoreau, escaping to the woods and Walden Pond to find some inner peace or a deeper meaning to her life? She did know one thing that guaranteed inner peace and was much quicker. A nice bottle of Bordeaux.

She started to turn back toward the cabin when she saw something move down by the lake. She strained to see. It looked like a man moving, sneaking between the trees, almost as if hiding.

Her stomach plunged and her knees went weak. She crouched down so suddenly she crunched leaves and almost lost her flashlight.

Did he hear that? Could he see her? She held her breath and listened. Behind the shrubs she could barely see. She pushed herself up on wobbly knees, just enough to see down by the lake. He wasn't there. Was he hiding? She couldn't see him. Her eyes darted around the shore, up and down the steep edges, between the trees.

The man was gone. He had disappeared as suddenly as he had appeared. She stayed crouching, waiting as though she expected him to appear again. Then she wondered, Had there been anyone there at all? Or was it simply her stressed and overactive imagination? They said her grandfather had started to hallucinate before the madness.

She needed to stop this or she would really drive herself mad. He could be a groundskeeper or a hiker or someone simply enjoying an evening stroll around the lake. It was a beautiful evening, after all. Not everyone went mad after dark.

The cabin was rustic but cozy with a fireplace, kitchenette, one small bedroom and modern bath that included a shower. The back door walked out onto an attached screened-in porch that overlooked the treetops and the lake. The moonlight illuminated the cabin through the windows and skylights. The reflection off the lake lit the entire porch.

Shadows of branches danced on the walls and suddenly they looked too much like skeleton arms reaching down for her. Maty flipped on every light switch and every lamp. Then she started to unpack her staples. She needed to get something to eat. Or more important, pour something to drink. Settle in. Lock down.

She didn't remember falling asleep.

There was a scream and then a clap of thunder. Maty woke with a jerk, almost knocking herself out of the lounge chair on the porch. At first she didn't know where she was. Her head felt heavy, her vision blurred from too much wine. It took a flicker of lightning to remind her.

But why was it dark? She glanced back inside the cabin. She knew she had left every single light on. She reached for the lamp she had dragged out onto the porch and turned the switch. Nothing. She tried again as another flash of lightning forked across the black sky. The thunder that followed rattled the floorboards. William had warned her about thunderstorms. She hated when he was right. Another clap of thunder and the rain started, a torrential downpour, with no signs of letting up. She liked the sound of rain. There was something comforting about its natural rhythms and the fresh scent of scrubbed wood and dirt.

That's when she remembered the scream. She was sure it was a scream that had awakened her.

Maty tried to get out of the chair, but her head begin to twirl. The wine. She must have drunk the whole bottle. She pushed against the arms of the chair. She tried the lamp switch again. Nothing. The electricity was off. In the dark she fumbled around and found her flashlight. What she really wanted to find was the Advil.

The downpour continued, but now the wind pushed it through the screen of the porch. She grabbed her book and blanket before they got soaked. She started to retreat inside, but as she reached for the wineglass she saw a flash of light down by the lake.

Not lightning, or was it?

She gulped what was left in the glass, snapped off her flashlight and sat back down, waiting and staring at the spot where she had seen the flash. There it was again. It looked like a tunnel of light from a flashlight. Then she saw him. A man carrying something flung over his shoulder, something that looked large and heavy. He really was crazy to be out on a night like tonight.

Maybe the wine really had made her mellow, because his appearance didn't frighten her. Quite frankly she didn't care if someone was stupid enough to be out in a night like tonight.

She was sober enough to realize she was drunk. She actually didn't mind the wet wind coming in on her. It felt good, fresh, and erratic. Her head no longer hurt. Her fingers found the wine bottle. She tipped it, pleased to see a bit left. She poured and sipped and continued to watch.

The man had a long stick and was poking the ground. No, wait, it wasn't a stick. The lightning flickered off the metallic end of a shovel. Wasn't he afraid of being struck by lightning? It certainly wasn't smart digging in the middle of an electrical storm. Maybe it wasn't a shovel at all. Suddenly tired again, she made her way to the bedroom. On the other side of the lake she thought she saw a light, a lamppost shining bright through the trees. How was that possible? The electricity was out. Her eyelids couldn't stay open and her head was too heavy to care. She climbed into bed and collapsed into a wonderfully deep, alcohol-induced sleep devoid of thunder and lightning and strangers digging in the rain.

When Maty woke a second time the digital bedside clock glowed 4:45. The lightning had been reduced to a soft flicker and the thunder, a low rumble in the distance. The full moon broke through the clouds, illuminating the small bedroom. She reached for the bedside lamp and twisted the on switch. It took her a second to remember that the storm had knocked out the electricity. She looked at the clock again and watched it click to 4:46 and realized it must be battery-operated.

The pain in her head reminded her of the wine. And worse, she had forgotten to take her pills. Out of his sight for less than twenty-four hours and Maty was already breaking her promises to William. But instead of regret or remorse, it felt more like defiance and victory. Silly and childish, but if he insisted on treating her like she was a patient or a child, he couldn't blame her for acting like one.

She lay in bed, staring out the window. All she could see from this angle were the shadows of treetops swaying in the breeze. It sounded like the rain had stopped entirely. All was quiet and peaceful, nature's wrath finished for tonight.

Then she heard footsteps.

Maty held her breath and listened. Had she imagined it?

No, there it was again, slow and hesitant—the soft groan of floorboards. Someone else was in the cabin.

She didn't dare sit up. Couldn't move if she wanted to,

paralyzed by fear. Her mind reeled. Had she locked all the doors? Yes, as soon as she'd arrived. But maybe not the porch door when she stumbled to bed.

Oh God, had she left it unlocked?

She strained to hear over the thump-thumping of her heart. Her eyes darted around the room. She had left her backpack and everything in it in the other room.

Minutes felt like hours. She willed herself to stay very still. She kept the sheet pulled up to her chin. Her hands were shaking. She could do this, she told herself, and tried to focus. She could ease off the bed and roll underneath.

Moonlight filtered in past the tree branches and illuminated the bedroom. Now was not a good time. She wanted to pull the curtains shut. Darkness was the only weapon she had. But she couldn't risk moving. Couldn't risk making a sound. So instead, she kept still. She would pretend to be asleep. Could she do that and not scream? Would it matter?

With the power still out there were no electrical whines of appliance motors turning off and on. She held her breath, straining to listen. She heard a distance train whistle. Leaves rustled in the breeze outside the window. A whip-poor-will called from the other side of the lake. No footsteps. No groaning floorboards. Had she imagined it? Was that possible? Oh God, maybe she was going mad.

Maty glanced at the clock and continued to lay still. Ten minutes. Fifteen minutes. It felt like a week. Twenty minutes. No footsteps. The thumping of her heart quieted. The banging in her head grew. Too much wine. Too much stress. And she'd forgotten to take her medication last night. Was that all it was?

She watched the darkness turn to dawn. The night

shadows started to fade and disappear from the bedroom walls. When Maty finally convinced herself that her imagination had gotten the best of her, she eased out of bed. Still, she monitored her movement, stopping and waiting, listening. After a few minutes of tiptoeing she felt ridiculous.

She stopped at the bathroom then marched into the kitchenette. She'd brought the staples for breakfast, had loaded the small refrigerator. Even without electricity everything was still cold. Her backpack sat on the counter where she'd left it. She poured herself a glass of orange juice and turned to go out onto the porch. That's when she saw the shadow of a man was standing by the door.

Maty gasped and dropped the orange juice, glass shattering.

"You forgot to take your pills last night," William said, walking into the middle of the room where she could see his face.

"You scared the hell out of me. What are you doing here?"

"I reminded you."

It was like he hadn't heard her. He looked tired. His clothes were wrinkled and damp. His shoes muddy.

"How long have you been here? How did you get in?"

"You drank a whole bottle of wine." he held up the empty bottle she had left on the porch. "But you forgot to take your pills."

"William, what are you doing here?"

"I'm not really here," he said this with a grin. "I'm checked in at a conference in Kansas City. I did that yesterday morning. Everyone thinks I'm in my hotel room, behind the do-not-disturb sign, preparing my presentation. My car's in the hotel's parking lot. I rented one to come back."

"But I don't understand. Why are you here?"

"Because I had a feeling you wouldn't take your fucking pills."

"William?"

"I changed them out, you see. A nice little concoction that wouldn't go so well with alcohol. Actually it probably wouldn't go so well with anything, but the alcohol would just be another indication of you going over the edge."

He tossed the bottle aside and that's when Maty noticed he was wearing gloves. And in his other hand he carried a knife, a wide-bladed hunting knife that he held down at his side as if he didn't even realize he had it there.

Panic forced Maty to step backward, slowly away from him until the small of her back pressed into the countertop. Trapped. There was nowhere for her to go.

"I don't understand," she found herself saying out loud. It only seemed to make William grin more.

"Of course you don't. You've been so self-involved in your own stressed-out madness that you haven't noticed anything or anyone around you. Where's your pill bottle?"

"But if you haven't been happy—."

"Where the hell are your pills, Madeline?"

In two steps he grabbed her by the hair and shoved the knife to her throat. His breath hot in her face, his eyes wide. He smelled of sweat and mud. He looked like a madman.

"It was you. Last night in the woods," she whispered and felt the metal press against each word. "Why?"

This time he laughed.

"I had to make sure you took them, that it looked like you'd gone over the edge. Everyone was supposed to be gone, but that boy ranger was still here. He saw me."

"Oh my God. William. What did you do?"

"The son-of-a-bitch would have ruined it all. Then after the storm when I came inside and found you still breathing . . ." He dragged out the last word like it disgusted him.

"You're the one who took the key from the park office door."

"I knew you'd stop at work. It gave me plenty of time to get here."

"You called me from here. The train whistle . . ."

"Make it easier on both of us, Maty. Where are your pills?"

He yanked her head against the cupboard and she thought she might black out.

"Okay," she managed. "Stop, just let me get them."

He let go. Shoved her away and backed up.

Maty rubbed at the back of her head and the tangled knot of hair. She eased herself toward the other end of the counter, hanging on for fear her knees might give out. She kept an eye on William even as she opened the zipper of her backpack and dug her hand inside. He stayed put, waiting, looking tired, impatient. She hardly recognized this man, his hair tousled and face dirty. He wasn't her husband anymore. No, he was some deranged madman who had killed the park superintendent and was about to kill her.

When Maty pulled the Colt revolver from her backpack William's eyes grew wide. Before he could react, before he could move, Maty shot him twice in the chest. The blasts made her jump each time.

She didn't cry. She didn't scream. Her hands weren't even shaking.

She laid the revolver on the counter. Stepped back, opened the refrigerator and poured herself another glass of orange juice. This time she sat down. She wondered if this was what it felt like for her grandfather when the madness took over.

She sipped the juice and said to herself, "Now, where to dump the body."

*

ALEX KAVA has built a reputation writing psychological thrillers full of authentic details that blend fact with fiction. In Kava's words, "If readers can't tell where the facts left off and the fiction begins, I've done my job." She is the *New York Times* bestselling author of seven novels featuring Special FBI Agent Maggie O'Dell, as well as two stand-alone thrillers. Before writing novels full-time, Alex Kava spent fifteen years in advertising, marketing, and public relations. She divides her time between Omaha, Nebraska, and Pensacola, Florida.

DEB CARLIN spent twenty-five years in the hospitality business, ranging from bars and restaurants to hotels, retiring with a stellar fifteen years at Darden Restaurants, where she helped write technical manuals and nonfiction business articles. She is the owner of eWeb-Focus, where she consults on business strategies for online presences. Her foray with *After Dark* is her first fiction endeavor, and she has plans to continue.

Wednesday's Child

KEN BRUEN

Had.

Funny how vital that damn word had become in my life.

Had . . . An Irish mother.

Had . . . Big plans.

Had . . . Serious rent due.

Had . . . To make one major score.

I'd washed up in Ireland almost a year ago. Let's just say I *had* to leave New York in a hurry.

Ireland seemed to be one of the last places on the planet to still love the good ol' USA.

And, they were under the very erroneous impression that we had money.

Of course, until very recently, they'd had buckets of

the green, forgive the pun, themselves. But the recession had killed their Celtic Tiger.

I'd gone to Galway as it was my mother's hometown and was amazed to find an almost mini–USA. The teenagers all spoke like escapees from *The Hills*. Wore Converse, baseball T-shirts, chinos. It was like staggering onto a shoot for The Gap.

With my accent, winning smile, and risky credit cards, I'd rented an office in Woodquay, close to the very centre of the city. About a mugging away from the main street. I was supposedly a financial consultant but depending on the client, I could consult on any damn thing you needed. I managed to get the word around that I was an ex-military guy, and had a knack for making problems disappear.

And was not averse to skirting the legal line.

I was just about holding my head above water, but it was getting fraught.

So, yeah, I was open to possibilities.

How I met Sheridan.

I was having a pint of Guinness in McSwiggan's and no, I wasn't hallucinating but right in the centre of the pub is a tree.

I was wondering which came first when a guy slid onto the stool beside me. I say *slid* because that's exactly how he did it. Like a reptile, he just suddenly crept up on me.

I've been around as you've gathered and am always aware of exits and who is where, in relation to the danger quota.

I never saw him coming.

Should have taken that as an omen right then.

He said, "You'll be the Yank I hear about."

I turned to look at him. He had the appearance of a greyhound recovering from anorexia and a bad case of the speed jags. About thirty-five, with long graying hair, surprisingly unmarked face, not a line there, but the eyes were old.

Very.

He'd seen some bad stuff or caused it. How do I know?

I see the same look every morning in the mirror.

He was dressed in faded blue jeans, a T-shirt that proclaimed *Joey Ramone will never die* and a combat jacket that Jack Reacher would have been proud of. He put out a bony hand, all the veins prominent, and said, "I'm Sheridan, lemme buy you a pint."

I took his hand, surprisingly strong for such a wasted appearance, said, "Good to meet you, I'm Morgan."

Least that's what it said on the current credit cards.

He had, as he put it, a slight problem, a guy he owed money to and the how much would it cost to make the guy go away.

I laughed, said, "You're going to pay me to get rid of a guy who you owe money to? One, why would you think I can do it, and two, how will you pay me?"

He leaned closer, smelled of patchouli, did they still make that old hippy shit? Said, "You've got yerself a bit of a rep, Mr Morgan, and how would I pay you, oh, I'd pay you in friendship and trust me, I'm a good friend to have."

Maybe it was the early pint, or desperation or just for the hell of it, but I asked, "Who's the guy?"

He told me, gave me his name and address and leaned back; asked, "You think you can help me out here, Mr Morgan?"

I said, "Depends on whether you're buying me the pint you offered or not."

He did.

As we were leaving, I said, "I'll be here Friday night; maybe you can buy me another pint."

Like I said, I didn't have a whole lot going on so I checked out the guy who was leaning on Sheridan.

No biggie but on the Thursday, his car went into the docks and him in it.

Some skills you never forget.

Friday night, I was in McSwiggan's; Sheridan appeared as I ordered a pint and he said to the barman, "On me, Sean."

He gave me a huge smile; his right molar was gold and the rest of his teeth looked like they'd been filed down.

We took our drinks to a corner table and he slapped my shoulder, said, "Sweet fooking job, mate."

I spread my hands, said, "Bad brakes, what can I tell you."

He threw back his head, laughed out loud, a strange sound, like a rat being strangled, said, "I love it, bad break. You're priceless."

That was the real beginning of our relationship. Notice I don't say friendship.

I don't do friends.

And I very much doubt that anyone in their right mind would consider Sheridan a friend.

We did a lot of penny-ante stuff for the next few months, nothing to merit any undue attention but nothing either that was going to bankroll the kind of life I hoped for.

Which was

Sea

Sun

And knock-you-on-your-ass cash.

An oddity, and definitely something I should have paid real attention to. I'd pulled off a minor coup involving some credit cards I had to dump within twenty-four hours. With Sheridan's help, we scooped a neat five thousand dollars. And at the time when the dollar had finally kicked the Euro's ass.

See, I do love my country.

You're thinking, "Which one?"

Semper fi and all that good baloney. It pays the cash, it gets my allegiance.

So, we were having us a celebration; I split it down the middle with him, because I'm a decent guy. We *flashed* up as Sheridan termed it.

Bearing in mind that the Irish seven-course meal is a six pack and a potato, we went to McDonagh's, the fish-and-chipper, in Quay Street.

We sat outside in a rare hour of Galway *Sun;* Sheridan produced a flask of what he called Uisce Beatha, Holy Water. In other words, Irish Moonshine, Poteen.

Phew-oh, the stuff kicks like one mean tempered mule.

Later, we wound up in Feeney's, one of the last great Irish pubs. Here's the thing: I'd sometimes wondered if Sheridan had a woman in his life. I didn't exactly give it a whole lot of thought, but it crossed my mind. As if he was reading my mind he said, "Morgan, what day were you born on?"

I was about to put it down to late night-drink speak, but I was curious, asked, "That's a weird question, what day, how the hell would I know what day?"

He looked sheepish, and when you add that to his rodent appearance, it was some sight, he said, "See, my girl, she has this thing about the nursery rhyme, you know, Monday's child is fair of face and am . . . . Thursday's, is, yeah, has far to go, she judges people on what their day of birth is."

My Girl!

I was so taken aback by that it took me a moment to ask, "What are you?"

No hesitation, "Thursday's child."

We laughed at that and I don't think either of us really knew why.

I asked, "Who is the girl, why haven't I met her?"

He looked furtive, hiding something but then, his whole life seemed to be about hiding stuff, he said, "She's shy, I mean, she knows we're mates and all, but she wants to know your birth day before she'll meet you."

I said, "Next time I talk to Mom, I'll ask her, ok?"

As Mom had been in the ground for at least five years, it wasn't likely to be any time soon.

Another round of drinks arrived and we moved on to important issues, like sport. Guy stuff, if ever you reach any sort of intimacy, move to sports, move way past that sucker, that intimacy crap.

I meant to look up the nursery rhyme but, as far as I got, was discovering I was born on a Wednesday.

Told Sheridan it was that day and he said, "I'll tell her."

He was distracted when I told him, the speed he took turning him this way and that, like a dead rose in a barren field.

I'd noticed he was becoming increasingly antsy, speed fiends, what can I tell you? But he was building up to something.

It finally came.

We were in Garavan's, on Shop Street; still has all the old stuff you associate with

Ireland and even . . . whisper it, Irish staff.

And snugs.

Little portioned off cubicles where you can talk without interruption.

Sheridan was on Jameson; I stay away from spirits, too lethal. He was more feverish than usual; asked, "You up for the big one?"

I feigned ignorance; said, "We're doing ok."

He shook his head, looked at me, which is something he rarely did, his eyes usually focused on my forehead, but this was head on; said, "Morgan, We're alike, we want some serious money and I know how we can get it."

I waited.

He said, "Kidnapping."

Without a beat I said, "Fuck off, that is the dumbest crime on the slate."

He was electric, actually vibrating; said, "No, listen, this is perfect, we . . . well me really, snatch a girl, her old man is fooking loaded and you, as the consultant you are and known, as such, you're the go between; we tell the rich bastard the kidnappers have selected you as the pick up man, you get the cash, we let the girl go and hello, we're rich."

I picked up the remnants of my pint; said, "No. Kidnapping never works. Forget it."

He grabbed my arm, said, "Listen, this is the daughter of Jimmy Flaherty; he owns most of Galway; his daughter, Brona, is the light of his life and he has no love of the cops; he'll pay, thinking he'll find us later, but we'll be in the wind and with a Yank as a broker for the deal; he'll go along, he's a Bush admirer."

I let the Bush bit slide.

I acted like I was considering it, then said, "No, it's too . . . out there."

He let his head fall, dejection in neon, and said, "I've already got her."

It's hard to surprise me. You live purely on your wits and instincts as I've always done; you have envisioned most scenarios. This came out of left field.

I gasped. "You what?"

He gave me a defiant look, then, "I thought you might be reluctant and I already made the call to Flaherty, asked for one million and said I'd only use a neutral intermediary, and suggested that Yank consultant."

I was almost lost for words.

Almost.

Said, "So I'm already fucked; you've grabbed the girl and told her father I'm the messenger."

He smiled; said, "Morgan, it's perfect, you'll see."

I was suddenly tired; asked, "Where's the girl now?"

His smile got wider; he said, "I can't tell you, see, see the beauty of it, you really are the innocent party and . . . here's the lovely bit, he'll pay you for your help."

Before I could answer this he continued, "You'll get a call from him asking you to help, to be the bag man."

I asked, "What if I tell Mr Flaherty I want no part of this?"

He gave me that golden tooth smile; said, "Ah Morgan, nobody says no to that man; how he got so rich."

I left early, said to Sheridan, "I don't like this, not one bit."

He was still shouting encouragement to me as I left.

I waited outside, in the doorway of the Chinese café a ways along. Sheridan had never told me where he lived, and I figured it was time to find out.

It was an hour or so before he emerged and he'd obviously had a few more Jamesons. A slight stagger to his walk and certainly, he wasn't a hard mark to follow.

He finally made it to a house by the canal and went in and I waited until he'd turned on the lights.

And I called it a night.

Next morning, I was the right side of two decent coffees, the *Financial Times* thrown carelessly on my desk, my laptop feeding me information on Mr Flaherty when the door is pushed open.

A heavily built man in a very expensive suit, with hard features and two even heavier men behind him, strode in.

I didn't need Google search to tell me who this was.

He took the chair opposite me, sat down, opened his jacket, and looked round.

The heavies took position on each side of the desk.

He said, "What a shit hole."

I asked, "You have an appointment?"

He laughed in total merriment, and the two thugs gave tight smiles; said, "You don't seem overrun with business."

I tried. "Most of my business is conducted over the phone, for discretion's sake."

He mimicked, "Discretion . . . hmm, I like that."

Then suddenly he lunged across the desk, grabbed my tie, and pulled me halfway across, with one hand, I might add. He said, "I like Yanks, otherwise, you'd be picking yer teeth off the floor right now."

Then he let go.

I managed to get back into my chair, all dignity out the window, and waited.

He said, "I'm Jimmy Flaherty and some bollix has snatched me only child; he wants a million in ransom and says you are to be the go-between."

He snapped his fingers and one of the thugs dropped a large briefcase on the desk.

He said, "That's a million."

I took his word for it.

He took out a large Havana and the other heavy moved to light it; he asked, "Mind if I smoke?"

He blew an almost perfect smoke ring and we watched it linger over the desk like a bird of ill omen till he said, "This fuckhead will contact you and you're to give him the money."

He reached in his pocket, tossed a mobile phone on the desk, said, "Soon as you can see my daughter is safe, you call that number and give every single detail of what you observe."

He stood up; said, "I'm not an unreasonable man, you get my daughter back, and the bastard who took her, I'll throw one hundred large in your direction."

He'd obviously watched far too many episodes of *The Sopranos* and I was tempted to add, "Caprice."

But reined it in.

I said, "I'll do my best, sir."

He rounded on me, near spat. "I said I liked Yanks, but you screw up, you're dead meat."

When he was gone, I opened my bottom drawer, took out the small stash, did a few lines, and finally mellowed out.

My mind was in hyper drive.

I had the score.

One freaking million and all I had to do was . . . skedaddle.

Run like fuck.

Greed.

Greed is a bastard.

I was already thinking how I'd get that extra hundred-thousand and not have Flaherty looking for me.

That's the curse of coke, it makes you think you can do anything.

I locked the briefcase in my safe and moved to the bookshelf near the door.

It had impressive looking books, all unread, and moving aside *Great Expectations,* I pulled out the SIG Sauer.

Tried and tested and of a certain sentimental value.

I'd finalized my divorce with it, so it had a warm history.

I headed for Sheridan's house on the canal, stopping en route to buy a cheap briefcase, and when the guy offered to remove all the paper padding they put in there, I said, no need.

I got to the house just after two in the afternoon and the curtains were still down.

Sheridan sleeping off the Jameson.

I went round the back and sure enough, the lock was a joke and I had that picked in thirty seconds.

Moved the SIG to the right-hand pocket of my jacket and ventured in. This was the kitchen. I stood for a moment and wondered if there was a basement, where Sheridan might have put the poor girl.

Heard hysterical laughter from upstairs and realized Sheridan was not alone.

"Way to go, lover," I muttered as I began to climb the stairs.

Sheridan as late afternoon lover had never entered my mind but what the hell, good for him.

I got to the bedroom and it sounded like a fine old time was being had by all.

Hated to interrupt, but business!

Opened the door and said, "Is this a bad time?"

Sheridan's head emerged from the sheets and he guffawed, said, "Fooking Morgan."

The woman, I have to admit, a looker, pulled herself

upright, her breasts exposed, reached for a cigarette and said, "Is this the famous American?"

There was a half-empty bottle of Jameson on the table beside Sheridan and he reached for it, took a lethal slug, gagged; said, "Buddy, meet Brona."

She laughed as my jaw literally dropped.

She said, in not too bad an American pastiche, "He's joining the dots."

I put the briefcase on the floor and Sheridan roared. "Is that it, fook, is that the million?"

He didn't enjoy it too long; Brona shot him in the forehead; said, "You come too quick."

Turned the gun on me and was a little surprised to see my SIG leveled on her belly.

Nicely toned stomach, I'll admit.

She smiled, said, "Mexican standoff?"

In Galway.

I said, "You put yours on the bed, slowly, and I'll put mine on the floor, we have to be in harmony on this."

We were.

And did.

I asked, "Mind If I have a drink?"

She said, "I'll join you."

I got the bottle of Jameson and as she pushed a glass forward, I cracked her skull with it; said, "I think you came too quick."

I checked her pulse and as I'd hoped, she wasn't dead. But mainly, she wouldn't be talking for a while.

I did the requisite cleaning up and now for the really tricky part.

Rang Flaherty.

First the good news

I'd got his daughter back and alive.

Managed to kill one of the kidnappers.

Got shot myself in the cluster fuck.

The other kidnapper had gotten away.

And . . . with the money.

He and his crew were there in jig time.

The shot in my shoulder hurt like a bastard and I hated to part with the SIG, but what can you do.

Wrapped it in Sheridan's fingers.

I don't know how long we were there; Flaherty's men got Brona out of there right away and I had to tell my story to Flaherty about a dozen times.

I think two things saved my ass

1. . . . his beloved daughter was safe.

2. . . . One bad guy was dead.

And I could see him thinking, if I was involved?

Why was I shot?

Why hadn't I taken off?

I even provided a name for the other kidnapper, a shithead who'd dissed me way back.

He produced a fat envelope; said, "You earned it."

And was gone

Four days later, I was, as Sheridan said, "In the wind."

Gone.

A few months later, tanned, with a nice unostentatious villa in the South of Spain, a rather fetching beard coming in, as the Brits would say, and a nice senorita who seemed interested in the quiet English writer I'd now become; a sort of middle list cozy author persona. I was as close to happy as it gets.

One evening, with a bag full of fresh-baked baguettes, some fine wine, and all the food for a masterful paella, I got back to the villa a little later than usual; I might even have been humming something from *Man of La Mancha*.

Opened the door and saw a woman in the corner, the late evening shadows washing over her; I asked, "Bonita?"

No.

Brona, with a sawn off in her lap.

I dropped the bags.

She asked, "What day were you born on?"

I said, "Wednesday."

She laughed; said, "Complete the rhyme . . ."

Jesus, what was it?

I acted like I was thinking seriously about that, but mainly I was thinking, how I'd get to the Walther PPK, in the press beside her.

Then she threw the said gun on the floor beside my wilted paella feast, smiled, said, "Here's a hint, Tuesday's child is full of Grace . . . so . . ."

Now she leveled the sawn off, cocked the hammer; said, "You get one guess."

*

KEN BRUEN was a finalist for the Edgar, Barry, and Macavity Awards, and the Private Eye Writers of America presented him with the Shamus Award for the Best Novel of 2003 for *The Guards,* the book that introduced Jack Taylor. He lives in Galway, Ireland. To learn more about Ken and his novels go to www.ken bruen.com

Eddy May

THEO GANGI

Eddy tells me we can make money together. Eddy is the best police impersonator there is. He hangs out in police bars. He goes into police stations and talks to cops in perfect jargon. He goes down to court and gets search warrants and arrest forms and types them up. Eddy's fed himself since the seventies by sending little kids into bathrooms to solicit pedophiles. Then he'd go in like a cop and shake them down.

I'm hanging out on Christopher Street with Eddy. He's by the phone booth in plainclothes, a sport jacket and black shoes. Eddy told me that's how you dress like a detective. So now I'm also wearing a sport jacket and plain black shoes.

I'm going to Brooklyn today and I'm pissed about it. I haven't crossed that water since I moved to Washington Heights and my father cursed me as a traitor.

It's early on a Tuesday afternoon. The lower west side teems with productivity; Starbucks supports a line out onto the sidewalk. People steadily file down into the subway. Busses yawn, stretch, and lumber up and down avenues. Eddy whistles an old song, "If I were a Bell," the way Miles Davis played it. It's a show tune, pretending to be jazz genius, about a man, pretending to be a bell. Eddy catches a glimpse of something through the dark window of the bar on the corner. He gets up close to it. I am still by the phone booth, being a detective. He curses, and starts pacing, fixated on the bar window. I go over to him. He curses again, rolling his eyes and smacking himself on his pocket keys.

"Problem?"

He wipes the sweat from his old, wrinkled brow.

"The fuckin' unit. Gave up three fuckin' homers in a row."

The Big Unit. The Yankees' biggest disappointment this year. Eddy and I are Yankees fans. We're both from Brooklyn, home of the former Ebbet's Field, where Brooklyn's own Dodgers once played, now a large project. You ask me it's just as good, replaces bums with more bums. Most native Brooklynites are Mets fans, as if obeying some law of transfer from one non–Yankee New York team to another. The Brooklyn bitterness toward the frequent champions is deep. Eddy chose the Yankees because some aspect of his life deserved to be aligned with a winner. My preference came at greater cost. To my father it was evidence of a great betrayal.

Many of my teenage years were spent explaining why Mickey Mantle was better than Snider, Pee Wee, Robinson, and Campanella combined. "They're bums, Pop," I would tell him. "It's common knowledge." His hurt was palpable. I told him it's only baseball, but he didn't believe me. "Bums? That what you think of me?"

The dark bar at daytime reminds me of my father. Three or four drunks sit at the bar stools, faces tilted to the blue wash of the TV screens above. Could be any time of day; it will always be the same time inside. Pop was like that; no matter the pitch, it was always a strike.

On the three mounted sets, Randy Johnson paces with his hands on his hips, spitting as though the homer was anybody's fault but his. The Big Unit irritates the hell out of me and Eddy. After he blows a game, I find myself making up my own *Post* and *Daily News* headlines. *Big Disaster. Flop of Fame.*

"Cocksucker ain't worth half what we gave for 'em," says Eddy.

"Got that right."

I'm a *New York Times* reader. Eddy reads *The Daily News* and *The New York Post*. But when the Big Unit loses, I buy *The News*, too, so I can fully absorb the crass, ruthless abuse my team deserves. Then I talk to Eddy about this year's two-hundred-million-dollar joke.

"No word though?" I ask.

"He'll be here."

Eddy is right about that. He thinks so, but I know for sure. I step back and the TV disappears in darkness, the glass opaque now, with my reflection on its surface. I like to dress a bit better, clean shaven, cuff links now and then, how my wife likes me. She's Puerto Rican, likes a little shine, some cologne. But Eddy told me how to dress like a detective, so I'm dressed like a detective.

"Ho shit!" barks Eddy, attention back on the TV on the other side of the glass. I go up beside him and look through: a replay of a White Sox player who I never heard of knocking an unhittable pitch, up by his eyes, clean out of the ballpark. The big unit, with his giant, gangly frame and trailer-park dismay, stands on top of the wheat shade mound of dirt in utter incredulity.

"Four!" says Eddy. "Four goddamn dingers in one inning? That pitch wasn't even a strike. It wasn't even close, damn near over his head! How'd he hit that? Fucking impossible. Four homers."

I shake my head.

"I can see the headlines. Four! four-get it!"

"Four-gone conclusion," says Eddy. "Just four-fit already."

I see the kid as Eddy goes on about how the Unit keeps throwing his flat, useless slider. The kid has bleached blonde hair and light eyes, with a don't-give-a-fuck apathy way beyond typical adolescence. His attitude puts him going on thirty, a couple of jail bids already behind him. In reality, the kid is maybe fifteen, though not even he knows for sure. Got more miles on him than a '89 VW.

"Yeah, he was unhittable in the National League, but so fuckin' what? My friend, you and I could have fifteen wins and an ERA under three with those pansy-ass hitters."

My father and Eddy were cast from the same boilerplate, even though Eddy is a European mutt and Pop was one-hundred-percent Sicilian. It must be the Brooklyn in them, the streets that taught them both how to hustle and talk, doing funny things with the letter H, adding it to the end of some words and striking it from the beginning of others. *Fuck outta 'ere*. Even their stooped countenance is the same: short necks, slumped shoulders, heavy faces pulled to the sidewalk as if losing money at dice.

Eddy's cast-iron eyes look just past me as he speaks,

just how a real cop might. Though a real cop would notice the kid already. Even when Eddy is pissed, he can't manage to make those dark, drooping bags of his look anything but sad.

I nudge him.

"That the kid?"

The kid makes eye contact with me. I hope he doesn't give it up. I hope I don't give it up. He smirks at me, teasing—a demon with the face of a cherub.

"Yeah. Hey, kid."

"Hey."

"What you got for me?" asks Eddy. The kid holds out a tan Ferragamo wallet. Eddy takes it, and opens it up.

Edward Schalaci.

"Mr. Edward Schalaci," says Eddy. For a moment, I think he's talking to me. "Would you look at that," he says, "guy's name is Eddie, like me. One-hundred fifty Columbia Heights. Yeah. Would you look at that, Brooklyn Heights, that's real money. Guy's probably married. Wife's got no clue. Right? Let's get a move."

As Eddy starts to walk down to the subway, the kid turns and smirks at me. Kid's got a crazy sense of his own power. He's an orphan from Poughkeepsie who came to The City to live off wealthy pedophiles. Got thrown out of a few downtown lofts and been selling his ass ever since. There's something supernatural about the way he seems to get younger every time I see him, as though he started at sixteen and now looks fourteen. Pretty soon he'll be reduced to shaking down sickos from a stroller.

The thought makes me queasy. My wife is ready, I mean *ready* for a baby. I'm hesitant, and days like this I know why.

We have done this a couple of times: we go into the

bathroom and pretend to be from the Youth Squad, I take The Kid outside while Eddy talks the guy into giving him money, to avoid being arrested. Eddy has been making money like that all over the west side of Lower Manhattan for years. His biggest moneymaker is this kid.

Eddy hooked up with The Kid on one of his fugazi raids, took him under his wing and taught him how to hustle, taught him how to get paid without giving it up. The Kid still did his own thing, and this wallet represented the coup de grace of their partnership. It meant that The Kid had consummated a transaction and then ripped the john off, 'cuz there are just no good deals left in The City.

When I see the wallet I think of this and only this. I try to joke in my head, but I cannot smile. I see the kid reduced to a baby and wrapped in my wife's tan arms: a bundle of joy, shock, and heartbreak. Is there a parent alive or dead who hasn't been heartbroken?

The wallet now is the source of the evil, clear evidence that Eddy knows exactly what this kid is doing and is an accessory. Eddy takes this confession in his hand like a ticket at a deli. I cannot decide if Eddy is magnificently in tune to his hustle or just facile as cardboard.

We join the heavy flow of traffic, heading toward the inevitable. There is no point in talking business in front of these strangers, so the three of us keep quiet. Eddy gives me commiserating glances as we squeeze on the crowded train, reminding me of Pop again. Old and red faced, Pop would raise his eyebrow and shrug like that with me, often reduced to the basics of interaction, like we spoke different languages.

The crowd thins before we leave Manhattan. We get off at the Clark Street station, stepping into the open

Brooklyn air beneath the old sign for Hotel St. George. Nothing tastes different about the air, but I'm aware of it. I'm breaking an old promise I made my father by coming here. I didn't want to see him in Brooklyn, with his Bensonhurst lowlifes and me trying to be a cop. I wonder what borders of mine my wife's unborn bundle will cross. The Kid looks around, stark baby-blue eyes restless and pissed.

"Who's this guy, anyway?" he asks, gesturing to me.

"That's Ron."

"Hi," I say.

"*Detective* Ron?" says The Kid, being smart.

"As far as you're concerned," says Eddy, "yeah, he's a fuckin' detective." Eddy clears his throat with a thick, nasty hack. Then, as if his throbbing throat reminds him, he lights a cigarette.

"You want one?" he asks me, already putting his pack of Marlboro menthols away. It is a running joke between us. I don't smoke. He offers anyway, hoping someone will join him in being self-destructive.

"Yeah," I say.

"You serious?"

"Yeah. Calm my nerves a bit. I got to act like you anyway, right?"

Smiling, his old movie star dimple like a crater in his cheek, Eddy takes his pack back out, and looks inside. He shakes it. Then reaches in, and gives me one, a bit bent. Then he throws out the pack, and motions toward me with his lighter.

"Wait," I say. "Your lucky?"

When he opens a new pack, Eddy always flips the first cigarette upside down, and saves it for last, his "lucky."

"It's no problem," says Eddy. "It's lucky. So maybe you won't get addicted."

He lights it. The minty smoke burns down my throat, and bites my lungs. I cough.

"Damn," I say. "What you smoke these for? Things have teeth."

The smoke clears way for more to come. The feeling is old and familiar. Pop smoked cigars, so I smoked cigarettes.

"You got a preference?"

"Used to smoke regular cigarettes," I say. "Parliaments."

"Heh. Pansy ass."

We keep walking, following The Kid's little sinister swagger.

"When you were a cop, you ever want to be a detective?" he asks me.

"Sure," I say, thinking. "But I most likely woulda gone upstate, you know? Been a trooper. Easy work, man. Good money."

"Heh. No angle in a fugazi state trooper, though, I'll tell you that. Looks like you got to settle for a detective."

"A detective's good," I say. "Just never thought I'd score good on the test."

"You scored fine on my test, heh."

I repeat this to myself: I am a laid-off cop. I still have my shield. That is why Eddy wants to work with me. He needs identification. I am bitter about being laid-off. I repeat this to myself.

We reach Pineapple Street. The neighborhood is a residential haven, with grand old architecture in muted red and earth tones. No home is higher than four stories on the tree-lined blocks, with ceremonial staircases, ornate banisters, and columned entrances. The doors and windows are huge, dark chandeliers dangling within, and brick fills in the rest of the expanding block.

"Let's go check out the promenade," suggests Eddy.

The Kid rolls his eyes. I agree, I want to get this over with, but Eddy is already on his way. Over his shoulder, I see Manhattan. From a distance, the towering shapes and rectangles look like an immaculate geometric drawing, a conception impossible to build. Then the murky gray water comes into view, the moat separating the boroughs from The City, as it's simply referred to by those who don't call it home.

The water reminds me of Pier 4 Bush, the day my father took me to learn his routine. Looking out at the mercury water and stacks of identically shaped, multicolored crates, Pop introduced me to what seemed like half the ILA Union. Augie, the plan clerk who told what crates wouldn't be missed; Patty, the dock boss who told the checkers where to carry them; Eddie, the checker who took the crates off to a truck; and Ernie, the rounds man who was on the job twenty-three years without making one arrest. Then Pop and Ernie collected on some gambling debts. Nobody got violent around me, least of all Pop, whose hands had already begun to shake and couldn't intimidate a child—he approached the dockworkers, as they would say, with two feet in one shoe. That day he told me I had a choice about whether I wanted to follow in his footsteps. As far as he was concerned, I chose wrong.

Now look at me. He'd be real proud.

The Kid leans over the banister, dangling a ball of spit at his lips and letting it fall below. I want to discipline him, smack him around. Not that my father ever laid a hand on me, though I know he wanted to. Couldn't ever bring himself to do it, no matter what instance of open defiance.

Looking on the water, Eddy takes out a small bottle

of Scotch and takes a sip, offering it to me, his blue hands shaking. I glance around.

"What're ya looking fer? We're the law," he says.

"You think we seem like cops if we smell like liquor?"

"Like a crooked cop, yeah. Fuck, they smellin' yer breath fer anyway?"

I sip it.

"My pop," I tell Eddy, the swallow stiff in my throat, ahh, "was a Scotch man. He worked on a dock. Long-shoreman. Worked by the water every day."

"Yeah? How'd he do?"

"Did okay. Had to hustle, though."

I drink again from the gold liquor and it drops to my stomach like a warm dagger.

"Longshoreman makes good money now," says Eddy.

"Yeah. Now."

The Statue of Liberty stands at the end of the island like Manhattan's toy. Tuesday is a bright, lazy day for some people; bachelors walking their dogs, mothers or nannies pushing strollers, and ghetto teens making out in big coats. It's difficult to look at The City and see Eddy's city. I can imagine some crimes more than others. I see professionals and I naturally imagine their drug habits, and the violence that brings them what they need. For every person, there is a logical shadow. For every BlackBerry-carrying, Bluetooth wireless talking professional, there is a messenger-bag middleman, bringing him goodies from some well connected, nickel-plate Ruger-carrying mover-shaker. What scares me about Eddy is how he sees the shadow side of sexuality. For every flower-buying, wife-fucking father, there's a child-buying, prepubescent-molesting deviant. It bothers me. I try not to be naive about things, but it bothers me. Drugs and violence are tolerable, but touching children is just another animal.

"We're gonna get a good thing goin', Ron," Eddy tells me. "Get this thing here down to a science."

"Yeah."

A science. This guy must have a wardrobe's worth of skeletons in his closet.

I have to wonder how Eddy sees and uncovers this aspect of The City with such ease. He knows where to go. He can find and spot his mark. Eddy is no protector of children. Unlike The Kid, Eddy does not know his own power. What some men do to children is an unchangeable truth in Eddy's life. He is a perpetual witness. His triumph is that he then hurts the aggressor by taking his money. Eddy is proud of this solution. Eddy then pays the children. He is their friend.

Or maybe he doesn't care. Maybe it's just a hustle like any other hustle, like any of Pop's hustles. There's money, and a game to get it.

I turn from the water and see the building we will go to from behind. It is one of two old buildings that shoot up into the sky like cylinders—one red, and the other beige. I'm not sure which color we will enter.

We walk back up to the residential avenue, The Kid with his blonde hair in tow. Eddy checks the license again, and looks up at the contrasting cylinders. There are two doorways, the red one a staircase above street level, the beige a staircase below. Red, I guess. Red makes sense. Eddy drops his cigarette, crushes it with his plain black shoe, and then begins down the steps toward the burrowed cavelike beige door. He rings the buzzer, takes out his badge, and folds it in his breast pocket so it shows clearly. He gestures for me to do the same.

"Yes?" says the filtered voice.

"Is this Mr. Edward Schalaci?"

"Who's this?" says the voice, sounding like a woman.

"This is Detective May with the NYPD. Does a Mr. Schalaci live there?"

"Yes."

"To your knowledge, did he lose his wallet, ma'am?"

A pause. He should have said, *might* we have a word, ma'am?

"I think so," says the woman.

Eddy smiles at me.

"Mark can't deny it's his now. Love when the wife's home."

The buzzer rings and the three of us walk up the creaky stairs, the air hot and damp. I sweat. I hear Eddy wheezing ahead of me. His feet drop heavily on the steps.

"Cocksuckin' walk-up," mutters Eddy.

He reaches the top and lets out a huge exhale. He turns to The Kid.

"Wait here," he says, and then turns to me. "Follow me. Let me do the talkin'."

The door opens and a pretty older blonde opens the door, her face inquisitive but pleasant.

Rebecca Schalaci.

"Hello, detectives, I'm Rebecca Schalaci."

Rebecca Schalaci is Margaret Gallo.

"Good morning, Ms. Schalaci. Sorry to disturb you. Is Mr. Schalaci at home?"

"Uh, yes," she says, and glances at me. "I'll get him."

She walks off. Eddy holds the door open.

"Ms. Schalaci," he says, "you mind if we come in?"

"No," she says, hesitant. "Not at all. Can I get you anything?"

"We're fine, thank you Ms. Schalaci."

She disappears into the back. The home is top notch,

with natural light, neutral walls, ornate molding, a display case with ancient plates, next to a plasma-screen TV. Eddy smiles.

"Wow. What you think we can get outta this guy? Quick, Ron."

I think.

"Thirty."

"We can beat thirty."

He is right.

"We can do better than thirty for sure. Good-looking broad, huh?"

He turns to look at me, his eyes finding mine for a moment, then looking off again.

"Shame. Good-looking broad like that, got no idea what she's into." Eddy nods to himself, repeating "shame."

The mark shows. The man is half gray, half bald, half concerned, and half dressed. He inserts a cuff link into the sleeve of his open shirt as he walks in.

Edward Schalaci is Woodrow Collins.

"Can I help you, officers?"

"Mr. Schalaci," begins Eddy, "we found a wallet with your ID inside." Eddy holds up the wallet. "Mr. Schalaci, does this wallet belong to you?"

Schalaci examines the wallet suspiciously.

"Uh, yeah, thank you. That's my wallet."

Eddy turns to me and nods.

"Better go get The Kid," he says.

I nod officially, like a detective.

"Sir, can we go to a more private part of the apartment?" asks Eddy.

I go back out into the hallway. I see The Kid.

"Time," I tell him. He seems younger still, skim-coated

skin—a child's sharp teeth. He looks back at me like, fuck you.

I lead The Kid inside and find Eddy and Schalaci in what looks like a study. Schalaci sees The Kid and his jaw drops.

"Mr. Schalaci, do you recognize this child?"

Schalaci is speechless.

"Mr. Schalaci, answer the goddamn question. Do you recognize this child?"

Schalaci nods, slowly.

"I thought you did, Mr. Schalaci."

The Kid looks bored.

"Is this the man?" I ask The Kid.

The Kid nods, and points as if he is in court.

"This boy, Mr. Schalaci, has identified you, and his parents are making a formal complaint against you, that you had sex with him, and that you abused him."

"Are you . . ." mutters Schalaci, losing his voice.

"I am very serious, Mr. Schalaci." Eddy reaches into his pocket and takes out the phony arrest warrant he has written up, and shows it to Schalaci. Schalaci takes it. He seems impressed.

"Do you understand the severity of these charges?"

"I . . . I'm sorry . . ."

"Take The Kid back out," Eddy tells me.

I walk The Kid back out of the room, and let Eddy do his thing. We go out in the hallway, and as I turn to go back inside, The Kid gives me the finger. I don't control myself this time. My open hand flies and cuffs the back of his head; a wisp of blonde hair springs up. His face gets red and he bites his lip with his sharp teeth, sizing me. He smirks, like he got what he wanted. I don't care. It felt good.

In the study, Eddy is into his routine.

". . . bail on the warrant there is set at forty thousand. Now, I'm a reasonable man, Mr. Schalaci. I want this taken care of, but I don't see the need to disrupt your life, or haul you in or anything like that. I can go back, I'll change a few numbers on the warrant and it'll just get lost in the paperwork. If you want, I'll even send you the warrant and you can rip it up, frame it, or wash you widows with it, point is you won't hear from us."

Eddy begins to sound like a salesman. Schalaci thinks hard about this, leaning back against his desk.

"They'll never call you again."

Schalaci nods slowly and a sense of relief washes over him.

"They won't call me?"

"No, sir. It'll be taken care of. I can promise you that."

Schalaci has not looked at me once this whole time. He gets up off his desk and walks past me, putting the cuff link into his other sleeve.

"Honey, I'm stepping outside with these gentlemen for a moment."

Eddy whispers to me.

"Guy's loaded. Shame about her."

Schalaci puts on his blazer and we follow him out the door. We leave The Kid in the stairwell playing with his gum, shooting knives at me from his eyes. We go back down the stairs and outside. We follow Schalaci past a silver Corvette, a couple of blocks over, around the corner and into a Citibank. Eddy hops in a corner store quickly and buys a pack of cigarettes. He pounds it into his palm, drops the cellophane on the sidewalk, and flips his lucky. He pops one in his mouth and offers me another. I take it.

"Why you smoking all of a sudden?"

"Don't know. Big job, you know. Got me nervous."

I don't know, I really don't. Eddy is smoking, so I want to smoke, too.

"Figure in a month or two, call the guy up, tell him it's taken care of. He'll be happy, you know, thank God nothing happened to him. Rest of his life he'll think some policeman took money, fixed the case and that's that."

I look at Eddy's unassuming face and think of Pop, the transformation after the police and Waterfront Commission raided his docks; outraged beyond baseball, beyond a Puerto Rican wife. A few bosses and many of his friends did some serious time behind that raid. Pop came to The City to look in my face with his hound eyes. "You know how that made me look?" he demanded of me. "I didn't know," I told him. I didn't, I swore I didn't.

I think of The Kid and wonder, if Pop had smacked me just once, let me know who was in charge, let me know how he felt. Enough of the hound dog eyes, the lovable loser. Softest crook I ever knew. If he'd laid it down, shown some *huevos,* maybe it wouldn't be as hard as it was. Maybe I wouldn't have even tried to be a cop.

Eddy inhales a menthol with vacant confidence, a man who isn't wrong even when he's wrong.

"Eddy," I tell him, "something's not right about this guy. You know?"

"Hey, Ronny, I been at this a long time, I know when something's off. This guy's perfect. He assumes he can throw money at anything, make it go away, so he can act any way he wants. Didn't even hesitate, like, forty? That's it?"

"I don't know. The guy never looked at me, never once. Wasn't right."

"Trust me. This is right as it gets."

Schalaci comes back out of the Citibank.

"Let's go back up to my apartment," he says.

Eddy nods like it's a good idea and charges forward, heavy eyes squinting in the morning light.

Eddy is spent when we get back up to the apartment, wheezing and coughing. Ms. Schalaci gets him a paper towel from the kitchen and Eddy wipes himself down.

"Detective?" asks Schalaci, pushy. "This way."

We follow him into the study. I see Ms. Schalaci out of corner of my eye, following us. Margaret Gallo.

Schalaci turns. I mean, Woodrow Collins turns. Woody. Asshole.

I leave the door open behind us. Eddy coughs and coughs. He doesn't notice the door. Eddy is the best police impersonator. But he doesn't notice a lot.

Schalaci holds out an envelope. Eddy coughs.

"Forty?" he asks.

Schalaci nods. My pulse is a jackhammer.

Eddy covers his mouth with the paper towel. He reaches with his other hand, nodding. He coughs into the towel. He takes the envelope.

My name is Eddie Schalaci. I am Eddie Schalaci again.

Detective first-grade Woody Collins, a.k.a. the phony Schalaci, takes out his badge and shows it to Eddy, whose eyes swell with disbelief.

"Eddy May, you're under arrest for impersonating a police officer, extortion, accessory to child prostitution, and child abuse."

Detective third-grade Margaret Gallo, a.k.a. Ms. Rebecca Schalaci, covers us from behind, her badge in one hand, her service pistol in the other.

I'm detective second-grade Eddie Schalaci, a.k.a.

Ronny Hertz. I don't pull out my badge. Mine is already showing in the breast of my detective's blazer.

For Pop's eulogy, I talked about his humor, how when I began going bald he told me, "Ed, I got a way you can save your hair." He showed me an empty cigar box. "Save it in here." I talked about how he loved giving people nicknames, he called his brother Whiney because his friend Whiney left Bensonhurst and Pop missed him. He called a guy Johnny Once, because he only came around once in a while. I talked about his devotion to my mother, who died when I was born, and how that was the first of the many ways I disappointed him. Some laughed, but others just stared with hard, narrow brows. I didn't mention the raid, less than a year before his death and the start of the indulgence that killed him. I didn't mention his devotion to Scotch, and the other powders and pills that he unsuccessfully hid from me. All I could think of was the night in that Midtown bar when he told me about the raid, and I told him I didn't know.

Shackled, head hanging in defeat, Eddy stares at the floor between his plain black shoes as Detective Woody Collins tries to get him to confess to more crimes. That was how Pop looked. He was beyond the rage he had a right to. He was broken, too old or helpless to even be mad about it. Eddy, his frown heavy like wet clay, is unreachable.

"We're gonna appeal to the pedophile community, Eddy. Make a deal. They'll come out the woodwork once they find out about you."

Collins looks at me. It was his idea to call the mark Eddie Schalaci, my name. He didn't want to be the only one who had to feel like a filthy child molester.

"We know you got a scrapbook, Eddy, of all your little bullshit scams."

Collins is an asshole.

I fish in my pocket for Eddy's pack of cigarettes, from when we took his belongings earlier. I toss the menthols on the table in front of Eddy. His callous fingers pick out a cigarette, and put it in his dry mouth. I light it for him with his lighter. His hands shackled, he raises the pack to me. I take one, and light it myself, then pace over to the mirror.

Eddy breaks his silence.

"I feel like The Unit, you know? When that cocksucker hit that goddamn pitch. Over his head, Ron. Pitch was over his goddamn head."

I nod, without the heart to tell him my real name, and turn to the mirror. There are the three of us. Eddy looks betrayed, as he always does. I look a bit like me again, Eddy Schalaci. Eddie Schalaci. Undercover works like that. Looking in a mirror. You never know when someone's behind it, looking back at you.

*

THEO GANGI is the author of *Bang Bang* (Kensington Publishing), a hard-boiled New York City–based crime thriller. His stories have appeared in *The Greensboro Review* and the Columbia University *Spectator*. His articles and reviews have appeared in the *San Francisco Chronicle, Inked* magazine, and *Mystery Scene* magazine. Visit him at www.theogangi.com.

The Plot

JEFFERY DEAVER

When J. B. Prescott, the hugely popular crime novelist, died, millions of readers around the world were stunned and saddened.

But only one fan thought that there was something more to his death than what was revealed in the press reports.

Rumpled, round, middle-aged Jimmy Malloy was an NYPD detective sergeant. He had three passions other than police work: his family, his boat, and reading. Malloy read anything, but preferred crime novels. He liked the clever plots and the fast-moving stories. That's what books should be, he felt. He'd been at a party once and people were talking about how long they should give a book before they put it down. Some people had said they'd endure fifty pages, some said a hundred.

Malloy had laughed. "No, no, no. It's not dental work,

like you're waiting for the anesthetic to kick in. You should enjoy the book from page one."

Prescott's books were that way. They entertained you from the git-go. They took you away from your job, they took you away from the problems with your wife or daughter, your mortgage company.

They took you away from everything. And in this life, Malloy reflected, there was a lot to be taken away from.

"What're you moping around about?" his partner, Ralph DeLeon, asked, walking into the shabby office they shared in the Midtown South Precinct, after half a weekend off. "I'm the only one round here got reason to be upset. Thanks to the Mets yesterday. Oh, wait. You don't even know who the Mets are, son, do you?"

"Sure, I love basketball," Malloy joked. But it was a distracted joke.

"So?" DeLeon asked. He was tall, slim, muscular, black—the opposite of Malloy, detail for detail.

"Got one of those feelings."

"Shit. Last one of those *feelings* earned us a sit-down with the Dep Com."

Plate glass and Corvettes are extremely expensive. Especially when owned by people with lawyers.

But Malloy wasn't paying much attention to their past collars. Or to DeLeon. He once more read the obit that had appeared in the *Times* a month ago.

J.B. Prescott, 68, author of thirty-two best-selling crime novels, died yesterday while on a hike in a remote section of Vermont, where he had a summer home.

The cause of death was a heart attack.

"We're terribly saddened by the death of one of our most prolific and important writers," said Dolores Kemper, CEO of Hutton-Fielding, Inc., which had been his publisher for many years. "In these days of lower book sales and fewer people reading, J.B.'s books still flew off the shelves. It's a terrible loss for everyone."

Prescott's best-known creation was Jacob Sharpe, a down-and-dirty counterintelligence agent, who traveled the world, fighting terrorists and criminals. Sharpe was frequently compared to James Bond and Jason Bourne.

Prescott was not a critical darling. Reviewers called his books, "airport time-passers," "beach reads," and "junk food for the mind—superior junk food, but empty calories nonetheless."

Still, he was immensely popular with his fans. Each of his books sold millions of copies.

His success brought him fame and fortune, but Prescott shunned the public life, rarely going on book tours or giving interviews. Though a multimillionaire, he had no interest in the celebrity lifestyle. He and his second wife, the former Jane Spenser, 38, owned an apartment in Manhattan, where she is a part-time photo editor for *Styles,* the popular fashion magazine. Prescott himself, however, spent most of his time in Vermont or in the countryside of Spain, where he could write in peace.

Born in Kansas, John Balin Prescott studied English literature at the University of Iowa and was an advertising copywriter and teacher for some years while trying to publish literary fiction and poetry. He had little success and ultimately switched to writing thrillers. His first, *The Trinity Connection,* became a runaway hit in 1991. The book was on *The New York Times* bestseller list for more than one hundred weeks.

Demand for his books became so great that ten years ago he took on a co-writer, Aaron Reilly, 39, with whom he wrote sixteen bestsellers. This increased his output to two novels a year, sometimes more.

"We're just devastated," said Reilly, who described himself as a friend as well as a colleague. "John hadn't been feeling well lately. But we couldn't get him back to the city to see his doctor, he was so intent on finishing our latest manuscript. That's the way he was. Type A in the extreme."

Last week, Prescott traveled to Vermont alone to work on his next novel. Taking a break from the writing, he went for a hike, as he often did, in a deserted area near the Green Mountains. It was there that he suffered the coronary.

"John's personal physician described the heart attack as massive," co-author Reilly added. "Even if he hadn't been alone, the odds of saving him were slim to nonexistent."

Mr. Prescott is survived by his wife and two children from a prior marriage.

"So what's this feeling you're talking about?" DeLeon asked, reading over his partner's shoulder.

"I'm not sure. Something."

"Now, *there* is some evidence to get straight to the crime lab. 'Something.' Come on, there's some real cases on our plate, son. Put your mopey hat away. We gotta meet our snitch."

"Mopey hat? Did you actually say mopey hat?"

A half hour later, Malloy and DeLeon were sitting in a disgusting dive of a coffee shop near the Hudson River docks, talking to a scummy little guy of indeterminate race and age.

Lucius was eating chili in a sloppy way and saying, "So what happened was Bark, remember I was telling you about Bark."

"Who's Bark?" Malloy asked.

"I *told* you."

DeLeon said, "He told us."

"What Bark did was he was going to mark the bag, only he's a Nimrod, so he forgot which one it was. I figured it out and got it marked. That worked out okay. It's marked, it's on the truck. Nobody saw me. They had, I'd be capped." A big mouthful of chili. And a grin. "So."

"Good job," DeLeon said. And kicked Malloy under the table. Meaning: Tell him he did a good job, because if you don't the man'll start to feel bad and, yeah, he's a little shit Nimrod, whatever that is, but we need him.

But Malloy was remembering something. He rose abruptly. "I gotta go."

"I dint do a good job?" Lucius called, hurt.

But he was speaking to Jimmy Malloy's back.

Jane Prescott opened the door of the townhouse in Greenwich Village. Close to five-eleven, she could look directly into Malloy's eyes.

The widow wore a black dress, closely fitted, and her eyes were red like she'd been crying. Her hair was swept back and faint gray roots showed, though Malloy recalled that she was only in her late thirties. Three decades younger than her late husband, he also recalled.

"Detective." Hesitant, of course, looking over his ID. A policeman. She was thinking this was odd—not necessarily reason to panic but odd.

"I recognize you," Malloy said.

She blinked. "Have we met?"

"In *Sharpe Edge*. You were Monica."

She gave a hollow laugh. "People say that, because an older man falls in love with a younger woman in the book. But I'm not a spy and I can't rappel off cliffs."

They were both beautiful, however, if Malloy remembered the Prescott novel correctly. But he said nothing about this, she being a new widow. What he said was, "I'm sorry for your loss."

"Thank you. Oh, please come inside."

The apartment was small, typical of the Village, but luxurious as diamonds. Rich antiques, original art. Even statues. Nobody Malloy knew owned statues. A peek into the kitchen revealed intimidating brushed-metal appliances with names Malloy couldn't pronounce.

They sat and she looked at him with her red-rimmed eyes. An uneasy moment later he asked, "You're wondering what a cop's doing here."

"Yes, I am."

"Other than just being a fan, wishing to pay condolences."

"You could've written a letter."

"The fact is, this is sort of personal. I didn't want to come sooner, out of respect. But there's something I'd like to ask. Some of us in the department were thinking 'bout putting together a memorial evening in honor of your husband. He wrote about New York a lot and he didn't make us cops out to be flunkies. One of them, I can't remember which one, he had this great plotline here in the city. Some NYPD rookie helps out Jacob Sharpe. It was about terrorists going after the train stations."

"*Hallowed Ground.*"

"That's right. That was a good book."

More silence.

Malloy glanced at a photograph on the desk. It showed a half dozen people, in somber clothing, standing around a gravesite. Jane was in the foreground.

She saw him looking at it. "The funeral."

"Who're the other people there?"

"His daughters from his first marriage. That's Aaron, his co-writer." She indicated a man standing next to her. Then, in the background another, older man in an ill-fitting suit. She said, "Frank Lester, John's former agent."

She said nothing more. Malloy continued, "Well, some folks in the department know I'm one of your husband's biggest fans, so I got elected to come talk to you, ask if you'd come to the memorial. An appreciation night, you could call it. Maybe say a few words. Wait. 'Elected' makes it sound like I didn't want to come. But I did. I loved his books."

"I sense you did," she said, looking at the detective with piercing gray eyes.

"So?"

"I appreciate the offer. I'll just have to see."

"Sure. Whatever you'd feel comfortable with."

"You made him feel bad. He nearly got capped on that assignment."

Malloy said to his partner, "I'll send him a balloon basket. 'Sorry I was rude to my favorite snitch.' But right now I'm on to something."

"Give me particulars."

"Okay. Well, she's hot, Prescott's wife."

"That's not a helpful particular."

"I think it is. Hot . . . and thirty years younger than her husband."

"So she took her bra off and gave him a heart attack. Murder-by-boob isn't in the penal code."

"You know what I mean."

"You mean she wanted somebody younger. So do I. So does everybody. Well, not you, 'cause nobody younger would give you the time of day."

"And there was this feeling I got at the house. She wasn't really in mourning. She was in a black dress, yeah, but it was tighter than anything I'd ever let my daughter wear, and her red eyes? It was like she'd been rubbing them. I didn't buy the grieving widow thing."

"You ain't marshalling *Boston Legal* evidence here, son."

"There's more." Malloy pulled the limp copy of Prescott's obit out of his pocket. He tapped a portion. "I realized where my feeling came from. See this part about the personal physician?"

"Yeah. So?"

"You read books, DeLeon?"

"Yeah, I can read. I can tie my shoes. I can fieldstrip a Glock in one minute sixteen seconds. Oh, and put it back together, too, without any missing parts. What's your point?"

"You know how if you read a book and you like it and it's a good book, it stays with you? Parts of it do? Well, I read a book a few years ago. In it this guy has to kill a terrorist, but if the terrorist is murdered there'd be an international incident, so it has to look like a natural death."

"How'd they set it up?"

"It was really smart. They shot him in the head three times with a Bushmaster."

"That's fairly *un*natural."

"It's natural because that's how the victim's 'personal physician' "—Malloy did the quote things with his fingers "—signed the death certificate: cerebral hemorrhage following a stroke. Your doctor does that, the death doesn't have to go to the coroner. The police weren't involved. The body was cremated. The whole thing went away."

"Hmm. Not bad. All you need is a gun, a shitload of money, and a crooked doctor. I'm starting to like these particular particulars."

"And what's *particularly* interesting is that it was one of Prescott's books that Aaron Reilly co-wrote. *And* the wife remembered it. *That* was why I went to see her."

"Check out the doctor."

"I tried. He's Spanish."

"So's half the city, in case you didn't know. We got translators, *hijo*."

"Not Latino. *Spanish*. From Spain. He's back home and I can't track him down."

The department secretary stuck her head in the door-way. "Jimmy, you got a call from a Frank Lester."

"Who'd be? . . ."

"A book agent. Worked with that guy Prescott you were talking about."

The former agent. "How'd he get my number?"

"I don't know. He said he heard you were planning some memorial service and he wanted to get together with you to talk about it."

DeLeon frowned. "Memorial?"

"I had to make up something to get to see the wife." Malloy took the number, a Manhattan cell-phone area code, he noticed. Called. It went to voice mail. He didn't leave a message.

Malloy turned back to his partner. "There's more. An hour ago I talked with some deputies up in Vermont. They told me that it was a private ambulance took the body away. Not one of the local outfits. The sheriff bought into the heart-attack thing but he still sent a few people to the place where Prescott was hiking just to take some statements. After the ambulance left, one of the deputies saw somebody leaving the area. Male, he thinks. No description other than that, except he was carrying what looked like a briefcase or small suitcase."

"Breakdown rifle?"

"What I was thinking. And when this guy saw the cop car, he vanished fast."

"A pro?"

"Maybe. I was thinking that co-author might've come across some connected guys in doing his research. Maybe it was this Aaron Reilly."

"You got any ideas on how to find out?"

"As a matter of fact, I do."

Standing in the dim frosted-glass corridor of a luxurious SoHo condo, Jimmy Malloy made sure his gun was unobstructed and rang the buzzer.

The large door swung open.

"Aaron Reilly?" Even though he recognized the co-author from the picture at Prescott's funeral.

"Yes, that's right." The man gave a cautious grin.

Which remained in place, though it grew a wrinkle of surprise when the shield appeared. Malloy tried to figure out if the man had been expecting him—because Jane Prescott had called ahead of time—but couldn't tell.

"Come on inside, detective."

Reilly, in his late thirties, Malloy remembered, was the opposite of Jane Prescott. He was in faded jeans and a work shirt, sleeves rolled up. A Japanese product, not a Swiss, told him the time and there was no gold dangling on him anywhere. His shoes were scuffed. He was good-looking, with thick longish hair and no wedding ring.

The condo—in chic SoHo—had every right to be opulent, but, though large, it was modest and lived-in.

Not an original piece of art in the place.

Zero sculpture.

And unlike the Widow Prescott's abode, Reilly's was chock-a-block with books.

He gestured the cop to sit. Malloy picked a leather chair that lowered him six inches toward the ground as it wheezed contentedly. On the wall nearby was a shelf of the books. Malloy noted one: *The Paris Deception*. "J.B. Prescott with Aaron Reilly" was on the spine.

Malloy was struck by the word, "with." He wondered if Reilly felt bad, defensive maybe, that his contribution to the literary world was embodied in that preposition.

And if so, did he feel bad enough to kill the man who'd bestowed it and relegated him to second-class status?

"That's one of my favorites."

"So you're a fan, too."

"Yep. That's why I volunteered to come talk to you. First, I have to say I really admire your work."

"Thank you."

Malloy kept scanning the bookshelves. And found what he'd been looking for: two entire shelves were filled with books about guns and shooting. There had to be something in one of them about rifles that could be broken down and hidden in small suitcases. They were, Malloy knew, easy to find.

"What exactly can I do for you, detective?"

Malloy looked back. "Just a routine matter mostly. Now, technically John Prescott was a resident of the city, so his death falls partly under our jurisdiction."

"Yes, I suppose." Reilly still looked perplexed.

"Whenever there's a large estate, we're sometimes asked to look into the death, even if it's ruled accidental or illness related."

"Why would you look into it?" Reilly asked, frowning.

"Tax revenue mostly."

"Really? That's funny. It was my understanding that only department of revenue agents had jurisdiction to make inquiries like that. In fact, I researched a similar issue for one of our books. We had Jacob Sharpe following the money—you know, to find the ultimate bad guy. The police department couldn't help him. He had to go to revenue."

It was an oops moment, and Malloy realized he should have known better. Of course, the co-author would know all about police and law enforcement procedures.

"Unless what you're really saying is that you—or somebody—think that John's death might not have been an illness at all. That it was intentional . . . But how *could* it be?"

Malloy didn't want to give away his theory about the crooked doctor. He said, "Let's say I know you're a diabetic and if you don't get your insulin you'll die. I keep you from getting your injection, there's an argument that I'm guilty of murder."

"And you think somebody was with him at the time he had the heart attack and didn't call for help?"

"Just speculating. Probably how you write books."

"We're a little more organized than that. We come up with a detailed plot, all the twists and turns. Then we execute it. We know exactly how the story will end."

"So that's how it works."

"Yes."

"I wondered."

"But, see, the problem with what you're suggesting is that it would be a coincidence for this 'somebody,' who wanted him dead, to be up there in Vermont at just the moment he had the attack . . . We could never get away with that."

Malloy blinked. "You—?"

Reilly lifted an eyebrow. "If we put that into a book, our editor wouldn't let us get away with it."

"Still. Did he have any enemies?"

"No, none that I knew about. He was a good boss and a nice man. I can't imagine anybody'd want him dead."

"Well, I think that's about it," Malloy said. "I appreciate your time."

Reilly rose and walked the detective to the door. "Didn't you forget the most important question."

"What's that?"

"The question our editor would insist we add at the end of an interrogation in one of the books: Where was *I* at the time he died."

"I'm not accusing you of anything."

"I didn't say you were. I'm just saying that a cop in a Jacob Sharpe novel would've asked the question."

"Okay. Where were you?"

"I was here in New York. And the next question?"

Malloy knew what that was: "Can anyone verify that?"

"No. I was alone all day. Writing. Sorry, but reality's a lot tougher than fiction, isn't it, detective?"

"Yo, listen up," the scrawny little man said. "This is interesting."

"I'm listening." Malloy tried look pleasant as he sat across from Lucius the snitch. Before they'd met, Ralph DeLeon reminded him how Malloy had dissed the man earlier. So he was struggling to be nice.

"I followed Reilly to a Starbucks. And she was there, Prescott's wife."

"Good job," DeLeon said.

Malloy nodded. The whole reason to talk to the co-author had been to push the man into action, not to get facts. When people are forced to act, they often get careless. While Malloy had been at Reilly's apartment, DeLeon was arranging with a magistrate for a pen register—a record of phone calls to and from the co-author's phones. A register won't give you the substance of the conversation, but it will tell you whom a subject calls and who's calling him.

The instant Malloy left the condo, Reilly had dialed a number.

It was Jane Prescott's. Ten minutes after that, Reilly slipped out the front door and headed down, moving quickly.

And tailed by Lucius, who had accompanied Malloy to Reilly's apartment and waited outside.

The scrawny snitch was now reporting on that surveillance.

"Now that Mrs. Prescott, she's pretty—"

Malloy broke in with "Hot, yeah, I know. Keep going."

"What I was *going* to say," the snitch offered snippily, "before I was interrupted, is that she's pretty tough. Kind of scary, you ask me."

"True," Malloy conceded.

"Reilly starts out talking about you being there." Lucius poked a bony finger at Malloy, which seemed like a dig, but he let it go—as DeLeon's lifted eyebrow was instructing. "And you were suspecting something. And making up shit about some police procedures and estate tax or something. He thought it was pretty stupid."

Lucius seemed to enjoy adding that. DeLeon, too, apparently.

"And the wife said, yeah, you were making up something at her place, too. About a memorial service or something. Which she didn't believe. And then she said—get this. Are you ready?"

Malloy refrained from glaring at Lucius, whose psyche apparently was as fragile as fine porcelain. He smiled. "I'm ready."

"The wife says that this whole problem was Reilly's fucking fault for coming up with the same idea he'd used in a book—bribing a doctor to fake a death certificate."

He and DeLeon exchanged glances.

Lucius continued, "And then she said, 'Now we're fucked. What're you going to do about it?' Meaning Reilly. Not *you*." Another finger at Malloy. He sat back, smugly satisfied.

"Anything else?"

"No, that was it."

"Good job," Malloy said with a sarcastic flourish that only DeLeon noted. He slipped an envelope to the snitch.

After Lucius left, happy at last, Malloy said, "Pretty good case."

"Pretty good, but not great," the partner replied slowly. "There's the motive issue."

"Okay, *she* wants to kill her husband for the insurance or the estate and a younger man. But what's Reilly's motive? Killing Prescott's killing his golden goose."

"Oh, I got that covered." Malloy pulled out his BlackBerry and scrolled down to find something he'd discovered earlier.

He showed it to DeLeon.

Book News.

The estate of the late J.B. Prescott has announced that his co-author, Aaron Reilly, has been selected to continue the author's series featuring the popular Jacob Sharpe character. Prescott's widow is presently negotiating a five-book contract with the author's long-time publisher, Hutton-Fielding. Neither party is talking about money at this point but insiders believe the deal will involve an eight-figure advance.

Ralph DeLeon said, "Looks like we got ourselves a coupla perps."

But not quite yet.

At 11:00 P.M. Jimmy Malloy was walking from the subway stop in Queens to his house six blocks away. He was thinking of how he was going to put the case together. There were still loose ends. The big problem was the cremation thing. Burning is a bitch, one instructor at the academy had told Malloy's class. Fire gets rid of nearly all important evidence. Like bullet holes in the head.

What he'd have to do is get wiretaps, line up witnesses, track down the ambulance drivers, the doctor in Spain.

It was discouraging, but it was also just part of the job. He laughed to himself. It was like Jacob Sharpe and his "tradecraft," he called it. Working your ass off to do your duty.

Just then he saw some motion a hundred feet head, a person. Something about the man's mannerism, his body language set off Malloy's cop radar.

A man had emerged from a car and was walking along the same street that Malloy was now on. After he'd happened to glance back at the detective, he'd stiffened and changed direction fast. Malloy was reminded of the killer in Vermont, disappearing quickly after spotting the deputy.

Who was this? The pro? Aaron Reilly?

And did he have the break-down rifle or another weapon with him? Malloy had to assume he did.

The detective crossed the street and tried to guess where the man was. Somewhere in front of him, but where? Then he heard a dog bark, and another, and he understood the guy was cutting through people's yards, back on the *other* side of the street.

The detective pressed ahead, scanning the area, looking for logical place where the man had vanished. He decided it had to be an alleyway that led to the right, between two commercial buildings, both of them empty and dark at this time of night.

As he came to the alley, Malloy pulled up. He didn't immediately look around the corner. He'd been moving fast and breathing hard, probably scuffling his feet, too. The killer would have heard him approach.

Be smart, he told himself.

Don't be a hero.

He pulled out his phone and began to dial 9-1-1.

Which is when he heard a snap behind him. A foot on a small branch or bit of crisp leaf.

And felt the muzzle of the gun prod his back as a gloved hand reached out and lifted the phone away.

We're a little more organized than that. We come up with a detailed plot, all the twists and turns. Then we execute it. We know exactly how the story will end.

Well, Prescott's wife and co-author had done just that: come up with a perfect plot. Maybe the man on the street a moment ago was Reilly, acting as bait. And it was the professional killer who'd come up behind him.

Maybe even Jane Reilly herself.

She's pretty tough . . .

The detective had another thought. Maybe it was none of his suspects. Maybe the former agent, Frank

Lester, had been bitter about being fired by his client and killed Prescott for revenge. Malloy had never followed up on that lead.

Hell, dying because he'd been careless. . . .

Then the hand tugged on his shoulder slightly, indicating he should turn around.

Malloy did, slowly.

He blinked as he looked up into the eyes of the man who'd snuck up behind him.

They'd never met, but the detective knew exactly what J.B. Prescott looked like. His face was on the back jackets of a dozen books in Malloy's living room.

"Sorry for the scare," Prescott explained, putting away the pen he'd used as a gun muzzle—an ironic touch that Malloy noted as his heart continued to slam in his chest.

The author continued, "I wanted to intercept you before you got home. But I didn't think you'd get here so soon. I had to come up behind you and make you think I had a weapon so you didn't call in a ten-thirteen. That would have been a disaster."

"Intercept?" Malloy asked. "Why?"

They were sitting in the alleyway, on the stairs of a loading dock.

"I needed to talk to you," Prescott said. The man had a large mane of gray hair and a matching moustache that bisected his lengthy face. He looked like an author ought to look.

"You could've called," Malloy snapped.

"No, I couldn't. If somebody had overheard or if you'd told anyone I was alive, my whole plot would've been ruined."

"Okay, what the hell is going on?"

Prescott lowered his head to his hands and didn't speak

for a moment. Then he said, "For the past eighteen months I've been planning my own death. It took that long to find a doctor, an ambulance crew, a funeral director I could bribe. And find some remote land in Spain where we could buy a place and nobody would disturb me."

"So you were the one the police saw walking away from where you'd supposedly had the heart attack in Vermont."

He nodded.

"What were you carrying? A suitcase?"

"Oh, my laptop. I'm never without it. I write all the time."

"Then who was in the ambulance?"

"Nobody. It was just for show."

"And at the cemetery, an empty urn in the plot?"

"That's right."

"But why on earth would you do this? Debts? Was the mob after you?"

A laugh. "I'm worth fifty million dollars. And I may write about the mob and spies and government agents, but I've never actually met one. . . . No, I'm doing this because I've decided to give up writing the Jacob Sharpe books."

"Why?"

"Because it's time for me to try something different: publish what I first started writing, years ago, poetry and literary stories."

Malloy remembered this from the obit.

Prescott explained quickly: "Oh, don't get me wrong. I don't think literature's any *better* than commercial fiction, not at all. People who say that are fools. But when I tried my hand at literature when I was young, I didn't have any skill. I was self-indulgent, digressive . . . boring. Now I know how to write. The Jacob Sharpe books taught me how. I learned how to think about the audience's needs, how to structure my stories, how to communicate clearly."

"Tradecraft," Malloy said.

The author gave a laugh. "Yes, tradecraft. I'm not a young man. I decided I wasn't going to die without seeing if I could make a success of it."

"Well, why fake your death? Why not just write what you wanted to?"

"For one thing, I'd get my poems published *because* I was J.B. Prescott. My publishers around the world would pat me on the head and say, 'Anything you want, J.B.' No, I want my work accepted or rejected on its own merits. But more important, if I just stopped writing the Sharpe series my fans would never forgive me. Look what happened to Sherlock Holmes."

Malloy shook his head.

"Conan Doyle killed off Holmes. But the fans were furious. He was hounded into bringing the back the hero they loved. I'd be hounded in the same way. And my publisher wouldn't let me rest in peace either." He shook his head. "I knew there'd be various reactions, but I never thought anybody'd question my death."

"Something didn't sit right."

He smiled sadly. "Maybe I'm a better at making plots for fiction than making them in real life." Then his long face grew somber. Desperate, too. "I know what I did was wrong, detective, but please, can you just let it go?"

"A crime's been committed."

"Only falsifying a death certificate. But Luis, the doctor, is out of the jurisdiction. You're not going to extradite somebody for that. Jane and Aaron and I didn't actually sign anything. There's no insurance fraud because I cashed out the policy last year for surrender value.

And Jane'll pay every penny of estate tax that's due. . . . Look, I'm not doing this to hurt or cheat anybody."

"But your fans . . ."

"I love them dearly. I'll always love them and I'm grateful for every minute they've spent reading my books. But it's time for me to pass the baton. Aaron will keep them happy. He's a fine writer . . . Detective, I'm asking you to help me out here. You have the power to save me or destroy me."

"I've never walked away from a case in my life." Malloy looked away from the author's eyes, staring at the cracked asphalt in front of them.

Prescott touched his arm. "Please?"

Nearly a year later Detective Jimmy Malloy received a package from England. It was addressed to him, care of the NYPD.

He'd never gotten any mail from Europe and he was mostly fascinated with the postage stamps. Only when he'd had enough of looking at a tiny Queen Elizabeth did Malloy rip the envelope open and take out the contents: a book of poems written by somebody he'd never heard of.

Not that he'd heard of many poets, of course. Robert Frost. Carl Sandburg. Dr. Seuss.

On the cover were some quotations from reviewers praising the author's writing. He'd apparently won awards in England, Italy, and Spain.

Malloy opened the thin book and read the first poem, which was dedicated to the poet's wife.

Walking on Air
Oblique sunlight fell in perfect crimson on your face
that winter afternoon last year.

Your departure approached and, compelled to seize
your hand, I led you from sidewalk to trees
and beyond into a field of snow—
flakes of sky that had fallen to earth days ago.
We climbed onto the hardened crust, which held
our weight, and, suspended above the earth,
we walked in strides as angular as the light,
spending the last hour of our time together
walking on air.

Malloy gave a brief laugh, surprised. He hadn't read a
poem since school, but he actually thought this one was
pretty good. He liked that idea: Walking on the snow,
which had come from the sky—literally walking on air
with somebody you loved.

He pictured John Prescott, sad that his wife had to return to New York, spending a little time with her in a
snowy Vermont field before the drive to the train station.

Just then Ralph DeLeon stepped into the office and
before Malloy could hide the book, the partner scooped
it up. "Poetry." His tone suggested that his partner was
even more of a loss than he'd thought. Though he then
read a few of them himself and said, "Doesn't suck."
Then, flipping to the front, DeLeon gave a fast laugh.

"What?" Malloy asked.

"Weird. Whoever it's dedicated to has your initials."

"No."

DeLeon held the book open.

"With eternal thanks to J. M."

"But I *know* it can't be you. Nobody'd thank you
for shit, son. And if they did, it sure as hell wouldn't be
eternal."

The partner dropped the book on Malloy's desk and sat down in his chair, pulled out his phone, and called one of their snitches.

Malloy read a few more of the poems and then tossed the volume on the dusty bookshelf behind his desk.

Then he, too, grabbed his phone and placed a call to the forensic lab to ask about some test results. As he waited on hold he reflected that, true, Prescott's poems weren't bad at all. The man did have some skill.

But, deep down, Jimmy Malloy had to admit to himself that, given his choice? He'd rather read a Jacob Sharpe novel any day.

*

A former journalist, folksinger, and attorney, **JEFFERY DEAVER** is an international number-one bestselling author. His novels have appeared on bestseller lists around the world, including *The New York Times, The Times* of London, Italy's *Corriere della Sera, The Sydney Morning Herald,* and the *Los Angeles Times.* His *The Bodies Left Behind* was named Novel of the Year by the International Thriller Writers Association, and his Lincoln Rhyme thriller *The Broken Window* was also nominated for that prize. He's been nominated for six Edgar Awards from the Mystery Writers of America, an Anthony Award, and a Gumshoe Award. He was recently short-listed for the ITV3 Crime Thriller Award for Best International Author.

His book *A Maiden's Grave w*as made into an HBO movie starring James Garner and Marlee Matlin, and his novel *The Bone Collector* was a feature release from Universal Pictures, starring Denzel Washington and Angelina Jolie. His most recent books are *Roadside*

Crosses, The Bodies Left Behind, The Broken Window, The Sleeping Doll, and *More Twisted: Collected Stories, Vol. II.* And, yes, the rumors are true: he did appear as a corrupt reporter on his favorite soap opera, *As the World Turns.* Readers can visit his website at www.jefferydeaver.com.

Eye of the Storm

JOHN LUTZ and LISE S. BAKER

In the dimness of the depths, Rob McKenzie felt a tug at his air hose. Turning, he couldn't believe his eyes. A giant hundred-pound squid was doing the dance of death with him at sixty feet below. Then, as if in ghostly display, another fifty squid circled behind their comrade.

Red Devils. Rob recalled reading about this phenomenon. But he had never seen anything like this, right off the coral reef of Key Largo. It had something to do with global warming, climate imbalance, and the increasing number of tropical storms and hurricanes.

Well, this is sure proof, he thought. He wouldn't have to write his local politician, since he was the Keys' congressman.

The squid nudged him again, this time tapping on his

face mask. Rob felt a thrill course through his body. It was a will-I-survive moment and possibly the diving experience of a lifetime.

Maybe the end of a lifetime. For a split second he thought about the good times with Mira, and the bad times. The better times with—

A ripple of bubbles, one final push, and the entire school of squid was gone.

Rob shook his head in disbelief, the adrenaline still pumping. This was going to be a great story to tell at work next week. He didn't want to head for the surface yet, but knew he should. Mira, his wife, had been increasingly irritated with his ocean forays lately. Had she clued into the fact that his midnight swims had become something more?

Engrossed in thought, Rob failed to notice he now had another visitor. This time it was in human form. Another diver, armed with a razor-sharp fish-gutting knife, was swimming up behind him. And yet another form swam behind that diver.

Mira McKenzie had just driven in from the deserted boathouse out on Shell Road. Sometimes she went there to think, other times for assignations with her pool boy. Fighting fire with fire regarding her failed marriage hadn't worked. It had only served to make her feel bitter and cheap. Now she climbed the stairs to the third floor of a faded pink-stucco office building a block off Highway One. She was wearing spike heels. She tried to tell herself it was a good workout for her calves and not for her vanity.

The frosted glass door was exactly as she had pictured it, like something out of a tawdry detective novel.

L. S. CRUM
PRIVATE INVESTIGATOR

The office smelled faintly of mildew and rot, an odor redolent of the Keys. On a corner of the ancient wood desk was a seashell ashtray full of bent and broken cigarette butts that made Mira think of maggots. A stout woman sat behind the desk, sorting through file folders. Mira's eyes caught one with her name on it. A word careened through her mind: *Evidence*.

"I need to see Mr. Crum," she said. "I'm a client."

The woman put the folders down, clasped her hands in front of her, and checked Mira out up and down. Her expression suggested she was confirming what she'd already figured out. It made Mira uncomfortable for a few seconds, then she decided what the hell did it matter?

"There is no 'Mister,'" the stout woman said.

"I spoke to a man on the phone when I first hired your agency," Mira insisted. A framed certificate on the wall caught her jumpy gaze. *Florida Highway Patrol*, it read. *Lucy S. Crum*. It was dated ten years previously.

"That was my ex. He keeps the books and signs up the cases. I'm the detective." The woman puffed out her massive chest like a strutting peacock.

"I'm Mira. Mira McKenzie." Mira had one hand in her purse. "I wanted to thank you for the job you did."

"Ah, the wayward spouse case." Crum got up from behind the desk. She was a good six feet tall and three feet wide.

Mira shuddered, but she'd be damned if she'd let this mountain of a woman make her feel small. "You got me the proof I needed. I don't know why, but I had felt it was my imagination."

"Nope, it was all too real, Mrs. McKenzie. Sorry. They did a lot of diving together, and more than that."

"It's a funny thing, but somehow I felt like everything that had happened was *my* fault."

"Lots of women in your position feel that way. A victim mentality, we call it."

This was Rob's fault, all of it, thought Mira. She had divorced herself from emotion, instead of actually divorcing him. It would be cheaper that way, she reasoned. "I came to give you a bonus." Mira pulled out her nine millimeter Glock handgun with a silencer.

Crum was quick as well. She hadn't spent a lifetime on the Florida Keys roads without developing an intuition for people. Trouble was, she'd seen too often the aftermath of bad decisions. This time, she was a second too slow as Mira shot her three times as if she was target practice.

I'll show you victim mentality, Mira thought. *You're the victim.* She shoved the file into her purse and set out to look for the cabinet where Crum kept her DVD master copies. *And don't forget the computer backup file,* the hard little voice inside her that she was coming to know so well told her.

Once she destroyed the file, the only link between her and her husband's death would be gone. The pool boy she'd hired to kill Rob had been paid off in untraceable cash, left for him to pick up where it was hidden in the deserted boathouse. By this evening he'd be California-bound. They would never see each other again. That was the deal, and he'd stick to it because he had no choice. He was the actual killer.

Mira's BlackBerry rang just as she was turning her Mercedes convertible into the red paving stone driveway.

The house on Key Largo's Millionaires Row was picture perfect. The manicured St. Augustine's grass, the sheltering oleander hedges, the hibiscus trailing in front of the white shutters. There was also the massive party barbecue area out back where scores of famous people had been wined and dined. And of course there was the requisite yacht, a forty-foot Sea Ray, *Second Chance*, tied up at the private dock. Rob's Jaguar was still in the garage. A nice reminder of the fact he hadn't surfaced for air since yesterday. Mira silenced the ring tone: Michael Jackson's "Don't Stop 'til You Get Enough." She smiled.

You got enough, Rob.

"Is Dad home?" Mira winced at her stepdaughter Trisha's voice on the cell phone. Then she steeled herself. It was time to make life go on as if *everything was* normal. The only difference was she'd be twice as rich and Rob was swimming with the fishes.

"Your dad didn't make it home last night, sweetie," Mira said innocently.

"Where is he?" There was a plaintive note in Trisha's voice that Mira had heard all too often. Trisha was obviously upset. Mira was unconcerned.

"Have you tried calling him?"

"I did. I left two messages. I failed the GMAT."

"Oh, honey, I'm sorry." Mira unlocked the front door and got the burglar alarm shut off all in one practiced movement.

"I really need to talk to Dad."

"Well, as soon as I see him or hear from him, I'll make sure he calls you."

There was a silence on the other end. Trisha knew all was not right with her father. He had a definite eye for the ladies. Mira was his fourth wife. *And his last.*

The shamus's videos depicted Rob in a dark, shadowy Key West dive bar having cocktails with a healthy looking blonde young enough to be another daughter. She'd been identified as a grad student majoring in marine biology, and she was a member of the Coast Guard Reserve.

Trisha was speaking . . . "I need to see this in a different light."

"See what?" Mira tried to pay attention. "Sorry, the connection went dead for a minute."

"Yeah, the storm will be coming through there soon."

"Storm?"

"Mom, you need to keep up and watch the news. Hurricane Damon. You need to follow the storm warnings. You're in the Florida Keys, for Chri'sakes."

Mira gave a little laugh. "We'll batten down the hatches like we always do. And I'll keep a lookout for your dad. Maybe he's in poker game with his cronies."

"I think I'm going to switch to law. Maybe the GMAT was an aptitude test."

"Like in that movie with Melanie Griffith," said Mira. "A mind for business, but a body for sin." Mira felt she was blabbing, but Trisha actually laughed before she cut the connection.

She called me Mom, thought Mira. For the first time she felt the beginning of doubt about her actions. She had always hoped for a relationship with Trisha. She had always wanted a daughter.

The thought was quickly followed by another: *No going back now.*

The storm hit at four in the morning. It woke Mira from a troubled dream in which half-decayed humans chased her down an alley. In the nightmare, she had frantically scratched at her arm. When she rolled up the sleeve of her nightgown, she found an oozing bloody tattoo of zombies.

Still a dream . . .

Awake completely now, she lay on the sweat-dampened sheets with her eyes open wide, staring at walls alive with the wild shadows of palm fronds dancing in the storm outside the window.

She put her sleep mask on, but it didn't help. It was as if she could still see the shadows. As if they were *inside* the mask.

Drenched in perspiration, she listened to the wind howl like banshees and the rain pound at the storm shutters. There was no going back to sleep without help. She climbed out of bed, plodded barefoot into the kitchen, and washed down an Ambien with two fingers of gin.

The last thing she was conscious of before sleep finally claimed her was the constant roar of the wind.

When she awoke again at daybreak, she looked outside. She blinked and looked again. The yacht was gone from its moorings!

The wind was still roaring and Mira felt like going back to bed. Maybe she could go back to sleep and when she woke again it would all be a bad dream. Maybe that was what life really was—dreaming, waking, dreaming, waking. Maybe none of it was real.

Wouldn't it be nice if you could choose which dream was real?

She slipped back into the satin sheets and put her sleep mask back on. For good measure, she slathered on some neck cream. Possibly the storm would serve some type of purpose. She was getting her beauty sleep. And the boat, as she called it, was insured, after all

At one in the afternoon, utter silence awakened her. Yes, this was more like it. But when Mira looked outside for the second time that day, a worse sight greeted her. The yacht was still MIA. But now flood waters had crawled over the pilings and were at the back glass French doors. She pulled on a robe and hurried to check it out more closely.

The doors were not doors anymore, just gaping holes where the storm debris was rushing inside. Glass shards littered the Persian rugs.

Hurricane Damon had been worse than anyone had anticipated. There had been no order to evacuate the Keys, as usually happened when a really powerful hurricane was headed toward the islands. At least no order that Mira, in her fury of activity, had been aware of. When you were orchestrating the murder of your husband, you tended to block out a lot of whatever else was going on around you. Damon must have gained intensity with unexpected rapidity as it approached in the night.

Mira couldn't get a signal on her cell phone or even on a landline.

You're a bastard, Damon!

She hurriedly pulled on some jeans and a shirt and got her purse. The gun was still in there; perhaps she should leave it home. But she felt naked without it, as if it were a talisman that could protect her.

She took the gun. If anyone questioned it, she'd say looters were always a threat.

The garage, the Jaguar, and Mira's Mercedes were still dry, thank God.

She backed the Mercedes out of the driveway, plowing into what seemed like a shallow lake. Highway One was flooded to the north, in the direction of Miami. She headed south, toward what she hoped was higher ground.

Daytime, but the sun hadn't actually come out and the sky was a mustard-colored burnt haze. Fallen palm fronds, coconuts, and chunks of plywood littered the road. Mira felt like the last survivor on earth.

Punishment. Retribution. Had she caused all this somehow? The victim mentality, the P.I. had termed it. Everything was all her fault. What she was learning was that it was difficult to know whose fault just about *anything* really was. Life kept getting more and more confusing. What it came down to was that a person had to take care of his or herself. That was about all the moral compass Mira carried.

She pulled abruptly to the right into a parking-lot swale. Lorelei's Bar and Restaurant. Maybe they were open. There were actually a couple of cars in the parking lot. Hurricane Party? Mira had heard about them but had never been to one. She hurried into the bar.

A decorator had gone berserk and designed the entire interior nautical. Right now, Mira didn't really want to think about the ocean. The decor made her seasick just looking at all the life preservers and lighthouse paintings. There was even an aquarium full of what looked like baby squid.

"We're closed, lady," said a grizzled man from the corner shadows.

"No party?" Mira's teeth wanted to chatter. "Why not? The storm's over."

"Lady, don't you know what's going on?"

Mira shook her head.

He got off his bar stool and walked over to her. Big mistake. She could smell a week's worth of sweat, tequila, and tacos. "It's the eye now. We're right in the middle of the eye of the storm."

"I don't understand."

"You're not from around here. Not a Conch. But I knew that." He sneered and looked over at her Louis Vuitton purse.

"What's going on?" she asked. "Why don't you just tell me?" She wanted to actually pull out her gun and give him the second surprise of his day. Shooting people could become a habit, a bad habit. Worse than shopping too much.

"You see, the storm will *seem* for a while like it's stopped. But don't let it fool you. It's like a woman who's in a fury. It *can't* stop. It'll swirl around and around. Lull you into thinking it's not deadly. Then when you least expect it . . . One thing I learned is, hell hath no fury like a woman scorned, except maybe a hurricane. If you ask me, they should go back to namin' them all after women."

Mira didn't wait to hear the rest. She hurried back outside and, gunning her Mercedes, broke every speed law in the books in getting back to the house.

The eerie calm was worse than anything she had ever felt. The waters had risen higher. She wondered when the storm hit again, when the eye passed, would the house withstand the winds? She got out of the car into ankle-deep water.

The sky had turned a gunmetal gray. Her skin crawled as the barometric pressure began to drop. The eye of the storm was passing, taking with it any false sense of security.

Off to her left she could see two police cruisers, lights flashing as if they were at the gates of hell. They had tried to approach the house from another direction, where the water was higher, and were stalled or stymied by the depth of the flood. Another police vehicle was approaching cautiously behind one that was stalled. Her rescuers attempting to reach her?

She knew they didn't have a chance to get to her before the killing storm, and a chill of fear passed through her. The feeling intensified as she saw that the police were otherwise occupied. They hadn't come for her. Instead they were looking down at a figure in a wetsuit washed up near the deteriorating shoreline. Was it Rob? Mira squinted, staring. A bushy mustache caught her gaze as they flipped the figure onto its side. Pedro the pool boy?

As if on cue, the sky continued to darken and a seagull appeared out of nowhere. Dive-bombing, it headed for Mira's hair as if it were a nest. She'd heard that the seabirds could go crazy when there was a hurricane, especially the gulls. There was a screaming sound and Mira couldn't tell if it was the bird or herself.

Then she became aware of another noise, not the screaming of a gull but a strange mechanical beating sound, and all at once a helicopter appeared. It maneuvered until it was directly overhead. The pilot was looking down and pointing at her.

She'd been seen!

She was saved!

She waved at the chopper frantically. The helicopter dipped, steadied, and a cable with a safety hitch was thrust down at her.

"Any others?" A man barked down to her through a small yellow bullhorn.

Mira knew when to seize opportunity.

"My husband," she yelled. "Oh, God, I warned him not to take the boat out! He's not a very good swimmer!"

The man with the bullhorn nodded to let her know he'd understood.

Jagged lightning rent the sky and the pilot looked away worriedly. The lightning hit again and again. The copter lurched and a female face peered down at Mira.

The blonde from the surveillance videos!

Mira remembered L. S. Crum's report: *Grad student . . . Marine biology . . . Did a lot of diving together . . . Coast Guard Reserve . . .*

Did a lot of diving together!

Over the beat of the thrashing helicopter blades, she didn't hear the gull's scream this time. With its sharp beak, the bird was rushing at her again, right at Mira's eyes.

The last thing she saw before she closed them was a familiar face next to the blonde's in the open 'copter doorway. It was a face that did not regret its owner's sins of omission nor his sins of commission. It was the face of a most unworthy sinner.

It was Rob's face. And if he had been close, she would have seen herself reflected in his eyes.

*

JOHN LUTZ is the author of more than forty novels and 250 short stories and articles. He is a past president of both Mystery Writers of America and Private Eye Writers of America. Among his awards are the MWA Edgar, the PWA Shamus, The Trophee 813 Award for best mystery short-story collection translated into the French language, the PWA Life Achievement Award, and the Short Mystery Fiction Society's Golden Derringer Lifetime Achievement Award. His *SWF Seeks Same* was made into the hit movie *Single White Fe-*

male, and his *The Ex* was made into the HBO original movie of the same title, for which he coauthored the screenplay. His latest book is the suspense novel *Urge To Kill.*

LISE S. BAKER is a licensed private investigator and a member of the World Association of Detectives. She has been nominated nine years in a row for California Investigator of the Year by CALI (California Association of Licensed Investigators). Her award-winning novel *The Loser's Club* was inspired by John Lutz's fictional detective, Fred Carver. Collaborating with Lutz on the short story "Eye of the Storm" is a dream come true for this writer/detective.

Currently, Detective Baker is working on a murder case for the Northern California Innocence Project. This is in addition to running her agency, L. S. Baker Investigations, which specializes in fraud investigations.

The Dead Club

MICHAEL PALMER and DANIEL JAMES PALMER

I've always loved Vegas. And not just in a "I love going there" kind of way, which I do. It's really much more than that. Vegas is like a second home to me. In the same way some people turn all warm and tingly inside when they stroll into, say, a knitting shop, that's how I feel as soon as I take my first footsteps onto the blood-red carpeting of a Vegas casino.

I'm home.

Funny thing is, I'm a doctor, a general practitioner, and a darn good one. So you'd think after seeing my fair share of emphysema cases and a battalion of concerned parents whose teenage kids have just started lighting up, that I'd despise the cigarette smoke that clings to the ceiling and the table felt. But you'd be wrong. I love it, despite having quit the nasty habit to win a bet some twenty years ago.

And who says gambling can be dangerous to your health?

The sounds of chips plinking against one another are like birdsongs to me. I love watching the waitresses work the room—the ones destined to seduce some high roller and those still strutting their stuff, despite being as well-worn as flea market furniture. I love the unending sea of lights and the symphony of the slots, praising the winners with their bells and chimes, while goading the losers into pointlessly dropping more down the hatch. But what I love most about Vegas is winning money and that's something I've always been very good at doing.

Now, Lee Anne, she's my wife, might be quick to disagree with that last claim, but she tends to focus on the negative. See, as any real gambler knows, you've got to take the bitter with the sweet and that means the losses with the wins. What Lee Anne can't seem to grasp is that even with the expected dry spells over the years, if you add it all up, I've won more money than I've lost, which is more than most players could honestly claim.

Some folks who know me best, Lee Anne for one, might argue that I had no business attending the AMA symposium on osteoporosis, held at the Luxor in Vegas, but Lou (he would be the head of my group, and the one flipping the bill) didn't seem to mind since I needed the continuing medical education credits.

"Bobby, do you really have to go for a whole week?" Lee Anne asked, while I was packing.

One thing to know about my wife, she only calls me Bobby if she's really unhappy about something I've done. To my friends, I'm Bob and at work I'm Dr. Robert Tomlinson, but at home, at least lately, I'm far more Bobby than I am Bob. Over the years, I've come to use Bobby myself whenever my behavior veers a few degrees from the center.

Yeah, I told her, I had to go. But of course, that was white lie. I did have to go, but not for the CMEs. I mean, Vegas wouldn't be Vegas without a little bit of sin thrown into the mix. You know, take the sweet with the bitter.

My first night in town, I skipped out on the Cardinal Healthcare–sponsored cocktail hour and rolled into the Bellagio's vast casino. I wanted to wet my whistle with a little blackjack at the fifteen dollar table just to get the juices flowing. Since most of us docs were staying at the Luxor, I had no desire to bump into any of them out on the floor. See, I was harboring a wee bit of guilt about spending my practice's hard earned money on the conference and not being the all-functions, all-the-time sort of guy. I figured, so long as I didn't run into anybody who recognized me, I wouldn't have to feel bad about having skipped out on the cocktail hour. Of course, even at the Bellagio I was spotted. But later I'd be glad because that was how I got introduced to The Dead Club.

The cocktail hour back at the Luxor was only half-cocked and already I was down three hundred on a string of hard-luck hands. The thing about strings, though, for good or bad, is that they're destined to end. The MIT math wonks who claim that sort of thinking is nothing but a gambling fallacy are full of S-H-I-T, if you ask me. I can feel when a win streak is coming on. It starts in my toes and buzzes up my legs like electricity; I had that feeling now. The first two cards of my next hand were the six of clubs and four of spades. Naturally, I doubled down, intending to cut my current losses in half with a win. My next card was the jack of clubs. The dealer bust hitting on thirteen, and just like that, I heard that bad-luck streak snap like the string of an overplayed guitar.

That was when I met Grover.

He sat down on the empty stool to my left and placed a hundred dollar initial bet, which he proceeded to lose in seven seconds. His follow-up was an even two hundred smackers.

"Looks like you've soaked up all the good luck this table's dishing out tonight," he said to me.

I'd won my fifth straight hand and he'd dropped his third.

"There's more luck to be had," I replied.

Now Grover was the sort of fellow you didn't easily forget and I knew that I'd seen him earlier in the day at the symposium registration booth. He had a grizzly-bear frame, a thick Santa Claus head of snow-white hair, and a matching snowy goatee. I was pretty confident he didn't recognize me.

"So what sort of doc are you?" he asked.

Guess I was wrong.

"GP," I said. "You?"

"Orthopedist. Name's Grover Theodore Marshall. Friends just call me Grove."

Grove had a vise for a handshake and a deep Southern accent. I never bothered asking where he was from, or what hospital he worked at, and he never bothered to tell me.

"Look at that," Grove said.

"What?"

"That woman over there."

My eyes followed his finger until I spotted an attractive thirtysomething brunette at the craps table.

"What about her?" I asked.

"She keeps touching her hair with her left hand. Hundred bucks says the next time she does it, it'll be with her right."

"You serious?"

I let my attention wander and the dealer had to ask if I wanted to set down a bet. I hated passing on a deal when I was so hot, but there was something compelling about Grove. We left the table together.

On closer inspection, the woman was well into her forties, and wore too much makeup.

I reasoned that either Grove was lying to me and she had been touching her hair with her right hand all along, which made it a sucker bet, or he was thinking that I was thinking he was lying, in which case he'd expect me to double the stakes, but only if I got to bet the right hand—a wager he'd politely decline. Trusting my gut, I went with the left-hand touch. Three seconds later I was a hundred richer.

"Goddamit!" Grove said, slapping my back hard enough to rattle my lungs. "I was so sure she was going to go right."

He slid a hundred from a thick wad and pressed the crisp bill into my palm.

"Just dumb luck," I said.

"No way," he said. "Hell, I got you pegged. You're a player. I've gotta hang with you, man. You think you can teach this old dog a few Vegas tricks so I don't get my clock cleaned all week?"

"Of course," I said.

"Sorry, I didn't catch your name," Grove said.

"It's Bobby," I said. "Bobby Tomlinson."

Grove and I spent the rest of the conference as inseparable gambling buddies. It helped that he shared my conferencing habits, which involved attending a morning session or two, skipping the afternoon sessions entirely to hit the tables, and breaking briefly for dinner, with more gambling until well past the witching hour. I shared all my trade secrets for blackjack (best odds for the player) and craps (a game I've affectionately renamed, "Lose All Your Money Fast"). By the week's end, I was up over fifteen-hundred and Grove, good God, had socked away almost four grand thanks to his willingness to place bets that doubled mine.

We were drinking vodka tonics, lounging on a couple of cushy chairs, and watching an array of forty television sets broadcasting what seemed to be every sporting event taking place in the world at that moment. Of course, we could bet on all of them, which we did for some. Grove won five-hundred bucks when Baltimore returned a punt for a touchdown.

"Hey, G.P.," he said, jabbing at my specialty, "didn't your mama ever tell you that the real money's in surgery?"

I guess I invited that taunt. All week long I had complained about not having deep pockets—the kind that would let me make the sort of bets Grove made without batting an eye.

"My wife is scared to death of the tables," I said. "I thought it might be a good idea to stay married and see my two kids through college." Each time I said something even half-funny, Grove laughed roundly and pounded my back.

"I like you, Bobby," he said. "I wish we could keep playing."

"Got to get back to reality."

"You know," Grove said. "You're a really great player. A gamer's gamer. You're like a craftsman on those tables."

"Hardly. I just helped educate you about some commonly held beliefs."

I took an extra long sip of my vodka because I wanted Grove to think I was that casual about my skill.

"If you're as good a doc as you are a gambler, you could make a killing in our club."

He voiced the thought almost as an aside, but he got my attention.

"What club?"

"Huh? Oh, I'm sorry, I was thinking out loud."

"Yeah? What club?"

Grove shifted his weight in his chair, glancing about as if the security cameras were as interested in his mysterious club as they were in the blackjack card counters.

"It's sort of a private club for doctors," Grove said, in a conspiratorial whisper. Then he added, "Doctors who like to gamble."

"I'm a doctor and I like to gamble."

"Yeah, well, we don't bet on cards."

"Yeah? What do you bet on, death?"

I laughed. Grove didn't even break a smile.

"Holy shit," I said. "Is that what you really do?"

Grove shifted his gaze down to his feet and spoke even softer.

"It's not exactly what you think. It's not even really illegal or anything. But ethically, well, it would be a bit awkward if word ever got out."

"I think I want to know more."

"Look, I'll tell you," Grove said, "but I need you to swear, Bobby, I mean swear to me, that you'll never breathe a word of this to anybody. Heck, I might even be able to sponsor you if you want in. That's how much I like you. We haven't admitted a new member in over five years."

"So what's the club?"

"It's called 'The Dead Club.'"

"Sounds sinister. Tell me more."

"Okay, here's how it works. Each month you get an email with a link. The link is to a password protected website. You'll have to download an application first before you can use the site. That way we can erase any record of the club on your computer in case of emergency."

"By emergency I assume you mean detection. What's on the site?"

"Each month there's a new medical file for a terminally ill patient in some hospital somewhere in the world."

"The world?"

"It's sort of a global club."

"And you're all betting on terminally ill patients?"

"That's right. We're using our considerable doctoring skills to wager, based solely on the information in their medical records. Like I said, we bet on precisely when they're going to die."

"That's a quite a new twist on the old line, 'I'm sorry Mrs. Smith, but I regret to inform you you've only got six months to live.'"

Grove's smile was far from his signature warm grin. This one was etched with profound mischievousness.

"See, that's how the club started, Bobby," he said. "A bet between two docs on just that and, well, it's sort of grown from there."

Right then and there I wished I had introduced myself as Robert, or at least Bob. But I kept thinking—*How can I get in on this action?*

"How many in the club?" I asked.

"I have no idea. Don't even know how long the club

has existed. Membership is on a trial basis and you have to be nominated by an existing member to be considered. Then you get vetted by a committee, all secret stuff, don't ask me how they do it and if you make it past them, which apparently few do, your name goes before the board for approval."

Grove was shockingly cavalier describing the club, given that it crossed fairly broad ethical lines.

"Where do the records come from?" I asked.

"Member-supplied. I have put up a few records myself. Of course you can't bet on your own."

I wanted to say something, but I was too stunned to speak. Grove continued.

"When you break the club down, there's really nothing wrong with what we do. It's all anonymous, supervised by the competition committee, which changes members every four months. We take pains to remove anything that could tie a record to the actual patient. No names, addresses, hospital, next of kin, exact birthday—none of it. All of that information is removed before it gets posted."

"How much have you won?" I asked.

"Let's just say if, like you say, you're worried about college tuition, a few winning bets in The Dead Club could take care of all that—all four years, both kids."

"Sounds intriguing," I said. "But what if the patient dies of something else. A slip and fall, say."

"Hey, in our world, dead is dead."

Fast-forward now. Two months slip by since I met Grove and his twisted little club. I had sunk back into my life dominated by sore throats, snoring problems, unexplained and unexplainable chest pains, equally mysterious muscle and joint aches and of course, parents concerned about their teenagers' smoking and pill-popping habits, refusing to look at their own.

Lee Anne and I fell back into step; that lost week in Vegas is now just a fuzzy memory, made even fuzzier by the routines of life—household duties and shuttling our children (Jake, twelve and Max, ten) to and from basketball practice, piano lessons, and the like. Then, on Christmas morning, no less, I get this email from tdc0529@aol.com. The message simply read: "YOU'RE IN" and there was a link for me to click. By this time, I had pushed Grove and his crazy betting pool to the back of my mind. I clicked the link anyway, and then panicked when it was clear some application was being installed on my computer. I was about to power off the machine when a Web browser popped open and the Web page that loaded read:

THE DEAD CLUB
Login:
Password:
First-time visitors, click here

When I clicked the first time visitor link, I was asked to enter my social security number, which to my surprise, I actually did. What's even more astounding is that it recognized my social and then returned a username/password combo, which allowed me to log on to the site successfully. I guess Grove had nominated me and I had been vetted by some committee and approved for membership in The Dead Club.

The site, itself, was a marvel. There were bets being tracked in real time from what I gauged to be nearing a hundred cases, some stretching back several years. The older cases were locked for any new action, but you could still track the current odds to win. To get into a betting pool, you had to bet on the current, active case, which for January was an eighty-eight-year-old man with stage-four pancreatic cancer, which, according to his biopsies, had spread to several adjacent organs, the most deadly of which was his liver. He was already showing signs of hepatic inflammation and obstruction.

My whole body started tingling with a mix of anticipation and excitement, but there was some revulsion, too. It was a feeling I knew well from Vegas, as though a thousand army ants had taken up residence underneath my skin and were now burrowing long tunnels alongside my veins and arteries. Grove was right, I thought, as I read through the anonymous record. There really wasn't anything wrong with what the club was doing.

The poor patient had endured the usual barrage of treatments, including chemotherapy, radiation, and even biological therapy. I looked up the statistics. Rarely did survival for Stage IVA pancreatic cancer, even with aggressive treatment, exceed one year. I modified the rate of deterioration, taking into consideration the man's medical history, general condition, and chemotherapy regimen that included Gemzar and Camptosar, both fairly recent. I weighed each factor, most importantly, his advanced age and thirty years of type-two diabetes. For this guy to make it six months would be a miracle.

Lee Anne popped her head inside my home office. I was so engrossed in reviewing the medical file that I didn't even hear her calling my name.

"Bobby, are you going deaf?" she said. "Dinner's on the table."

I jumped at the sound of her voice and quickly hid the browser with a well-placed click of my mouse.

"Just give me a minute," I said, without bothering to turn around.

My heart pounded in my chest. Lee Anne departed with my assurance that I'd follow, but I went back to the site as soon as she had left the room. The betting system for The Dead Club was even more ingenious than Grove had described. It was a kitty-based system, five-thousand-dollar uniform bet for all players wagering on an open case. Players were allowed to pick a time period from the options given, in this case, every two weeks for a year, and then every month. And just like *The Price is Right,* the winner had to be the closest without going over. There were already at least twenty doctors involved in this case, because the kitty was up to one hundred thousand dollars.

At risk was my five grand. If I won, I'd split with any doctor who picked the same time period as I did. Whoever was behind this operation possessed some serious computer chops to make the site so sophisticated, but still easy to use.

I had a bank account with ten grand in it that Lee Anne didn't even know existed. I was planning to use it for a surprise mega-trip to Italy in celebration of our fifteenth wedding anniversary. My mouth went dry thinking about what we would do in Europe when I won this bet, and every nerve in my body told me I was going to. I never for a moment considered we might end up celebrating our anniversary at an Outback Steakhouse.

The Dead Club wasn't luck, it was skill.

I imagined gondolas, floating down a river of champagne, with Lee Anne nestled in my arms, and then the two of us touring the lush English countryside in a rented Bentley. I felt a sudden rage at all those arrogant surgeons in The Dead Club with their gilded lives, looking down with disdain on my chosen specialty. But what they didn't know was that I possessed skills to interpret medical records in ways the other docs simply could not. I decided then and there that I'd mail a bank check, as required, to the post-office-box address provided, to give myself a minimum kitty of five-thousand dollars to play with.

One measly bet couldn't hurt.

I won.

John Doe died two months and twenty-five days from my first Dead Club bet. I wasn't the only winner, though. Competition was tougher than I had anticipated. Fifteen of us split a hundred-fifty-thousand-dollar kitty. Just like that, I had doubled my money, and those army ants were now dancing the Lambada in my head, but at 75 r.p.m.

I hadn't bet on another case since my inaugural John Doe play, but now I couldn't wait for April the first to arrive, because that meant a new record would be posted for betting. The pool would be open again and I was ready and willing to take the plunge.

I won again.

This time, I split the kitty with only two other docs who agreed with me that the woman, halfway into her fourth year with ALS, or Lou Gehrig's disease, would be gone in four months. The safe bet would have been eight months, given that the average life expectancy for ALS sufferers was between three and five years. But this Jane Doe had a subtle abnormality on her cardiogram and an elevation in her serum calcium that I decided was worth at least a deduction of six weeks.

It was a tough bet, given that 10 percent of ALS patients live ten years or longer. Still, there were enough indicators that, like me, two other skilled docs had calculated death would soon be knocking on her door. Her demise netted me sixty-three thousand dollars. Forget gondolas. Now, it was the Riviera that was flooded with champagne.

But winning streaks, even a streak of two, run the risk of ending and mine came to a crashing halt that August. I lost four in a row. Four! Two Jane Does and two John Does. It would have been a twenty-five-thousand-dollar loss, five thousand dollars per bet. But I didn't bet five thousand dollars. The Dead Club also had a high rollers game with a thirty-thousand-dollar minimum ante and my winnings qualified me for that club membership as well. For a man of my income and means, the rush of placing a thirty-thousand-dollar bet was indescribable. I was sure my winning ways were going to continue. I never would have started playing the thirty-thousand-dollar kitty game otherwise. Never has being wrong about a hunch hurt so much.

A mere twelve months after placing my initial wager on the stage IVA John Doe, I had blown not only my winnings, but a second mortgage on my house and a chunk of my kids' college fund. Lee Anne hadn't found out just yet, but she was suspicious, that's for sure.

Confessing to her my involvement with The Dead Club would be akin to signing my divorce papers. Just when I thought my luck had officially run out, I saw the January bet.

The unimaginable had happened.

I couldn't believe what I was seeing. The name of a consulting neurologist for a terribly ill man had been left in at the bottom of his note. Ivan Dworsky, a neurologist I knew well. Barring an incredible coincidence, the case was a patient at my hospital! All I had to do was determine and confirm the identity, and that I was quickly able to do. The gondolas were floating again.

Richard Generoso—sixty-seven years old with invasive glioblastoma multiforme, a grade-four malignant brain tumor.

I had only three days to place my bet. This was like betting blackjack while seeing the dealer's hand. It was one thing trying to predict the outcome by reading a medical record, but another thing entirely to have access to the actual patient. I could review his CT scans with the best radiologists around.

It was no problem tracking Generoso down. I was standing by his bed when in came my second pot of gold. His doctor, whom I happened to have played racquetball with on a few occasions, entered the room with his patient's latest lab results. I explained that Generoso and I were acquaintances. The invasive radiologists had just performed a spinal tap, I was told, and the results were bad—very bad. Cancer cells were filling the spinal canal—a quick ticket to heaven. The news was as good as gold, because it was fresh and not something included in the medical records the rest of The Dead Club had reviewed. It was better than seeing the dealer's cards. This was knowing I had blackjack on my next hand.

Three weeks, that's what I gave him—no more than twenty-one days to live. The cancer itself wasn't that large, and sure enough, I was the only one to bet his end would come so soon. I took out a third mortgage on my house, forged Lee Anne's signatures, and put the money in the kitty. If I lost, I'd be over a hundred grand in the hole. But I had no intention on losing this one.

Fast-forward nineteen days. Richard Generoso is beginning to fail, but not that rapidly. He has finally been readmitted, but he is hanging on and still conscious most of the time. I've checked on him enough so that he thinks

I'm his new physician and his doc thinks that he's my long-lost uncle.

"How're you feeling today, Richard?" I asked. It was less than forty hours before I was going permanently under water if he didn't die.

"Feeling okay," he replied dreamily. "My daughter is looking into hospice care."

Richard's eyes were rheumy with memory.

He knew he was going to die and I knew he was going to die, but for him to pointlessly pass away three days or a week or a month from now in hospice care would have thrown my life into an unrecoverable tailspin. The money was already gone, and trying to find The Dead Club, let alone trying to blow the whistle on them, was fruitless.

The next day, with less than twelve hours remaining on my bet—make that life as I knew it—Richard was still alert most of the time.

It simply wasn't going to happen.

I went to my office and returned with just fifteen minutes left, as panicked as I had ever been about anything.

Generoso's doctor and nurse had just left. I walked nonchalantly down the hall and into his room, closing the door behind me.

I don't really remember injecting the Diprivan into his IV port. In less than two minutes, his eyes closed. Moments later, his breathing stopped. His face turned waxy and pale. I notified the nurses and they called the attending physician. There was no resuscitation. I watched as the time of death was logged.

11:58 P.M.

Two minutes later and I would have killed the man for nothing.

Grove sat across from me.

"You look well," he said.

"I've been better."

"I can imagine," he said.

I hadn't seen Grove since that week in Vegas, but somehow his hair looked even whiter, the goatee fuller; same for his belly.

For a few awkward minutes, we didn't say anything to each other; then he broke the silence.

"I came here to thank you," he said.

"For what? I tried to shut down The Dead Club. But I never could find you."

"Yeah, well, our application makes it easy to erase all information about the club from a member's computer. And Grover Marshall isn't my real name."

"Figured that. So what are you here thanking me for?"

"Well, you made me a lot of money."

"Yeah? How's that?"

I asked the question, but I already had a knot forming in my stomach. I knew what his answer would be.

"You deserve to know that you were never in The Dead Club, Bobby."

I swallowed hard. My throat was tightening, but I still managed a slight, near-imperceptible nod.

"You *were* The Dead Club, Bobby."

I caught a devilish gleam in his eyes and it made me shiver.

"You were betting on me?" I croaked.

Grove didn't budge, but he did jump in his seat when I smacked my hand hard against the reinforced Plexiglas that separated us.

"Hands off the glass, Tomlinson!" A guard's voice boomed from a crackly PA system.

I glanced down the long hallway, past the row of other prisoners on my side of the glass, toward the guard's station. I waved my hands in the air, the well-understood signal that I promised no further breech of prison protocol.

"I wouldn't tell you this if they recorded our conversation," Grove said, smiling again. "But I thought you'd appreciate knowing that a lot of members were betting you wouldn't go through with it. I mean, they really didn't think you could. But I gambled with you in Vegas, Bobby. I guess I had the inside skinny. I doubled down and bet half a million that you'd kill that guy to win the bet. I really owe you for coming through."

"My win streak, the neurologist in Generoso's hospital record not being blanked out, all part of the set up to suck me in?"

Grove nodded, real slow and deliberate.

"I also bet a bundle that you'd get caught," he said. "Gotta hand it to you, Bobby. You don't disappoint."

"This isn't over, Grove, or whatever your name is. Not by a long shot. Five years from now I'm up for parole. When I'm out, I'm going to track you down and make sure you're either sitting on my side of the glass, or lying somewhere six feet underground. You hear me? That's what's going to happen."

Grove laughed in a jolly, warm guffaw that reminded me of the week we met in Vegas.

"You're not going to do anything of the sort, Bobby. And don't count on making parole either."

"Oh yeah?" I replied.

My eyes narrowed on Grove as I balled my hands into tight fists.

"Yeah," Grove said.

"You want to bet?" I said.

*

Massachusetts native **DR. MICHAEL PALMER** is the author of fourteen novels of medical suspense, all international bestsellers. His books have millions of copies in print worldwide, and have been translated into thirty-eight languages. Palmer was educated at Wesleyan University and Case Western Reserve School of Medicine. His most recent novel is *The Last Surgeon,* dealing with Post Traumatic Stress Disorder. His novel *Extreme Measures* was made into the hit film of the same name starring Hugh Grant, Gene Hackman, and Sarah Jessica Parker. Palmer also works as an associate director of the Massachusetts Medical Society's Physician Health Services, helping doctors with physical and mental illness, as well as drug dependence, including alcoholism. He has three sons, two cats, and some fish.

DANIEL JAMES PALMER holds a master's degree in communications from Boston University, and is a musician, songwriter, and software professional. His debut thriller novel, *Delirious,* is scheduled to be published by Kensington Publishing in early 2011, part of a three-book contract with the publisher. He lives with his wife and two children in one of those sleepy New England towns.

Underbelly

GRANT McKENZIE

Shorty Lemon poked his index finger between tiny nylon teeth and gave it a wiggle. The teeth parted easily and the brass slider ran smooth, but it still took some dexterous finger kung fu to unzip the suitcase from the inside.

Once he negotiated the first awkward corner, the lid opened wide enough for him to peek out.

The compartment was dark and noisy.

Just beyond thin metal walls, a Cummins diesel roared as the transaxle drove eight massive steel-belted radials. On the other side, wind slapped against baggage doors, desperate to force its way inside. And below, the pavement whined as if protesting the weight of twenty-eight thousand pounds of fast-moving steel.

Noise was good. It stopped the passengers in soft seats

a short distance above Shorty's head from hearing his movements.

Shorty finished unzipping the case and stood to stretch. Even at three feet ten and one-quarter inches, a suitcase was a tight fit.

Dressed in black cargo pants and turtleneck, Shorty liked to believe he looked as cool as Steve McQueen in *Bullitt*. With an excited grin, he pulled on his spelunking lamp, tightened the headband, and flipped the switch. Three super bright LEDs lit up the cabin to reveal a mountain of luggage.

He hoped at least one of them contained chocolate. Milky Swiss was his favorite, but he had to be careful. Two months earlier he wolfed down a full box of festive Irish whisky liqueurs. The alcohol-filled chocolates had sent him into a near sugar coma and he was barely able to zip himself back inside the case before passing out. When his partner retrieved the case at the terminal, he discovered Shorty had puked all over his favorite McQueens.

The memory still made him shudder.

After rubbing his hands together to get the blood flowing, Shorty ripped bags open.

He started with the largest one, but was disappointed to find that all it contained was a collection of old lady clothes. And from the look of them, they would have found more use in a landfill than in somebody's wardrobe.

He rolled his eyes. "Freakin' loser."

He shoved the bag aside.

The second bag contained a slick digital camera, a superthin Mac laptop, and a snack pack of Ritz Crackers with the fake cheese goop in the middle. A nest of rolled socks protected the crackers as though they were some kind of luxury treat.

"Loser number two."

Shorty crushed the crackers in his hand before sprinkling the disgusting remains over the owner's clothes. Whoever ate that garbage, he decided, deserved to wear it, too.

He slipped the camera and laptop inside his own suitcase and moved to the next.

Unzipping the bag, he stared at a gun . . . attached to a hand . . . pointing at a spot between his eyes.

"Shorty." A familiar scratchy voice was attached to the hand that was aiming the gun.

"Twinkle?" Shorty lifted his head and exposed the gunman's face to his headlamp. "What the hell are you doing? You're Wednesdays on the Washington run."

Twinkle squinted against the light and his upper lip curled in a sneer. "Change of plans."

Jonathon "Twinkle" Toews climbed out of the suitcase, his gun never wavering from Shorty's head. Shorty had heard Twinkle brag he had a quarter-inch on him in the height department, but he suspected the lying dwarf wore lifts.

"Well fuck me blue," Shorty said with a laugh. "This is some mix-up."

"No mix-up, Shorty. Big haul on this bus and I want my cut."

"Big haul?"

Twinkle snorted. "Don't play dumb. The horse is trotting cross-country, but it ain't gonna make the stable."

Twinkle cocked the hammer. Even amid the blanket of engine noise, it was decidedly menacing.

"Whoa, back up." Shorty raised his hands in surrender. "I ain't part of your circus, so what the fuck?"

Twinkle snorted again. "You don't know, for real?"

Shorty shook his head and the light from his lamp danced around the cabin like the return of E.T.

Twinkle resettled the hammer and lowered the gun. "Guess that's why you ain't packing."

"Exactly," Shorty agreed. "I'm not packing because . . ." He hesitated, then sighed. "Really, I don't know what the hell you're talking about."

"Heroin," said Twinkle. "Sixty keys."

"That a lot?"

"When it's pure, uncut bone, baby. One hundred Gs a key."

Shorty whistled. "Six million dollars. And somebody put it on a bus?"

Twinkle grinned, his Hollywood caps reflecting the light. "Who's gonna rob a bus?"

"Except you."

Twinkle shook his head. " 'Cept you, Shorty. I work Wednesdays, 'member? The Washington run. Ask anybody."

As the double-crossing realization hit, the blood drained from Shorty's face. It didn't have far to go.

"Keep opening bags." Twinkle lifted his gun into the light as a reminder. "Find me the barking dogs."

Shorty tossed suitcases and boxes aside, searching for the likeliest suspects, until he discovered four black canvas bags with reinforced seams and heavy-duty zippers.

"Here's your barkers," he said.

"Dogs," corrected Twinkle. He moved in closer. "Heroin is called 'dog.' "

"Ahh," said Shorty as if he understood. "Because you have to be barking-mad to use it?"

Twinkle was unamused. "You're a lost cause. Always have been. Open the damn bags."

Shorty turned his attention and his headlamp to the bags. They were each locked with a tiny padlock.

"Who, in their right mind, thinks these locks do any good?" he said. "I mean, really. You can get better ones out of a gumball machine."

"Just open them," Twinkle growled. "Save the commentary for your eulogy."

Shorty pulled a pair of folding snips from his pants pocket and snipped off all four locks.

"Open them," Twinkle ordered.

The first bag contained twenty vacuum-packed squares of white powder. The next two bags contained the same, but the fourth bag held money. Lots of it. One hundred dollar bills, crisp and smooth, bundled in packages of 50. If Shorty's math was right, and it usually was, there were at least 120 bundles.

Shorty whistled. "That's not pocket change."

"I wasn't expecting any money," said Twinkle.

"Oh, good. Can I have it?"

Twinkle sneered. "You can't use it where you're going."

Shorty sighed and zipped up the bags. Bigger men than Twinkle had threatened him in his time, but none rankled quite so much.

"So how you getting off?" he asked.

Twinkle nodded toward the large loading doors that ran along the side. "I sure as hell ain't going all the way to Boston. Open the doors."

"They're locked."

Twinkle lifted the gun and pointed it at Shorty's crotch.

"I hear you only got one ball, Shorty. Want me to even you up?"

Grumbling to himself, Shorty slipped the snips back into his pocket and returned with a stubby screwdriver that held six different bits. With the flick of his thumb, he made the Torx head shoot out of the compact handle and lock in place. Shorty settled in front of the loading door and worked his magic. Within seconds, the doors were ready to be opened.

"What about the driver?" Shorty asked. "He's bound to notice."

Twinkle cut him off with a snort. "He's gettin' paid enough to ignore what's in his mirrors."

Shorty spun around. "So everybody's in on this except me?"

Twinkle grinned. "Somebody had to be the fall guy."

"Fuck!"

Twinkle brought the gun barrel close enough to caress Shorty's cheek. "What you waitin' for?"

Shorty heaved open the doors to bathe the compartment in blinding daylight. A hurricane rushed inside, ripping open the lids of unzipped suitcases and forcing the loose contents to take flight.

Twinkle screamed as a giant pair of old-lady bloomers leeched onto his face. Its breathable cotton crotch stuffed itself into his mouth and became lodged in his throat. When Twinkle finally yanked the choking garment free, Shorty's clenched fist was closing in.

Shorty hit him with everything he had, sharp knuckles against soft cartilage, powered by arms, legs, feet, and toes. The punch was a beauty.

Twinkle grew two inches, his gun flying from his hand to the rear of the cabin as his nose was crushed against his cheek and his upper teeth pierced his upper lip. He flew backward, landing hard on the four black bags.

Before he could recover, Shorty was on him again. The

second punch sent Twinkle's nose to the other side of his face and the bones in his cheek went *crack*.

"You were going to kill me, you son of a bitch!" Shorty scored another hit. "How the fuck do you like it?"

Twinkle cowered, his hands rising to cover his ruined face as snot, blood, and tears dripped from his chin.

Shorty wasn't in the mood for mercy. He raised his fist again, but before he could land a fourth blow, a gunshot pinged off the wall just inches from his head.

Shorty spun to face the open doorway. A black motorbike and convertible sidecar bore down. His ex-girlfriend, LoLa, hung over the side. She fired again.

Shorty dove behind the avalanche of luggage as the second shot ricocheted around the cabin. Cursing his luck, he peered out and felt his heartbeat stutter. LoLa was looking good in tight black leather and a silver helmet with an iconic honeybee painted on its crown. That had always been his nickname for her when they shared an apartment in the Village. She had a singing voice as smooth as honey, but a temper that stung like . . .

Another bullet whizzed by his head.

"Your ass is grass now, Shorty," Twinkle mumbled through a bloody mouth. "My sis knows how to hold a grudge."

Shorty peeked from behind his wall of soft-sided cloth and cheap plastic. LoLa was closing in, her voluptuous pale bosom peeking from the unzipped V of the leather jacket as she strained against the sidecar to gain more reach. The muzzle of her .45 searched the interior for a kill.

LoLa had always possessed an unshakable will. Even when they wandered the country from sea to shining sea, LoLa working the clubs and bringing the house down while Shorty emptied the pockets of enraptured drunks, she was determined to be a star. Shorty always admired that, although he secretly wished she could just be happy with who she was: his passionate little honeybee.

Shorty yanked the lamp off his head and threw it into the darker recesses of the hold. As the headlamp flew through the air, LoLa fired another shot. The light exploded in midair.

Shorty rocked back on his heels. It was one hell of a shot, and Shorty hoped for his own sake it was more luck than skill.

He looked out again and their eyes met. LoLa was smiling behind a transparent visor, her teeth as white and perfect as he had paid for. She flicked her soft, pink tongue, proving she still knew how to use it.

Shorty automatically returned the smile, lost in remembrance of times past when they had adored every quarter-inch of each other. Then, he saw her driver. The man on the motorbike was a hairy monster with a full ginger beard and a grin that was a few kernels shy of a cob. Dressed in full leather biker gear, he must have stood at least five foot six in boots, and the sight churned Shorty's stomach. LoLa had always liked them full-sized and the memory of catching her cheating ass writhing on top of the rent-to-own portable dishwasher was a sight he wanted burned from his brain.

LoLa shouted, "Give us the bags, Shorty."

"Fuck you."

LoLa laughed. "Not anymore. I've moved on."

Shorty heard movement to his left and crawled over the luggage to get a better look. Twinkle had staggered to the open doors, his face a mess and his movements unsteady.

"Get the bags, Twinkle," LoLa yelled. The motorbike kept perfect pace with the bus.

"I can't," Twinkle cried. "He busted me good."

"Get the fucking bags, brother."

"I can't!" Twinkle moved closer to the edge. "I want off this damn bus."

Shorty yelled: "Hey, Twinkle!"

Twinkle turned.

Shorty swung one of the heavy black bags in the air and let go. "Don't forget your luggage."

The bag hit Twinkle square in the chest, knocking him off balance. Twinkle screamed as he fell out the open doorway with the bag clutched in his arms.

LoLa's driver swerved, but the sidecar still bore the brunt of the impact as Twinkle's head slammed into the windshield and the bag he was holding burst open in a giant cloud of white powder.

With a fierce determination, the driver managed to maintain control even as the sidecar's wheel crunched over Twinkle's broken body. A windowless black van following behind didn't even attempt to brake.

When the bike caught up to the bus again, its sidecar was dented and its windshield cracked. Streaks of blood dusted in powder flowed over LoLa's leathers. Even her pretty silver helmet was webbed with gore.

Angry tears filled LoLa's eyes when she raised her gun again.

Shorty threw a blue backpack at her. With its light-weight aluminum frame, the pack hit the pavement and bounced high, almost removing his former lover's head from her compact body.

She fired in hasty retaliation, but the bullet pinged harmlessly off the side of the bus.

Shorty followed with a volley of a half-dozen open suitcases: boxer shorts, pajamas, blouses, underwear, a smart tuxedo, and a rubber diving suit all flowed through the doorway and sailed down the freeway.

LoLa and her driver backed off after the bike nearly went into the ditch, when a small blue box exploded and a flock of errant panty liners got stuck on the bearded monster's goggles.

Best of all, Shorty found a large, unopened Toblerone bar. It was the size of his left arm.

As Shorty contemplated ripping open the triangular packaging, the dark, windowless van pulled up level with the bus. Its side door slid open to reveal three men dressed in head-to-toe body armor, complete with knitted balaclavas that showed only their eyes, and holding paramilitary-style submachine guns.

Shorty gulped and dropped the chocolate. "Y-you want the drugs?"

The three men nodded as one.

Shorty crawled back over the scattered luggage and pulled one of the black bags to the door. The van moved closer to the bus. One of the men grabbed the bag and yanked. Shorty instantly let his end go before he was pulled out of the bus along with it.

"Get the others," yelled the shortest of the three. It was difficult to tell the man's exact height, but in Shorty's estimation anything over four feet was a waste of vertical.

Shorty retrieved the third bag, but this time, when he went to hand it over, the head of the reaching gunman imploded, his balaclava mask becoming a sieve of blood.

Gunfire and broken glass rained from the passenger compartment above. The other two gunmen quickly ducked inside the van and returned fire. Both vehicles swerved and the dead gunman slid out of the van to vanish in a pink mist, but he left something behind snagged in the nylon handle of the drug bag—his submachine gun.

With the sound of two-way automatic gunfire filling the air, Shorty picked up the gun and grunted. It was heavier than he expected.

Shorty had never fired a machine gun before, but he'd seen plenty of movies. Getting used to the weight, he turned it on its side. A small dial marked in red pointed to two symbols. One showed a single bullet, the other showed three. He reasoned this toggled the gun between single-shot and full-auto modes.

Shorty flipped the switch to full-auto and pointed its barrel out the open doorway. People were screaming in their seats above as the bus continued to barrel on at top speed and bullets flew in both directions. Shorty imagined the greedy driver, knuckles white as he gripped the steering wheel, desperately searching for help and cursing the day he met a crooked dwarf with a Hollywood smile and an offer too rich to refuse.

Shorty drew in a deep breath and squeezed the trigger. Rounds spat from the gun like a horde of angry wasps with lead stingers. His first bullets chewed up the road before the gun's unexpected kick drew the muzzle skyward. Shorty released the trigger before a volley stitched the metal ceiling. Fortunately, the van had been an impossible target to miss. His stray bullets shredded its front tires, windshield, and roof.

Without tires, the van's front rims dug into the road and its ass end flew into the sky for a series of cartwheels that would have made an overweight gymnast proud. Two screaming bodies flailed into the air as the van exploded. Its flaming carcass careened off the road and rolled down a sharp ravine to a farmer's field below.

Shorty looked at the gun in surprise. It packed a lot of wallop for such a small—

A bullet smashed through the ceiling and tore a chunk of meat from his arm. Shorty cried out and dropped the gun, only to watch in stunned horror as it bounced once on the floor before sliding out the open doorway.

Shorty's cries were silenced when another bullet pierced the ceiling and puckered the floor between his legs. It was followed by an angry voice.

"You little bastard! Think you can steal from me?"

Another bullet, this time less than four inches from his head. Shorty dove into the remaining luggage and scrambled toward the rear of the hold . . . where he found Twinkle's handgun. He snapped it up in both hands as the drug dealer pumped another hole through the ceiling.

This time, instead of retreating, Shorty sprinted to the fresh hole, jammed his gun against it, and squeezed the trigger.

A loud scream echoed through the hold and a heavy thump hit the ceiling as the gunman fell.

"You shot my fucking bal—"

Shorty aimed his gun where a bump had suddenly appeared in the ceiling and fired again. By the time he ran dry, the screaming had stopped.

"Nice work," said LoLa. "You always did overcompensate."

Shorty spun. The motorbike and sidecar was matching pace outside again, while LoLa was armed and pissed and standing in the doorway of the baggage compartment.

"And you were always nimble." Shorty dropped his empty gun to the floor and cradled his wounded arm.

"So what do we have left?" LoLa asked.

"Between us or—"

"Drugs, numbnut."

Shorty indicated the lone black bag sitting near the open doorway. "Twenty kilograms of uncut heroin. Worth around two million."

"Hardly seems worth the trouble."

Despite himself, Shorty grinned. "You've come that far up in the world, huh?"

LoLa smiled. "Never walked taller."

She lifted her gun and fingered the trigger.

Shorty blurted, "There's a fourth bag."

LoLa's smile brightened and she eased off the trigger. "Oh?"

"Six hundred thousand in cash. I figure you take the drugs, leave me the dough. I've earned it."

"Earned it? You cost me four good men, transportation, weapons, and dry-cleaning, not to mention my brother."

"You never liked Twinkle much."

"No, but I loved him."

Shorty and LoLa stared at each other for an endless moment, a thousand memories shared in the blink of an eye.

"We'll always have Paris," said Shorty.

LoLa snorted. "A fishbowl fuck in Tennessee doesn't count, Shorty, don't you get that? I need more than road trips in a broken-down VW van, nightclubs with putrid toilets, and hiding from the landlord on rent day. You always thought too small. I plan to live large."

"You've gone hard."

"No, Shorty. The problem is, you've stayed soft." She waved the gun at his chest. "Get me the bag."

Shorty tilted his chin. "It's just back there."

"Do I look like I do heavy lifting? Get it."

Shorty scrambled over the remains of the unopened

luggage and pulled out the last black bag. He hefted it onto his shoulder, wincing at the pain, and returned to the woman he'd once loved.

"Pity it has to end this way, honeybee," he said.

LoLa thumbed back the hammer.

When the bus pulled into the Texaco station ten minutes later, a squad of eight patrol cars swarmed around it. The men and women in blue were bundled in armor-plated protection, riot helmets, and enough firepower to ventilate a crack den.

They removed the traumatized passengers first before rushing the luggage compartment.

They didn't meet any resistance.

Inside was a lone body dressed in head-to-toe black, its lifeblood coating a duffel bag filled with twenty kilos of pure, uncut heroin.

The dead woman had a tiny screwdriver protruding from her chest and half a Toblerone bar stuffed in her mouth.

*

GRANT McKENZIE was born in Scotland, lives in Canada, and writes U.S.-based thrillers. As such, he wears a kilt and toque with his six guns. His debut novel, *Switch*, was lauded by author Ken Bruen as "Harlan Coben on speed" and quickly became a bestseller in Germany. It has been published in seven countries and three languages so far.

The Gato Conundrum

JOHN LESCROART

The Uffizi Gallery—Florence

Don Matheson, also known as Nishion der Matosian in Armenia and Nishi ibn Matos throughout the Arabian world, was starting to develop museum fatigue.

And no wonder. Every wall of the Uffizi was essentially wall-papered with masterpieces by Botticelli, da Vinci, Michelangelo, Raphael, Titian, and (Matosian's favorite, mostly because of his name) Fra Filippo Lippi.

All the art in one place wore a guy out.

Even if, like Matosian, you were a thirty-eight-year-old ex-Navy SEAL in perfect physical condition who ran six miles in under an hour every morning before the sun was up. And even if, as happened quite frequently, you'd enjoyed phenomenal, acrobatic, and oftentimes tantric sex the night before.

But conjuring up a deep artistic appreciation for fifty

or sixty paintings should not be the work of an hour, or even of a day. Matosian much preferred the Rodin garden in Paris, where you could go outside and sit looking up at *The Thinker* and let the power and meaning of the sculpture get inside your head and heart and leave you, somehow, changed for the better.

Enriched.

In truth, he wasn't here to enjoy the art, but to meet a contact who was driving up that morning from Rome. When that contact hadn't arrived by the appointed hour, he'd decided—since he was here—to take advantage of the opportunity to check out the art, which he'd been doing now for nearly forty minutes.

It occurred to him that the late contact might not be the fault of Italy's roads or the Florentine traffic, but a deliberate attempt to lull him into the semisoporific state in which he now found himself. Museum fatigue could not literally kill, of course, but it could leave you dullwitted and exposed.

And in Matosian's life, these states were often the precursor to disaster.

Matosian tore his eyes away from Raphael's *Madonna of the Goldfinch* and quickly but surreptitiously scanned the milling crowd of tourists surrounding him. Nothing untoward caught his eye on the first sweep, but then, in the limit of his peripheral vision, a flash of blond hair appeared and then disappeared behind the entrance to the next room.

He turned, but had only taken his first step in that direction when he heard a scream. In that first second the crowd around him froze, and he used that moment to push his way through the press of people. By now others had taken up the cries, but Matosian ignored them, getting over to where a beautiful young woman lay where she'd fallen.

Matosian was the first one at her side. He felt the slight pulse in her neck, noted the shiny pallor and heat of her skin. Clearly, she'd been poisoned, probably right here in the Uffizi while she was waiting to make contact with him. Now her eyes opened and even through her obvious pain, he detected a softening in her expression— she recognized him. "Veni," she gasped. "Come." And lifting her arm, she brought him down close to her lips.

"Gato," she whispered.

The agreed upon password. Cat.

She pressed something now into his hand—it felt like an ancient key—and closed his fingers over it. "Gato," she repeated.

And then she went still.

Hyde Park—London

There had been no time to search for the woman's killer in Florence. It would have been a futile exercise in any event. No doubt, the assassin had done his damage and disappeared into the crowd even before Matosian had gotten out of the museum.

And there was no time to waste.

But the good news was that Matosian had received the key and immediately recognized it for what it was—as a youth, he'd been trained by traveling gypsies in the arcane art of lock picking, and now could not only pick any lock, ancient or modern, that he encountered, but he could identify by sight or touch any one of the 314 closely guarded discrete patterns used by ancient guild of locksmiths in setting the internal tumblers in locks since the late Middle Ages.

Now, in the swiftly darkening evening of the same day that he'd left Florence, and dressed in a low-key gray business suit, Matosian walked along the calm waters of the Serpentine in a deep fog. His destination: the shelter/pump house for the Italian Fountain at the north end of the park.

As he walked, something began to nag at the borders of his consciousness. Walking at this time in this weather, he wouldn't normally expect to have any company on this gravel path. But his training let him hear things that others could not, and now he came to an abrupt full stop.

Sure enough, steps sounded behind him. They kept on for one or two steps before they, too, stopped. But that was enough for Matosian.

Side-stepping over to the grass, he waited until the steps began again. And another set of them, clearly several men, converging from in front of him as well. And then—he sensed rather that actually heard them—another set of footfalls registered from directly behind him on the grass.

They were closing in on him now from three directions, with the freezing waters of the Serpentine as his only escape.

Even now the shadows were beginning to appear out of the fog. Big men in trenchcoats. Matosian could take care of himself in any fight, but now he estimated a force of at least six men bent on taking him down.

And then he heard his name, in a female key. "Don," the voice said. "Gato."

He turned and saw her, frail and beautiful, yet somehow strong and competent, sitting on the metallic bench that bounded the gravel walk. With no time to reason it out, he went over to her. She had wrapped herself in a heavy scarf over her peacoat, and now she brought it up around his neck, and brought her lips to his. As her tongue probed his, he realized that she tasted of almonds.

His pursuers had by now converged on the path, thirty feet away from them. He could hear them talking as the kiss continued. And then, as a group, they began to come down toward the bench.

"Excuse me," one of the men said, "have you seen . . . ?"

The woman broke their kiss and, holding Matosian's face against her shoulder, snapped out in a rich Cockney accent. "Does it look like we're looking out for somebody here, guvnor? Now piss off."

And then she came back to the kiss.

After the men had gone, spreading out to find their quarry, the kiss finally ended. And now Matosian saw that tears filled her eyes. "Daphne," she said. "The girl in Florence this morning? She was my sister."

The pump house for the Italian Fountain did not get a lot of traffic. Matosian and Chloe—for that was the name of the woman who'd saved him with her kiss, Daphne's almond-scented sister—had no trouble finding the door that was the match for the key he'd carried from Florence.

Once they were inside, Chloe turned to him. "What's supposed to be hidden here?" she asked. "Daphne never told me before . . ." Her voice broke as the sentence trailed off.

Matosian took her in his arms. "It's all right," he said. "She felt no pain. They were professionals. As for what's hidden here, we'll find it. I'll know it when I see it." He flashed his laser penlight around the dark room. The pumps churned hundreds of gallons of water and most of the space was filled with pipes and plumbing. The light traced what looked like ancient graffiti on the walls, and suddenly Matosian came forward to examine the writing more carefully.

"This is it," he announced. "It's not graffiti, though they've done a good job of making it look like it."

"What is it then?"

"Cyrillic. Early Bulgarian Cyrillic."

"What does it say? Can you read it?"

"Yes, of course," he answered abstractedly. Matosian could read sixteen different alphabets and was fluent in twenty-two languages. "It's . . . just a minute. It's non-sense. 'Roses are pie, are is the area of a circle.'"

"'Are is'? Is that what it really says?"

"There's no doubt about the words," Matosian said.

"Maybe it's a code," Chloe offered.

"No, not a code. A puzzle." His voice became more animated. "That's it, a puzzle! Roses are . . ."

"Red!" she said.

"Yes they are." Getting into it now, Matosian came back to the script. "So what's left?"

"'Pie are is the area of a circle.'"

"But it's not," Matosian exclaimed breathlessly. "That's $pi\ r$ squared." A pause. "So what two words are left out."

"Red Square," she said.

"Exactly."

The Kremlin—Moscow

Matosian normally worked alone, but Chloe now clung to him, both of them shivering in the north wind that whipped through the square. She had refused to leave him in London even as they'd sped to the private airfield just outside Dover—bereft over the loss of her sister, and fearful for her own life, she saw him as her last ray of hope.

On Matosian's personal jet, she'd fallen asleep until they were making their descent into Russia, and now suddenly, as an early morning crowd of tourists and bureaucrats hurriedly brushed by them, the enormity of their situation seemed to strike her for the first time.

"So Daphne never got to tell you what this was ultimately about?" she asked.

Matosian shook his head. "They got to her two steps ahead of me. She barely managed to get out the password and pass me the key before . . . before she was gone."

"Do you think it might have something to do with the password itself? Gato."

"Shh." He put a gentle finger to her lips. "Let's let that remain unspoken until we need it." He looked around at the milling crowd. "But yes," he went on, "I don't think that's impossible. My initial contact . . ."

She stopped him. "Who was that?"

A grim smile. "People say it as a joke, but in this case it's as real as a heart attack. I could tell you, but then I'd have to kill you. But let's say it's a high-ranking official of my country's government. Very high-ranking, and all but invisible."

"And he told you something about . . . the password?"

"Not in so many words. At Langley . . ."

"So it's CIA then?"

"Forget I ever said that." Matosian cast around, checking the faces in the crowd. Then, back to Chloe, he lowered his voice. "I don't know if it started there. Just that it came through there."

"I understand," she said. "I'll tell no one. Ever."

He looked at her for a long moment. Then, coming to the decision that he would trust her, he went on. "When he mentioned the password to me, I got the feeling that a cat, or the symbol of a cat, would play some role in what we were trying to locate, but when I asked, he just smiled that enigmatic smile of his and said, 'I think you'll find out when you need to.' And then I was off to Florence." He shook his head in apparent disbelief. "It's hard to imagine that was only three days ago."

"So what are we looking for here? This venue—Red Square—is a lot bigger than the pump house back in London. Whatever it is could be anywhere."

"You're right." Again, Matosian shook his head. "All we know is that somebody wanted me here and believed I would find and recognize whatever it was." Now his face grew somber. "I feel like I'm letting my people down, that they might have picked the wrong man, that I wasn't up to the job."

"But no one's told you what the job is!"

"That," Matosian said, "comes with the territory."

Suddenly a large black car pulled up and six men in heavy trenchcoats appeared from its doors almost simultaneously in front of them. Matosian took Chloe's arm and started to turn when he realized that one of the men had already gotten around directly behind him. He smiled in a relatively pleasant fashion and said in heavily accented English, "I have a gun and I will use it. You are both please to come with us."

Somewhere Underneath the Kremlin—Moscow

Matosian had been tortured before—in Iran, Afghanistan, Syria, and Colombia. He liked to think of himself as somewhat of an aficionado of torture. He knew that he would probably survive whatever they had in mind, but he wasn't sure he could say the same thing about Chloe. And, now that she was in his care, he couldn't live with that scenario.

He was going to have to break out and find her.

But currently he was in a dark subterranean room, the doors closed behind his captors after they'd tied him up on the simple wooden chair. They were obviously going to work first on his feet, and to that end, they had removed his shoes. But they'd thrown them to the side and left them against the wall. He was far better trained than they were and he'd already loosened the ropes with which they'd bound his legs and arms, but he wanted the ropes still to appear tight when they came back in to question him, so when he was sure he'd sufficiently weakened the knots, he rested.

He didn't have long to wait. The big man with the heavy accent opened the door and turned on the light, one glaring bulb in the center of the ceiling.

"Mr. Matosian," the man said as he came to stand in front of his captive. "I am Viktor. My last name, unimportant."

"But enough about you, Viktor. What have you done with her?" Matosian asked.

"She's safe. We haven't touched her. Yet."

"You don't have to hurt anyone," Matosian said. "I'll tell you whatever you want. Whatever I know."

"You care very much for this woman, no?"

"Very much, yes. But you know, these ropes, they are too loose. You should know I can slip out of them whenever I want."

"Very funny, that is. I watched Vladimir tie you up myself, of which no one is better."

"Still," Matosian said, "maybe you'd better check again. If you're going to be tickling my feet, you wouldn't want me to come undone from laughing too hard."

Chuckling without any humor, Viktor took a step closer, bringing him into Matosian's range. In a series of lightning moves, the seated man struck twice with his fists, once in the neck and the second shot to the nose, crushing the cartilage there. Before the blows had completely straightened Viktor up, Matosian had stepped out of the ropes binding his legs as well and now kicked out, hitting his captor again in the chest. Viktor went down in a silent hump.

Quickly donning his shoes and socks, Matosian was out into a narrow, dimly lit corridor within five seconds. Chloe had still been with them when they'd turned into his room, so she must be farther down the hall the way they'd been walking. So, turning in that direction, he started jogging, stopping to check the doors.

She was behind the third one, bound as he'd been, hand and foot, though they'd left her shoes on, and had put duct tape over her mouth.

Where had her captors gone? Where were the rest of them?

There was no time to ask those questions, and Matosian wasted no movement wondering about it or getting her untied. When he gently removed the duct tape from her mouth, he paused for a half second to touch her lips with his own. Then, taking her by the hand, he pulled her from her chair, and they were off and running down the hallway, toward a stairway beyond which shimmered the glow of sunlight!

They came out into an all-but-deserted alley that led off Red Square, and a fortuitous one at that. At the end of the block, as they were just coming out into the crowded square and the view of the Kremlin again, Matosian suddenly stopped, looking up.

"What is it?" Chloe asked.

"Look." He was pointing to an ornate iron streetlight right above their heads. Matosian had almost run into it. The light was off since it was daytime. But its spherical bulb was held up by an amazingly realistic sculpture of the Sphinx. "This is it," Matosian cried.

"I don't see it," Chloe said.

"Sure you do," Matosian answered gently. "It's the face of a woman and the body of a lion. And what is a lion?" he asked.

"A cat!"

His face lit up into a huge smile. "Hurry," he said urgently. "There's still time." And taking her hand again, he started to run.

The Louvre—Paris

"I didn't even realize that there was a Sphinx here," Chloe said.

"They're all over the place," Matosian answered. "Santorini and Thebes in Greece, Giza in Egypt, St. Petersburg in Russia, and many, many more."

"But then, how did you . . . ?"

"As they knew I would, I recognized that the specific Sphinx on that streetlamp was based on the one here at the Louvre." He stared for a moment at the enormous stone carving. "I really do think we're getting close now," he said.

"But who are 'they'?"

"Yes," he said. "Who are 'they'?" He sat on a stone bench across from the ancient sculpture, patting the space next to him in invitation.

Chloe lowered herself down next to him, close enough so that their thighs touched. She took his hand and after a moment, he turned to her. "When I thought they were going to hurt you," he began, and then could not go on. She reached up then and touched his lips with her free hand, and then that hand went back around his neck and brought his face down to where their lips could again meet—this time not as a ruse to fool Matosian's pursuers as their first kiss had been in London, nor out of relief as the kiss they'd shared under the Kremlin. This time, their bodies lingered, their mouths locked in a transporting kiss of passion and connection.

When at last they broke it off, it had grown dark in the museum.

Restaurant Le Jules Verne, The Eiffel Tower—Paris

Matosian savored the first bite of his foie gras, the first sip of their twenty-five-year-old Chateau d'Yquem as he looked across the room at the beautiful woman who was returning from the ladies' room, walking toward him 125 meters above Paris. "I don't know how we've gotten to here," he said when she got to the table and sat down, "but I'm so glad that we have. I never thought that this—a feeling like this—would happen to me. Here's to you."

She raised her own glass. "And to you. And us." She tasted her foie gras, quickly seared and served with candied figs and a balsamic *gastriche,* and seemed to nearly swoon at the flavors. But then, abruptly, her face clouded over. "But where exactly are we?"

He knew, of course, that she wasn't speaking literally, and he came forward and lowered his voice, his food for the moment forgotten. "All my senses tell me that we're where we're supposed to be."

"But where do we go next? And to look for what?"

"Whoever's running this hasn't let us down yet," Matosian said. "We're here because they drew us here. I think that even though it goes against my every instinct, the best move now is simply to wait until they contact us. Otherwise, the trail simply ends here, and that I can't accept. Not after all we've been through."

As though on cue, the tuxedoed waiter appeared at the table. "Mr. Matosian?" he queried.

Matosian looked up expectantly. "Guilty."

"There's a phone call for you at the reception kiosk."

Flashing a quick and knowing glance at Chloe, Matosian stood and turned to accompany the waiter back to the small podium near the restaurant's entrance. There he picked up the headset of the old-fashioned telephone and said hello.

"Gato," came the cryptic reply in an electronically scrambled male voice.

"Gato yourself," Matosian snapped, "and the horse it rode in on. Tell me what this is all about right now or I'm out of it. We're both out of it."

"How do you know you can trust the woman?"

"You killed her sister, damn you. That's how I know. She wouldn't be in this at all if it weren't for that."

"Her sister was collateral damage," the voice said. "It couldn't be helped. And unless you're very careful, the same fate may befall her, too. And in the very near term. Do you hear what I'm saying?"

Matosian, suddenly now as close to panic as he'd ever been, raised his eyes and found Chloe still seated at their table, finishing her foie gras, relaxed and beautiful. "I hear you," he managed to get out. "What are my instructions?"

The voice didn't hesitate. "The best thing you can do is get to your hotel as soon as you can."

"Who are you?"

"Call me Honest Abe, but don't waste any time thinking about me. Time is of the essence now. *Now! This second.*" The voice repeated with metallic urgency. And then, with a click, the connection went dead.

Matosian hung up and walked as quickly as he could without calling attention to himself back to his table. Chloe looked up at him questioningly as he took out his wallet. He was just dropping a thousand-euro bill on the table when the waiter reappeared with an *amuse-bouche*, some sort of superlight looking spoon-sized quenelle in a saffron broth, which he placed in front of Chloe.

Matosian leaned over her and rasped out, "Don't touch that. Don't take another bite."

"But monsieur . . ." the waiter demurred.

Matosian straightened to his full height. "Non, monsieur. Pourquoi pas vous même le mangez?"—"Why don't you eat it yourself?"

The waiter went white.

"Je suis sérieux," Matosian said. "I'm serious. Just take that little bite." Then, suddenly, the tension and danger of the past few days took over and Matosian took the little proffered spoon and in one fluid and lightning motion forced the waiter's hand up to his mouth, where he stuffed the little ball of dough and held the man's jaw shut for another couple of seconds.

As soon as he let go, the waiter spit the dough out and grabbed for one of the glasses of water on the table. At the same instant, Matosian grabbed Chloe's hand and forcibly lifted her out of her seat. "We're out of time here," he told her.

Behind her, the waiter had taken one step back toward the kitchen before his knees seem to give out from under him and he fell headlong into the spirits tray.

"Now! Now! Now!" Matosian pulled Chloe along behind him as the crowd in the restaurant rose almost as a single unit to see what had caused the disturbance. They were both walking double-time, holding hands, past the standing, sometimes screaming, panicking patrons and toward the exit and the long elevator ride down. But then Matosian, thinking better of using the elevator, led her back even farther to the little-used stairway with its three hundred or so steps to the ground.

When that door had closed behind them, Chloe pulled her hand away, stopping him. "What was that about?"

"This is about believing the warning I got over the phone. And, by the way," he added, "I've got my instructions now, or as good as I'm going to get them."

"What are they?"

"It's still not completely clear. But one thing is."

"What's that?"

"We've got to get to the hotel. Like yesterday."

And taking her hand again, he led her down the clanging and darkened stairway and out at the base of the Eiffel Tower.

L'Hotel George V — Paris

"Something's changed," he said.

"What do you mean?"

"This isn't the way we left this room," Matosian said as soon as they'd come through the door and double-locked it behind them.

"What's different?" Chloe said. "I don't see . . ."

But he had already crossed to the table in front of the couch. It held a variety of magazines and travel guides fanned out artistically. But within the fan, two of the magazines were folded open rather than to their covers. Matosian picked up the first one, glanced at its description of fine hotels in Washington, D.C., and then immediately grabbed the second, opened to an article on Abraham Lincoln called "The Great Emancipator."

He stood stock-still for a long moment. Chloe came up behind him and put her arms around him. "What is it?" she said.

But, his heart breaking, Matosian kept his face straight as he turned to her. "I've got to go now," he said. "You'll be safe here."

"But. . . ." Her doe eyes filled with tears. "I thought that you and I . . ."

"We will," he said. "But I've got to finish this. And it won't be safe for you where I have to go. If the warning we got in the restaurant meant anything, that much was clear. I've got to do this alone."

And so saying, he kissed her one last time and strode for the door. "Whatever you do," he said as he turned at the door, "lock this behind me and don't let anyone in, not even hotel staff. I've paid for your room for a week, and I'll be back to you before then."

"Don!" She ran across to him. "I'm afraid. I don't know . . ."

He quieted her with a last kiss. "Wait for me," he said. "Trust me."

And with that, he was gone.

The Lincoln Memorial—Washington, D.C.

It was close to 4:00 A.M. when Matosian mounted the steps at the end of the Capitol Mall. When he got near to the top, he moved into the shadow of the imposing structure and could just make out in front of him the looming bulk of the sixteenth president of the United States, Abraham Lincoln.

The night was dead quiet and surprisingly warm. Matosian still wore his tuxedo from the Restaurant Jules Verne in Paris—there had been no time to change, and certainly not as he flew his own jet alone over the Atlantic, wrestling with his unanswered questions, his demons, and most of all, least familiarly, with his emotions.

But now he was at the end, and there was no time for emotion.

He got to the last step, paused, took a breath, and then continued forward under the massive stone ceiling and into the monument. The place seemed to be made of darkness itself. Then, steeling himself, he came forward more and then more, step by step. Finally, he stopped.

With the laser light that had served him so well in the pump house in London, now he shone its beam over the words of the Gettysburg Address on his right, then over to the Second Inaugural Address on the left. He stopped on the words, "with malice toward none; with charity for all" and somehow he felt anew that however this whole terrible affair turned out, he was proud to be doing this important work for his country, proud to be an American.

They could never take that away from him.

For some reason, he became aware of the feel of water evaporating from the reflecting pond behind him, sending a chill down the back of his neck.

There was no sound. He was alone.

It was all as it should be.

He drew in a breath as though it might be his last. Finally: "Gato," he whispered into the cavernous emptiness. And then again, more loudly. "Goddamn it, gato."

And from behind the statue, he heard the footsteps—a light tread, but businesslike, echoing within the semienclosed chamber.

A figure began to emerge from behind the sculpture. Matosian raised his laser beam, hesitated, and then pressed the button, bathing the figure in a green fluorescent light.

"Hello, Don." How Chloe had beaten him here from Paris he didn't know and couldn't imagine. And she also had managed to find the time to change her clothes, for now she wore a well-tailored dark business suit. "Well done," she said, stopping ten feet in front of him. "Congratulations. You've passed."

"I've *passed*?" A slow, deep rage seemed to settle into the middle of his chest. "What do you mean? Has this all been some sort of a game?"

"Not some sort of a game, Don. The most important game in the world. We had to know what you were capable of, what motivated you, how you reacted under pressure. And we had to see it ourselves, not hear about it from some questionably reliable third source. This is the last round before you're allowed to do the really important work, the work no one can ever know about."

"But what . . ." The world seemed to be whirling about him. He brought his hands up to his forehead and closed his eyes against the sensation of vertigo. He became vaguely aware of another set of footsteps emanating from the opposite side of Lincoln's body. Opening his eyes, he pointed his light in that direction and was not surprised to see his original connection from Langley, call him Honest Abe now, rounding the corner by the emancipator's right foot. "Hi, Don. Glad you could make it."

"*You're glad I could make it?*" Again the rage threatened to undo Matosian. "But what about your sister?" he said to Chloe. "What was that?" He whirled on his CIA contact. "Was that simply collateral damage, as you called it, Abe?"

"Easy," Chloe said. "We expected you to be upset, Don. Most people who get to this stage in their training are upset. It's natural. But first, know this. She wasn't my sister, and . . ."

"That doesn't forgive . . ."

But she raised her hand imperiously, stopping him. "Second, and perhaps more important, she's not dead. She took a small pill we provided that mimics death very effectively for the better part of an hour. Her job was to get the key to you and then to appear to die. Your job, which you performed spectacularly, I might add, was to forget about her as an acceptable loss and move on with the mission. If you'd have stayed around long enough for her to recover, you wouldn't be here now. You'd be lateraled into career oblivion and never even know what happened."

Matosian shook his head. "You people are cold," he said.

"Cold is a virtue," Chloe answered. "Cold is a necessity. And you're a few degrees below lukewarm yourself."

"For a while there I wasn't," Matosian replied.

"No. That was clear."

Their eyes met. Even in the dark, Matosian thought he could still detect a spark there.

But Honest Abe spoke up, breaking the palpable tension of the moment. "Your mention of Langley was your only mistake. We thought of shutting down the mission then."

"So why didn't you?"

"Because you played it right, plain and simple. Of course, it only makes sense that someone had given you your marching orders, and you being an American, they could rationally have only come from one source. You telling Chloe about it the way you did established your credibility and gave away nothing she wouldn't have already known if she were on the other side anyway. You may have even let the information slip on purpose. It would be interesting to know if that were the case."

"I'll keep that as my own secret," Matosian said, "if I'm allowed to have any, that is."

"We'll give you just the one," Honest Abe said, and Matosian thought he could detect the trace of a smile in the gash of his mouth. Agency humor.

"Don," Chloe said. "We're done here unless you've got any other questions."

"Just one," Matosian said. "What was the deal about the password. It had nothing to do with the mission."

"It helped bring you to Paris," she said. "Otherwise, it was meant to be a conundrum."

"You mean a riddle?"

"Well, not precisely. You know that a conundrum is a riddle whose answer is a pun. For example, when is a door not a door?"

"When it's ajar, of course," Matosian said.

"Right. So we knew we were going to keep you running around. Everywhere you went, you checked out your surroundings, and if you were going to succeed, you had to say, 'Got to go.' Gato go. It suggested itself."

"And on that note," Matosian said. "I've gato go now. You'll know how to reach me again, I'm presuming."

"Bet on it," Chloe said.

Little Dix Bay—British Virgin Islands

Twenty-four hours later, Matosian walked out of his beachfront bungalow and across the white sand into the crystal clear and warm Caribbean water. Navigating by the bright full moon, he swam straight out from the beach for four thousand strokes, then nearly out of sight of land, turned and began the long swim back.

By the time he got to where it was shallow enough for him to stand, the sky to the east was just lightening to a nacreous glow. He could make out the tracks he'd made in the sand on the walk down from his bungalow, but now standing in those tracks was a woman, facing away from him, wearing a diaphanous white shift and nothing else.

When he finally made it back to the hardened sand where the water lapped the shoreline, she turned around and tentatively walked down to where he stood, stopping in front of him, looking up at him with a mixture of trepidation and longing.

"In Paris, I thought you were with them," he said.

"I know. When you took the phone call. Then with the waiter."

"Would you have let me eat that little spoonful?"

"I knew you wouldn't, by that time. Would you have let me?"

"I didn't, if you remember. Even though I'd been convinced you were the enemy." He paused, then came out with another question. "And I presume the waiter, like the woman who wasn't your sister, is all right?"

She nodded. "And ten thousand dollars richer." A pause. "But that was when you were sure, wasn't it? At the restaurant?"

He nodded. "Yes. No one else but you could have known where we were. You called Abe when you went to the bathroom."

She put a hand on his arm. "By that time, I wanted to tell you, but I couldn't. I didn't want you to leave me, but you had to. We were both trapped in the maze we'd helped create."

"And," Matosian asked, "are we still trapped in it now?"

"No," Chloe said. "I've gotten word of a secret mission involving the Vatican that we'll need to see to soon, but until we get the call from Abe, our time is our own. One day, maybe even two, if we want to take them." Her eyes pleaded with him. "If you could find it in yourself and in your heart to trust me again."

"If you put your arms around me," Matosian said, "maybe you can convince me."

She did as he'd suggested, and after holding her body

against his for a moment, he pulled away enough to let him lean over.

And their lips came together.

She tasted like almonds.

*

JOHN LESCROART is a *New York Times* bestselling author of twenty-one novels, including most recently *Treasure Hunt,* which is the third book in the San Francisco–based Wyatt Hunt series. His books have been translated into seventeen languages in more than seventy-five countries, and his short stories have been included in many anthologies.

His first novel, *Sunburn,* won the San Francisco Foundation's Joseph Henry Jackson Award for best novel by a California author, and *Dead Irish* and *The 13th Juror* were nominees for the Shamus and Anthony Best Mystery Novel, respectively. *Guilt* was a Reader's Digest Select Edition choice, and *The Suspect,* chosen by the American Author's Association as its 2007 Novel of the Year, was also the 2007 One Book Sacramento choice of the Sacramento Library Foundation.

The Princess
of Felony Flats

BILL CAMERON

I

Barely a year into his sentence—ninety-nine moons for felony skullduggery and aggravated bloodletting—Frank Pounder's barrister gets wind of an impending shit storm in Newcastle CID. Detective Inspector Dale Dingus is about to be brought up on charges for falsifying evidence in a connivance and brigandage case he's been chasing alongside the Crown Bureau of Revelation and Arrest since before dirt. Not too bright, our boy Dingus. Suddenly his cases going back five years are getting a fresh look, and the Crabs are none too happy about it.

I can't say as I blame them, but unlike the linear thinkers in the Bureau, I have a knack for sniffing out openings in the misfortune of others. I'm already noodling the angles before a whiff of the Dingus travail goes public, even before Frank's shark moves for dismissal. The prosecuting magistrate knows no way Frank gets convicted in a retrial without Dingus's tainted evidence, so the legal wranglings don't figure to take long. Frank expects to be sprung in time to see his unborn baby mapped via UltraSound, and he spares no breath bragging about how he'll be on hand to learn whether his offspring is a pointer or a setter.

But don't get the idea Frank is some kind of sentimental doily muncher. Trust me, the man's a black-hearted ogre with a chest like a beer keg and fists of seasoned oak who runs everything from Newcastle Deeps to the slopes of the West Hills, even from gaol. Kingpin of Felony Flats, territory he took by force from Old Man Miller himself. Ended up with Miller's daughter too, a double-handful of hell named Dahlia with the personality of a wolverine and a body that looks like it was molded from the finest grade ballistic gel. That Frank's looking forward to progeny is evidence of little more than his well-earned reputation for getting what he wants and then some.

Sure, he's had his setbacks, getting pinched by Dingus in the first place not the least of them. Then, when he arrived at Little Liver Creek Penitentiary full of grandiose plans of conquest, the ruling camarilla, the Incandito Banditos, let him know they took their notions of seniority plenty serious. In the course of ensuing combat operations, some unidentified miscreant stuck a sharpened toothbrush between Frank's ribs one night right before lockdown.

But Frank survives—no surprise to anyone who knows him. The surprise is that during his recovery, he experiences what your more educated types call an epiphany. Life is a tenuous, fragile thing that could end any time: shiv, heart failure, meteor ricochet off the moon. That's when he makes his plans for immortality via reproduction, with Dahlia Miller anointed brood mare.

Only problem is there's no place to breed in the gaol commons, and the warden's a hard case. No conjugal visits, period. Bastard was immune to bribes too, some kind of miter hat with an overdeveloped sense of right and wrong. But if the warden is a stone, guards are made of squishier stuff. Frank arranges to smuggle his squirt out in a plastic cup so Dahlia can take it to some high-priced, honeypot medico over on the west side. Doc Ciconi is as good as they come in the field of procreation at a distance. Once the good doctor performs his magic, Frank can look forward to a little tucker waiting for him at the ass end of the slam. In the meantime Dahlia has something to keep her busy. Too busy to screw around, Frank figures. Clever plan, you ask me, except for the part where it doesn't work for shit.

People tell me I know too much about this crap, that the way I stick my nose into things is gonna get it cut off. I figure a man has to make a living somehow. In the realm of criminal endeavor, I'm what you might call a knowledge worker. A dangerous business to be sure, especially since when presented with foreknowledge of Frank Pounder's unscheduled early release, I do something only the first little pig would do. I nail his girl.

II

Even from prison, Frank means to keep Dahlia on a short leash, but she's not some compliant lap dog. Before she knew Frank she was a busy girl: stripper, high-priced call girl, roller derby queen. With him behind bars she figures she's got some elbow room. Her only problem is one of coinage. The allowance he provides isn't enough for her live in the style to which she's accustomed.

I catch up with her not long after Frank got shivved. She's standing at one end of the rail at the High Tail Inn, the titty bar in the Flats. Typical joint. Central catwalk, three poles, smoke-dimmed stage lights on the ceiling. Twenty, thirty horn dogs nursing pickling gin or industrial beer and staring slack-jawed at the jiggling silicone on stage. Vinyl booths that smell of diluted pine cleaner in the back for private dances. Dahlia is arguing with Biff Steele, the joint's owner of record. She got her start right there on that stage, and she wants another run. Just a few nights shaking her rubber boobs for sweat-drenched tips, little something to buff the bank account. Biff wants nothing to do with it. Being the owner of record doesn't count for much when Frank Pounder is the owner of benefit.

"No way, Dahlia. Frank'd feed me my nuts."

"Don't be a pussy, Biff. I need money."

"You wanna drink, I'll set you up from the top shelf. But I ain't going against Frank, no matter that he's up to Little Liver."

Top shelf at the High Tail is barrel scrapings most anywhere else. Pissed, Dahlia spins and stalks off. Even angry, she's worth a second look. A floor-to-ceiling beauty, just enough curves, blond hair from an expensive bottle and indigo eyes from Aphrodite's paintbrush. I watch her take up a post at the other end of the bar and yell for a bottle of champagne. Biff winces. He's going to have to order in.

Given a choice, most folks would take sliding down a razor blade into a vat of alcohol over crossing Frank Pounder. I choose to sidle up to her, nudge her ass. "Hey, baby. Sounds like you got a problem. Maybe I can help you out."

She looks me up and down like she's inspecting road kill. "I'm way outa your price range, pipsqueak."

Dahlia Miller can have her pick if looks are all she's after. Tall, dark, and handsome I'm not. But I have something your typical boy toy can't offer.

"You'd be surprised at my price range." I lean back, show her the round edge of a roll of green in my pocket. "It might be even bigger, but Frank lived through the shank . . ."

Her indigo eyes flash. I have her attention. Dahlia Miller might be Frank's plaything, but it's no secret the two have a volatile relationship built on a foundation of antagonism. Everyone knows she was basically a peace offering from Miller so Frank would let the old man keep his book after he lost the war for control of Felony Flats.

"You shivved Frank?" Dubious.

I show her a saucy grin. "You can hardly expect me to make an admissible admission in a public place like this."

"One phone call and you don't live to see outdoors again, admissible or otherwise."

"Now where's the fun in that?" I make a frowny face. "Besides, who says the Incandito Banditos don't have some reach outside Little Liver themselves?"

She looks around the bar, tries to figure out which of the drooling slam-hounds might be my cover. All eyes are either glazed over or fixed on the pole grinders. I see no percentage in letting her know it's none of the above.

"You're taking a big chance, no matter who's looking out for you."

"Hey, if you're not interested—" I slip the wad of cash back into my pocket.

She puts a hand on my forearm, wavering. "How long were you inside?"

"Coupla years on a cook-and-book. Got busted trying to move some meth. My buyer didn't show and I tripped over my dick into a sting looking for a backup sell."

She's thinking about my roll of cash, thinking I ain't seen a woman who wasn't in halftone for two years. Thinking she can lead me anywhere she wants to go by my ugly duckling. And she's bored. That may be what finally sells it. She's a bored, broke ex-stripper more in love with provoking her man than the man himself. "What's your name, sailor?"

"Call me whatever you like, Dahl."

"That's the way it's gonna be, huh?" She laughs, puts an arm around my waist. One of her nipples pokes through fabric into my right ear. "Let's get out of here, find somewhere with a little class." And so we're off. On the way out, I see Biff Steele giving me a look, and I know this little scene is going to get back to Frank. I'm fine with that.

III

Dahlia and I head downtown, hit a string of gold-plated joints where she can dance and inhale expensive hooch bought with my green. I'm not drinking as much as she is, but then she's got a couple of stones on me. By the time we catch the last cab of the night from Old King Cole's she's barely walking. We go back to her place, a leather-and-lace dollhouse in the neutral zone between Miller's Crossing and the Flats. The first bang is quick, which pisses her off, but I have a couple more in me. We both get my money's worth, and the next morning I'm gone before she even realizes she's hungover.

Sure, I've given in to my baser instincts. Man in my line of work gets few enough perks. But in the days and weeks that follow, I avoid the Flats and stay on the move, one eye cocked over my shoulder, ear to the rails. I have no illusions Dahlia has any interest in me personally, but given the bankroll in my pocket and my hints about the shank in Frank's back, I'm sure she'll come looking for me.

Takes her a while though. Long enough for Frank to recover and achieve his epiphany.

Meanwhile, folks living in Newcastle's underbelly gossip like ladybugs at a house fire. By the time I get a call from this simpleton I know who works at Leech and Humors Medical Testing, I've already heard the broad strokes of Frank's seminal conception. Simon sorts test results for the courier, then files the lab copies. He knows just about everyone on staff at clinics and medico offices around town.

"Doc Ciconi has Dahlia Miller scheduled to come in for weekly prenatal vitamin shots," he tells me.

"And I'm supposed to care because . . . ?"

"Well, I heard you got a sniff of that blossom. Thought you'd be interested."

"Street talk. If you believe that I got some magic beans to sell you."

He giggles, then says, "Did you hear about Dingus?"

Dale Dingus is something of a legend around Newcastle, the super cop who first put the squeeze on Old Man Miller's operation, weakened him enough that

Frank was able to push him out. Then Dingus up and takes Frank himself off the street after catching him in the act of dispensing a little Pounder justice on the leader of the Red Riding Hoods over a demand for a piece of the meth trade. Dingus followed up on a tip that took him to a riverfront foundry just as Frank was dipping the errant biker boss feet first into molten lead. At least the poor bastard still had his boots on.

I already know the poop, but I let Simon tell me anyway. Dingus is local law, but his knowledge of the Flats is such that the Crabs brought him on board the task force targeting all the top guys in Frank's operation. When they learn he's been presenting paper trail evidence cooked up in his own office to the grand jury, the whole case collapses.

"Kinda like how your lungs will collapse," Simon adds, "once Frank finds out about you and his sweetie."

Maybe he's not so simple after all. I hang up. Frank's legal situation is still sorting itself out, but I know he'll be released back into the wild soon. It's time to make an appearance in the Flats.

IV

I'm sitting alone at the bar in the Sugarplum Haus, brooding on the dark walnut and the smell of wood smoke, when Dahlia finally tracks me down. She slips onto the stool next to me, grabs my bourbon and tosses it back. She must not have read the brochure on what to avoid while heavy with child. Not that I say anything. For now, I'm content to let her think it's her little secret.

"Where you been, sailor? You haven't called."

I'm sure she can guess why, so I order another

bourbon, and one for her so she'll leave mine alone. When the bartender sets us up, I sip my drink and watch Dahlia in the mirror over the back of the bar. She strokes her long neck like she's got something on her mind. I keep my yap shut, figuring sooner or later she'll need to fill the silence.

"Remember when you told me you got sent up for that meth thing?"

"What about it?"

"I was thinking maybe you could help me out."

I look at her like she's a pockmarked street gretel, not a statuesque blond rapunzel. "What, you wanna score some speed?"

She rolls those big indigos like she thinks my wit matches my stature.

"So what then?"

"Well, it might be I got a line on a truckload of decongestant. The real thing, not that fake crap they sell over the counter nowadays."

"Sufa-Dream, something like that?"

"Exactly like that."

"Where the hell did you get a truckload of Sufa-Dream?" I make my voice sound dismissive, like I think she's full of shit. But I already know such a truck exists. The news criers on teevee glossed over it, no doubt because Drugs and Vice doesn't want to trouble Newcastle's citizenry with facts. But the street has been buzzing about the truck that never arrived at Pharma-City's central warehouse. A mixed shipment, everything from eye drops to recreational lubricants. And barrel after barrel of Sufa-Dream. Her father boosted the truck, and now the sweet flower beside me has her hands on a hundred thousand packs of sinus medicine, one-point-two million doses of name-brand pseudo-ephedrine. She wants me to cook it for her.

I tell her there ain't enough bourbon in all of Kaintuck for this conversation. "Besides," I add, "I can't believe you don't know someone else for this. With your connects?"

She swirls her bourbon and I watch her, curious what's going on behind those eyes. She tosses back the hooch at last. "Everyone I know Frank knows."

And there it is.

When her pop boosted the truck, all he figured on was a big payday, something to reset his fortunes now that his nemesis was in the can. What Old Man Miller didn't count on was Frank already had his sights on the pseudo. Had a team and a plan. Cops on the come would divert the truck off the I onto surface streets and Frank's boys would take it under the Billy Goat Bluff Bridge. Frank was already the biggest supplier of meth on the coast. This much pseudo would keep his distributors in crank for a year.

Old Man Miller worked the deal from the other end. He knew the truck driver, or more precisely he knew the driver's son. The kid had lost enough bullion betting the ponies at Miller's book that he gave the kid's father a choice: give up the shipment or give up his boy's hands. So when the night of the delivery comes, the pseudo never makes it onto the I for Frank's pet cops to divert. Next day, the driver turns up in the river. No one has seen the truck or its contents since.

"I don't know, Dahl. This doesn't sound like the kind of thing I want to get into the middle of."

She leans into me, presses her double-barreled acorns into my back. "Come on, baby. I'll make it worth your while." I feel her hand run along my thigh. Stroke by stroke, I'm warming up to her touch. But I need to keep my focus.

"Answer me one question."

"What's that, honey?"

"How does the gingerbread man baking in your oven fit into all this?"

She catches a handful of testicles. It's all I can do not to squeal. She's got a grip like a tin woodsman.

"Who told you that?"

I can't answer until she eases off a little, but when she does I gasp, "You think it's some kind of secret? In this town?"

She ponders that, her face a chart of unexplored territory. After a moment, she withdraws her claw and sighs. Looks away. I cross my legs and take a chance.

"It's not Frank's, is it?"

I can actually see the anxiety in her plasticine countenance, but she only shrugs. "Could be yours for all I know."

I don't think she really believes it's mine. Or at least, she doesn't believe it's any more likely to be mine than any number of other fellas. An active young woman, our Miller's daughter.

"Tell me," I say. She orders another bourbon and runs it down.

She explains that Ciconi couldn't artificially inseminate her because she was already expecting. Not for long, but hormones don't lie. So she's scared, because if Frank finds out, molten lead will be the least of her troubles. Unless the kid is late, Frank could get suspicious of the timing and demand a paternity test. So she wants me to cook the meth. Even wholesale, she's thinking she can make enough money to escape with her father, who won't survive long himself once the truth about the Sufa-Dream truck gets back to Frank.

"I suppose you're in a hurry," I say.

"They won't be able to keep him in for much longer. Another week, two at most, before his conviction is vacated. I need this done." She looks at me, and now her indigos have gone all dim and watery. "Can you help me? I'll split the sell with you. That's some serious bullion."

I let my own eyes soften and give her a smile. "Okay, bring me the pills."

"And you can work fast?"

"Don't worry. I have a tight operation."

I ask for a number where I can reach her. She writes it on my hand. I think we're done, but she leans in one more time, whispers in my ear. "So, sailor, you gonna tell me your name now that we're partners?" Hand on my thigh again.

I shake my head. "All things considered, I think I'll stick with anonymous."

She pulls back, lips a thin line, and I realize she knows what I'm thinking. "Frank will find you if he wants to."

She leaves me there, balls aching and stomach on fire. I know she's right. But in the short run, keeping my identity under wraps is the one thing I got going for me.

V

The next day I call Dahlia from a clean pre-pay cell and we meet at a pub out on the edge of the Old Forest. I expect her to bring the pseudo, but that's not how it's going to work. Old Man Miller doesn't know about me, and she wants to keep it that way. He's so skittish with

Frank on his way out of the slam he'll never let a stranger near his boost. Once upon a time he'd have had his own people to do the work, but between Frank and the Crabs, his operation is down to two twigs in the wind. Apparently he's been angling to just sell the pills and be quit of the whole mess, flee Newcastle before Frank returns. Dahlia insists she can cook the crystal herself, make them some real bullion, but he's unconvinced.

She tells me I'll start with one case of Sufa-Dream only. I'm to make a batch overnight and get it back to her first thing so her old man can check it out. I'm not thrilled and tell her so. "I'm taking a chance every time we meet. I'm not gonna do this piecemeal."

"He says I have to prove I can do it before he'll give me the rest."

"I'm surprised he's willing to let you near this stuff, a lady in your condition."

The look she gives me makes it clear what she thinks of her condition.

I insist Dahlia provide the red phosphorus and iodine too, but that stuff's easy enough to get, and cheap. I don't even have to explain I don't want a chemical trail following me into the Flats. She delivers everything in the back of a stolen wagon. Next morning, I drop the jar of crystal in a locker at the bus livery, then wait to hear how good my work is.

Dahlia and I meet in the courtyard square, lunch time. Lots of citizens around. She's pleased as Goldilocks with a bowl of perfect porridge, and brings us each a container of kung pao mutton to celebrate. "Dad's alchemist says it's super clean. He says we can step on it all day, it'll spread like butter."

"So you're happy."

"We're gonna be end of the rainbow rich." She chopsticks a chunk of meat into her mouth and bats her eyes at me. To add cream to the pudding, her blouse is unbuttoned almost to her waist. "What do you say I come along when you make the big batch, help you out?"

"I work alone."

"How are you gonna cook that much crystal in two days?"

"I have my methods."

"And you can't use some help?" She leans forward so I can see all the way to the bottom of her golden valley. I figure she's not nearly as interested in helping me as finding out where my lab is.

"Not gonna happen, Dahl."

"What if I insist?"

"What if I walk away?"

"What if I tell Frank I'm carrying your baby?"

I gnaw mutton. Neither one of us would live through that confession and she knows it. She's not worried about my fate, but self-preservation runs strong in her genes. She stands abruptly and drops her lunch on the cobblestones at my feet. Greasy sauce splashes across my shoes. She heads off across the square, ass hard as stone.

"Don't dawdle, Dahl," I call after her. "The wheels of justice are turning."

VI

I'm not troubled by the idea that Dahlia is cooking up a double-cross. I know she won't move against me until I deliver the finished meth—she can't help but be jacked about the quality of my crystal and the bullion it'll command. So the next day the transfer of the pseudo goes off without a hitch. I even pretend not to find her transmitter

in the wheel well of the delivery truck. It's easy enough
to drop it down a storm drain as I drive away.

A few hours later, I get wind of a couple of Dahlia's
trolls prowling the Flats looking for me. Guess they figured out I don't live in the sewer, so they're dropping
green and asking for a name, a location, anything they
can get on me. I take the news in stride. They're not
alone. Frank's shark is working double-time, and word
is already out on the street about the dwarf who picked
up his girl at the High Tail. That hurts, to be honest.
Five-four is hardly a dwarf. I leave my pre-pay cell
turned off on the theory she has enough juice to arrange
a track on the phone's GPS. Even if she doesn't, I know
Frank does.

I don't have time to chit-chat on the phone anyway.
The delivery Dahlia is expecting is a big one. The arrangements make for a busy couple of days, but that's
good. Before I know it, the truck is packed with the
goods and all I have to do is get ready for the meet. It's
supposed to be a three-way exchange: me, Dahlia, and
her buyer. I'm to call a number an hour beforehand with
the location, enough time for Dahlia and her guy to get
there but not enough time to arrange anything untoward. Even with that precaution, it's a bad set up for me.
But what Dahlia doesn't know is I don't care about the
money. From where I sit, it's long odds the meet will even
occur.

I stop by the High Tail a little after noon. A risk, but
it's too early for Biff, and no one else would think to
look for me there. I've got my eye out for a particular
guy, a big-eared street gnome I know from around the
Flats. Good source of poop, and not too expensive. He's
sitting at the rail, a pint of piss-yellow ale in each paw.
Only one listless nymph works the pole.

"What do you hear?" I say. The I.D. of Dahlia's buyer would be nice, but I don't expect that. Mostly I just want a sense of the street.

"You hear about Frank?" he says without taking his eyes off the g-string three feet from the end of his nose.

"His conviction was formally vacated yesterday afternoon. They're supposed to let him out today."

"Bet you're glad it's a long drive down from Little Liver."

"You could say that."

He grins and quaffs ale. "He arrived back in New-castle this morning." The place is only a quarter full, and even though the mopes around us all seem to be concentrating on the nipples on stage, I still feel like I got Argus eyes staring at my back. I'd hoped for one more day.

"Thanks. What do I owe you?"

"You live to see next week, you can buy me a steak."

I walk down to my garage. Another risk, but one I've calculated. I can see from half a block away that the padlock is on the ground. I lower my head and turn, head back the way I came. In that instant, lead hits into the wall beside me, right about where my head would be if I was of average height. I break into a run without looking to see who's shooting. I hear more gunfire, pretty damned brazen in broad daylight, but it's not like Felony Flats sports a neighborhood watch. As I move, I pull out my cell and thumb the power. I'm not worried about GPS now, and in any case once I make my call I won't need the phone any more.

I turn at the next corner and run flat out. A bullet tears through my jacket under my arm as I lift the phone and press the only speed dial number I have programmed, a number Dahlia wouldn't be happy to know I'm calling.

I zig left into the street in front of a taxi, horn blaring. I hear footsteps behind me as the phone rings in my ear.

"I'm hot," I huff when the call connects.

"Where?"

"West pickup, and make it now."

I drop the phone as I turn into an alley mid-block. Two hundred feet, straight shot. Dangerous, but necessary. One of my pursuers yells, "Where you think you're going, munchkin!" The voice echoes against brick. My hands are starting to shake.

A vehicle appears at the opposite end of the alley, a black van. The side door opens as I break out across the sidewalk, a helmeted man in black Kevlar waves me in. Another bullet cracks past my ear as I tumble inside. The driver hits the accelerator. For a split instant as the van surges off, I can see back into the alley. Two guys, no one I recognize. Their eyes bulge, though with anger or surprise I don't know.

Takes me a minute to get my breath, then I say, "Who got the truck?"

"Your girlfriend did, but those were Frank's boys on you back there."

I know Dahlia will stay on me. She can't take a chance Frank's goons won't make me talk before they plant me, so she's gotta plant me first. And I'd hate to disappoint so enchanting a lady.

VII

I decide on an upscale noodle joint on Breadcrumb Boulevard, the nice end of the strip. I'm eating a mixed stir fry as she sits down across from me. The satisfied smirk on her face tells the tale.

"What's doing, Dahl? You here to bring me my money?"

"I don't think so, Stilt," Her expression makes me think of a rat with a chicken egg. "That's right. I know who you are."

What can I say? The convicts and lowlifes I deal with are hardly an imaginative lot when it comes to street monikers.

Her indigo eyes have gone black, but when she grins, her teeth are so white I can read the menu by them. "I have a car outside. We're going for a ride."

I spear a shrimp with my fork and wave it at her. "Can I finish my dinner first?"

"Don't be a smart ass. And don't try anything funny either. I got guys at the front and back. All I gotta do is . . ."

Her voice trails off because I'm shaking my head, sad little smile on my face. Apparently Dahlia believed me when I told her I work alone.

"Your old man's soldiers are going to have a hard time doing your bidding from the back of a patrol car." I reach up to my ear and pull out the ear piece receiver, show it to her. "Weapons charge at the least, since we both know they got no permits for those ice cold gats they're packing." I inhale a noodle. "Other charges too, once we get to digging."

Dahlia is looking at me like I'm a dingleberry hanging off her tampon. I guess I can't blame her. "Who the hell are you?" she says.

"You said you know who I am. Stilt, remember? Though I'd rather you call me Sheriff Popper."

She sags back in her chair. "You're law."

"Royal Witness Protectorate, temporarily seconded undercover to the Crabs to help clean up the Dale Dingus

fiasco. But after tonight, with your help, that'll be done."
And not a minute too soon. Crabs were born with a rod
up their ass. But considering the way Dingus burned
them I guess I can understand why they're tetchy.

She's quiet for a moment, then says, "So what's in the
back of my truck?"

It's sinking in. "A little meth, actually. Same as the first
batch, cooked up in the Crab lab. I didn't want to con-
fuse your alchemist." I smirk, head canted to the side.
"But mostly what you got is powdered laxative cut with
kosher salt. You know, for body."

She's not amused.

"Now that I got your attention, Dahl, what say you
and me have us a little chat?"

"I have nothing to say to you."

They never do. Not at first. Not until I play my hole
card, which I don't waste time doing with Dahlia. I'm
tired and I want this finished.

"You're not pregnant."

That throws her. I can see the confusion in her big
blues. "But the doctor said—"

"What we told him to say, after he spilled Frank's
juice down the lab sink. Ciconi has been ours ever since
he got busted trading his script pad for blow jobs. When
you go in each week for those vitamin shots he's pumping you fulla hormones and other crap to make you
bloat up. It wouldn't fool you for too much longer, but
it was enough to keep you puking in the morning and
regretting your lax enforcement of no glove, no love."

The news has the effect I expect. The air goes out of
her. Hell, it almost looks like her silicone boobs deflate
along with her imperious demeanor.

After a long moment, she says, "You never actually
shivved Frank, did you?"

"Not me. We got the Bandito that did on ice out in the forest. He'll be available when the time comes, same as I expect you to be."

"You're a bastard."

I can't argue with that. It's part of my job description. "Here are your options, Dahl. You help us, we'll take care of you. Relocation, protection, the works. All you hafta do is roll on Frank, your dad, and your crystal buyer, help us tie them all to the Sufa-Dream boost and the meth traffic round about Newcastle. And not just them. I expect you to name names up and down the organization." We had the shattered remains of a banditry case to clean up, after all. Plus my own broken meth sting, the one I pretended I went to Little Liver for.

"And if I say no?"

I shrug and signal the waiter for a to go bucket. "Your choice, Dahl." I'm not worried. Between the kingpin, the old man, and the scheming dwarf, we both know which one offers the shot at happily ever after.

*

BILL CAMERON is the critically acclaimed author of the dark, gritty Portland-based mysteries *Lost Dog, Chasing Smoke,* and *Day One.* His stories have appeared in *Spinetingler, Killer Year,* and *Portland Noir.*

Savage Planet

STEPHEN COONTS

Adam Solo wedged himself into the chair at the navigator's table in the small shack behind the bridge and braced himself against the motion of the ship. Rain beat a tattoo on the roof over his head and wind moaned around the portholes. Although the seas weren't heavy, the ship rolled, pitched, and corkscrewed viciously because she was not under way; she was riding sea anchors, being held in one place, at the mercy of the swells.

Through the rain-smeared porthole windows Solo could see the flood and spotlights of another ship several hundred feet to port. She was also small, only two hundred forty feet long, roughly the size of the ship Solo was aboard. Carrying massive cranes fore and aft, she was festooned with flood lights that lit the deck and the water between the ships, and was also bobbing like a cork in a maelstrom.

Through the open door to the bridge Solo occasionally heard the ringing of the telegraph as the captain signaled the engine room for power to help hold the little ship where he wanted her.

Johnson was the captain, an overweight, overbearing slob with a sneer engraved on his face and a curse on his lips. Solo ignored the burst of mindless obscenities that reached him during lulls in the wind's song and concentrated on the newspaper before him.

Possible alien spaceship found in Atlantic Ocean, the headline screamed. Beneath that headline, in slightly smaller type, the subhead read, *Famous Evangelist Funds Salvage.*

Solo was a trim man with short black hair, even features, and skin that appeared deeply tanned. He was below average in height, just five-and-a-half feet tall, and weighed about 140 pounds. Tonight he was dressed in jeans, work boots, and a dark green Gortex jacket. Looking at him, one would not have guessed that he was a very successful engineer, and the owner of twenty patents.

He read the newspaper story carefully, and was relieved to see that his name wasn't mentioned. The story told how Jim Bob Bryant, the preachin' pride of Mud Lick, Arkansas, had raised millions to fund the salvage from the sea floor of the flying saucer discovered six months ago by a oil exploration ship taking core samples. Bryant was quoted extensively. His thesis seemed to be that the flying saucer would lead to a new spiritual renewal worldwide.

On the editorial page Solo saw a column that denounced Bryant as a charlatan promoting a religious hoax. The writer stated that only the ignorant and gullible believed in flying saucers.

Solo had just finished the pundit's column when the door opened and a heavyset man wearing a suit and tie came in. He tossed a coat on the desk.

"Reverend," Solo said, in greeting.

The Right Reverend Jim Bob Bryant was so nervous he couldn't hold still. "This is it, Solo," he said as he smacked one fist into a palm. "This saucer is the key to wealth and power beyond the wildest dreams of anyone alive."

"You think?"

"Gettin' into heaven has always been expensive, and the cost is gonna keep risin'. People who get somethin' for free don't value it—that's human nature. Only value what they pay for, and I'm gonna make 'em pay a lot."

Bryant braced himself against the roll of the ship and glanced out the porthole at the heaving sea between the ships. "You still think you can make the computers talk to you?"

Solo nodded. "Yes, but you've never told me what you want from them."

"Miracles, man—that's what I want. I want to learn to do miracles."

"I don't know that there are any miracles in the saucer," Solo said mildly. "We never found any in that saucer we took apart. What we found was extremely advanced technology from another world, another time." Solo had become Bryant's right-hand man by convincing him that he had been a lead engineer on the top-secret examination of a saucer the government had secreted in Area 51 in Nevada.

Bryant, a con man himself, had taken a lot of convincing. Solo had drawn diagram after diagram, explained the functioning of every system and the location of every valve, wire, nut, and bolt.

Tonight, Bryant said, "You dig out the technology and I'll do the miracles. Gonna turn prayer and song into money, Solo, and believe me, that's the biggest miracle of them all."

Solo waggled the newspaper. "I thought you were trying to keep the recovery of the saucer a secret."

"The newshounds sniffed it out," Bryant said with a shrug. "You gotta admit, after the news of this discovery, it was just a matter of time before someone sailed out here to raise the saucer. We're here first, which is the important thing. Life is all about timing, Solo." Bryant turned to the porthole and rubbed the moisture from the glass with his sleeve. "This alien ship may be torn all to hell, smashed into bits, but there's a sliver of a chance that one or more of the computers is intact, or at least their memory core. If that's the case, we're in this with a chance."

Jim Bob Bryant jammed his hands in his pockets and stared out of the porthole into the night with unseeing eyes. The possibilities were awe-inspiring. Space travel experts all agreed that if man were to attempt a voyage between the stars, aging was going to have to be retarded or prevented altogether for the travelers to arrive alive. The distances were vast beyond any scale that could be grasped by the twenty-first-century mind.

Bryant smacked a fist into the palm of his other hand. "*Yes, the people of the saucers must have possessed an anti-aging drug, and the formula might be in this saucer's computer.*" The possibility of using such a drug in religious services gave him the sweats. He could found his own church. He could . . .

If the saucer crew were people.

Solo had assured him they must have been, based on

the design and operation of the government's secret saucer, the one no government official had ever admitted existed.

He glanced over his shoulder at Solo, who was flipping through the rest of the newspaper. He knew so much . . . or pretended to.

Bryant sighed. If Solo had been lying all along, he wouldn't really have lost anything but some credibility, and in truth, he didn't have much of that beyond the circle of the faithful. This whole expedition was financed with donated money. All Bryant had contributed was his time and lots of hot air.

From his pocket he pulled the photo of the saucer taken by a camera lowered over the side of the salvage ship. In the glow of the camera's spotlight, he could make out a circular, round disk, thicker toward the middle.

Yes.

Bryant was staring at the photo when he heard Johnson, the captain, give a shout.

Out of the porthole, Bryant saw a shape even darker than the night sea break the surface for a moment, then ease back under.

"It's up!" he said excitedly. With that he dashed through the door onto the bridge and charged down the ladder to the main deck.

Adam Solo slowly pulled on a cap and stepped onto the bridge. Ignoring the captain, who was still at the helm, Solo walked to the unprotected wing of the bridge and gazed down into the heaving dark sea as the wind and rain tore at him. The wind threatened to tear his cap from his head, so he removed it. Jim Bob Bryant was at the rail on the main deck, holding on with both hands.

Floodlights from both ships lit the area between the

ships and the heavy cables that disappeared into water. From the angle of the cables, it was obvious that what they held was just beneath the surface. Snatches of the commands of the chief on deck shouted to the winch operators reached Solo. Gazing intently at the scene before him, he ignored them.

As Solo watched, swells separated the ships slightly, tightening the cables, and something broke the surface. It was a mound, dark as the black water; swells broke over it.

As quickly as it came into view, the shape disappeared again as the ships rolled toward each other.

It's real and it's there. We are so close, he thought, then remembered the other times when he had gotten his hopes up, only to see them dashed to splinters, leaving him bitter and forlorn. *Yet perhaps this time . . .*

Over the next five minutes the deck crews aboard both ships tightened their cables, inch by inch, lifting the black shape to the surface again, then higher and higher until finally it was free of the water and hung suspended between the ships. The spotlights played upon it, a black, saucer-shaped object, perfectly round and thickest in the middle, tapering gently to the edges, which were rounded, not sharp. It was huge—the diameter was about ninety feet—and it was heavy—the cables that held it were as taut as violin strings, and the ships listed toward it a noticeable amount.

Solo stepped back into the sheltered area of the bridge and wiped the rain from his hair with his hand, then settled the cap onto his head as he listened to the voices on the bridge loudspeaker. The deck chiefs of this ship and the other vessel were talking to each other on handheld radios, coordinating their efforts as the saucer was inched over the deck of this ship. The ship's radio picked up the conversation and piped it here so that captain could listen in and, if he wished, take part.

A moment later Bryant came up the ladder from the main deck.

"Well, we got it up, Reverend," Captain Johnson said heartily. "And they said it couldn't be done. Ha! You owe us some serious money."

"I will when you have it safely on the dock in Newark," Bryant shot back.

It took twenty minutes for the deck crew to get the dark, ominous disk deposited onto the waiting timbers and lashed down. The saucer was so large it filled the space between the bridge and the forward crane and protruded over both rails. It seemed to dwarf the ship on which it rode, pushing it deeper into the sea. The ship's floodlights reflected from the wet, black surface as pinpoints of light. From the bridge the canopy on top of the saucer was visible, some kind of clear material, but due to the glare, nothing could be seen inside.

On deck the crewmen were staring at the strange black shape, touching it tentatively, looking in awe . . .

Solo watched in silence, his face passive, displaying no emotion. On the other hand, Bryant's excitement was a tangible thing. "Oh, my God," Bryant whispered. "It's so *big*. I thought it would be smaller."

When the cables that had lifted the saucer from the sea floor had been released, the sea anchors were brought aboard and the ship got under way. Solo felt the ride improve immediately as the screws bit into the dark water. The other ship that had helped raise the saucer had already dissolved into the darkness.

"There you are," Johnson said heartily to Bryant, who had his nose almost against the window, staring at the spaceship. "Your flying saucer's settin' like a hen on her nest, safe and sound, and she ain't goin' *no place.*"

Bryant flashed a grin and dashed for the bridge wing ladder to the main deck.

Solo went back into the navigator's shack. He emerged seconds later carrying a hard plastic case and descended the ladder to the main deck.

As Bryant watched, Solo opened the case, took out a wand, and adjusted the switches and knobs within, then donned a headset. Carrying the instrument case, he began a careful inspection of the saucer, all of it that he could see from the deck. He even climbed the mast of the forward crane to get a look at the top of it, then returned to the deck. As he walked and climbed around he glanced occasionally at the gauges in his case, but mostly he concentrated on visually inspecting the surface of the ship. He could see no damage whatsoever.

Bryant asked a couple of questions, but Solo didn't answer, so eventually he stopped asking.

Solo crawled under the saucer and lay there studying his instrument. Finally he took off his headset, stowed it back inside the case, and closed it.

One of the officers squatted down a few feet away. This was the first mate. "No radiation?" he asked Solo. The sailor was in his early thirties, with unkempt windblown hair and acne scars on his face.

"Doesn't seem to be."

"Boy, that's amazing." The mate reached and placed his hand on the cold black surface immediately over his head. "A real *flying saucer* . . . I didn't think such things existed. Where do you think this one is from?"

"Not from our solar system."

"Another star . . ." The mate, whose name was

DeVries, retracted his hand suddenly, as if the saucer were too hot to touch.

Solo studied the belly of the saucer as the raw sea wind played with his hair. At least here, under the saucer, he was sheltered from the rain.

"Everything inside is probably torn loose, I figure," DeVries continued, warming to his subject, "when that thing went into the drink. Scrambled up inside there like a dozen broken eggs. And those aliens inside, squashed flat as road-killed possum and just as dead. Couldn't nothing or nobody live through a smashup like that. And how about germs, if you open that thing up? What if the bugs get out and kill us or contaminate the world?"

Solo ignored that remark.

The first mate turned to Bryant and asked, "So, Reverend, how come you're spending all this money raisin' this flyin' saucer off the ocean floor?"

Bryant said matter-of-factly, "I intend to make some money with it."

"Well, I hope," DeVries said thoughtfully, a remark Bryant let pass without comment.

As those two watched, Adam Solo donned self-contained breathing apparatus. He fiddled with the controls and adjusted the mask until he was satisfied with the airflow, then he motioned the other two back.

They waddled out from under the saucer. Satisfied, he placed his hand on the hatch handle and held it there. Now, after ten seconds or so, he pulled down on one end of the handle and rotated it. The hatch opened above his head. Water began dripping out.

Not much, but some. The saucer had been lying in 250 feet of water; if the integrity of the hull had been broken, seawater under pressure would have filled the interior. This might be leakage from the ship's tank, or merely condensation. Solo wiped a drip off the hatch lip, jammed his finger under the breathing mask, and tasted it. He was relieved—it wasn't saltwater.

Now Solo inspected the yawning hole. He stuck the wand inside and studied the panel on his Geiger counter. "Background radiation," he told Bryant, who had also donned breathing apparatus. The preacher rubbed his hands together vigorously, a gesture that Solo had noticed he used often.

Solo turned off the Geiger counter. He carefully wrapped the cord around the wand and stowed it in the plastic case, then shoved the case up into the dark belly of the saucer.

DeVries craned his neck, trying to see inside the saucer. "Like, when you going to climb into this thing?"

A smile crossed the face of Adam Solo. "Now," he said. He raised himself through the hatchway into the belly of the ship.

Jim Bob Bryant crawled under the ship, then squirmed up through the entryway. He closed the hatch behind him.

The first mate slowly shook his head. "Glad it was them two and not me," he said conversationally, although there was no one there to hear him. "My momma didn't raise no fools. I wouldn't have crawled into that thing for all the money on Wall Street."

The first mate made his way to the bridge. Captain Johnson was still at the helm. "Well, did you ask him?" the captain demanded.

"Wants to make money, Bryant said."

"I already know that," the captain said sourly. "Oh, well. As long as we get paid . . ." After a moment the captain continued, "Solo's weird. That accent of his—it isn't much, but it's there. I can't place it. Sometimes I think it's eastern European of one kind or another, then I think it isn't."

"All I know," DeVries said, "is that accent isn't from Brooklyn."

The captain didn't respond to that inanity. He said aloud, musing, "He's kinda freaky, but nothin' you can put your finger on. Still, bein' around him gives me the willies."

"They got money," DeVries said simply. In his mind, money excused all peculiarities, an ingrained attitude he had acquired long ago because he didn't have any.

"Imagine what that thing must have looked like flying."

They fell silent as they stared at the craft, looked from right to left and back again, trying to take it all in, to understand, as the sea wind whispered and ocean spray occasionally spattered the windows.

DeVries finally broke the silence. "It's heavy as hell. Like to never got it up. We almost lost it a dozen times."

"Notice how the ship's ridin' ? Hope we make harbor before the sea kicks up."

DeVries grunted. After a moment he said, with a touch of wonder in his voice, "A real, honest-to-God flying saucer . . . Never believed in 'em, y'know?"

"Yeah," the captain agreed. "Thought it was all bull puckey. Even standing here looking at one of the darn things, I have my doubts."

The only light inside the saucer came through the canopy, a dim glow from the salvage vessel's masthead lights. It took several seconds for Solo's eyes to adjust.

The room was large, almost eight feet high in the middle, tapering toward the edges. In the rear of the room was a hatch, one that apparently gave entry to the engineering spaces. Facing forward was a raised instrument panel and a pilot's seat on a pedestal, one with what appeared to be control sticks on each side, in front of armrests. As Solo had told Bryant, the seats were sized for humans. The pilot could look forward and to each side about 120 degrees through a canopy made of an unknown material.

Solo used a small flashlight to inspect the cockpit compartment, then the instrument panel. There were no conventional gauges, merely flat planes where presumably information from the ship's computers was displayed. There were a few mechanical switches mounted on one panel, but only a few.

Lying carelessly on the panel, where the impact of the crash or the jostling of salvage had carried them, were two headbands, almost an inch wide, capable of being easily expanded to give the wearer a tight fit.

Hope flooded him. At first glance the ship seemed intact. *If only the computers and communications systems are in order!*

Solo was still standing rooted in his tracks, taking it all in, when Jim Bob Bryant crawled up through the entry and closed the hatch behind him. As he looked around, he said something under the breathing mask that Solo didn't understand. Solo slowly removed his own mask and laid it on the instrument panel.

Bryant kept glancing at Solo, the mine canary, for almost a minute as he tried to take in his surroundings. Then he removed his mask, too, and stood looking around like a lucky Kmart shopper.

"Amazing," he said under his breath, then said it again, louder. He reached out to touch things.

Solo moved the flashlight beam around the interior of

the ship, inspecting for damage. The cockpit was so Spartan that there was little to damage.

"Does it look like that one the government has in Nevada?" Bryant asked.

"Very similar," Solo said, nodding.

"Where is the crew? How did they get out with this thing in the ocean?"

Solo took his time answering. "Obviously the crew wasn't in the saucer when it submerged. I can't explain it, but that is the only logical explanation." The flashlight beam continued to rove, pausing here and there for a closer inspection.

"Reverend Bryant, I know you've had a long day and have much to think about," Solo continued. "My examination of the ship will go much faster if you leave me to work in solitude."

Bryant beamed at Solo. "I didn't think it could be done," he admitted. "When you told me you could raise this ship and wring out its secrets, I thought you were lying. I want you to know I was wrong. I admit it, here and now."

Solo smiled.

"I leave you to it," Bryant said. "If you will just open that hatch to let me out." He took a last glance around. "Simply amazing," he muttered.

Solo opened the hatch and Bryant carefully climbed through, then Solo closed it again.

Alone at last, Solo's face relaxed into a wide grin. He stood beside the pilot's seat, grinning happily, apparently lost in thought.

Finally he came out of his reverie and walked to the back of the compartment, where he opened an access door to the engineering compartment and disappeared inside. He was inside there for an hour before he came out. For the first time, he retrieved a headband from the instrument panel and donned it.

"Hello, *Eternal Wanderer*. Let us examine the health of your systems."

Before him, the instrument panel exploded into life.

The first mate DeVries strolled along the bridge with the helm on autopilot. The rest of the small crew, including the captain, were in their bunks asleep. The rain had stopped and a sliver of moon was peeping through the clouds overhead. The mate had always enjoyed the ethereal beauty of the night and the way the ship rode the restless, living sea. He was soaking in the sensations, occasionally crossing the bridge from one wing to the other, and checking on the radar and compass, when he noticed the glow from the saucer's cockpit.

The space ship took up so much of the deck that the cockpit canopy was almost even with the bridge windows. As the mate stared into the cockpit, he saw the figure of Adam Solo. He reached for the bridge binoculars. Turned the focus wheel.

Solo's face appeared, lit by a subdued light source in front of him. The mate assumed that the light came from the instruments—computer presentations—and he was correct. DeVries could see the headband, which looked exactly like the kind the Indians wore in old cowboy movies. Solo's face was expressionless . . . no, that wasn't true, the mate decided. He was concentrating intensely.

Obviously the saucer was more or less intact or it wouldn't have electrical power. Whoever designed that thing sure knew what he was about. He or she. Or it. Whoever that was, wherever that was . . .

Finally the mate's arms tired and he lowered the binoculars.

He snapped the binoculars into their bracket and went back to pacing the bridge. His eyes were repeatedly drawn to the saucer's glowing cockpit. The moon, the clouds racing overhead, the ship pitching and rolling monotonously—it seemed as if he were trapped in this moment in time and this was all there had ever been or ever would be. It was a curious feeling . . . almost mystical.

Surprised at his own thoughts, DeVries shook his head and tried to concentrate on his duties.

This is Eternal Wanderer. I am Adam Solo. Is there anyone out there listening?

Solo didn't speak the words, he merely thought them. The computer read the tiny impulses as they coursed through his brain, boosted the wattage a billionfold, and broadcasted them into the universe. Yet the thoughts could only travel at the speed of light, so unless there was an interplanetary ship, or a saucer relatively close in space, he might receive no answer for years. Decades. Centuries, perhaps.

Marooned on this savage planet, he had waited so long! So very long.

Solo wiped the perspiration from his forehead as the enormity of the years threatened to reduce him to despair.

He forced himself to take off the headband and leave the pilot's seat.

Opening the saucer's hatch, he dropped to the deck. He closed the hatch behind him, just in case, and went below to his cabin. No one was in the passageways. Nor did he expect to find any of the crew there. He glanced into one of the crew's berthing spaces. The glow of the tiny red lights revealed that every bunk was full, and every man seemed to be snoring. They had had an exhausting day raising the saucer from the seabed.

In his cabin Solo quickly packed his bag. He stripped the blankets from his bunk and, carrying the lot, went back up on deck. Careful to stay out of sight of the bridge, he stowed his gear in the saucer.

A hose lay coiled near a water faucet, one the crew routinely used to wash mud from cables and chains coming aboard. Solo looked at it, then shook his head. The water intake was on top of the saucer; climbing up there would expose him to the man on the bridge, and would be dangerous besides. He couldn't risk falling overboard, which would doom him to inevitable drowning—certainly not now. Not when he was this close.

He removed the tie-down chains one by one and lowered them gently to the deck so the sound wouldn't reverberate through the steel ship.

Finally, when he had the last one off, he stood beside the saucer, with it between him and the bridge, and studied the position of the crane and hook, the mast and guy wires. Satisfied, Adam Solo stooped, went under the saucer, and up through the hatch.

The first mate was checking the GPS position and the recommended course to Sandy Hook when he felt the subtle change in the ship's motion. An old hand at sea, he noticed it immediately and looked around.

The saucer was there, immediately in front of the bridge. But it was higher, the lighted canopy several feet above where it had previously been. He could see Solo's head, now seated in the pilot's chair. And the saucer was moving, rocking back and forth. Actually it was stationary—the ship was moving in the seaway.

DeVries's first impression was that the ship's motion had changed because the saucer's weight was gone, but he was wrong. The antigravity rings in the saucer had pushed it away from the ship, which still supported the entire mass of the machine. The center of gravity was higher, so consequently the ship rolled with more authority.

At that moment Jim Bob Bryant came up the ladder, moving carefully with a cup of coffee in his hand.

He saw DeVries staring out the bridge windows, transfixed.

Bryant turned to follow DeVries's gaze, and found himself looking at Adam Solo's head inside the saucer. Solo was too engrossed in what he was doing to even glance at the bridge. The optical illusion that made the saucer appear to be moving gave Bryant the shock of his life. Never, in his wildest imaginings, had he even considered the possibility that the saucer might be capable of flight.

Like DeVries, Bryant stood frozen with his mouth agape.

For only a few more seconds was the saucer suspended over the deck. As the salvage ship came back to an even keel the saucer moved toward the starboard side, rolling the ship dangerously in that direction. Then the saucer went over the rail and the ship, free of the saucer's weight, and rolled port with authority.

Bryant recovered from his astonishment and roared, "*No!* No, no *no!* Come back here, Solo! It's *mine*. Mine, I tell you, *mine!*"

He dropped his coffee cup and strode to the door that led to the wing of the bridge, flung it open, and stepped out. The mate was right behind him. Both men grabbed the rail with both hands as the wind and sea spray tore at them.

The lighted canopy was no longer visible. For a few seconds Bryant and DeVries could see a glint of moonlight reflecting off the dark upper surface of the departing spaceship; then they lost it. The night swallowed the saucer.

It was gone, as if it had never been.

"If that doesn't take the cake!" exclaimed the Reverend Jim Bob Bryant. "*The bastard stole it!*"

"Adam, this is *Star Voyager.* So good to hear from you."

"I am alive. I have a saucer. I can meet you above the savage planet."

The voice from the starship told him when their ship would reach orbit. Solo mentally converted the time units into earth weeks. *Three weeks,* he thought. *Only three more weeks.*

"I must pick up the others," he thought, and the com system broadcast these thoughts.

Adam Solo topped the cloud layer that shrouded the sea and found himself under a sky full of stars.

*

STEPHEN COONTS is the author of fifteen *New York Times* bestsellers, the first of which was the classic flying tale *Flight of the Intruder.*

Stephen received his Navy wings in August 1969. After completion of fleet replacement training in the A-6 Intruder aircraft, Mr. Coonts reported to Attack Squadron 196 at Naval Air Station Whidbey Island, Washington. He made two combat cruises aboard USS *Enterprise* during the final years of the Vietnam War as a member of this squadron. His first novel, *Flight of the Intruder,* published in September 1986 by the

Naval Institute Press, spent twenty-eight weeks on *The New York Times* bestseller lists in hardcover. A motion picture based on this novel, with the same title, was released nationwide in January 1991. The success of his first novel allowed Mr. Coonts to devote himself to writing full-time; he has been at it ever since. He and his wife, Deborah, enjoy flying and try to do as much of it as possible.

Suspended

RYAN BROWN

Howard Boyd's time was up.

Twilight had descended on the mountain by the time he exited the dining hall at the base of the slopes, clipped back into his skis, and returned to the chairlift.

He was met with disappointment.

"Lift's closed, pal," said the terminal operator as Howard approached. The man was clearing dirty sludge from the loading area with a shovel.

"Already?" Howard skied forward until his waist met the yellow rope blocking the line entrance. "But can't I just make one more run, buddy?"

"It's Freddy, and no you can't." The operator dodged an empty lift chair moving past. "It's five o' clock. Last skiers are coming down now."

Howard slid his sleeve off his Rolex. "I got four

fifty-one. And I can make this run in a hell of a lot less than nine minutes."

"Swell. Trouble is it's an eighteen-minute ride to the top."

"Come on, man. The cell service up here is for shit; I had to go inside to phone the office, and I just got tied up. Give me a break, will ya?"

"Forget it, we're closed." The operator jammed the shovel into the snow. "Marvin's probably already left the terminal up top anyway."

"Marvin, eh? Well can't you check if he's still working up there? Come on, Freddy, have a heart." Howard unzipped the breast pocket of his bib and presented a fifty-dollar bill to help change the man's mind. It wasn't until he brought out a second fifty that Freddy finally gave in.

"Ah, hell." The operator brought his walkie-talkie to his lips. "Marvin, come in . . ." Getting no response, he banged the squawking radio against his knee and tried again. "Marvin, you reading me up there?"

"Go ahead," came a voice through thick static.

"Yeah, Marvin, you still up top? Got another asshole down here, wants to make a run. It'll mean fifty . . . uh, twenty-five bucks to you if you'll wait."

Seconds passed before the radio squawked again and Marvin's voice came back. "Yeah . . . go ahead."

Freddy switched off the walkie-talkie with a shrug and cut his eyes back to Howard. "It's your funeral." He took his time approaching, but was quick to snatch the two bills from Howard's glove. He unhooked the rope and allowed Howard to push past. "I's you, I'd ski down with Marvin. He's the best skier on the hill, knows every inch of this mountain."

"I hardly need a babysitter," Howard scoffed. "Been riding black diamonds for more than twenty years."

"Yeah? In the dark? With weather moving in? We'll be under an avalanche warning come tomorrow, mark my words."

"Piece of cake," Howard said, swishing through the maze of rope leading to the loading area.

"Just get down quick, fella, or it's my ass." Freddy waved him off and disappeared into the bull-wheel shack.

Howard allowed an empty chair to pass, then side-stepped into the loading space and let the next chair scoop his backside. The chair accelerated through a sharp ascent before rattling over the sheaves of the first tower and slowing into a smooth, quiet glide.

He closed his eyes and drew crisp air into his lungs, a grin tugging at the corners of his mouth. Snow began to flurry as the chair crept over a steep, pine-wooded peak. The terrain then fell away sharply, opening into a wide treeless valley already clear of all ski traffic.

Minutes passed.

The chair chattered past another tower and continued on for seventy-five more yards before the drone of the lift suddenly muted and the cable came to a gentle halt. Momentum swung the chair back and forth some until it eventually hung motionless.

Howard cursed under his breath. The clouds seemed to close in more quickly in the stillness. The base of the slopes and the resort village far below were already completely obscured.

Boredom set in immediately. He took out his cell phone hoping to check messages, but when he saw that he still wasn't getting a signal, he set the phone down beside him, thinking he'd check again from a higher elevation.

The snow fell more heavily now, landing thick and wet against his goggles, stinging his cheeks. He huddled his arms across his chest to fight the chill that was seeping through his clothing like acid.

Christ, what I would give for a . . .

He paused, then fumbled into the breast pocket of his coat. To his relief there remained a crumpled box of Salems pressed against his monogrammed Zippo. Setting his gloves on the seat next to the phone, he tapped out the single remaining cigarette and thumbed the lighter until it sparked a flame. He drew quickly and heavily off the cigarette, burning it down to the filter.

Three minutes later, still chilled to the marrow, he flicked the dead butt away and cursed again. "Come on, Freddy, Marvin, you asshole, crank 'er up."

Looking down to check his watch, he caught movement through the gauze of cloud between his knees—a lone skier, some two hundred feet below, swishing with perceptible skill down the slope. Howard watched the man until he disappeared under the chair.

Hell of a skier, he thought. *Quite a pro.*

Then he jumped, startled by the unexpected sound of laughter.

"I think your fate has just been sealed, Howard."

Howard turned toward the voice and found sitting on the other side of the chair a man he'd watched die months before.

"Jesus Christ!" He yanked his goggles down to his neck and looked the man up and down, his eyes wide with horror, his jaw hanging slack.

Another liquid chuckle left the dead man's throat. "Miss me, Howard?"

It was Terry Choate, Howard's former business partner, in the flesh.

Only the flesh was gunmetal gray, slightly transparent,

and peeling off of grossly mangled bones. The dead man's smile was toothless and glistened red. His misshapen skull was split open at the crown. Gray liquid oozed from the ghastly wound and trickled down past sunken, ink-drop eyes.

Howard's heart became a piston in his chest. He tasted a bitter sickness rising in his throat. "Terry, what are you . . . how can you be—"

"I'd say Freddy was right, wouldn't you, Howard?" The corpse's words slithered off a sluglike tongue. He aimed a thumb over his shoulder. "That Marvin might truly be the best skier on the hill. Certainly looked like an expert to me."

Howard could only stare at the dead man, stunned with terror, until at last he blinked back to attention. "What . . . what did you say?"

Terry pointed toward the slope behind the chair. "Marvin. It doesn't appear that he waited for you."

"Marvin?" It took a moment for Howard to understand the corpse's meaning. He turned slowly around in the seat. The skier he'd seen a moment ago had long since vanished under the cloud. "Marvin." Howard blinked again. "Yes. Marvin. But . . . but he said—"

"*Yeah, go ahead,*" Terry finished. "I believe those were the exact words Marvin used. But the static coming through that radio was rather heavy, wasn't it Howard? Couldn't it be that Marvin's words were not an instruction for you to proceed, but an indication that he was still awaiting a response from his coworker below?"

Howard's stomach knotted, his terror now compounded. He spun around in the chair and screamed Marvin's name until his voice went hoarse. In response he heard only a desperate echo. It wasn't until he turned back that he realized he'd just knocked the gloves and cell phone off the seat.

"Looks like we're in for a long, cold night, Howard." Terry grinned with malice . . . then vanished.

Howard's gaze darted all around. He called out to Terry, but heard only the corpse's cryptic laughter, which seemed to come at him from all directions, taunting and threatening at the same time.

Darkness fell quickly then, even as time stretched out.

It wasn't long before the weight of Howard's skis began to pull painfully on his tired knees. Deeming the skis useless, he kicked them off into the night and listened, to no avail, for their contact with the ground.

Faced with the knowledge that he would never survive a drop from the chair, he was left to wait and listen and watch as the storm rolled in.

The dead man didn't appear again until seven hours and nine inches of snow later.

"I see you haven't gone far, Howard." The corpse's voice snaked out of the darkness. "In truth, neither have I. I have always been with you, every minute of every day. Since the very beginning . . . or end, I should say, *my* end."

Curled with his knees tucked under his chin, back pressed against the armrest, Howard lifted a trembling hand. With fingers made bloodless by the cold, he pried open an eyelid, sealed shut by frozen tears. Through his blurred vision he saw only swirling snow on a field of black.

"I suggest you reach into your pants' leg pocket," Terry said. "Down by your right calf. Go on, Howard."

It was some time before Howard mustered the energy to do as instructed. Struggling with dead hands on the zipper, he reached into the pocket and came out with the plastic glow stick he had mindlessly tucked away three days before—a precautionary handout from the ski-rental shop in a place where avalanche warnings were not uncommon. Howard bent the stick until it clicked, bathing the space around him with its green luminescent glow. He hooked the stick to the shoulder strap of his bib, then raised his head to face the man across the chair.

"*Boo!*" A grin parted the corpse's livery lips. "That's much better, isn't it, Howard?"

"You . . . are . . . not . . . real," Howard rasped.

Terry's laugh was guttural, yet eerily childlike. "Search your conscience, Howard. I think you'll find I most certainly am real. You've only been stranded a few hours; delirium couldn't have possibly set in yet. Anyway, I know you too well. You'd never allow your mind to go. No, never your mind! It's that mind for which I partnered with you in the first place. Such a brilliant architectural mind, it is . . . a mind clever enough to get away with murder."

"I . . . didn't . . . murder—"

"Stop it!" Terry spat. "You've already killed me, Howard, don't insult my intelligence."

"The hook . . . the safety hook on your lanyard . . . it was just an accide—"

"Yes, my fall did appear a terrible accident, didn't it? I must say, as you read my eulogy, I almost believed you'd even convinced yourself that it was accidental. Fortunately for you everyone thought so. Makes sense, after all. It's dangerous work we do, marching in our slick-soled Italian loafers across the narrow beams of our towering structures, only a hardhat and a measly nylon strap to insure our safety." His face contorted into a scowl. "Who knew that the hooks on those straps could ever prove faulty, right?"

Howard studied the corpse's designer suit, once spotless and impeccably tailored, now shredded and caked with spilled entrails. "What do you want, Terry?"

"Only the same privilege you were granted last September. To look into the eyes of my partner as he falls."

"Fuck you!" The words shot from Howard's mouth in a voiceless hiss.

"You have already done that, Howard. Now it's my turn to return the favor."

"You deserved everything you got, Terry. You rode on my coattails for a decade, taking credit for my work. The vision was mine!"

"The vision *was* yours, Howard, I never failed to grant you that. But we were partners, and your vision was nothing without me to sell it, to make others see it and feel it."

Howard looked away, hugging his arms close, his teeth chattering.

"I'm curious to know, Howard, if you're prepared to freeze to death arguing with me, or if that creative mind of yours is considering how you're going to get off this chair."

Howard leaned forward and looked into the black void below.

"I think you've already determined that you'd never survive a voluntary fall," Terry said. "And of course you'll never make it through the night in these temperatures." He leaned across the seat and winked a pupil-less eye. "Not without a fire, anyway."

Howard met the corpse's gaze for a beat, then dug hastily into his pocket for the lighter, wondering why he hadn't thought of it before.

"There's that brilliant mind at work!" Terry said. "I knew you still had it, Howard."

It took several tries for Howard to get a flame out of the lighter. With a cupped palm, he guarded the struggling flame against the wind and relished the warmth it brought to his frostbitten fingers. But within seconds, the flame died in the icy gusts.

"Don't you have anything to burn, Howard?" Terry tapped his jaw in thought, then snapped his bony fingers. "A cigarette box, perhaps?"

Howard came out with the box of Salems and crushed it flat. He thumbed the Zippo repeatedly until he was able to bring a flame to the box, but in the whipping wind the cardboard wouldn't catch. After some consideration he pulled the lighter apart, exposing its inner workings. He removed the soaked piece of rayon from the canister and squeezed a few drops of fuel onto the cigarette box. Then he closed the lighter again, raked the flint, and instantly set the box aflame.

The paltry fire turned the box to ash in less than a minute, and provided only a scant amount of heat.

Still, at the corpse's urging, Howard employed the same procedure to his lift tickets, which burned even more quickly than the cigarette box.

Four business cards and six-hundred-and-thirty-dollars worth of folding money went next. When Howard's credit cards refused to catch fire, the corpse raised a finger and made another suggestion.

"Your clothing, Howard," he said. "It might produce a bigger flame that would act as a signal fire. Isn't there anything you can spare?"

There wasn't. But Howard's body was stiff with cold, and the promised warmth that a fire would provide was just too hard to resist. Within minutes he had forcibly ripped his thermal undershirt and his boxer shorts from beneath his outer clothing and burned them both down to smoking embers. The corpse went on to tempt Howard into sacrificing his stocking cap, and, finally, his thick woolen socks, on which he'd had to squeeze the last drops of fuel left in the lighter in order to spark a flame.

The corpse's grin widened when only a faint whiff of smoke remained between the two men. "Well, Howard, it appears you're out of recourses."

The dead man's cackling laugh was infuriating, but Howard refused to let Terry see his rage.

He looked into the corpse's cobalt eyes and shook his head with pointed resolve. "No."

"What's that, Howard?"

"I said no, Terry! This isn't over."

The dead man clasped his hands with a bony click. "Of course it isn't! It's only getting more fun."

Howard swallowed a fistful of snow from his lap to wet his parched throat. He straightened his legs, sending searing pain to his frozen knees. He reached up and took hold of the center pole from which the chair hung. His hand slipped twice from the bar as he attempted to hoist himself up on cramped legs.

"So, what's the plan now?" Terry asked. "Climb up to the cable above, then go hand over hand back to the tower, right? Yes, it is the only way. There's a ladder on the tower that would lead you all the way down. But it must be nearly a hundred yards back, maybe more—not an easy journey for a man of your size." His tongue made a rueful click. "Those four-course lunches and hourly lattes have done you no favors over the years, Howard. I suggest you use your ski poles, bridge them over the cable and zip along the line."

It was a thought that had occurred to Howard just seconds before. He raised his backside off the seat and reached beneath him for the poles, which he had been protecting at all costs. But just as his hand fell on them, the corpse leaned across the chair, yanked the poles from Howard's grasp, and tossed them away.

"What are you . . . No!" The poles were out of sight before Howard could even scream the word. Fury erupted inside of him. "You son of a bitch!" In a burst of madness he lunged across the chair, hands outstretched for the corpse's neck.

But his hands—in fact his entire body—moved straight through the specter unimpeded. With nothing to halt his momentum, Howard toppled forward out of control. The lower half of his body slipped off the front of the chair. His hands clawed madly for the rear edge of the seat and somehow took hold. The next instant found him dangling in open air, legs kicking in the wind, arms outstretched across the seat.

The corpse spoke when Howard's girlish scream finally faded. "Take it easy, Howard. Calm down. I've been waiting far too long to allow this to end so quickly for you." His tone was level. "Just bring one leg up at a time, slowly and carefully. You'll be fine."

Howard did as Terry directed and eventually make it back onto the seat, quivering with exhaustion. He refused to grant the corpse so much as a look. When he regained his wind he brought his feet back onto the chair and finally made it to a standing position. Again, he attempted to climb the pole, but got only inches off the seat before sliding back down.

"Your boots, Howard. You will never make it with your boots."

Howard reached down with palsied hands and unclamped the boots enough to slip his feet out. Snow crunched on the seat beneath his bare toes. Taking hold of the bar again he looked up and paused, paralyzed by the prospect of leaving the relative safety of the chair.

"What's wrong, Howard? Don't tell me you're getting cold feet," Terry chuckled.

Howard ignored the cruel taunt. Using his feet for extra leverage now, he hoisted himself off the chair. His muscles spasmed from the strain. The bones of his spine creaked like the turn of a ratchet handle with every upward thrust.

When at last he reached the cable, he took hold and eventually summoned the courage to release his legs from the bar. Dangling freely now, he swung back and forth, trying to build enough momentum to swing his feet up on to the cable and relieve his hands of some of the burden.

The effort proved futile, and expended more energy than Howard could afford. He had no choice but to continue using only his hands.

Three minutes gained him little more than ten feet along the cable. His fingers quickly stiffened into inflexible claws around the bundled steel wires. His heart drummed behind his ribs. His lungs labored with every breath.

Four more minutes elapsed.

He thought that if he could just reach the next chair he could stop and rest, perhaps shake some feeling back into his hands. But beyond the faint green light of the glow stick, he saw only darkness.

His right hand slid forward another inch. Then his left. Right. Then . . .

His left hand slipped from the cable, leaving him hanging by the floundering grip of his right.

An instant before Howard fell, the corpse appeared before him again, taking hold of Howard's jacket collar and jerking him upward with unfathomable strength.

Howard reached out with grabbing hands until once again he had secured a firm grip on the cable.

The corpse hung only inches in front of Howard by a single rotting hand, showing no strain in his effort. His expression remained a sneering, cadaverous grin. No longer just a specter, the dead man had become something shockingly more tangible. The torn flesh of his scalp flapped in the wind. His stench was foul, nauseating.

The corpse reached inside his tattered suit coat. "Recognize this, Howard?"

Howard's eyes fell to the nylon lanyard rolling out of Terry's free hand. At each end of the six-foot cord was a copper rebar hook. It was identical to the safety strap worn by Terry on the day of his fatal fall. One end of it had been hooked onto itself, forming a loop. Howard's eyes came back up.

"Now it's my turn." The corpse slipped the loop over Howard's right foot, then pulled it up his leg to the top of the thigh.

"Terry, what the hell are you doing?"

The corpse answered with a hard upward tug, tightening the loop like a noose.

Howard cried out in pain. "Dammit, Terry, what are you doing to me?"

Terry proceeded to attach the remaining hook to the cable above, snapping it closed with a click. "It is time for your confession, Howard."

"I told you I have nothing to conf—"

A fist of stripped bone struck Howard across the jaw. "Say it, Howard!"

Howard shook his head furiously, the coppery taste of blood filling his mouth. "I told you, I did nothing! The hook was faulty. The locking mechanism just snapped . . ."

Another punch struck Howard's opposite cheek.

"These things don't just snap, Howard! Or . . . do they?" The corpse yanked downward on the lanyard.

"No!" Howard screamed. "Don't, please! Terry, whatever you think happened that day—"

"You gave me the harness, Howard. Fifteen years together, never once had you provided me my safety harness on a building site."

"It wasn't my fault!"

"Liar! You looked me in the eyes as I fell, and I saw it on your face. You took pleasure in my fall, didn't you? Say it!"

"Terry, I didn't—"

"Say it!" The corpse yanked again on the lanyard, harder this time. "Say it!"

It was guilt as much as terror that finally broke Howard. "Yes! I killed you! Is that what you wanted to hear?" Hot tears welled in his eyes.

"Is it the truth?"

"I swear on my life it's the truth!" He lost another precious inch of his grip on the cable. He now clutched it with only the tips of his numb fingers. "I've confessed, Terry, now please! I'm sorry. I'm so sorry!"

"Sorry isn't good enough, Howard! Not for me, nor for my wife and son who have cried on your shoulder all these many months as I was forced to look on."

Howard looked into Terry's eyes, his mind racing. "Your son . . . yes . . . Kyle! Terry, I saved Kyle from—"

The corpse drove a fist into Howard's stomach. "Don't you ever mention my son's name, Howard!"

Howard's breath shot out of him. He fought to draw air back into his constricted lunges. "But it's the truth!" he sputtered. "Four years ago. The third story collapse on the Donovan project. It was your birthday, Terry, I know you remember! Kyle was to surprise you at the site, but I called him that morning and told him not to come! I knew that the structure wasn't completely sound and I told him not to come. We were all nearly killed, Terry; I know you haven't forgotten it! Kyle and I agreed never to mention it to you. But it's true, Terry, you have to believe me!" Tears streaked Howard's face as he searched for mercy in the corpse's lifeless eyes. "You have to believe me!"

"After hearing the lies you've told my friends and colleagues all these months? The lies you've told my wife and children? Why should I believe you?"

"Because it's the truth! Oh God, Terry, you have to believe me!"

Silence fell between them, each man holding the other's bitter glare.

It was the corpse who finally looked away. "You'll find out soon enough whether or not I believe you, Howard. It's time for us to part now."

"No! You can't leave me!"

"I'm not going anywhere."

"But I can't hold on any longer!"

"That's the idea."

Howard's eyes moved to the hook above his head. "Is it secure, Terry? I have to know if the lanyard will hold when I let go!"

"There's only one way to find out."

"What! What does that mean?"

"It means your moment of judgment has finally come, Howard."

"Wait! Please wait!"

Gazing into Howard's frantic eyes, Terry offered a

slow nod. "I will wait, Howard . . . for as long as it takes. All I have left now is to look into your eyes and wait . . ."

*

As an actor, **RYAN BROWN** has held contract roles on *The Young and the Restless* and *Guiding Light*. He has also appeared on *Law & Order: SVU*, and starred in two feature films for Lifetime Television. His first novel, *Play Dead,* a comic supernatural thriller, was published in May 2010, and his short story "Jeepers Peepers" appeared in ITW's Young Adult Anthology.

Invisible

SEAN MICHAEL BAILEY

nvisible ain't easy, man. Takes years of practice, years of trying, failing, and all the pain comes with being caught.

Took me six years of hiding from Momma, hearing her call me so sweet, that boiling water sloshing out the pot onto the floor while she looked for me all over the house. Her carrying the hot pot, or those things she stuck in me. Learned a lot in them two thousand days. First, I just hid. Ha. Can't hide from Momma. Can't run, can't hide.

Only thing that works is invisible.

Daddy did it. Went out for that peppy pizza, left it on the front porch, and just vanished. She never did find him. But that wasn't invisible. That was cheating. He just ran away. He had a car.

Nobody taught me. Learned invisible by myself. I

would sneak off to a closet or slide under the bed, trying to hide, pretending I wasn't there, all the time secretly praying Momma would put down the pot, drop the fireplace shovel, and just hug me.

That don't work. I was still me, hiding, scared of Momma. That ain't invisible. She could see into my mind, find me every time. Burn me, hit me. Hurt me.

I found out I couldn't wait 'til Momma started heating the water and singing her hymns. I had to work at it all the time, planning, concentrating, watching. Had to learn not to be me, to become a thing with no thoughts. A couch, laundry in the cellar, dust in the cedar closet. Dust don't want to be found by nobody, laundry don't want to be hugged. Still not invisible, but when I did that, it took Momma longer to find me, so it was, like progress, you know? Then I figured how to plan, make it seem like I couldn't be in the house. Leave open the door, a window. Make her think I could not be where I was. Had to find the right spot at the right time, too. Made it harder for her, but that made her madder. Still wasn't invisible.

Not 'til I stopped being dust and became Momma.

She would open up that sink cabinet, look right down at me in a ball, and not see me. I wasn't there. I was her, not seeing me. Looking at only a can of Ajax and a bucket and some moldy junk. No boy.

That did it.

Invisible.

Later, I was so happy I done it. If I did my work right, thought it all out, made the house feel like I was gone, found the right spot to go and be Momma, singing about God, boiling water, looking for that dirty, sinful boy, she never found me. Later, when Momma *was* gone, I had to learn how to be invisible to other people in other places.

It was hard, but that was my new job and I was, like the doctors say, motivated.

Now, I got it down to about three months, give or take.

First, I told the doctors about it, but their eyes got all scared. They wrote it down but didn't believe me. Thought I was crazy as Momma. I showed them good. I watched, planned every day, watching from the prison yard at the homes beyond the concertina wire fences. People coming and going from the homes outside. Men, women, kids. Cars, trucks. Dogs, cats. Worked out, waited 'til it was cold. Daylight Saving Time Monday night. Wore lots of clothes, layers, long sleeves. Taped myself all over, under my sweats, under my orange jumpsuit, like a mummy, so there would be no blood, no good scent for the dogs to follow. Guards stayed inside for the first time 'cause it was cold, dark, cloudy. I did my runs to and from the fence, until my smoker went off behind the fire extinguisher. By the time they looked back in the yard, I was gone, flying up the fence, the blades ripping my layers, then up the second fence, like in the Olympics, over and out.

They found my clothes next to the big road, everything but the pizza. Right next to the big sign warning not to pick up hitchhikers because it was a correctional institution. Looked like I stripped, got into a car, and I was gone. Never thought I would run in the opposite direction, take a dip in the icy water of a pool in one of the backyards and then run the water off. Anyway, just a prison escape, looks like.

But I was invisible.

Deputies and cops came into the house where I was invisible, but I was in the right spot at the right time with the right people, who couldn't see me.

I was now Harold. He said his name was Harold. He let the cops in and they searched. One of them even looked where I was but didn't see me. Invisible, like I told you. I wasn't there. I wasn't curled up under the living room couch. I was Harold, sitting on top of the couch.

Harold listened as the guys with the shotguns and M16's told him about the inmate escapee. Did he see or hear anything unusual in the last thirty minutes? We told them no, nothing, just the siren from the jail and all the lights and helicopters and dogs. We went out into the backyard to see them. Who escaped, we asked them?

A bad guy, a real mutt from Down South, they told us. Serial killer. Crazy as a shithouse rat. Hard case, boiled his own mother, killed maybe fifteen people all over the country. Real escape artist. Desperate. Consider him armed and dangerous. They asked us about any strangers in the area recently, any other residents or weapons in the household.

We told them we saw no one suspicious recently, we lived alone, told them about the legal, licensed shotgun in the bedroom closet upstairs. Then we talked all racist, how those minority people were all trash, not even human, those people. How all those scum lowlifes should get the death penalty.

The cops were uncomfortable. They cut us off, told us this guy wasn't black or Latino. He was white.

We just said, oh.

They gave us a description of the fugitive, a name. Showed us a picture. We didn't recognize me. We said we had never seen the guy, but if we did, we'd blow his ass away. Better not come around here.

The deputies said that was a bad idea. Told us to just keep our doors locked. If we saw anything, call 911 right away. We offered them coffee and booze, for the cold, but they said they had to continue their search, even though the skel probably got into a waiting car out on the highway and was long gone. There was a big alert out, roadblocks.

We felt safe with all the cops in the house. When they left, it was good to see them still driving around the neighborhood on patrol. Past midnight, they moved on, looking for the guy somewhere else. The clock on the mantle clicked gently after we shut off the TV news. We checked all the doors again, to make sure they were locked, and went upstairs to the bathroom.

That's when I stopped being invisible, quietly crawled out from under Harold's couch, and softly mounted the stairs. I knew Harold would go to the bedroom closet and get his shotgun soon, to have it by the bed while he slept. When he opened the closet door I would be inside. I wouldn't be invisible then. I'd let him see me.

Then we would be one.

*

SEAN MICHAEL BAILEY is the pen name for the *New York Times* bestselling author of crime nonfiction who went from the dark side to the darker side to write the thriller *1787*. He has completed his second novel, *Triad*, and is working on another.

When Johnny Comes Marching Home

HEATHER GRAHAM

It was eighteen sixty-five when the terror came to Douglas Island.

Eighteen sixty-five when Johnny came home.

Naturally, it was a time when few people cared what was happening on a small, barely inhabited southern island off the coast of South Carolina.

So much tragedy had already come to the country; there were so many dead, dying, maimed, and left without home or sustenance that a strange plague descending upon a distanced population was hardly of note.

Unless you were there, unless you saw, and prayed not just for your life, but your soul.

The war was over, but not the bitterness. Lincoln had been assassinated, and all hope of a loving and swift reunion between the states had been dashed.

Brent Haywood, Johnny's cousin, had made it home

the week before. A government ship—a Federal government ship—had brought him straight to the docks. He limped. He was often in pain. Shrapnel had caught him in the right hip, and he'd be in pain, limping, for the rest of his life.

Brent had been a prisoner a long time, and he told me that he hadn't seen Johnny since Cold Harbor, and that he wasn't sure if he wanted to see Johnny; he hadn't known that his cousin had survived until we had received the news. "There's something not—right with Johnny," he told me.

The world, our world, or that of our country, was in a sad way, desperately sad. On Douglas Island, we had survived many years of the travelers who had come from far and wide to see the beauty of our little place, to ride over the sloping hills, to fish and boat and hunt. The war had barely begun before we had ceased to care who won or lost. Now, far too many people were struggling just to survive. The South was in chaos.

And so it was on the day that Johnny MacFarlane came home.

At first, nearly the whole town came out, two hundred odd of us came to the docks to meet the boat that had brought him home. A letter had been received the previous week, and we knew just when the schooner the *Chesapeake* was to bring him home. A kindly surgeon Johnny had come upon somewhere in his travels home after the surrender at Appomattox Courthouse had written that Johnny MacFarlane was not well, but friends were helping and would be sending him home with all possible speed, and they made arrangements for his travel.

Came the day. I was there with my father, eager, barely able to wait through the moments that would bring him back to me. From the widow's walk of Johnny's home, Janey Sue, his sister, had seen the schooner out on the horizon, and so we had gathered. Our town band was playing welcome songs, and it was no matter that he'd been one of the last battered soldiers of Lee's army, we were one country now, and the band played for him, using all the songs we knew. People sang at the docks, and it was momentous. Federal song, fine. They played, "When Johnny Comes Marching Home."

Except that the schooner stopped far out to sea, and it was strange, for even the music ended by the time Johnny rowed himself to shore in a small boat.

There was deep dockage at the island, and throughout the war, we'd been visited now and then by ships from both sides, and it was only the fact that we were, actually, so small and seeming to offer so little in support or importance that they all passed us by with little interest after docking. Sometimes, sailors wanted to loot the houses, but thanks to my father's brilliance at hiding all assets, they did not stay. We had never imagined that any ship would eschew the fine docks and send Johnny home in a longboat, but so they did.

No matter.

Johnny was coming home.

And we watched as he rowed, and we waited until the little boat reached the docks, and then we all raced to him, descended upon him, really, tying up the rowboat, and helping him to the dock. His dear little sister, Janey Sue, immediately threw herself into his arms, nearly knocking him from the dock.

He hugged her in return; over her shoulder, he looked at me.

I was shocked.

Johnny and I had been together forever. We'd both

been born and raised on the island. We had dreamed great visions for our future, and in those dreams, we would travel, but always return to our island. He wanted to be a teacher. Knowledge gave a man power and strength, he believed. Oh, Johnny had always been a thinker, and I had loved following the processes in his mind.

But he'd been more than a thinker. Johnny had been a doer, a man who had always been strong, in a way, the typical Southern gentleman of his age. He could drink, ride, and shoot with the best of them, and also been able to repair any leak or damage done to Fairhaven, his estate on the island.

He was a man ahead of his time; he had joined the Confederate forces because he had believed in states rights. He had never believed in slavery—how could one human being, one soul, ever own another?—but he had also believed that change had to come about with laws that would help newly freed individuals make a living— survive, in short.

He had been . . . Johnny. Beautiful, such a handsome man. Smart, always careful in his thoughts and words. Strong, a man's man, a woman's man, independent, powerful, capable.

And now. . . .

Johnny was a shell of the man he had been. My father had warned me—war changed people. It brought out their strengths and their weaknesses, but either way, it changed a man for good. We had heard that Lee's troops had been starving, so his emaciated shape shouldn't have shocked me. His pallor had come about, certainly, because of his illness.

But I had never expected the look in his eyes.

Once, they had been the blue of the sky on a summer's

day, as brilliant and vital as Johnny himself. Once . . .
they had brightened easily with laughter. Once upon a
time, they had looked at me in way that had awakened
every raw and erotic thought in my mind, and stirred my
heart to a thunderous pounding. Once. . . .

They had been alive.

He looked at me now with recognition, but even the
color in his eyes had changed. Now, they seemed so pale
a blue as to be almost colorless.

It was as if . . . the color within them was dead. It was a
ghost color, like the remnant of what had once been real
and tangible, but now was nothing more than a memory.

I gave myself a shake. The town was welcoming him,
but as he looked at me over his sister's shoulder, he
smiled slowly. A ghost of his old smile, but it was there,
and suddenly, as dead as his eyes might appear, I saw
that he had never forgotten what we had shared, that he
loved me. I told myself that I was crazy. I rushed forward
through the crowds, and he took me into his arms. Despite his fragile appearance, he swept me up in strong
arms and swirled me around, and held me close.

"Now," he whispered, "I have come home."

I smiled at him; I was jubilant. Johnny was home.

Once he had been greeted by one and all, we helped
him into the family carriage and headed to his home,
Fairhaven. We were greeted at the door by Brambles,
the butler, while in the foyer stood Brent, who had not
come to the docks to meet Johnny. Brambles was all
over himself, sputtering and crying as he greeted Johnny.
Brent was more reserved, shaking his cousin's hand. He
was cordial, but visibly cool. Johnny was polite to everyone, saying all the right things.

When my father, Janey Sue, and Brambles led Johnny

on into the dining room where a feast was awaiting his return, I held back, pulling on Brent's arm. "You are—a horse's ass!" I hissed to him. "What? Were you wishing that Johnny wouldn't make it home? What's the matter with you?"

I had grown up with Brent as well. He was lean and tall like Johnny, dark haired, handsome, light eyed, and he'd been bred with the same ethics. I couldn't understand him being so bitter and churlish, not about Johnny coming home. I knew he'd taken some hard hits. He'd married a girl in Virginia, and she'd died before any of the family had even managed to meet her. To be sad and even bitter seemed to be one thing; to be so cold to his cousin seemed quite another.

Brent studied me. I couldn't help but think that his eyes were green—not the beautiful blue Johnny's had once been. And yet today . . .

They were alive. Deep set and steady, and somehow, wise beyond all that I had seen before.

"I loved Johnny like a brother," he told me.

I frowned. "Then give him a hug and a real welcome, and be happy that he is home!" I told him.

He gripped my hands tightly. "Jules," he said, his voice suddenly heated and passionate, "be careful. Be very careful, please."

I jerked away from him, staring at him. "Be careful—of Johnny? Brent, you have lost your mind."

I swept on into the dining room.

Mable, the cook, had gone all out. Johnny's favorites were all on the table. There was ham, chicken, roasted lamb, cornbread, turnip greens, summer squash, tomatoes, fresh berries, and for dessert, sweet-potato-pecan pie.

Johnny barely touched his food. He thanked Mable and told her how delicious everything on the table tasted.

But he didn't really eat. He simply pushed his food around the plate.

When the meal had ended, Janey Sue and I gave the gentlemen a few minutes alone in the study for brandy and cigars. She and I were both chafing. Johnny had just come home. And so much that was innocent and traditional had already been lost—why were we delegated to the ladies' room?

"Time enough!" I said firmly. Janey Sue smiled, and she and I headed to the study.

Johnny was seated in his father's huge old leatherback chair behind the desk. Brent was at the settee, and my father was standing by the mantle, perplexed as he watched Johnny. "What's done is done. How would we change anything now?" My father was asking.

Brent seemed to be looking out the window, paying no mind to what was going on.

"Maybe the world needs a clean sweep," Johnny said. "A mighty flood to rise up, and clear us all out, those who were greedy and made their fortunes on the backs of other men, and those who will sweep down now to make their fortunes on the broken backs of those trying to come to terms with the war. What has been . . . the past is gone. It can never be relived."

He stood up. "My dear friends, and family," Johnny said, glancing tenderly at his sister, glancing at Brent, "I am exhausted. Forgive me."

Everyone agreed that he must rest. But I raced out into the hall after him. He didn't mean me, of course. He would need me. Naturally, a Southern lady did not sleep with her beau until they were married.

But such myths had gone away in the river of bloodshed that had been the war. I had lain with Johnny many times. I did not shout it from the rooftops, nor did other

Southern women, well aware that their opportunities for intimacy with their loved ones might be limited and quickly ended by a volley of cannon fire.

"Johnny!" I said, stopping, laying my head against his chest. "I will come up later, once we've settled for the night. Father will understand that I am staying with Janey Sue, and Janey Sue has long known that I stay with you."

He pulled away and stared at me, frowning. He shook his head. "No, no, you must go home tonight."

"Johnny—"

"Tonight, please. You must." His hands cupped my face. "You must go home, far from here. You are not . . . you must. I love you as I have always loved you. But tonight, go home."

He walked away from me. I stared after him, incredulous. I had missed our nights together. I had dreamed about them time and time again as I had prayed that he would return from the war.

My father emerged from the study. "Jules, we must go home, and let these fine folks rest for the night."

"But—" I began.

"Jules, please," my father insisted.

Brent stared at me. He was not going to help me. And even Janey Sue, next to Brent, appeared to be a little lost.

I had no choice but to leave with my father. I was not invited to stay.

The next morning, fishermen from Douglas Island boarded the schooner which had brought Johnny home, but not into the docks.

The schooner was empty. There was not a soul aboard her.

My father, commonly looked upon as the people's leader on the island as we had no mayor or other governmental structure there, listened gravely to the men, then announced that we'd be going out to Fairhaven to speak with Johnny while he sent other men in one of our fastest ketches to alert the proper authorities on the mainland.

Brambles, deeply distressed, opened the door. He told my father that Johnny was doing poorly. He would get Mr. Brent.

Brent, looking worn, came to the foyer and led us into the study. My father told Brent about the lack of a crew or other passengers on the schooner. Brent listened gravely. I thought his face became more ashen as he did so.

"That's quite a mystery," Brent said.

"Surely, Johnny can tell us something!" my father said.

"Johnny is sedated right now; he had a very hard night," Brent said. He grimaced. "I have laudanum, for my hip, you know. Johnny needed sleep, very badly," he said.

"Well, I must speak with him. Authorities will come from the mainland, and they will demand to know something," my father said.

Brent nodded. He looked like a man under torture. Still, I was resentful. I was convinced he was jealous of Johnny, and that he was hiding something.

"May I see Janey Sue?" I asked him.

He shook his head. "She is resting, as well."

"Brent, damn you—!"

"Jules!" My father said with horror. "The war is over. We will not become animals because it existed, or because it is over!"

Brent looked away. "It's all right, Mr. Shelby. I realize that my own behavior must appear far less than hospitable. Forgive me."

I wanted to slap his face. My father, however, had my

elbow. He apologized for me, and we were quickly out of the house.

"He's doing something to Johnny—it's Brent. Father! Maybe he's trying to kill him. Brent would probably like to inherit the property. You must stop him!"

My father looked at me. He was grave, but didn't share my fear or my passion. "Child, war is hard on the women who wait. It is devastating to the men who fight, who stare at their fellow human beings, sometimes look them in their eyes, and shoot them or stab them through with their knives or bayonets. Let it be; we will see. Brent knows that Johnny must answer to me. Give it the day."

I had no intention of giving it a day. I rode out to Johnny's beautiful Fairhaven, and I came around the back. I left Mathilda, my horse, behind the stables, grazing on long grasses, and I slipped through the kitchen door. I knew my way around the house, and I looked out for both Brambles and Mable as I climbed the stairs.

What I found horrified me.

Johnny's room had been boarded; there were nails imbedded in the wooden planks that now walled him in. I walked to the door and called his name.

He did not answer. I tried and tried, and then hurried down the hall to Janey Sue's room. Her door was not barricaded, but she wasn't there.

I slipped from the house, furious now. Brent was locking his cousin away! What had he done with Janey Sue?

I rode hard, straight back to my home, determined that my father was going to do something, and do that something now. But he wasn't there, and as I stood in the parlor of our home on Main Street, not far from the docks, I heard the shouting.

The sound was distant, but so loud it carried on the breeze. I left the house and ran down Main Street until I reached the long boardwalk that stretched out so that the larger ships could avail themselves of the deep harbor, and there, found the reason for the horror. People had backed away, but they were in a circle around something on the dock.

I pushed through the crowd.

And I saw what they saw.

Bodies. White, swollen, and bloated, and torn to shreds. They had been gnawed upon.

Eaten.

"Sharks," someone cried. "The water is infested!"

"This was not a shark attack," one of the older fishermen said. He shook his grizzled head, rubbing his chin. "This is not a shark attack. I've seen what the big fellows can do to a man left in the water. The bodies are . . . not missing any limbs. They've been chewed by something. But not a shark."

As I stood there, Brent arrived at the docks. He pushed his way through the crowd until he could stare at the bodies. He became the color of burnt ash, and he turned around without a word, and strode back to his carriage.

I ran after him. I caught him at the end of the dock, grabbed his shoulder, and forced him to face me. He stared at me for a minute as if he didn't even see me. I slapped him across the face, I was so scared and furious. "What is going on, Brent, damn you, what is going on? I went to the house. I saw what you did to Johnny, and I will not stand for it, do you hear me?"

He did then. The slap had angered him, but it had brought him back to the reality of the moment—and me, forcing the issue, in his face.

"Go away, Jules," he said duly. "Go away, and lock yourself in your house. Better yet, take your father and go far, far away."

"You have lost your mind, Brent. What are you going on about? What is happening?"

He hesitated, but then indicated the tavern on Main Street. He set an arm around my shoulder and led me toward it, and around to the benches that sat outdoors to where, in better times, many a fisherman and farmer had gathered together to drink beer and eat their noon meals.

Now, the area was empty, and he made me sit down.

Across from me, he closed his eyes for a moment as if gathering both his strength and his sense of sanity, then, he looked at me. "There's something really wrong with Johnny."

"What?" I demanded. "I know he has been at war. I know he might have been injured, I know that many men bear mental wounds, that they've seen things, but . . ."

"You saw the men on the dock," he said. It wasn't a question. It was a fact. "I've seen just a similar thing—before."

"Go on," I said, frowning, and truly puzzled. Maybe Brent had returned more damaged than any of us had imagined.

He let out a breath and looked at the moss dripping from one of the old oaks that bordered the small outdoor dining area. He didn't want to look at me.

"It was at Cold Harbor," he said.

I shook my head, still trying desperately to understand what he was talking about. I placed my hands on his. "Brent, Cold Harbor was a victory for Lee. I know that dead men are still dead men, and I know that more than two thousand of your own troops died as well, but—"

He looked at me, dead on. "Men die. It's how they die that's terrifying. We were near Bethesda Church, camped out there. Yes, it was a Rebel victory. But on the night of the tenth, there was a break, and two companies of Feds made it through the lines. We might have been slaughtered in our sleep, but Johnny was on guard duty."

"So he saved your lives!" I told him.

Brent said, "We woke up and found them. At least fifty of them. Torn to pieces. Like the men on the dock. It wasn't as if they had been killed; it was as if they had been eaten. I don't know what happened; I never will. They were bloated from the sea, but they were . . . gnawed. Chewed. Eaten."

I ripped my hands away from his and stood up. "Brent! You're trying to say that Johnny did it, that Johnny . . . *ate* the men on the schooner? You must be insane! I'm telling my father what you said, I'm . . . Brent! You're horrible, don't you see that? How dare you imply that Johnny could . . . and where is Janey Sue? She wasn't at the house."

He looked up at me, startled. "What?"

"Janey Sue isn't at the house," I told him.

Ignoring me, he jumped to his feet, and he was gone down the street. I saw him reach his horse, and in his wake, the road became dust.

I left him to find my father. At the docks, I was horrified to find that he'd left a message for me. He was gone. He had climbed aboard a boat with the bodies to take them back to the mainland.

I was frustrated beyond belief, but it was almost dark. I went back to my house, seething, trying to determine what I could do before he returned.

Finally, I determined that I would wait until the morning. In the daylight, I was going to find one of my father's friends to accompany me out to Fairhaven, and I would demand that Brent produce Johnny and Janey Sue.

I locked my doors carefully, and I went upstairs to sleep. I tossed about, but finally dozed, and I believed it was Brent's horrible story that made me dream. And in that dream, Johnny was outside. He was high in the branches of the massive oak beyond my window, begging that I let him in. I opened the window, deliriously happy to know that he was all right, and that he needed me.

But something was wrong with him.

His eyes. The color, the pale blue color, a dead color . . .

He was cold, although it was June, and he seemed strong, though he shouldn't have been so strong. He held me, he cradled me, and then he pulled away from me. Suddenly, he seemed tortured, and he pushed me away. "No, God no," he shouted. "Oh, God, no, oh, God, no!"

Then, he was gone. He leaped through the window, and he was gone.

I had been dreaming, of course. He had never been there. I opened my eyes and roused, and discovered that my window was open.

Through the open window, I heard the screams.

My father owned a Colt; he kept it in his drawer by his bed, and I raced to retrieve it, my fingers shaking as I loaded it with six bullets. I was in my nightdress, but I didn't care. With slippers on my feet I went tearing from the house and down by the docks.

I didn't believe what I saw.

Something. Something like a man.

I could *hear* him. I could hear him *eating,* hear him *drinking,* human flesh, for he had torn open one of the dock workers, and another lay at his feet, and a woman was torn in half just a few feet away. The creature, the *thing* on the docks had picked up human beings and ripped into them like a man might tear into ribs at a barbecue.

I was frozen. Then I came to life. Screaming, I headed for the thing, my father's very trusty Colt raised high.

I started shooting.

It didn't fall. It did stop eating. The horrible, frenzied slurping sound stopped.

The thing turned toward me and was staring. Then, with uncanny speed and agility, it was running at me, and running hard.

I was dead. Worse, I was about to be gnawed to death, ripped in half, my flesh consumed before my heart ceased to beat. I was so horrified that I was barely aware of the sound of the horse's hoof beats behind me, and I couldn't even scream when I was swept up off the street, and thrown over the neck of a horse.

It was then that I heard Brent, who had rescued me from the road, shouting above the sound of screams and terror. "Get into your houses. Get your swords, you have to remove the head . . . swords, people, swords, bullets do nothing, aim to decapitate!"

He whirled his horse around, and still, so casually rescued and tossed, I could see little. People came to the streets then bearing their infantry and cavalry swords. One fellow had his machete; he had once worked in the sugarcane fields.

I was righted at last. And I thought he was going to set me upon the ground. He looked at me and then did not. "Sit tight," he said. He drew his sword and we road hard down the docks, leaping to bit of poor shoreline at the end. I screamed as I saw something rise from the water; Brent did not. He swept his sword out in a mighty arc; the head of the thing went flying, and the body crashed down to the water, lifeless.

I heard screams of triumph, and knew that the island folk were now holding their own.

And then, it was over. Brent called out orders, and people started a bonfire, and the stench in the night air grew sickening. As the body parts were collected for the fire—those killed as well as those who had done the killing—I saw that some of the *things* had been Federal navy. *Men from the schooner.*

Daylight came. Exhausted, Brent sat back at the table outside the tavern again. I took the bench opposite him. He looked up at me miserably. "I think it was a girl in Richmond. Johnny was Johnny then. Soldiers on the street were harassing her, calling her a monster. Johnny stopped them, but the next morning, he looked like hell. He told me that she had been a monster."

"You still say Johnny did this? The men from schooner did this. I saw their bodies, Brent."

"And how do you think they became what they are?" he asked me wearily. "I found a doctor, a surgeon, a man with the Union. That's when I was captured. He'd seen it before; he was trying to find a cure. I prayed that Johnny would die, or that this man would find the cure. But . . ."

"I don't believe you," I told him. "Johnny didn't do this."

Brent started when we heard shouting again. He jumped to his feet. We ran back to the place where the smell of burning flesh was so terrible now, where the bonfire burned.

I heard Brent cry out and fall to his knees and I knew why.

He had found Janey Sue. Her throat had been ripped out; her left cheek was gone entirely.

I watched as Brent sobbed, and I was too numb to find tears myself for the girl who had been my best friend throughout the long years of the war.

Brent stood, ordering that she be burned like the rest. I set my hand on his shoulder. "Brent, you can bury her—"

He swung on me. "No, don't you understand yet? Johnny is—he's a zombie. And everyone he touches becomes the same."

I pushed away from him, still refusing to believe. "Stop it, Brent, stop it! Johnny would never, ever, in a thousand years, have hurt his sister."

It was daylight. I could no longer bear the horrid odor that rose to the fresh summer sky, or the sight of the bodies. I ran back to my house.

A few hours later, I decided that I was leaving. I would find my father. I would take one of the little sailboats, and if there was no wind that day, I would row. I was going in to Charleston.

The sun was falling; it was the perfect time to start the long journey. Night would save me from the heat, and the lighthouse would guide me. At first, my plan was perfect. I caught a bit of a breeze, and the darkness fell, but the air was balmy and I was fine. Then, I felt the first thump against the boat. Then another.

And, in that balmy breeze, with the sea so gentle and the stars blazing in the sky above, *the thing* crawled aboard. It was Johnny. For a moment, his eyes were dull and dead. He came toward me and I scrambled swiftly, ready to leap overboard. He caught my shoulders, his strength incredible. He opened his mouth, aiming for my throat.

Then he paused. To my astonishment, tears came to his dead eyes. "I don't want to, I don't want to, oh, God, I remember you . . ."

"Johnny, let me go, for the love of God, Johnny," I begged.

I felt the boat bump again.

Rescue, I thought, somehow, rescue.

Johnny jerked around. I looked past him.

It was another of the things.

I looked hard. My heart sank. It was one of *them*.

And it was my father.

He leaped at Johnny, rocking the small boat precariously, and I thought he had come to save me. But he wrenched Johnny from me, and then, I saw *his* eyes.

Dead eyes. Once, a dancing brown shade. Now, dead.

"Father, no!" I screamed in terror and misery. But he would have bitten down upon me, ripping and tearing, if Johnny hadn't pulled him away. Johnny was still crying, and suddenly, my father was crying, too. But still, they weren't battling to save me.

They were fighting over their prey.

I was desperate. I leaped off the small boat, though I knew that they could swim. I tried freeing myself from my cumbersome skirt and boots while they fought, unaware that I was gone. Then I set out for the island. I was a good swimmer, but still, I had come far from shore.

I was crying myself, gulping too much water, fighting the numbness of terror. I had left the island, and I had done so with the Colt, but little good that did me now. I'd never had a sword, nor had my father. I had to pray that I could swim hard enough, fast enough.

My exhausted limbs could barely continue moving, but I began to believe that I might make it.

Then, I felt the tug upon my ankle. And gasping for air, I went down. In the dark, murky seawater, I could barely see. But it was Johnny. Dead eyes blank, wide open, blank. No more tears. No sign of life or memory.

He took my shoulders. I was done in. I closed my eyes; he would rip out my throat. It wouldn't last long.

But I was ripped away from him. No matter; hope didn't even float in my soul. It would be my father, claiming his portion of the kill.

But I wasn't ripped to shreds. I was tossed back. I fell hard and realized I was almost on the little patch of beach south of the harbor area. I could stand, and I staggered to my feet. Then I saw Brent. He swung his sword, and Johnny's head was swiftly severed from his body, and lost to the waves. The headless body stood for a minute, then fell. Brent turned to me. He shouted, and lifted his sword. I thought he meant to kill me; that he believed that I had been bitten, infected, and that he meant to kill me, as well. But he strode past me.

"Don't look, Jules, don't look!" he shouted.

I didn't. I winced. I heard the plop of the head, and then the splash of the body, and I knew that my father was at peace as well.

Soaking, Brent and I staggered from the water together.

"I told you," he said sadly. "Something wasn't right with Johnny."

Federal troops came the next day; the incident was quickly over. At that point in history, none of us had the energy to argue much when the murders on Douglas Island were blamed upon the horror and stress of war.

Brent and I left soon after. We are a strange couple, but we do well enough. We manage in life, and like other couples, we sleep together at night.

Unlike other couples, we both sleep with swords at our sides. Johnny is at rest. But God knows who else might come marching home.

*

New York Times and *USA Today* bestselling author **HEATHER GRAHAM** was born somewhere in Europe and kidnapped by gypsies when she was a small child. She went on to join the Romanian circus as a trapeze artist and lion tamer. When the circus came to South Florida, she stayed, discovering that she preferred to be a shark- and gator-trainer.

Not really.

Heather is the child of Scottish and Irish immigrants who met and married in Chicago, and moved to South Florida, where she has spent her life. She majored in theater arts at the University of South Florida. After a stint of several years in dinner theater, backup vocals, and bartending, she stayed home after the birth of her third child and began to write. She has written more than 150 novels and novellas, including category, suspense, historical romance, vampire fiction, time travel, occult, horror, and Christmas family fare.

She is pleased to have been published in approximately twenty-five languages, and has had more than seventy-five million books in print, and is grateful every day of her life that she writes for a living.

On the Train

REBECCA CANTRELL

Joachim Rosen shifted on the wooden bench. He was lucky to have a seat at all. Most prisoners had to lean against the sides of the train car or sit on the floor.

He pulled his tattered striped jacket closer around himself, folding his arms over the bright yellow triangle. Despite the afternoon sun, he shivered, but the presence of the man leaning against the side of the car next to him weighed more heavily on his mind than the cold. He looked familiar, and he did not want to meet anyone from his old life.

Out of the corner of his eye Joachim noticed the man's pink triangle. The familiar face belonged to a homosexual. He avoided the man's gaze.

"I know you from before." The man pursed his lips.

Joachim tensed, but ignored him.

The man inhaled slowly. "I'm Herman Schmidt. We met at El Dorado on the Motz Strasse, in Berlin. Ernst Vogel was scheduled to sing. Remember?"

"No." Joachim watched the white puff of air that accompanied the word. "Never been to Berlin, except to get to Oranienburg." He glanced around the car. Had he told anyone of his shop in Berlin?

Herman stared at Joachim's yellow triangle. "I didn't realize you were Jewish."

He straightened on the bench. "Always was."

"Being different didn't used to be so difficult."

Both sat silently. Joachim listened to the clatter of the train's wheels and the high scream of the wind. The metal door clanked against the side of the car. Perhaps it had fallen off once and been refastened too loosely. Through the high window fragile black limbs of bare winter trees appeared and disappeared, each tree a sign that they were one step closer to their final destination.

"My name was in someone's address book." Herman's voice cut through the wind. "Some imbeciles didn't even know enough to throw them away."

Joachim flinched. If informers heard Herman, it could cost Joachim his life. "I don't know what you mean."

"I'm certain you don't," Herman said sarcastically. "Where are we going?"

He lied. "Don't know. Another camp. They're all the same."

Herman picked at his ragged cuticles. "I've never been to a camp. What are they like?"

Joachim looked at him for the first time. Herman suddenly seemed plump and healthy in the clear, cold afternoon light stabbing through the window. "Bad. For you, even worse."

Herman pointed to his pink triangle. "Because of this?"

"It's the worst kind to have." Joachim glanced involuntarily down the car at the bowed, bald heads of the other prisoners. No one paid them attention.

"You've been very careful, I see." Herman twisted the right corner of his mouth into a smile.

"I'm here because I'm Jewish."

Herman studied his face. "We could jump the guards when they stop the train. I'm still strong."

The man on Joachim's right shifted on the bench. Joachim froze. What if he overheard them?

"They have guns," Joachim whispered. "I've never seen anyone escape like that. But I've seen men die trying. It's reckless."

Herman sighed. "I was never very good at being careful."

Joachim stared blankly at the sliding door in front of him. Rust had bled deep lines into the metal. Loneliness howled through him like the wind through the open door. "I've always been good at it."

Herman ran his palms along his cheeks, as if he just woke. "Good at what?"

"Being careful."

Herman slid to a sitting position with his back to the door and wrinkled his nose. The smell of so many unwashed men crowded into the car obviously bothered him.

"It's not a simple thing to do," Joachim said.

Herman embraced his round knees. "I should be in Berlin. Studying for my degree in engineering or reading the paper and thanking the Führer for ridding the country of vermin like you. Of vermin like me."

Joachim scratched a flea bite on his shrunken calf. It itched, but he tried not to think about it.

"Then I'd have dinner with my landlady, Frau Biedekin. She's an exquisite cook. We'd have potatoes, smothered with butter. We'd have sauerbraten, since today is Sunday. For dessert, let's see—"

Joachim's stomach clamped into a tight knot. "Stop it!"

Herman snorted. "Is it more than you can stomach?"

Joachim glared at him until Herman stopped laughing.

"That's the only way you'll get it," Herman said. "By dreaming."

"Dreaming is not," Joachim hesitated, searching for the right word, "careful."

"I believe I mentioned that I was no good at being careful."

Joachim shrugged, the coarse material of his jacket scraping across his shoulders. "Dream, then. Just quietly."

"If you can't escape from them in dreams, they've defeated you."

"What do you know? You've never even been to a camp," Joachim said. "Tell me about dreams in a month, friend."

"If I can't tell you about dreams then, I hope to have the sense to end it."

Joachim drew in a sharp breath.

"Life," Herman said as he stood, "is more than mere survival."

Joachim shook his head. "Not right now."

"No!" Herman's voice echoed off the sides of the car. Several prisoners swiveled their heads toward him. No one spoke.

Joachim pretended to be asleep. He sat with his chin against his chest, swaying with the movement of the train, listening to the wind whine, and watching shadows cast inside the car by passing trees.

"You know it's about more than simple survival," Herman finally whispered at Joachim. "You were in Berlin with us. You remember good food and love and music and dance."

Joachim gripped his bony knees, knuckles whitening. "I wasn't there."

Herman studied Joachim. "Do you want to know what became of the rest of the group? Francis? Ernst? Kurt?"

Joachim inhaled. One, two, three times. "I don't know any Francis or Ernst or Kurt."

Herman stared at his own soft hands. "Not even Kurt? Everyone knows Kurt, even the Gestapo. They got my name from his address book. I'm surprised yours wasn't in there, too."

A hot pain stabbed Joachim's neck. *Relax,* he ordered himself.

"I saw you together." Herman pointed a pudgy finger at him. "Everyone was together with Kurt."

He concentrated on relaxing his muscles, despite the cold and Herman's voice.

"Remember how graceful Kurt was?" Herman's hands sketched arcs in the air. "He should have been a dancer, not a soldier. He flowed when he moved, like a cat."

Joachim clenched his right fist, the one that Herman could not see. "I don't know any Kurt," he answered in a level voice.

"That wasn't you holding his hand at El Dorado that February? Or was it Silhouette? One of those clubs. Weren't they wonderful? And the pianos. I love piano music, although I never learned to play myself."

Joachim said nothing. His mother had forced him to practice two hours a day.

"It's a wonderful thing to make beautiful sounds with your fingers."

Joachim shifted his gaze to the floor; the slats were coated with about a centimeter of freezing mud and criss-crossed with ridges created by his shoes. "It would do you no good now."

"Just knowing would be enough." Herman scratched his back against the door. "I could play the songs in my head and beat time on the ground."

Joachim wanted to warn him. "Will that help when you're hungry? Or tired? Or cold?"

Herman nodded. "If I can feel the music, I won't think about my stomach, or my body."

Joachim pulled his arms tighter around himself. His elbows cut into his hands, almost numbing them. "You will."

"I won't."

"You've never been there." Joachim crossed his legs, savoring the thin ribbon of warmth where his right leg lay on top of his left. "You can't know."

"I don't need to know what it's like there to know myself."

"You won't last long. Your kind never does."

"Is that why you're afraid that the people here will recognize you? Are you afraid they'll realize your trian-gle should be as pink as mine?"

Joachim prayed that the man on his right slept. That everyone in his end of the car slept. "No, it shouldn't. I'm Jewish, but I'm no fag." He stressed "fag," trying to make it sound hard and ugly.

"Wasn't Kurt the most exquisite fag?" Herman's voice caressed the word. "But not after the Gestapo was through with him."

Joachim's stomach cramped.

"They ruined those delicate cheekbones. He could barely walk when they were done." Herman watched Joachim, a gleam in his eye. "I think he escaped to Switzerland."

Joachim's stomach relaxed. The car rattled along.

"Where are they sending us?" Herman asked again.

"Dachau, I think," Joachim said, angry at himself for not lying this time. He'd also heard they might be going to Auschwitz, but he didn't tell Herman that.

"Dachau is only a few hours by train from Constance, from Switzerland."

"You wouldn't be allowed on a train."

"So I'd walk." Herman rubbed his palm over the rough stubble on his shaved head.

"A few hundred kilometers in the snow? Anyone who sees you will turn you in. Or shoot you. You are the enemy now."

"I'd reach the border."

"The Swiss won't let you in."

"I won't go through the checkpoint." Herman smiled. "I'd lift a boat and row across Lake Constance."

"Nazis guard the boats. You'd never make it."

"What a way to die." Herman sighed. "Free and on the water."

Joachim stirred on the bench. He had loved to swim as a boy and had been the best swimmer in his school. "You shouldn't think of dying," he said to the door. "It's not . . . careful. You have to be careful."

"Have you ever had Swiss chocolate?" Herman asked.

Joachim clasped his hands in his lap.

"I can almost smell it," Herman continued. "Thick dark chocolate with bitter marzipan."

"Or with—" Joachim did not finish his sentence, surprised that he had even begun it.

"Peppermint," Herman finished. "Crisp peppermint."

Joachim pushed his chin against his chest. His shoulders were taut and raised, and he forced them down. He would not think about chocolate.

Herman swallowed. "I wanted to go to school in Zürich. A friend of mine went. Came back in thirty-three as a Nazi. I was stunned."

Joachim raised his head. "It's hard to lose a friend that way."

Herman searched Joachim's face. "It's hard to lose a friend *any* way."

Joachim tried to imagine the friendship he could have had with Herman in Berlin. Then someone farther down the car coughed, and he forced his mind to go blank.

Herman rubbed his hands together. "When do we arrive in Dachau?"

"I don't know. Try to sleep."

Herman almost fell when the train abruptly slowed to climb a steep grade. "I could run faster than this train."

Joachim laughed, quietly and cynically. "What good is that? Do you want to run to the next car? Get there earlier?"

Herman's words tumbled out. "We can get out of that door. It's not wired on very well. We could jump off the train and no one would notice."

Joachim's stomach clenched again. His hands trembled. He could not remember when he had been so terrified. Even when the Nazis came for him, he was not so afraid. "The Nazis notice everything."

"Not everything," Herman said, staring at Joachim's yellow triangle. "Not everything."

"If they catch you, they will kill you. Slowly."

Herman smiled. Suddenly he looked very old, and Joachim flinched away from him. "Aren't we dying slowly now?"

Joachim thought of the cold outside, the Nazis who were sure to be around with rifles, the incredible distance to the Swiss border. They would never make it. Never.

He spoke to his worn wooden shoes. "Eventually the war will end, and Germany will lose. They will set us free then."

"Maybe," Herman said. "Eventually."

Joachim stared at a brown stain on top of one shoe. *Blood?* he wondered. "It won't be too long."

"Are you daring to dream?" Herman mocked him as he turned to the door. "You shouldn't do that. It's not *careful*."

Joachim's voice trembled. "I don't want you to go."

"By this time next week we could be in Switzerland, with Kurt."

"Or we could be dead."

"Or we could be dead," Herman repeated. "We could be dead anyway. At least this way *we* get to decide."

Muscles tightened in the backs of Joachim's legs. He wanted to stand. But he did not know what kind of death waited outside. It would be a death, probably a sooner death than awaited him at Dachau. A sooner death.

Herman dropped his warm hand onto the crown of Joachim's head. "I'm leaving. Are you coming with me?"

Joachim shook his head. He needed time. He hated his cowardly survival instinct.

"Kurt didn't escape to Switzerland," Herman said abruptly. He withdrew his hand, the spot he'd warmed now colder than the rest of Joachim's head. "Kurt died."

Joachim's stomach convulsed. His voice almost broke when he spoke, but he brought it under control. "I don't know any Kurt and I don't care what he did."

He gazed into Herman's eyes, surprised that they were such a vivid blue. They reminded him of a mountain lake he swam across as a child. Joachim dropped his eyes first.

"Be careful then, Joachim Rosen."

Herman forced the door out, grunting as his arms shook with the strain. Slowly, the wire stretched. Joachim admired his strength. He could never force the door like that.

"Good-bye." Herman dropped out of the train into the snow.

For the first time since they took him, Joachim wept. He did not cry with the loud, wet wails of his childhood. He sat and wept the dry, silent sobs of a new grief.

The prisoner next to him reached over and put a cold hand on his arm. Joachim slowly brought himself under control.

The train jerked to a stop and knocked him to the floor. He pulled himself back onto the bench. Whispers ran the length of the car. Why were they stopping?

Were they in Dachau already? Herman had escaped at the last instant. Joachim tried to imagine him rowing across Lake Constance to a land filled with chocolate, but instead pictured him bleeding in the snow.

The familiar aroma of cigarette smoke wafted in. Behind him several prisoners inhaled the smell greedily, but Joachim shrank back. That odor meant soldiers.

The car door jerked open, and Joachim threw up an arm to shield his eyes from the scalding light. Dark profiles of three soldiers with guns loomed in the doorway, a prisoner sagged between two others. They heaved a body in and slammed the door.

Joachim alone crossed to the inert figure, giving up his precious seat on the bench. He knelt and rolled him over. Dim light from the window illuminated a battered face. Herman.

Joachim shook him, thinking of Kurt's beautiful face broken by the Gestapo. Herman's head lolled on his shoulders. He looked dead.

Joachim put a finger under Herman's nostrils to check for breath just as the car jolted back into motion. Off balance, he fell across Herman's body. Herman's heart beat against Joachim's chest. Joachim smiled. He lay there a moment, remembering other men and other nights.

He pulled himself to a sitting position and peeled off his own jacket, shivering. He wiped blood from Herman's face with its tattered sleeve, tracing the angle of his cheekbone. Herman moaned.

Joachim's shaking fingers unbuttoned Herman's jacket. He lifted Herman with one hand and pulled his jacket off, wincing at the darkening bruises on his ribs.

Another prisoner put a skeletal hand on Joachim's naked arm. "Careful," he said. "You don't want to be pink at Dachau."

Joachim squeezed his hand.

The prisoner pulled back. Joachim finished switching jackets with Herman. Now his own jacket bore a pink triangle, Herman's a yellow one.

The prisoner turned away.

Joachim cradled Herman's head in his lap until the train stopped hours later. The doors opened onto darkness.

"*Raus!*" yelled the guards. The prisoners stumbled out.

The guards marched through the weary prisoners, separating them into two long lines. They sent Joachim to one line, Herman to another. Joachim looked at the pink triangle on the man next to him. Herman was safe.

But then Joachim noticed the other triangles in his line: red, black, and purple, but no yellow. Herman stood in a line of all Jews.

Joachim read the station name off a sign. Not Dachau at all. Not a work camp.

The sign read Oswiecim. He closed his eyes. The German name for Oswiecim was Auschwitz. A death camp. He smelled sweetish smoke from the crematorium.

Joachim opened his eyes and searched for Herman. Herman's blue eyes met his. Herman nodded. He knew, too.

Joachim's line moved toward a convoy of trucks, Herman's into the darkness. Joachim realized that the yellow triangles were never coming back. He pulled his jacket closer around his thin frame, one hand lingering on the pink triangle. Strains of Wagner drifted through the cold air surrounding both of them.

*

REBECCA CANTRELL writes the critically acclaimed Hannah Vogel mystery series set in 1930s Berlin, including *A Trace of Smoke* and *A Night of Long Knives*. She lives in Hawaii with her husband, son, and too many geckoes to count. For more details, see www.rebeccacantrell.com.

Children's Day

KELLI STANLEY

Golden Gate International Exposition
Treasure Island, San Francisco Bay, 1939

Shorty was complaining about the grift around Midget Village when Miranda saw the clown. Sad eyes. No smile. The Gayway wasn't always gay, even for a clown and the little blonde girl with him, waiting in line for cotton candy.

Too many kids, too many clowns. Monday, April 3, Children's Day, and Miranda wondered why the fuck she'd come back to the fair on her one day off. Maybe because she had nowhere else to go.

"You take it up with the bulls?" she asked Shorty.

The little man shook his head, the red light of the cigarette dancing at the end of his mouth.

"You know how it is. Don't take us serious. Come in for a belly laugh and drift over to Sally Rand's or Artists and Models for a tweak of some tit. Christ Almighty, I can't blame 'em for that, but we need protection, not a goddamn babysitter."

Miranda nodded, looking over his head. The clown was crouched at the side of the refreshment booth, talking to the kid, pink sweat dripping on his dirty white collar. Puffs of spun candy hid her face. A stout woman in a green plaid coat smiled at them through her peanuts.

Miranda dropped her Chesterfield and rubbed it out in the dirt next to a wadded-up napkin from Threlkeld's Scones. "I'll do what I can. I don't have much pull with the cops—"

"You got pull where it counts, sister. You got in the papers, you got your shamus license, you caught your boss's killer. That's enough for Leland Cutler, and it's enough for Shorty Glick."

She bent down to shake the midget's hand. "I'll do what I can. Be seeing you, Shorty."

He nodded, put the ten-gallon hat back on, hoisted up the chaps and kid's gun belt with dignity, and waddled into the compound. Singer's Midgets, carted around from sawdust heap to sawdust heap, stared at, laughed at, gee whiz, they're tiny, Bob, just like kids. Fuck you, too, lady. How's that for kid talk?

She walked down the fairway, leaned against the wall of Ripley's Odditorium and lit another Chesterfield, staring down at the line waiting for Sally Rand's Nude Ranch. Sally's girls needed protection as much as the midgets, and the only kind they'd get from the cops came with a price. Miranda just charged money.

Women were clutching their hats against the cold Bay wind, and some Spanish flamenco dancers from the Alta California exhibit huddled, laughing, in front of the fortune teller. Miranda pressed herself against the stucco wall, closing her eyes. No fortunes left, not for Spain. Not for Miranda. Fortunes meant future, and she didn't think about the future anymore, not since '37. Johnny wasn't in it.

Poor, tired Spain, poor tired world, tired, so tired of war, and yet more coming, more fucking wars, more corpses, white flesh bloated and ruptured, rotting in farm house wells, mangled bodies on the streets of Madrid. No future, no fortune. No Johnny. Just the carnival. Listen to the calliope and it'll all go away.

Step right up, folks, one thin dime, neon and fishnets, girls in G-strings, babies in incubators. Welcome to the Gayway, Leland Cutler's Pageant of the Pacific, pride of 1939, and who gives a fuck if New York has a world's fair, too.

She blinked, watching the cigarette ash burn closer, Laughing Sal's mechanical cackle drifting on the wind. No treasure on Treasure Island. Just another world's fair. Another goddamn calliope.

She walked back again toward Midget Village. The line at the refreshment stand was shorter. The clown and the kid, still in sight, headed toward Heather Row. But the clown was pulling the kid's arm, the girl crying, upset. Fat lady in green nowhere to be seen.

Miranda gulped the cigarette, nicotine hitting her lungs. Burnett hadn't taught her much. Wiggle when you walk, Miranda, you know how to be an escort. Fuck being a detective. Wrong again, Burnett, you bastard, rest in fucking peace.

They all needed help, midgets and Sally's girls and sideshow freaks and monkeys in race cars. She dodged two sailors and a marine, and hurried toward the clown.

You pays your money and you takes your choice.

Couple of fraternity boys pushed an elderly couple by in the fifty-cent chairs, almost running down Miranda. The clown pulled the kid toward La Plaza Avenue, rounding the corner by the Owl Drug Store and Ghirardelli Chocolate.

A sharpie in a cheap suit pried himself away from a souvenir booth, eyes on Miranda's snug navy jacket, as if looking would make it go away. She tried to side-step him, but he jumped in front, blocking her.

"Lady, why the hurry? A looker like you—"

"Get out of my way—"

He stroked his thin mustache with one hand, and put his other one on her left shoulder, straight arm, sliding up and down, out and in.

"Sally's that way, girlie—you could make a bund—"

Miranda shoved his hand off her breast with her right, backhanding him hard in the face with her left. He tumbled, off balance, and hit the dirt.

By the time she heard the angry "Fucking bitch!" the clown and the girl had disappeared.

Ghirardelli Building, sign of the giant parrot. It perched above the door, hawking chocolate malts and candy. Café sat one hundred, about twenty people were waiting for seats. No clowns. A lot of children.

A blonde in a hat and brown jumper was leaning over the candy belt, watching the chocolate bonbons. Miranda pushed her way through. Not her.

Eight people, understaffed, handing out samples to quiet the kids. Five-year-olds all looked alike.

Miranda's stomach tightened, started to hurt. She headed for the Owl, checked the lunch counter, toy department, searched the aisles.

Too late.

The White Star Tuna Restaurant was quiet, almost empty. Found a table by one of the windows, stared out at the enormous sparkling walls of Vacationland until the tuna-tomato salad and coffee arrived.

It was too early for tuna, too early for the Chicken of the Sea star on top of the bright round building, too early for the "Romance of Tuna" story that hung on the walls and filled a page in the takeaway souvenir menu.

Early didn't mean much to Miranda. Late night at Sally's, boyfriend trouble for one of the girls. Now she'd lost the clown. Tuna romance was just the fucking ticket.

Back and forth, back and forth across the knots of people. She looked down at her cup. Kaleidoscope of black. Maybe she was wrong.

Around and around, spinning, shiny, colors too dark. Five years old, first encounter with fingers in wrong places. Hard fingers, hard laps, persistent. Little girl, bouncing on an old professor's lap, friend of her father. Bouncing hard.

Around again to ten. Old Hatchett asleep, father away, drunk or at an academic conference or both. Escape the dungeon, get out, get out to the streets. Muddy San Francisco, horse shit on Market Street, ten years after the quake. Man in a dirty suit, sudden smile, all in the eyes. Eyes that scared her, hands that scared her, come on, little girl, I'll give you a present. Don't you want to play?

Fourteen and she learned how to fight, how to bite a finger, how to squirm out of a grasp, learned where to look and what to look for, curious, but not enough to return to the professor's lap, or the Santa Claus with his own bag of toys. Around and around she goes, and where she stops . . .

The kaleidoscope dissolved, carousel no longer turning. No farther, not today.

Miranda drained her coffee, shoved the tuna away un-
touched, and left half a dollar on the yellow Formica
table top. Walked back to the Plaza and lit a Chesterfield, still scanning the crowds. Maybe she'd been wrong.

A uniformed cop was walking up from the Court of
Pacifica, heading toward the Gayway, nodded when he
saw Miranda.

"You busy, Corbie?"

She inhaled the cigarette, blew a stream of smoke behind her. "It's my day off. Why?"

His brown eyes were somber. "Lady says her daughter's been kidnapped. We're looking for a clown."

Silk dress from Magnin's under a shoulder-length fur,
head of a dead animal dangling from the back. Gloved
hands. Whiff of My Sin when she sobbed.

She was a little older than Miranda, about thirty-five.
Brown hair, more than a touch of henna.

Grogan looked at her, his mouth curled around a cigar, then back over at Miranda.

"You here to add the woman's touch, Corbie, or because you got something?"

She blew a smoke ring, watched it float behind his left
ear. "How about the human touch, Grogan—or is that
beyond you?"

He shrugged, eyes on the victim. One of the uniforms
coughed.

"Says she turned her back to buy her kid some cotton
candy at the Gayway, and next thing she knew the kid
was gone. The kid's name is Susie. I thought Donlevy
gave you the low-down."

"What he knew of it." She pulled Grogan's chair from his desk and sat next to the woman.

"Any enemies, Mrs. Hampton? Demands for money, threats?"

The face that jerked toward Miranda was sharp, still pretty. "N-no. Not that I know—and please, don't tell my husband. He'll—Geoff is so impetuous, I'm afraid he'll—don't tell him!" She gasped, the sable quivering.

Miranda ground the Chesterfield into the arm of Grogan's chair. Waited for Mrs. Hampton to breathe again.

"Did Susie ever run away—or get lost?"

"No. Please, please, just find her. I don't even care if you find that—the monster who took her, just find my little girl."

Miranda leaned forward. "Exactly what happened?"

"I—I told them already. Sergeant, why do I have to—"

"—you don't have to do nothing, Mrs. Hampton. This here's Miranda Corbie. She's what they call a private eye in them fairy tales people read."

The woman held the handkerchief up to her face.

"Are you going to help get my Susie back?"

"I need the truth, Mrs. Hampton—in your own words."

The woman took a deep, rattling breath, closed her eyes for a moment. "Cotton candy. Susie likes it. She just turned five last week, I—I was looking for a smaller bill—the man at the counter didn't have change for a twenty—"

Miranda looked up, exchanged glances with Grogan.

"—and by the time I sorted it all out, I turned around and she was—was gone."

"Where does the clown come in?"

She closed her eyes again, shaking her head, hand to her heart. "He'd been following us. I'd noticed him, he'd made Susie laugh earlier, and we threw him a dollar. I thought he was just, you know, performing as those people do, but I can see now that he was following us."

Miranda pulled out the pack of Chesterfields, offered one to Mrs. Hampton. She shook her head. Miranda's lighter sputtered, and one of the uniforms stepped forward with a lit match, while another one sniggered. Miranda grabbed his hand for a moment, looked up, and said, "Thanks."

She inhaled, leaning back in Grogan's chair. Said it casually. "So you didn't actually see him take Susie."

Lois Hampton fixed her large brown eyes on Miranda's, all reproach and a mother's dignity, surrounded by the faint odor of Choward's Violets and Sen-Sen.

"Miss Corbie—I didn't need to see him. I know. My daughter's in danger." She bent forward, placing a gloved hand on Miranda's sleeve. "Please—please help me."

Rick wasn't at the Press Building. Miranda hung up the payphone, watching husbands pull wives into the Ford Building. Hit the receiver, asked the operator to try the *San Francisco News*. Shook out another Chesterfield from the crumpled pack.

"Rick—Miranda. I've got something."

He paused for a moment then, laughed, Irish lilt always so goddamn irritating.

"It's not like you ever call and ask me over for a drink. What is it? Need some help with that shiny new PI license of yours?"

She struck a match on Ford's wall.

"You were over two weeks ago."

"Don't worry, honey, you don't have to ration me. What is it?"

"Little girl kidnapped by a clown."

He whistled, and she held the phone away.

"Don't fucking whistle. Woman's name is Lois Hampton. Lives in the city. Five-year-old daughter, blonde. Susie. Husband is Geoff, they've got money. I need you to look her up."

Silence, while Rick scribbled. "What about the clown?"

"He's not a clown by now. I tried to tell Grogan to search the restrooms, but he's still out looking for circus acts. Just check Lois Hampton."

He hesitated. "Miranda—"

"Yes?"

"—should I look for—you know—"

"Molesters? Rapists? Another Albert Fish in a clown costume?" Her voice was heavy, and her hand shook when she brought the cigarette up to her mouth. "Check everything. I'll call you back in half an hour."

"OK."

She hung up the phone, taking a last shuddering inhale of the Chesterfield. Squinted up at the giant National Cash Register, the two-foot numbers marking attendance. Twenty-three thousand and counting. A lot of them five-year-olds.

Children's Day. Four hundred fucking acres of it.

She lost them at La Plaza. Nearest restroom was across the road at Vacationland. He'd sneak into the ladies room, use the girl as an excuse.

Clean-shaven, late thirties, dressed oddly. Maybe baggy pants and a souvenir shirt. Unless he'd planned it, and was hiding more than a trick hanky in his clown suit.

A guide stood outside, buttons still shiny on the uniform. College kid.

She asked: "You see any clowns this morning?"

He rolled his eyes. "Lady, I could tell you—"

"Don't. This one kidnapped a little girl."

Jaw dropped. "Geez, lady. I've seen maybe three or four. All the kids, you know. Children's Day."

"Any come in here?"

"Maybe. I've been moving around."

She headed inside the curve of the building. Women's and men's restrooms, side by side, across from the cafeteria and barbershop.

Attendant a slow, stooped woman with a Russian accent. *Da,* there was a clown. *Da,* he come in with a child. She stroked the dollar bill like it was a pet.

The other one, younger, dark-haired, lounge help. Another dollar. Yes, miss, told him it ain't proper. No mother, I says, and he says she's sick in bed, and he's off work, needs to wash up. Washed up right there in the sink. Felt sorry for him, miss. I ain't done nothin' wrong.

Another dollar, help the guilt along.

Little girl was crying, miss. Hungry. Talked about doughnuts. What's this all about? I ain't done nothing wrong, miss, I can't lose my job, gotta feed my own kids. No, don't remember what he looked like without the face on. I ain't done nothing wrong. He was just an average Joe, miss. Just an average Joe.

Miranda ran out of the powder room, the door banging behind her.

Doughnuts meant the Gayway, Maxwell House building, hot coffee and crullers, the Doughnut Tower's fat red neon stripes slicing through the fog.

Couple of hundred in the restaurant, maybe forty kids. No little blonde girl. No clown, ex or otherwise. No luck. Spilled out like coffee, good to the last drop.

Miranda checked the Penny Arcade next door, then up and down the strip, past the Glass Blowers and Loop-A-Swing, the diving bell and flea circus. Her ankle twisted on a souvenir kewpie doll dirtied from sawdust and cigarette butts. She stopped, breathing hard, picked it up. Maybe from a kid in Children's Village, the Gay-way's official nanny service, complete with on-duty nurse and riding ponies. Perfect for when the parents ogled nipples at Sally Rand's.

She stared at the painted face. Midget Village, Chinese Village, Children's Village. Too many goddamn villages. The clown would be in the big villages by now, San Francisco or Oakland. He'd gotten by her, gotten by them all.

Miranda walked to a phone by the Fun House and dialed Rick. Set the kewpie doll on the phone ledge.

"Sanders? You got anything?"

"Yeah. Half a goddamn hour, Miranda—"

"Fucking tell me."

He grunted. "Lois Hampton. You said the kid is five, right?"

"Turned five last week. Why?"

"She married Geoff Hampton, finance attorney, four years ago. Methodist service. No parents for the bride. She worked at Emporium—probably counter girl, from what the society column left out."

"So she married up. And the kid's not his."

"Or is, but nobody waited for the license."

Miranda tapped her second-to-the-last cigarette out of the Chesterfield package. "What else?"

"What the hell do you want for thirty minutes? No child killers. So far."

She took out the Fair lighter, lit, and inhaled, blowing smoke and watching it drift by the Headless Girl stand.

"See if you can find a birth certificate for Susie. And call Whitney—the concession director. Lean on him for a list of clowns working Treasure Island today."

Rick hesitated. "Listen, I want her found as much as you do. But I can't spend all day—"

"Yeah, I know. Give it another hour, Rick. OK?"

He grumbled. "Yeah, Miranda. Don't I always?"

She hung up the phone, staring at the two giant Ferris wheels turning side by side. Shielded her eyes to make sure. A little blonde girl and a dark-haired man were sitting in a top car, laughing.

Shoved her way to the front of the line, eyes on Susie, insults behind her.

The operator leered, all teeth. "Your money's worth, missy. One dime. I'll make sure you get a good, long ride."

Miranda showed him her ID. "Stop the goddamn wheel."

Face red, he pulled one of the long handles. She leaned on his shoulder, the line behind her starting to whisper.

"Step aside when you get to the car with a little blonde girl. I'll tell you when."

He nodded, easing the cars to a stop, one at a time, one at a time. Three more to go before Susie.

A fat lady in the car before them had difficulty getting out. Susie's hat was off. The clown's hand stroked her hair, greasepaint still filling the cracks in his face.

Their car swung into line. Miranda poked the operator in the back with the kewpie doll, and he opened the gate, got out of the way. The clown gave Susie a small push and she walked forward. Miranda stepped in front of her, held out the doll.

"This is for you, Susie."

The little girl stared at her, confused. Miranda grabbed Susie's hand, eyes raised to the clown. He looked from one to the other, panic twisting his face. Then he jumped off the platform, running into the Gayway crowds while a woman behind them screamed.

It took three minutes to find a cop. She gave him Susie, ran past Greenwich Village toward the opposite end of the zone. Where the hell could a clown go to be inconspicuous? Except he wasn't a clown anymore.

She stopped in the middle of the grounds, breathing hard. Susie was safe. Not harmed. But the clown . . .

She looked up at the complex called Children's Village. And took out her last cigarette.

He was slapping on greasepaint when she walked in the room. Jumped up, shrank against the wall, eyes large without the makeup, focused on the .22 in her hand. Still sad.

"Please, please, lady. I was just trying to see her. She don't even know I'm her father."

She stared at him, smoke from the Chesterfield curling toward the cracked mirror.

"Some fucking father. You expect me to believe you? You kidnapped a little girl, goddamn it—"

"There's proof. Loie's got it. She showed it to me. Before—before she got married."

He wiped his forehead, his hand shaking. Sank slowly into the chair, the bare yellow lightbulb throwing shadows across his face.

"Made me promise never to see her. Susie's chance. Loie's chance. My little girl could have the good things . . . I ain't never gonna be able to buy her what he can. And

I kept my promise. I ain't seen her since she was a baby."

Miranda gestured with the .22. "Keep your hands on the counter. I saw *Stella Dallas,* and it plays better with a woman. You broke your goddamn promise. Why? Got religion, all of a sudden? Or did you figure you'd be Daddy for a day?"

Face, mouth, voice, pleading, looking at her, not the gun. "Loie brought her here, to the Village. I make balloons for the kids . . . Loie was leaving for Sally's, didn't recognize me with the face and all. I stopped her, asked about Susie, but she was worried 'bout people seein' us together. So's I took Susie when she left, tried to—to spend a little time with her. Knew they'd probably look for me as soon as Loie figured it out, washed my face, took my street clothes with me."

Miranda blew a stream of smoke toward the cheap pine wardrobe in the corner, the pistol steady and pointed at the clown.

"What were you going do with her? Tell me that— what were you going to do with her?"

"I weren't gonna keep her, lady. I just wanted to see my little girl. Give her some fun, something to remember her old man by. She said she likes cotton candy. Please don't lose me my job. I like kids. I'm good with kids. Ask Anderson—didn't he tell you? Didn't he tell you I'm good with—"

"Fuck the job. Worry about San Quentin."

Face whiter than makeup, shadows under the eyes, dark pools. Hands trembling on the counter. The Tower of the Sun carillon played the hour, "Flow gently, sweet Afton, disturb not her dream."

His voice croaked, reedy, strong, sure.

"All right. Go ahead. I'm not sorry for tryin' to see Susie. I'm glad I did it. I'd do it again. And at least she'll know her old man was willin' to pay the price for seein' her."

Miranda took a long drag on the Chesterfield, studying his face. He met her eyes, breathing hard, defiant. *Disturb not her dream . . .*

She said: "Put some makeup on."

She thought about Susie, and about what Susie would want. But fuck, Susie was five years old, and it didn't matter what she'd want. Children's Day was make-believe, and only once a year.

At least she had a father who loved her. That put her ahead. Put her ahead of Miranda.

She called Lois Hampton, calmed her down. Met with her privately, lunching at the Women's Club, Susie still holding the kewpie doll. Suggested new terms for Susie's daddy, especially with Geoff away so much. No, no publicity, Mrs. Hampton. No publicity.

Called Rick. Got a liverwurst sandwich at Maxwell House, walked to the Owl for more cigarettes. Finally strolled over to Midget Village, watching Shorty twirl a six gun for some kids and their parents, the late afternoon sun stretching across the bay, the midgets making long shadows in the sawdust of the corral.

A cop ambled by, stood next to her.

"Hear you found the missing girl, Corbie."

"Yeah."

"Lost the kidnapper, though?"

Miranda shrugged, opened a new package of Chesterfields. "I don't know, Gillespie. Sometimes a clown is just a clown."

He stared at her. "What the hell does that mean?"

She blew a smoke ring, watching it rise high on the bay wind, drifting above the Gayway.

"It means Happy Children's Day."

He shrugged his shoulders, and moved on.

*

KELLI STANLEY is an award-winning author of two crime fiction series. *City of Dragons* (from Thomas Dunne/Minotaur Books in February 2010) continues the story of Miranda Corbie—private investigator in 1940 San Francisco—ex-escort, and the protagonist of *Children's Day*. Kelli's debut novel, *Nox Dormienda*, set two thousand years earlier in Roman Britain, won a Macavity Award nomination, and the Bruce Alexander Award for best historical mystery of the year. Kelli lives in foggy San Francisco and earned a master's degree in Classics. Discover more about Kelli and the worlds she writes about at www.kellistanley.com.

My Father's Eyes

WENDY CORSI STAUB

Things aren't always as they seem," my father liked to say, and when he said it, I would shake my head as if to say, no, they certainly are not.

Really, I was shaking my head because he was wrong. Dead wrong.

Dead—the irony should make me smile, but I don't dare, because they're watching me now. Every twitch of my mouth, every word that comes out of it, makes them wonder.

Let them.

Yes, my father was dead wrong. Most things—and people, too—are, I have learned, exactly as they seem.

Take Abby. Some might assume that beyond the triple chins and homely façade must belie a sparkling wit or a generosity of spirit. Why else would the most eligible bachelor in town—my widowed father—have married her?

Not for her money, though she had enough of it. But then, he does—rather, *did*—as well.

Not for her well-regarded family name, either. Our own name is equally—if not more—illustrious in this particular corner of the world.

Nor did he marry her to raise his motherless daughters. I was going on five when Abby moved in with us, but my sister was a decade older; she took better care of me than anyone. I have never needed—or wanted—a stepmother.

I barely remembered my own mother, having lost her when I was just a toddler. Yet I have always missed her. Does that make sense?

Never mind; I don't care if my feelings make sense to anyone other than myself.

My Uncle John told me once that my mother doted on me to the point where people whispered that I was spoiled. But who could blame her for indulging her third daughter when she'd buried her second just two years earlier?

As for her firstborn—if my sister had minded being overshadowed by my birth thirty-odd years ago, she either got over it or hid it very well, because I've never sensed resentment from her.

Not even now.

"Are you all right?" she asks anxiously from across the breakfast table, and I'm touched by the concern in her eyes, brown and somber, like our father's . . .

A terrible, wonderful fantasy sweeps through me, and then I realize it isn't a fantasy anymore. It's a memory now, a fresh one; I indulge it until my sister utters my name and repeats the question.

Do I look *all right?* I want to say in response, as I freely stir extra sugar into my morning tea; no one to protest that shred of self-indulgence.

I couldn't be better, I want to assure my sister—without an ounce of sarcasm, as it's the truth.

But I just nod at her, and I sip the hot, decadently sweet brew.

She arches a dubious brow, because, like most people, she subscribes to the theory that things aren't always as they seem—and because she herself couldn't be farther from "all right" on this hot and sunny August morning.

She will be, though, in time. The worst of our nightmare is over at last. What lies ahead is nothing compared to what we've been through.

I contemplate helping myself to another biscuit. There's no reason not to. I break one open and slather it with butter, then drench it in honey.

Before I can sink my teeth into the gloriously rich, sticky crumble, Maggie sticks her red head into the room to ask in her thick brogue, "Shall I open the drapes in the front room?"

"No!" my sister and I say in unison.

"Don't open the drapes in any room until we tell you otherwise," I instruct her. "Do you understand, Maggie?"

Something flickers in the housekeeper's blue eyes—eyes that seem sharper today, as they focus on me, than ever before. She used to look through me, through all of us, as the help should—and vice versa.

But now, as we exchange a glance—mine wary, Maggie's dangerously shrewd—I wonder whether she understands far more than just my orders to shroud the windows from prying eyes.

She slinks away, and I eat my biscuit in silent contentment. My scalp is soaked beneath my thick auburn hair; it must be ninety-five degrees outside already, and considerably warmer here in the kitchen.

This, however, is nothing compared to yesterday morning, when the red-hot stove threw off additional heat. My sister wasn't around to ask me why it was blazing away on the steamiest day of the year. Maggie was here, but of course it wasn't her place to question anything.

In the next room, the clock chimes the half hour.

"It's almost time." My sister pushes back her chair. Half past ten.

Nearly twenty-four hours ago, my father unexpectedly came home from the office. He wasn't feeling well, he said. Sick to his stomach. He was going to take a nap before heading back to work.

He didn't bother to ask where Abby was.

I didn't tell him.

"Aren't you going to come upstairs?" my sister asks from the doorway.

"No need, I'm ready," I tell her, smoothing my full skirt as I stand up.

My dress is, appropriately, black.

Earlier, I locked my bedroom door before I removed the dress from its designated hook at the back of the wardrobe in my room. Slipped beneath the dark black silk, snug as a lining, was the blue cotton dress I'd had on yesterday morning.

It will obviously have to be dealt with—but not today. So I took a plump goose-down pillow from my bed, remembering how many times I had futilely pulled it over my head to smother ghastly sounds in the dead of night.

Dead.

Again, the irony.

Even now, left alone in the kitchen, I don't smile. I am thinking about how I carefully slit open a pillow seam to create an opening just a few inches. After wadding the blue dress into a tight little ball, I tucked it through the opening, pushing it deep into the feathers. When I had carefully stitched the seam closed again, there was no sign of tampering, no telltale lump, even when I patted the pillow hard, all over.

I'm confident that no one will ever find the dress before I have a chance to destroy it.

I eye the cold iron stove.

Unlike fabric—and, for that matter, wood—metal cannot absorb telltale stains. But wood and fabric are so easily transformed to ashes, and ashes tell no tales.

I stood over that blazing stove yesterday morning, sweat pouring down my face with salty tears—not tears of grief, but of sheer relief.

It seemed to take forever to incinerate that wooden handle, its top freshly splintered, and all the while I was aware of father lying there on the sofa in the next room, Abby upstairs, Maggie in her third-floor quarters . . .

I knew that at any moment all hell could break loose.

It did—but on my terms: when the wooden handle had been thoroughly cremated.

I'm certain fabric will incinerate in no time at all.

I'll burn the blue dress tomorrow.

Today, wearing funereal black; I must attend to other things.

In the cemetery over on Prospect Street, two freshly dug graves wait in the family plot beside the dead mother I don't remember and the dead sister I never met.

They're better off there, I have often thought.

"When you came along, you healed your mother's grief," Uncle John told me once, years ago. "She adored you. So did your father—still does, as far as I can tell," he'd added.

Those words made my stomach churn, yet I said nothing. Neither did my sister, who was there. She didn't even look at me; there were some things we would never dare to discuss, close as we were.

But she knew. Of course she did. So did Abby, whom my father married not in spite of the fact that she was a fat, dour recluse, but because of it. He correctly assumed she was so grateful to have been spared an old maid's fate that she'd overlook his miserly flaws; forgive him anything.

I, on the other hand, have never forgiven him. Or *her*. Nor would I pretend to; that isn't my style.

Thus, it's no secret around town that ours is hardly a warm, cozy household. My father and Abby and my sister and I went about our daily business, merely co-existing under the same roof.

Until yesterday morning.

The night before had been sleepless, as so many are. I lay in my bed, cloaked in a quilt and a high-necked gown despite August heat as oppressive as my own familiar dread. When I was a girl, I would dress in layers and pile on the bedding, in a futile, pathetic attempt to shield myself. I've long since realized that was impossible, yet old habits die hard.

Waiting for the creak on the stairs that last night, I wondered whether he would come to my door this time, or to my sister's.

That I fervently wanted it to be her turn is perhaps the most shameful part in all of this. Yet I can make no apology for my feelings; they are what they are. I suppose it simply means that my hatred for him is even stronger than my love for her.

That night, it was my door he unlocked with the master key he kept in his black overcoat that reeked of sweet tobacco and sour sweat. There he stood, silhouetted in the doorway for a terrifying moment before he crossed the threshold and, as always, locked the door again behind him.

Even now, the memory of the key turning in the lock makes the biscuit churn with burning bile in my gut.

Every night . . .

Every single night, for as long as I can remember: the heavy tread of his boots on the stairs, the key in the lock . . .

I picture my sister waiting in the dark, praying he wouldn't come to her—or, more likely, that he would, because she's the better person and would want to spare me.

Then again, when faced with such unspeakable horror, is anyone really capable of such noble behavior? Maybe she was relieved to hear him enter my room and know that she was safe for that night.

I picture her with her head buried beneath her pillow, trying desperately to block out the repulsive sounds that would pierce the thin wall separating our bedrooms and a useless puff of goose down.

Useless no more, I remind myself, thinking of the blue dress as I leave the kitchen.

The first-floor rooms are dim, yet slats of golden sunlight fall across the rugs wherever draperies hang slightly parted.

Outside, wagon wheels rattle along Second Street. Voices rumble faintly from curious bystanders and gleeful ghouls.

Earlier, I peered through an upstairs window at the throng that's grown steadily since the news broke. The crowd is held at bay not just by our sturdy wooden fence, but by the police officers stationed around the property.

"Why do you think they're here?" I asked my sister last night.

"To keep the murderer out, should he reappear, I suppose."

Or perhaps, I thought to myself, to keep the murderess in, should she try to escape.

They *must* suspect.

Then again, even if they do . . .

Even if they were to find the broken-off hatchet head I so carefully wiped clean of any trace of blood, or the stained dress hidden deep in my pillow . . .

Even knowing what they know about our family, and my open contempt for my miserly father and for Abby, whom I haven't called "mother" in years . . .

They will never grasp the truth.

I am, after all, a woman.

A temperamental, sharp-tongued, spoiled woman trapped in a miserable, miserly household . . .

But a woman nonetheless.

No matter how damning the circumstantial evidence, should any of it come to light, they'll be sure to look beyond it. They'll be certain that things cannot possibly be as they seem. They believe, as my father did, that nothing ever is.

Fools.

I wander into the parlor and stop short, seeing a figure silhouetted before the sofa. In this faint light, I can't see the splotched upholstery and spattered wallpaper, but I know they're there.

"Maggie," I say, and she jumps, startled, whirling to look at me.

The room is too dim to betray the knowing flash in her eyes, yet it's palpable as bloodstain.

Will she hurtle an accusation?

If so, I'll deny it—just as I did yesterday, when the house was crawling with police wanting to know where I was when my stepmother and father were hacked to death so viciously that one of his eyeballs was flung from its socket.

Never again will I see that terrible glint in his brown gaze, betraying his hideous plans for the wee hours.

Never, never again.

The nightmare is over; at last, I am in control.

For a long time, Maggie just looks at me.

Perhaps she, too, suffered sleepless nights. Perhaps she, too, lay awake, listening in dread for the creak of a heavy masculine step on the stairs. Perhaps she, too, fantasized about making it stop.

"My name," she tells me in her soft brogue, "is not Maggie."

No, it isn't. But it's the only thing my sister Emma and I have ever called her. It was easier that way; the maid before her had been Maggie.

I look her in the eye. "I'm sorry . . . Bridget."

She nods, clearly satisfied.

No fool, Bridget Sullivan. She grasps what so many do not: that things are often exactly as they seem.

"I accept your apology, Miss Borden. Old habits die hard, I know."

At long last, I smile.

"Please," I tell her, "call me Lizzie."

*

The bestselling author of more than seventy novels, **WENDY CORSI STAUB** has penned multiple *New York Times* bestselling adult thrillers under her own name and more than two dozen young adult titles, including the current paranormal suspense series *Lily Dale*, which has been optioned for television. Her latest thriller, *Live to Tell*, received a starred review from *Publishers Weekly* and launches a suspense trilogy that will include sequels *Scared to Death* and *Hell to Pay*. Under the pseudonym Wendy Markham, she's a *USA Today* bestselling author of chick lit and romance.

Industry awards include a Romance Writers of America Rita, three Westchester Library Association Washington Irving Awards for Fiction, the 2007 RWA-NYC Golden Apple for Lifetime Achievement and the 2008 RT Book Reviews Career Achievement Award in Suspense. Readers can join her online at www.WendyCorsi Staubcommunity.com.

Program with
a Happy Ending

CYNTHIA ROBINSON

The worst part about dying alone in front of your TV is that you can't get to the remote control. Victor Secco learned this soon after he died in his Barcalounger. His TV was on. In fact, it was blaring. That's what the headlines said: *Mummified corpse found in front of blaring TV.*

It's hard to say when, exactly, Vic's pharmacological catatonia crossed over into the big sleep. He was up to six or seven Ativans a day, and a couple of Ambiens at night, and then Marina would give him a Ritalin when she wanted him to transfer funds or sign checks. It was all kind of like being dead already. Only you watch a lot of TV.

The first couple of girls who came over—the girls from the service—they would say things like, "Let's get you outside, Mr. Secco." Or, "How about some fresh air,

Victor?" He'd tell them, "Fuck you. Get out of the way of the TV."

They didn't get it. They thought Victor watched so much TV because of the stroke. They didn't get it when he said he wanted a happy ending, either. They thought he was talking about the TV show. Like he gave shit whether or not Crystal got back together with Jack.

Marina got it, though. She was the third or fourth girl the service had sent over. He waited until she was giving him his sponge bath. Then he said he'd like a happy ending. She smiled, slack-jawed and lupine, and she put a towel over him down there and worked her fist up and down until he was very happy.

"You are bad boy, Victor," she said in that crazy Russian accent. The accent made it better. He liked to pretend he was James Bond and she was a KGB operative trying to seduce government secrets out of him.

Sometimes he wished that had actually happened. If an operative had approached him when he was at TRW, he would have sold everything he could have copied onto a floppy disk. But no spies ever came forward. No windfall. No house in the Balearic Islands, no bank account in the Caymans.

Instead, Victor had to slog it out, stacking up commissions, one contract at a time. Ballistic-missile systems. Smart bombs. Nerve gas. You work like an asshole. Lots of overtime. Taking clients out for lunch, drinks, dinner, drinks.

And now, for what? So he could sit in front of the TV, goofed up on meds, with nothing to look forward to but his daily hand job.

Marina wasn't supposed to come over every day. But she said it was obvious to her that Victor needed her there. The people at the agency didn't understand. She said she'd work for him freelance. Off the books. Cash. She brought groceries, and meds, and she'd turn on the soft-porn station when he was ready for his happy ending. That made it go faster. And she started doing more things for him, extra things. Running his errands. Picking up around the house. Selling his car. Putting his golf clubs and stereo and the furniture he didn't need onto eBay.

"You're so alone, Victor," she'd say.

He'd point the remote at the TV and change the channel.

One day he looked down at his watch.

"Hey, Marina," he said. "What the fuck. This isn't my Rolex. This is some Mickey Mouse watch."

"Is yours, Vic," she said.

"Look at the second hand," Victor yelled. "The second hand of a Rolex sweeps. This is not a sweeping motion. This is ticking. It ticks. Like a fucking Timex! That's not sweeping. This is some cheap shit from Bangkok."

"Time for your meds, Vic."

"Some piece of shit knockoff," Victor said.

She popped a couple of Valiums in his mouth and tipped the Dixie Cup to his lips. Didn't I just take my pills, Victor wondered.

"Drink your Ensure," Marina said.

"It tastes funny," Victor protested.

Marina stuck the bendy straw in Victor's mouth and rubbed the crotch of his tracksuit until all the Ensure was gone.

"God damn it!" Victor said. "That shit tastes so bitter."

"Your detective show is on, Victor," she said, handling the remote control.

Victor loved that show. It was about a renegade cop

who uses psychic powers to find murder victims. The cop's powers led him to a 7-Eleven. He was convinced there was a corpse in the back of the standup freezer. Vic felt a touch of indigestion. They exhumed the body from behind the frozen Salisbury steaks. Vic felt prickling up and down his legs. It spread up his torso.

He heard a man's voice. A Mexican accent. Where's the Mexican? There's no Mexican on this show.

Then he recognized the voice. It was Pedro, the pool guy. He was talking to Marina. They were in the room, behind him. Victor heard the glass patio door sliding shut. Giggling. Marina and Pedro. He was whispering. She shushed him.

Next, they were standing in front of him. Marina was biting a hangnail on her thumb. Pedro bent down and peered into Victor's face.

"Why are his eyes open like that?" Pedro asked. He waved his hand in front of Victor's face. "I think he's dead."

"Get the laptop," Marina said. "And take those gold chains off of him. They could be worth something."

Pedro went to turn the TV off. Marina stopped him. She said they should leave it on, loud, like normal, so it looks like he's home, just watching TV.

"Should I turn off the AC?" Pedro asked.

"No," Marina said. "Leave it on. Or else he'll stink up the place and the neighbors will call police."

They left.

Baretta came on the TV. In the old days, back when he and Joanne still lived in Laguna Beach, Victor would come home from work and watch *Baretta*. Or *Kojak*. Those two were his favorites. Although, he also liked Rock Hudson in *McMillan & Wife*. That was before McMillan was a fag. That reminded him: he used to watch *Rockford,* with that guy who was *Maverick.* And, speaking of fags, Victor liked *Ironside* because Raymond Burr was a cripple and could still solve crimes without getting up. Victor thought he'd heard that Ironside was a fag, too.

And he liked *Cannon* because the show always got personal—Cannon was always solving a crime for some dame who was a former girlfriend.

"He sure gets a lot of action for a fat guy," Victor would call out to Joanne who was in the kitchen.

Plus, when it came time for Cannon to nail the perp, the crim would take off running and then they'd show Cannon start to run and cut right to Cannon grabbing the guy by the collar and tossing him on the ground. Every time that happened Victor would laugh and holler for Joanne to come in and see it.

"They never show the fat guy running," Victor would bray.

But Joanne didn't give a shit about *Cannon.* She wouldn't even look at the show.

All Joanne ever did was complain. Not shrill, but plaintive. Like a martyr. Saint Joanne, our lady of neglected sorrows. Victor couldn't even recall the sound of his ex-wife's voice. It had been muffled, always coming from over his right shoulder. Joanne always stood in the blind spot of Vic's recliner.

Joanne would pepper Victor with questions and demands. Did you get the car smogged? You need to talk to Ronny about his allowance. Look at what the girl did to my hair!

She never asked about Heidi. Victor wasn't even sure if Joanne knew her name. She always referred to her as "your secretary." "They call them 'administrative assistants' now," Vic would tell her. "Whatever," Joanne would say, "she's curt with me on the phone."

"What?" Victor would have to yell.

"Curt," Joanne would yell back from the kitchen. "She's rude and disrespectful when I call you at the office. Who does she think she is?"

When Joanne came home from work, she would always go straight to the kitchen. She'd take off her shoes and hang her blouse over the back of a kitchen chair. She'd cook dinner in her brassiere, and her skirt and her suntan pantyhose with the reinforced toe. Joanne would stand at the stove, stirring Ragu spaghetti sauce. The loose flesh at the back of her upper arms quivered. But her breasts stood high and firm in the cross bracing of her sturdy white brassiere.

Joanne stuck it out until Ronny went off to college.

One afternoon, while Victor was watching a sport-fishing program, Joanne entered the TV room. She was wearing her blouse, and carrying a suitcase. She said she was going to her sister's, and there were potpies in the freezer. After a month, Joanne hadn't come home. But Victor received a letter from her lawyer.

Victor continued to get mail after his death. Every morning, the postman slipped mail through the slot. It fell onto a pile drifting up against the door.

As a corpse, Victor received glossy brochures beckoning him to join other active seniors in their retirement communities. The retirees in the ads were always cutting up—spinning brodies in their golf carts or coasting on their bicycles with their feet kicked up in the air. And the active senior men were always with foxy active senior women who looked like forty-year-old models in gray wigs.

It was when he retired that Victor noticed Heidi started going out more. They'd only been married for a couple of years. But she was restless. She'd leave dinner for him, a plate covered in foil. He'd put it in the microwave and eat on a TV tray. When she got home, she'd turn off the TV and go to bed. She'd leave him sleeping in the Barcalounger.

They didn't start fighting until the move came up. Victor was ready to go to Palm Springs; he'd been looking forward to it for years. But Heidi said she was too young to go out there. "What about my career," she said.

"You're a fucking secretary," Victor said, "what career?"

Heidi got herself a townhouse up in Newport Beach with the settlement money. And Victor noticed that Ronny stopped calling him around that time. He suspected something he didn't even want to say out loud. Ronny and Heidi were the same age, and she did "confide" in him. That's what she'd called it. Fuck them, he said to himself. And he moved out to Palm Springs on his own.

A couple of days after Marina and Pedro split, Victor felt a tugging sensation at his abdomen. The TV was playing that show about the renegade cop who solves crime with his obsessive-compulsive disorder. The OCD cop worked with another cop who had Asperger's syndrome. He solved crimes with his overbearing nature. That autistic guy's going to get his own spin-off, Victor thought.

The tugging at his abdomen got stronger. And to Victor's surprise, a slender, glistening cord shimmied out from the elastic waistband of his tracksuit pants. It aspired up, toward the ceiling, pulling at his navel.

Then Victor was on the ceiling, looking down at himself sitting in the Barcalounger. He held his hand in front of him, and it shimmered silver and white, like a TV screen in the old days when the programming ended for the night.

He remembered how he'd often wake up in his chair and that static screen would be crackling. It made him feel kind of blue, kind of alone. Now the TV played twenty-four/seven, and Victor didn't wake up.

He looked down at the silver cord, tracing its trajectory. It looked so fragile—it was crimped and looping and it glistened wet. But it was strong. The cord anchored into Victor's navel and it tethered his silver, shimmering self—his self that was floating along the ceiling—to the brown, dry corpse in the Barcalounger below.

I am dead, Victor realized.

Vic sat dead in front of his TV watching more episodes of a psychic renegade cop. He also regularly saw a show about a gritty renegade cop. This guy had so much grit that he took on international terrorists—Towelheads, Victor identified them—all by himself. Gritty cop was always under the gun. For instance, he had just hours to locate a nuclear bomb no bigger than a burrito. Under this pressure, the gritty detective had to do the only thing that a real renegade can do. He tortured suspects with ordinary household items: duct tape, ballpoint pens, and, in one case, an electric nose hair trimmer.

The AC kept the ranch bungalow cool and dry. The Freon circulated, leeching the scant humidity out of the air, wicking the moisture out of Victor's body.

His skin cured into beef jerky. His eyeballs clouded over with a bluish white film, and they popped out of his eye sockets and rested on his cheekbones. They burst and flattened, so they looked like two hatched reptile eggs, dried under the desert sun into empty leather sacks.

Marina's face flashed onto the TV screen. It was an old police-file photo. Her blond hair looked very yellow, and her roots showed. She was pale and when it was frozen on film like that—when she wasn't talking or licking her lips—her jaw looked very long and narrow. A photo of Pedro appeared beside her. He looked frightened and bewildered, childish. Greasy fucking Mexican, Victor noted. A bright sheen bounced off the tight curls of Pedro's mushroom-cap hairdo.

Then a third photo appeared: a bald man with face like a boxer—broken nose, piggy little eyes, mean slash of a mouth. The newscaster said his name was Boris something or other. He was an "associate" of Marina's. Boris, Victor snorted. That's rich. How fucking cliché.

Boris was being sought by the authorities, the newscaster said. Live film of a desert scene rolled onto the screen: a black Lincoln, high-centered on the edge of an arroyo. The car doors were standing open. A couple of lumps were lying on the sand, covered in white tarps.

Dirt nap, Victor announced to himself.

Week after week, Vic floated dead, bobbing along the ceiling of his ranch style bungalow. Below him, his desiccated husk withered into the Naugahyde of the Barcalounger.

The TV blasted.

Program after program. Commercial after commercial. Season after season. Through live coverage, and summer reruns. Through hurricanes, murders, and high-altitude bombings. Through real cops, fake cops, fake real cops. Through makeovers, liposuctions, and boob jobs. Through entertainment, infotainment, and docudramas. Through re-enactments, dramatizations, and purely fictional events. Through summer, then winter, and then through summer again. The television glowed blue and white, flickering over Victor's lifeless face.

Marina had showed him how to set up his automatic payments. She'd been sure to leave enough money in the checking account to cover at least a year of utility bills. There were so many passwords, and clicks, and "I Agree" buttons—it was so easy to cash out the stocks and drain the 401K. And who had the money now? Maybe Boris.

It was two years before anyone came to the house. The visitor didn't come to see Victor. He came to read the meter. He let himself in the side gate and walked around the back of the house.

The pool was drained dry and full of palm fronds. They'd blown down from the date palms over the course of two spring seasons when the winds are high and fierce. The dried palm fronds crinkled and rustled in the arid cement bowl of the pool. Tree rats harbored in the withered leaves, burrowing into the arboreal necropolis.

The meterman stepped back from the pool. Where there are rats, there are snakes.

He heard a television blasting. It was a game show. A crowd roared; *Wheel of Fortune*.

Some old person, he thought. Can't hear.

He rang the back doorbell, then pounded on the door. He walked over to the glass sliding door, looked in the window through the gap in the vertical Levelors. He saw Victor—his profile sagging, his hair bristling, his leather hands were clamping black talons dimpling the armrests.

When the gurney wheeled out onto the driveway, the silver cord that attached Victor to the brown husk dissolved. He floated freely, into the cloudless sky, looking down at the streets in their tidy grids, the rows of palm trees lined up so neatly, so intentionally, and the swimming pools, blue and twinkling like merry gems.

As he floated higher, Victor realized, without alarm, that the shimmering silver pieces that suggested his form were drifting apart. The spaces between the silver became wider, and wider, until there was nothing but space. A brief thought flashed. Victor knew that he would, himself, be on television that evening. And he felt curiously happy, because he no longer cared.

*

CYNTHIA ROBINSON lives in San Francisco. She is the author of the Max Bravo series of black comedy mysteries. St. Martin's Press published *The Dog Park Club* in 2010 and *The Barbary Galahad* is forthcoming in 2011.

Killing Carol Ann

J. T. ELLISON

I've just killed Carol Ann. Sweet, innocent Carol Ann. Her blond hair flows down her back and trails in the spreading pool of blood. What have I done?

I've known Carol Ann for nearly my whole life. Every memory from my childhood is permeated by the blond angel who moved in across the street when I was five or so. Skipping up the street after the ice cream truck, getting lost in the shadows during a game of hide-and-seek, watching her sit in the window of her pink room, brushing that glorious hair. We were two peas in a pod, two sides of the same coin. Best friends forever. Forever just turned out to be an awful long time.

Our relationship started as benignly as you'd expect. I'd seen the moving truck leave and knew that a family had taken the Estes' house. Mrs. Estes died, left her son with bills and a dozen cats. I missed the cats. I'd wondered about the family, then went back to my own world.

Carol Ann spied me sitting on our front step, twirling my fingers through the dandelions in the flowerbeds. Mama had sent me out to pluck the poor, insignificant weeds from the ground, worried they'd ruin her prized flowers. Mama's flowerbeds were local legend. The best in three states. At least that's what the members of the garden club said about them. Full to the brim with the heady blooms of gardenias, azaleas, jasmine, roses, sweet peas, hydrangea, daylilies, iris, rhododendrons, ferns, fertile clumps of monkey grass, and a smattering of black-eyed Susans . . . the list went on and on. A green thumb, Mama had. She could make any flower grow and peak under her watchful gaze. All but me, that is. Her Lily.

I was crying about something that day, I don't remember what. It was past ninety degrees, a sweltering summer afternoon. A shadow cast darkness across my right foot. A strange girl stood on the sidewalk in front of the A-frame house I grew up in. A yellow-haired goddess. When she spoke, I felt a rush of love.

"Hey girl," she said. "Would you like to play?"

"Do I wanna play?" I answered, suddenly numb with fright. I'd never had a playmate before. Most folks' kids steered clear of me. The nearest child my age was a bed-ridden boy who smelled funny and coughed constantly. Mama made me go over there once, but after I screamed as loud as I could and pulled his hair, she didn't make me go back. Mama's garden-club friends didn't bring their spawn to visit with me while they played canasta under the billowing tent in the backyard. There was no one else.

"Are you simple or something?" the girl asked.

"Simple?"

"Oh, never mind." She turned her back and started away toward the river, skipping every third step. She wore a white dress with a pink ribbon tied in the back in a big bow—the kind I'd only ever wear on Easter, to go to church with Mama. Even from behind, she was perfect.

"Wait!"

My voice rang as true and strong as it ever had, deep as a church bell. She stopped, dead in her tracks, and turned to me slowly. Her eyes were wide, bluer than Mama's china teapot. Then she smiled.

"Well. Who knew you'd sound like that? I'm Carol Ann. It's nice to meet you."

She strode to me, her hand raised. I'd never shaken hands with a girl my age before. It struck me as awfully romantic. She grasped my hand in hers.

"How do," I mumbled.

"Now, is that any way to greet your dearest friend?" Her voice had a lilt to it, Southern definitely, but something foreign, too. She squeezed my hand a little harder, her little fingers pinching mine.

"That hurts. Stop it." I tried to shake loose, but she was like a barnacle I'd seen on Tappy's boat once. Tappy took care of the rest of the yard for us. He wasn't allowed to touch the flowerbeds, but someone had to mow and weed and prune. Mama could grow grass like nobody's business, too.

"Not until you do it right. My God, am I going to have to teach you manners as well as how to bathe?"

She wrinkled her nose at me and I realized how sweet she smelled. Just like Mama's flowers. I was lost. I looked her straight in those china blue eyes, my dull brown irises meeting hers. I cleared my throat, but I didn't smile.

"It's nice to meet you as well."

She dropped my hand then and laughed, a tinkling, musical sound like wind chimes on a breezy afternoon. She had me enthralled in a moment.

"Let's go skip rocks in the river."

"I'm not allowed. Mama says—"

"Oh, you're one of *those*." She dragged the last word out, gave it an extra syllable and emphasis.

"One of what?" My hackles rose. Two minutes and we were having our first fight. It should have been a warning. Instead it made my blood boil.

She smiled coyly. "A mama's girl."

Back then, I thought it was an insult. I reached out to smack her one good, but she pranced away, closer to the river which each skip.

"Mama's girl, mama's girl." She singsonged and danced and I followed, my chin set, incensed. Before I knew it, we were on the river, a whole block away from Mama's house. I wasn't allowed to go to the river. A boy drowned the summer past, no one I really knew, but all the grown-ups decided it wasn't safe for us to play down there. This girl was new, she wouldn't know any better. I didn't want to be a mama's girl anymore.

Mama skinned my hide that night. She'd called and called for me to come to dinner, had Tappy look for me. Carol Ann and I were too busy to hear. We skipped rocks, whistled through pieces of grass turned sideways between our thumbs, and dug for worms. I showed her how to bait a line and she nearly fainted dead away when I put a warm, wriggling worm in her hand. Tappy found us right after sunset and took me home screaming over his shoulder. The joy I felt wouldn't be suffused by

Mama's switch. Never again. I had a friend, and her name was Carol Ann.

It was the first of many concessions to her whims.

"My Goodness, Lily, can't you try to look happy? You're all sweet and clean, and we'll have some ice cream after, if you're good. All right?"

"Yes, ma'am," I mumbled, sullen.

Mama had me spit-shined and polished for a funeral service at church. I didn't want to go. I wanted to run off to the river with Carol Ann, skip rocks, have a spitting contest, something. Anything but go to church, sit in those hard pews, and listen to Preacher yell at the old folks who couldn't sing loud enough because their voices were caked with age and rot.

I didn't think that was fair to them. I remember my granny vaguely, who smelled like our attic and had a long hair poking out of her chin. She'd scoop me in her arms and sing to me, her voice soft like the other old folks. I liked that, liked to hear them whisper the words. It made the hymns seem dangerous in a way. Like the old folks knew the dead would reach out of their very graves and grab their hands, pull them down into the earth with them if they sang loud enough to wake them.

Mama wasn't hearing no for an answer today. We walked the quarter mile to the Southern Baptist, greeted our brothers and sisters, sat in the hard pews, and celebrated the death of Mrs. O'Leary. Preacher made sure we knew that we were sinners, and I felt that vague guilt that I was alive and Mrs. O'Leary was dead, though it was supposed to be glorious to have passed to the better side.

We finished up and put Mrs. O'Leary in the ground. I tried hard to hold my breath in the graveyard so no spirits could inhabit me, but the graveside service took so long I had to breathe. I took small sips of air through my nose, felt my vision blacken. Mama pinched my upper arm so hard I gasped.

I gave up trying to hold my breath. All the ghosts had been waiting, watching, patiently hovering, anticipating the moment when I took in a full breath of air. They're inside me now; they inhabited my soul, tumultuous and gray. I tried to fight them, until I couldn't find any more reason to.

I begged to be allowed to go home, to be with Carol Ann, but Mama kept a firm grip on my arm while I cried. Folks thought I was grieving for Mrs. O'Leary. I was grieving for myself.

Mama decided homemade ice cream was just as good as the Dairy Dip, after all.

One day a massive storm came through. The trunks of the trees were black with wet, the leaves in green bas-relief to the long-boned branches. Storms frightened me—the ferocity of the winds, the booming thunder felt like it was tearing apart my very skin, shattering my soul. Carol Ann and I had taken refuge in my room. She rubbed my stomach, trying to calm me, crooning under her breath. Nothing was working. I was shaking and sweaty, low moans escaping my lips every once in a while. Carol Ann was at a loss. She stood, leaving me on the floor, and went to the window.

"Come away from there, Carol Ann." My voice sounded panicky, even to me. She turned and smiled.

"Don't be a goose, Lily. What, do you think the wind's going to suck me right out that window?"

A flash of lightning lit up the room and the thunder shook the house. I whimpered in response, my eyes begging her to come back to me. She turned and stared out the window, ignoring my pleas.

Then she whirled around, a wide smile on her heart-shaped face. "I have an idea. Let's be blood sisters."

"Blood sisters? What's that?"

"What? You've never been blood sisters with anyone before, Lily? My goodness, where have you been hiding all these years?"

"There's no one to be sisters with, Carol Ann. You know that." I felt vaguely superior for a moment, but she ended that.

"We need a knife."

"Why?"

"My Lord in heaven, Lily, how do you think we're going to get at the blood?"

So I snuck out of my room, slunk down the stairs, gripping each with my toes so the wind didn't whisk me away when it tore the roof off the house. The storm was loud enough that Mama didn't hear me go into the kitchen, get a knife from the rack next to the stove, and make my way back up the stairs into my room. Carol Ann's eyes lit up when she saw the knife, the five-inch blade sharpened to a razor's edge.

"Give that to me."

I did, a sense of wrongness making my hand tremble. I think I knew deep in my heart that Mama wouldn't want me becoming blood sisters with anyone, no matter what the course of action that led me there. But that was Carol Ann for you. She could always convince me to see things her way.

Carol Ann took one of my sheer cotton sweaters, a red one, and laid it over the lamp, so the light fragmented like a lung's pink froth and the room became like thin blood. We sat in the middle of the floor, Indian-style, facing each other. She made sure our legs were touching. I was scared.

"Okay. Stop fretting. This will only hurt for a second, then it will be all over. You still want to be my blood sister, right?"

I swallowed hard. Would this make us one? I didn't want that. No, I didn't want that at all. A tiny corner of my mind said, "Go find your Mama, let Carol Ann do this by herself."

"I think so," I answered instead.

"You think? Now Lily, what did I say about you thinking? That's what I'm here for. I do the thinking for both of us, and everything always turns out just fine. Now quit being such a baby and give me your arm. Your right arm."

I didn't want Carol Ann to think I was a baby. I held out my arm, which only shook for a second.

Carol Ann was mumbling something, an incantation of sorts. Then she held up the knife and smiled. "With this blade, I christen thee." She ran the blade along the inside of her right arm, bright red blood blooming in the furrows created in her tender flesh. She smirked, a joyous glow lighting her translucent skin, and took my arm. The point of the knifed dug into the crook of my elbow. "Say it," she hissed.

"With this blade, I christen thee." My voice trembled. She drew the knife along my arm and I almost fainted when I saw the blood, dark red, much darker than Carol Ann's. Then she took my arm and her arm and held them together. We stood, attached, and walked in a circle, eyes locked, blood spilling into each other.

"Our blood mingles, and we become one. You are now as much Carol Ann as I am, and I am as much Lily as you are. We are one, sisters in blood."

Redness slipped down my elbow. Spots danced merrily in my vision.

Carol Ann's eye sparkled. "Quick, we need to tie this together, let our blood flow through each other's veins while our hearts still beat."

She grabbed a sock off the floor and wound it around our arms, dabbing at the rivulets before they splashed on the floor of my bedroom, then beckoned me to lay down next to her. I put my head in her lap, my arm stretched and tied to hers, and she held me as our blood became one. I felt at peace. The ferocity of the storm seemed to lessen, and I felt calm, sleepy even.

"LILY!" The scream made me jump. It was Mama. She saw what Carol Ann and I had done. I didn't care. I was tired. It was too much trouble to worry about the beating I was going to get.

I didn't get to see Carol Ann the rest of that muggy summer. Mama sent me away to a white place that smelled of antiseptic and urine. I hated it.

I came back from the white place in the fall, quieter, more watchful than before. The leaves were red and orange and brown, the skies were crisp and blue. I was worried that Carol Ann might have moved away; the drive was empty across the street, the window dark. When I asked Mama, she told me to quit it already. No more talk of Carol Ann. I wasn't allowed to see her, to play with her, anymore.

I went back to school that year. Mama had been keeping me home before, teaching me herself, but she figured it was time for me to leave the nest. I needed to be around more girls and boys my age. I was so happy that she sent me to school at last, because Carol Ann was there. She had moved, but only a couple of streets over. She was zoned to the junior high, just like I was.

We didn't exactly pick up where we left off. Carol Ann had many other friends now. But I'd catch her watching me as I stood on the periphery of her group of devotees, and she'd wink at me in welcome. Those moments warmed my heart and soul. She was still my Carol Ann, even though I shared her with my classmates.

The school year progressed without incident until Carol Ann came up with a new game. The pass-out game. Every girl in school wanted to be a part of it. We'd line up in the bathrooms, stand with our backs against the wall, and hold our breath until the world got spinny. Carol Ann would cover our hearts with her hands and push. Hard. We'd pass out cold, some sliding down the walls, some keeling over. Carol Ann reasoned that it stopped our hearts for a moment, that in that brief time we could see God. That's why the teachers got so upset when they found out.

Of course, they found out when *I* was doing the heart-pushing on a seventh-grader named Jo. I got suspended, and the fun stopped. No more pass-out game. No more Carol Ann, at least until I wasn't grounded anymore.

They rezoned us for the ninth grade; decided we were big enough to go to high school. I had to take the bus, which I normally hated, because it drove past the Johnsons' farm, and their copse of pine trees with the hanging man in them. I knew it wasn't a real dead man, but the branches in one of the trees had died, and they drooped brown against the evergreen—arms, legs, torso, and broken neck. Mama used to drive me to Doctor Halloway this route, ignoring my requests to go the long way past Tappy's place. I hated this road as a young girl; just knew the hanging man would get out of that tree and follow me home.

When the bus would pass it by, I'd try not to look.

Since I was a little older now, it wasn't so bad in the daylight. But as winter came along and the days shortened, the hanging man waited for me in the dusky gloom. He spoke to me, the deadness of the pine needles brown and dusty like a grave.

The next year, Carol Ann started taking the bus. Life got better. She was only on it some days, because she had a lot of dates now. Some days, after school, I'd watch Carol Ann riding off in cars with shiny, clean boys, throwing a grin over her shoulder as they faded into the gloaming. But there were times when she'd come out of the school, clothes rumpled, mouth red and raw, scabs forming on her knees. She'd jump on the bus just before it pulled away from the curb and wouldn't want to talk.

But mostly, we sat together in the back, in those idyllic days, talking about boys and teachers, the upcoming dances and who was doing it. I knew Carol Ann was. You could tell that about her. I was fascinated by sex, though I'd never experienced it. Carol Ann promised to tell me all about it.

She snuck vodka from her parents' house and slipped it into her milk some mornings. She'd share the treat with me, and we'd get boneless in the back of the bus, giggling our fool heads off. She taught me how to make a homemade scar tattoo, using the initials of a boy I liked. She took the eraser end of a pencil and ran it up and down her arm a million times until a shiny raw burn in the shape of a J appeared. She handed the pencil to me, and I tore at my skin until a misaligned M welled blood. I have that M to this day. I don't remember which boy it was for.

The bus driver, Mrs. Bean, caught us with the vodka-laced milk. Carol Ann wasn't allowed to ride the bus anymore. I didn't see her as much after that. I think the school and Mama really did their best to keep us apart. It was probably a wise decision. But I felt incomplete without her at my side.

Now that I'm grown, away from Mama's house, away from Carol Ann, I remember the little things. Spilling on Carol Ann's bike, scraping the length of my thigh on the gravel. The year she pushed me into the cactus while we were trick-or-treating. The day I nearly drowned when I fell through the ice on Gideon's Lake, and she laughed watching me panic before she went for help. Carol Ann did nothing but get me in trouble, and I was happy to leave her behind as an adult.

So you can imagine my shock and surprise when the doorbell rang, late one evening, and Carol Ann was on my front step. Somewhere, deep inside me, I knew something was dreadfully wrong.

I live in the A-frame house I grew up in. Mama's been in a home over in Spring Hill for a couple of years now. They have nice flowerbeds, and I visit her often. We walk amongst the flowers and she reminds me of all the terrible things I did when I was a kid. No one thought I'd ever grow out of my awkward stage, but I did. I went off to college and everything. Carol Ann went to a neighboring school. I'd see her every once in a while, working as a waitress in one of the coffee shops on campus, or shopping in the bookstore. I learned that it was best to ignore her. If I ignored her enough, she'd get the hint and leave.

But here she was, in the flesh, rain streaming down her face. Her blond hair was shorter, wet through, darker than I remembered. She was a skinny thing, not the radiant beauty I remember from my childhood.

I was frozen at the door, unsure of what to do. She

knew better than to come calling; that was strictly forbidden. We'd laid down those ground rules years before, and she'd always listened. I was saved by the phone ringing. I glared at her and motioned for her to stay right where she was. Carol Ann was not invited into my house. Not after what she did all those years ago. It had taken me forever to get over that.

The phone kept trilling, so I turned and went to the marble side table in the foyer, the one that held the old fashioned rotary dial. I picked it up, almost carelessly. It was Mama's nurse at the Home. I listened. Felt the floor rushing up to meet me. Everything went dark after that.

When I woke, the sun was streaming in the kitchen window. Somehow I'd gotten myself to a chair. There was coffee brewing, the rich scent wafting to my nose. Carol Ann stood at the counter, a yellow cup in her hands. She took a deep drink, then smiled at me.

"Hey, stranger." Her voice was soft, that semi-foreign lilt more pronounced, like she'd been living overseas lately.

"Hey, yourself," I replied. "You're not supposed to be here."

"You needed me." She'd shrugged, a lock of lank blond falling across her forehead. "I'm sorry about your Mama. She was a good woman."

I had a vision of Mama then, standing in the same spot, her hair in curlers, rushing to finish the preparations for a garden-club meeting, stopping to lean back and take a sip of hot, sweet tea and smiling to herself because it was perfect. She was perfect. Mama was always perfection personified. Not flawed and messy like me. My heart hurt.

I forced myself to do the right thing. To do what

needed to be done. My heart broke a little, and my head swam when I said, "Carol Ann, you need to leave. I don't need you. I never did."

She looked down at the floor, then met my eyes. Tears glistened in the corners, making the cornflower blue look like a wax crayon. "C'mon, Lily. We're blood sisters, you and I. We're a physical part of each other. How can you say you don't need a part of yourself? The *best* part of yourself? I make you strong."

"No!" I screamed at her, all patience gone. "You are not a part of me. You aren't . . ."

A fury I hadn't felt in years bubbled through my chest. There was only one way to get through to her. I grabbed the porcelain mug from her hand, smashed it on the counter, and swiped a gleaming shard across her perfect white throat. She fell in a heap, blood everywhere.

As I stood over her, watching her hair turn strawberry, I felt a tug and looked down at my leg. Carol Ann was trying to grab a hold of my foot. I kicked her instead, hard, in the ribs. She stopped moving then.

The thought is fleeting. What have I done?

I've just killed Carol Ann. She was never sweet, never innocent. She was a leech, an albatross around my neck. I didn't need her. Carol Ann needed me. That's what Doctor Halloway always told me. That's what they said in the hospital, too. The white place, so pristine, so calm. They told me I'd know when the time was right to get rid of Carol Ann once and for all. Mama would be so proud. She knew I didn't need Carol Ann, knew I was strong enough to live on my own. She always believed in me. I miss her.

The blood drips . . . drips . . . drips . . . from my arm. I feel lighter already.

*

J. T. ELLISON (*The Cold Room*) is the bestselling author of the critically acclaimed Taylor Jackson series. She was recently named Best Mystery/Thriller Writer of 2008 by the *Nashville Scene*. She lives in Nashville with her husband and a poorly trained cat. Visit JTEllison.com for more information.

Chloe

MARC PAOLETTI

Pull over," Dad says, voice barely audible over the hum of the air conditioner. "I have to go."

I shake my head. "It's too dangerous."

"Pull over. *Now*."

Dad knows I can't refuse a direct order. I pull off the deserted highway into an all-night gas station, and continue past the pumps to a pair of filthy white doors around the backside of the food mart. The left door reads *Men*. It's 1:00 A.M.

Dad doesn't get out of the car. Instead, he stays pressed into his seat, skeletal fingers clutching the dash. He twists painfully, and the LSU T shirt that once stretched tight across his torso shifts in a loose flurry of shadows. His head has only a few white strands left, and his sunken face looks tight, like it's been slammed shut.

"We're sitting ducks out here," I say.

Dad doesn't seem to care. "I need your help," he says, and then unlatches the glove compartment with a shaky hand; the tiny door falls open with a *thunk*. He burrows underneath a pile of maps until he finds something. A ballpoint pen.

"What's that for?" I ask.

Instead of answering, he pushes the pen at me with little stabs. "Cramps. Hurts." His voice is dreamy with morphine.

The pen is clear plastic, the kind you can see the ink through, and I take it to humor him. Due to medication and chemo, Dad hasn't been himself for months. A major liability if our rivals found out, which was why the family sent him to the middle of bumfuck nowhere to get better. Instead, he got so bad we had to take him back.

"Hurts," he says again.

"I heard you the first time." I pull the Colt .45 from underneath my seat and tuck it under my belt, then kick open the door and step into swampy night air that smells like motor oil and rotting green. Dad must be really out of it to take this kind of risk. Word could have already spread that he's weak. We could both be dead before reaching the men's room, but an order's an order.

I've been taking orders from Dad my entire adult life. He ordered me to switch my course of study from architecture to law, which I hate like poison now. He ordered me to stay loyal to the family, no matter what, and ordered me to steer clear of Chloe—a woman I fell deeply in love with in law school—because she was an "unacceptable risk." In other words, she wanted no part in the family business. Dad orders me like he fucking always does, and always has.

I scan the gas station. It's clear—for now.

I circle fast to the passenger door and open it, forgetting

that Dad isn't belted in because the tight strap hurts his skin. He falls toward me, and I catch him against my chest before he tumbles out. His nose presses against my right temple; his breath feels warm against my ear.

"We have to be quick," I tell him. "Think you can handle that?"

There's no way to pull his arm across my shoulders. Instead, I slide my arms forward to the elbows under his armpits. When I stand, it's like lifting a man made of cardboard tubes.

With him pressed nose-to-nose against me, I shuffle back blindly toward the restroom as smooth and quick as I can. I don't want to jar his bowels loose before we get there, but I also don't want to stay in the open longer than we have to. If the gas station attendant were watching, he might think we were two queers dancing.

I scan for threats to avoid looking into Dad's eyes. Moths swoop and click against a streetlight bulb, and I'm tempted to let the light draw me in, too. Away from Dad, this place, myself.

"Veer left," Dad says, slurring. He's the only one who can see the way. "Now right."

More orders. Or, as Dad might say, "proper direction." The only direction I ever wanted to travel was away from the family with Chloe by my side. I'd never met a woman like Chloe, then or since. Gentle and almost pretty, she did things as they came, which turned the grinding shuffle of life into a spontaneous, free-form expression. I remember wishing I had the confidence to be like that. At the time, it was enough to simply be around her. I try not to think about what I could have learned from Chloe, and the terrible things I've learned instead.

My back thumps against the restroom door. I let my left arm go lax so Dad can reach down and turn the knob. To my surprise, the door opens. After pulling Dad inside, I notice the door can't be locked without a key.

The room is twice the size of a broom closet and lit by buzzing fluorescents. I'd imagined graffiti-covered walls and an odor toxic enough to choke a horse, but the walls and floor gleam fish-belly white, and there's a pine-tree chemical smell that's almost pleasant. Water drip-drips into a clean sink below an unblemished mirror.

I shuffle Dad past a pair of sparkling urinals to the stall, bump open the door with my shoulder, and squeeze us inside. The toilet is to my right, his left, and has a thick black seat. The water is clear, but there's a brown streak along the inside of the bowl.

"Line me up," Dad says. Voice tight.

"Can't you take it from here?"

"I told you. I need your help."

I swing Dad around so the backs of his knees graze the rim of the bowl, and then use my right foot to kick his feet shoulder-length apart. He's wearing dark blue sweat pants, which he struggles to push past his bony hips. I let him struggle a few moments longer before helping, and glimpse gray pubic hair. I move to settle him onto the toilet seat, but he clings to me.

"Still need your help," he whispers, and points to his backside, elbow squeaking against the metal wall. "Hurry. Hurry. It won't take much."

"What are you talking about?"

"The morphine clogs me up."

He keeps pointing, pointing, and I look at him incredulously. The nurses didn't mention anything about clogs. "How the hell am I supposed to—?"

"The pen. Hurry."

I think he's kidding, but then he starts panting and wincing. Suddenly, I'm acutely aware of the weight of the pen in my breast pocket. My stomach goes cold. I'm not fucking ready for this. I'm ready to defend him from a rival-family's assassin, sure, but not for this.

I look at the wall, the ceiling, but his eyes are waiting for me. He grimaces; a thread of spittle traces down his lower lip.

I need time to prepare, but it seems like time is never in the cards when it comes to Dad. He gave me just one hour to tell Chloe it was over after we'd been seeing each other for two years. One fucking hour, and the rest of my life to regret it.

Holding Dad steady with one hand, I pull the pen from my pocket and hold it by the capless tip. Blue ink stains my thumb. I figure the blunt end is the "proper" end since it's less likely to catch, but who knows? I can't believe what I'm about to do as I reach around Dad's bony hip, and then trace the pen along the curve of his buttock. When I find the right spot, I pause, waiting for god knows what, and then I close my eyes and push slowly. Steadily. I feel strong, thick resistance.

As odd as it seems, when Dad sucks a breath, all I can think about is Chloe's face when I told her we couldn't be together any more. It was nearly the same look Dad had earlier in the car—face slammed shut, unable to believe what was happening. Normally, Chloe's eyes were full of indiscriminate wonder. Within seconds, I'd erased it all.

I push the pen deep, until half disappears, and then twist sharply, roughly. Not taking so much care now. Dad grunts a warning. I yank my hand and the pen clear, and the echo of splashing water fills the stall, followed by the reek of fermented waste. I let him fall back onto the toilet seat, and then drop the soiled pen into his lap.

"Hurry," I say, mimicking his earlier demand. His body trembles with effort.

Chloe had trembled, too, when asking for a reason. It was the first time she'd tried to pin me down about anything, the first time she'd attempted to divine a chain of precipitating events. I looked at her, my own face slammed shut, until she dashed away. I never saw her again. I'd let my soul mate go without a fight. How could I help her understand when I barely understood myself? Family members do as they're told. It's that simple and that complicated.

After letting Chloe go, I became an expert at letting other people go, too. At *getting* them let go, rather, as the family's criminal defense attorney. I freed con men, wise guys, hitters. Too many to count. My imposed law degree and loyalty put to use.

I found out later—still many years ago—that one of the men I'd helped free had dealt with Dad's "unacceptable risk." On the day I'd said goodbye, Chloe had been shot once in the head, once in the heart, and dumped in the Red River. To do something about it would have meant disloyalty to the family. So I did nothing. Like I said, it's that simple and that complicated.

I glance at the men's room door. Part of me hopes an assassin barges in, guns blazing. The splashing stops. Finished, Dad's commanding mien is all but gone. I tear free a few squares of toilet paper, yank him forward, and wipe him clean.

"Up," he says, but it's more of a question. He stares at his shoes. This time I support him with his left arm across my shoulders so we can both see. The pen clatters to the floor.

"This way," I tell him as we shuffle forward. I yank his

body closer to mine to better bear his weight, which has increased substantially somehow. "*This* way."

We bang through the door, and I keep a watchful eye. Still nobody around.

After I load Dad into the car, I climb into the driver's seat. Dad twists away from me toward the door. I draw my gun and point it at the back of his head.

I can kill him right now, and make up any story I want. Ambush, whatever. I can kill him—something I've dreamed of doing—before the cancer inevitably does.

But I don't. Instead, I slide the gun back under my seat, and crank the car into gear. In a way, I make the decision for Chloe. Better that Dad feels every agonizing moment he has left. Better that he continues to realize the waste our lives have become.

*

MARC PAOLETTI is the author of *Scorch,* a thriller that draws upon his experiences as a Hollywood pyrotechnician, and coauthor of *The Last Vampire* and *The Vampire Agent,* the first two books of the Annals of Alchemy and Blood series. His acclaimed short fiction has appeared in numerous anthologies, and, as a journalist, he has interviewed such notable figures as Sting and Beatles producer Sir George Martin. He has also published comic books and written award-winning advertising copy. For more information, visit www .marcpaoletti.com.

Cold, Cold Heart

KARIN SLAUGHTER

Even now, she could still feel the ice in her hand, a stinging, biting cold that dug into her skin like a set of sharp teeth. Had the flesh of her palm been that hot or the California climate so scorching that what had been frozen moments before had reverted so quickly to its original form? Standing outside his home, she had been shocked to feel the tears of moisture dripping down her wrist, pooling at her feet.

Jon had been dead for almost two years now. She had known him much longer than that, twenty-four years, to be exact—back when he spelled "J-o-h-n" properly, with an "h," and would never have dreamed of keeping his curly black hair long, his beard on the verge of hermitous proportions. They had met at a young adult Sunday school class, then become lovers, then man and wife. They had taught high school chemistry and biology, respectively, for several years. They had a son, a beautiful, healthy son named Zachary after John's grandfather. Life was perfect, but then things had happened, things she tried not to think about, and the upshot was that in the end, the good life had called, and Pam had not been invited.

Her hair was too long for a woman her age. Pam knew this, but still could not bring herself to cut it. The slap of the braid against her back was like a reassurance that she was still a person, could still be noticed if only for the faux pas of being a fifty-two year-old school teacher who kept her salt and pepper hair down to her waist. While women her age were getting pixie cuts and joining yoga classes, Pam had rebelled. For the first time in her life, she let her weight go. God, what a relief to eat dessert whenever she damn well wanted to. And buttered bread. And whole milk. How had she lived so long drinking that preposterously translucent crap they labeled skim milk? The simple act of satisfying these desires was more rewarding than any emotional joy that could be had from buttoning a pair of size six pants around your waist.

Her waist.

She made herself remember the good things and not the bad, the first few years instead of the last seventeen. The way John used to trace his hand along the cinch of her waist—rough hands, because he liked to garden then. The bristle of his whiskers as his lips brushed her neck, the gentle way he would move the braid over her shoulder so he could kiss his way down her spine.

Wending her way through various backwater towns for the third—and hopefully last—time in her life, she made her way toward the western part of the country; she forced her mind to settle on the good memories. She thought of his lips, his touch, the way he made love to her. Through Alabama, she thought of his strong, muscular legs. Mississippi and Louisiana brought to mind the copious sweating when they first joined as man and wife. Arkansas, the perfect curve of his penis, the way it felt inside her when she clenched him, her lips parting as she cried out. Oklahoma, Texas, New Mexico . . . these were not states on a map, but states of mind for Pam. As she drove across the Arizona line, she found herself suspended between the road and the heavens, and the only thing keeping her grounded was her hands wrapped around the leather steering wheel.

The car.

All she had left of him now was the car.

Two years ago, he had called late in the evening—not late for him, but the three-hour time difference put the ringing of the phone well into that block of time when a piercing ring caused nothing but panic. She foolishly thought of Zack, then the second ring brought more reason, and she thought of her father, a physically frail man who refused to live in a nursing home despite the fact that he could no longer do much of anything but sit in his recliner all day watching the History Channel.

"Papa?" she had cried, grabbing up the phone on the third ring. A fire. A fall down the stairs. A broken hip. Her heart was in her throat. She had read that phrase in so many books, but not understood until now that it was physically possible. She felt a pounding below her trachea; her throat was full from the pressure of her beating heart moving upward, trying to force its way out.

"It's me."

"John?" Even as she said his name, she imagined it spelled correctly, the "h" flashing like a neon sign outside a strip club.

In keeping with his new California lifestyle, he had said it so matter-of-factly, as if he were discussing the weather: "I'm dying."

She'd been glib, said something she had watched him say so many times on *Oprah* or *Dr. Phil*: "We're all dying. That's why we need to make the best of our lives now."

Such an easy thing for him to say. Independently wealthy people didn't tend to have as negative an outlook on life as those who had to get up at five every morning to get dressed so they could go out and teach drooling teenagers the periodic table.

"I'm serious," he had said. "It's cancer."

Her heart was no longer in her throat, but there was something stuck there that made speaking difficult. She managed, "What about Cindy?" The petite, dark-haired Pilates instructor who had been living with him for the last year.

"I want you to be there when it happens," he'd said. "I want that healing."

"Come to Georgia, then."

"I can't fly. You'll have to come to California."

Pam still cursed that day when they had first flown to California for a teachers' conference. It had been a way to get out of Atlanta; an exciting adventure, their first trip out west. Their grief counselor had suggested they do something "fun" to take their minds off what had happened and John had eagerly suggested the conference. Pam had stared out the window most of the flight, shocked at the vast and varied terrain beneath them. Dense forests with dirt roads cutting into them like lashes from a switch gave way to barren desert and nothingness. How could people live in such desolate places, she had wondered.

How could people survive with nothing but cacti and tumbleweed out their windows?

"Look," John had said, pointing out the oval plane window to the patch of red dirt that represented the state of Arizona. "That's where Ted Williams is."

Ted Williams, the baseball player whose decapitated head had been cryogenically frozen by his nutty children.

"Liquid nitrogen," John had explained. "His body's floating in a vat next to it."

Pam looked away from the window for the first time. She allowed herself a quick glance at John, his steely blue eyes, his long eyelashes that were more like a woman's. She loved him profoundly, but could not see her way across the chasm that had opened up between them. She wanted to touch his hand, to revel in the way his voice changed, got deeper, when he was teaching someone something new.

Instead, she asked, "Why did they have to decapitate him?"

John had shrugged, but she saw the corner of his mouth twitch into a smile.

"You know," he began, "The only other organ in the body with similar chemistry and composition to the brain are the intestines."

Pam should have laughed. She should have made some silly comment about how we all really *are* shit-for-brains, but she had simply said, "I know," and let the low hum of the plane's engines fill her ears as they flew into the unknown.

Zachary had never been on a plane. His life had revolved around the Atlanta suburb of Decatur where Pam and John had lived all of his life. This was where he played baseball, went to the mall, and, judging by the empty condom packets Pam found in his pockets when she washed his jeans, managed to screw every girl in his class.

At sixteen, he had his father's height, his mother's sarcasm, and his grandfather's addiction. The autopsy report revealed an alcohol level nearly six times the legal limit. The coroner had seemed to think it would comfort Pam to know that Zack had been so intoxicated that he had probably been unaware of any pain as his car had skidded off the road, tumbled down a ravine, and wrapped itself around a tree.

"I'm dying, Pam," John had said on the phone. "Please. I want you here with me."

Brain cancer. No pain, because there aren't any nerves in the brain. She wanted to make a joke, to remind him of what he had said about Ted Williams, the decapitated popsicle, but John had brought it up himself. "Remember when we first flew out to California?" As if she had ever been again after that conference. She was lucky if she could afford a vacation to Florida during the summer, and then it had to be with a couple of other teachers so she could afford to stay somewhere nicer than the roach motel eight miles from the beach.

"I want to be put into stasis," he'd told her. "I want to be cryogenically frozen so that I can be reanimated one day."

She had laughed so hard that her stomach had literally clenched. The tears in her eyes were from the pain, she had told herself, not from any sense of losing him.

Yet, she had not thrown away the ticket when it came, had not told him to go fuck himself with his first-class plane ride and his fucking millions the way she had so many times before.

Millions. It had to be several million by now. *Biologi-*

cal Healing was still on several bestseller lists and she knew that it had been translated into at least thirty different languages. At this very moment, people in Ethiopia were probably reading about John's theory of using the "mind-body connection" to overcome loss and suffering. The funny thing was, Pam was the one with the doctorate in biology. John was just a high school science teacher with a message and he had through some fluke taken his message to the world.

"Grief," John told an agreeable Larry King, "knows no one particular language."

He had written a book about losing Zack, then losing his wife. Pam thought that's what she resented most: being lumped in with Zack as if she had died, too. She hadn't had that luxury, had she? She had been left behind to go to the morgue so that she could identify her son's body because John could not. She had sorted through Zack's address book to find his friends from soccer camp and baseball camp and band camp so that they could be notified. She had been the one to go to the mailbox and find the letters, a hundred at least, from Boy Scouts and pen pals that Zack had accumulated throughout his sixteen years of life. Because John had been so incapacitated by grief, it had been Pam who had chosen the suit for Zack's eternal rest, then bought the new one when the funeral director kindly explained that it was several sizes too small.

The suit had been two years old. She had bought it when Zack was fourteen so that he could wear it to his cousin's wedding. Fourteen to sixteen was a lifetime. In two years, he had grown from a boy to a man and as she had taken the dark blue suit and tie out of the cleaner's bag where it had hung in the closet for two years, Pam had not even considered the possibility that Zack had outgrown it. The running jokes about his eating them out of house and home, the fact that he needed new shoes every two months because his feet kept getting larger, had been lost to her, and standing in his room, smelling his sweaty teenage smell that clung to his sheets and thickened the air, she had almost smiled at the thought of the old suit and taken it off the closet rod with some relief because that was one less decision out of the way.

John had to be sedated so that he could go to the funeral. He had leaned against her as if she were a rock, and because of this, Pam had made herself rocklike. When her mother had taken her hand, squeezed it to offer support, Pam had imagined herself as a block of granite. When a girl who had been in love with Zack— one of many, it turned out—had collapsed, sobbing, against Pam, she conjured in her mind several slabs of marble, cold, glistening marble, and built a fortress around herself so that she would not fall down to the ground, weeping for her lost child.

Pam had been the strong one, the one everyone turned to. She steeled herself against any emotions, knowing that if she allowed them to come, she would be overwhelmed, stoned to death by the guilt and grief and anger that would rain down.

"Write about it," she had told John, begged him, because she could not listen to his anguish anymore without unleashing her own. "Write it in your journal."

He had always kept notebooks, and just about every day he jotted down his thoughts like a little girl keeping a diary. At first, she had thought this habit strange for a man but later came to accept it as just another one of his endearing eccentricities, like his fear of escalators and belief that eating raw cookie dough would cause intestinal worms. When it started, she was glad when he stayed in his office writing all night instead of coming to bed, where he invariably cried himself to sleep, tossing and turning from nightmares, calling out Zack's name. She had ignored these terrible nights as long as she could, wished them away because to acknowledge them would be to acknowledge the loss, and she could not bring herself to do that, could not admit that they had lost their precious boy.

Finally, in the heat of an argument, she had mentioned John's fitful nights and he had turned on her like an animal, accused her of being cold, of not dealing with her emotions.

There was a switch.

John was always the rational one, Pam the emotional one. He had always used logic to defeat her and invariably won every argument because he didn't let his feelings get the best of him. Even nine years ago, when Pam had found out that he was cheating on her with one of the front office secretaries from school, he had outlogicked her.

"You're not going to leave me, Pam," he had told her, arrogance seeping from every pore. "You don't have enough money to raise Zack on your own, and you won't be able to teach at the same school as me because no one likes you there. They'll all be on my side."

Sobering to hear from the man you love, not least of all since every word he said was true.

Through almost twenty years of marriage, he had consistently been the more reasonable one, the one who said, "let's just wait and see" when she was certain that a raspy cough from Zack's room in the middle of the night was lung cancer or that the rolling papers that fell out of his notebook one day in the kitchen meant he was a meth freak.

"Let's wait and see," John had said when she told him she thought Zack had taken some wine from the refrigerator.

"Boys will be boys," John had said when she found an empty bottle of vodka in the back of Zack's closet. The cliché had made her want to scratch out his eyes, but she had listened to him, made herself calm down, because the irritated way John glanced at her, the quick shrug of his shoulders, made her feel like a hysterical mother instead of simply a concerned parent. At school, they both dealt with overreacting parents on a daily basis: mothers who screamed at the top of their lungs that grades must be changed or they would go to the school board; fathers who tried to bully teachers into not failing their sons by threatening to sue.

The phone call had come at nine o'clock on a Friday evening—not one in the morning, not a panicked, wake-up-to-catastrophe time of night. Zack had left home earlier with Casey and some friends, and John and Pam were watching a movie. *The Royal Tenenbaums.* Pam was making herself watch the entire movie—not because she enjoyed it that much but because she knew Zack did, and she wanted to talk to him about it in the morning. He was at that point in his teenage life where any sort of discussion with his mother was pained, and she sought out things—literally, things: movies, football games, funny articles in the paper—that they could comfortably talk about.

"I'll get it." John jumped for the phone—he always liked to answer it—as Pam fumbled with the remote control to mute the television.

"Yes, it is," John had said, his tone of voice low, slightly annoyed. A telemarketer, she thought, then John's face had turned white. What a silly phrase, Pam had thought, as she sat on the couch, her feet tucked underneath her, to say that someone's face turned white—but it had. She sat there watching it happen, a line of color draining down his neck like a sink being suddenly unplugged until all the red was gone from John's usually ruddy skin.

Then, he had whispered, "Yes, we have a son."

"We have a son." The first words John had said to her when she had come out of recovery. The birth had been difficult, and after sixteen hours of labor, the doctor had decided to do a caesarian. Pam's last memory had been the sweet relief of the pain being taken away by the drugs (she would have freebased heroin by then), and John's crouching trot beside the gurney as they rolled her into the OR, tears in his eyes as he whispered, "I love you."

He whispered again into the phone. "We'll be right there."

Only he wasn't right there. It was the ghost of John who had sat in the passenger seat of the car as she drove to the county hospital. It was his ghost who had floated through the front doors and waited for the elevator to come. Pam had taken his hand, shocked at how cold it was, the skin clammy, his calloused fingers like ice.

Zack, she thought. This is how Zack's hand will feel.

John had stood frozen outside the morgue. "I can't do it," he had told her. "I can't see him like that."

Pam had, though. She had looked at her son, stroked back his thick, black hair and kissed his forehead even though it was caked with dried blood. His eyes were slit open, his lips slightly parted. A long gash had flayed open the line of his jaw. She took his hand and kissed his face, his beautiful face, then signed the papers and took John home.

Pam's second trip to California had been very different from the first one. First-class was a whole new world to her, from the hot towel to wipe her face to the warmed nuts to the endless supply of alcoholic beverages. A well-dressed man stood in baggage claim, her name on the placard he held in front of him. The black Lincoln Town Car was spotless, a bottle of cold water waiting for her as she climbed into the back seat.

This was John's personal driver, she gathered. Bestselling millionaire authors didn't have to drive themselves around, especially when they lived in the Hollywood Hills. Pam took no delight in the palm-tree-lined streets, her first glimpse of the famous Hollywood sign. She felt like a whore for taking John's money. At the dissolution of their marriage, she had insisted they split everything down the middle: selling the house, the cars, their meager stocks so that it could all be done in cash. Money had been the noose he kept around her neck for years. They couldn't go on vacation or buy a new car or splurge on a dinner out because of money. To say John had kept a tight grip on the purse strings was an understatement. Everything was on a budget and even Pam was kept on an allowance. She seethed with hatred every time she thought about their life before, the way she had allowed him to control everything. How easy it must have been for him, how boring in its own way, to have so much power over her.

When John had gotten his first royalty check from *Biological Healing,* he had offered her a share of the money, but Pam had told him where he could deposit it. She had read the book at least three times by then, had gone to school where her students had read about the "pedestrian" sex life she had shared with her husband. Her colleagues had read about how she had simply walked away when John had accused her of not loving their son. Her drycleaner knew that she had once told John that she was disgusted by the thought of being with him.

"Take the money." John had reasoned, "I know you need it."

"You bastard," she had hissed. Her teeth were clenched, and she wished they were biting into his jugular, twisting it out of his neck like a root from the ground. She cursed him, something she never did, because she thought cursing was base and showed a lack of intelligence. "Fuck you and fuck your money."

"I'm sorry you feel that way, Pam." His tone was reasonable, the same tone he had used when she questioned him about where he had been until one in the morning, why there was a key in his pocket that didn't fit any of their locks. The tone that said, "Why are you being so silly? Why are you letting your anger ruin your life?"

She could even picture that smirk, that knowing smirk that said he knew that he had won. Money was his way back into her life, his way to control her again, to make her want nice things only so he could snatch them away at will.

As if she were a prostitute, he had offered: "I can send it to you in cash, if you prefer."

Pam had slammed down the phone before he could say anything else.

Mostly, she got news of her ex-husband from magazines, television shows, and helpful friends. "Did you see John met the Dali Lama? Did you see John spent the weekend with the president?"

"Did you see that I don't give a shit?" Pam had said to one of them, but this had been a mistake, because God forbid she should be bitter about the man who was helping heal the country. Funny how he never mentioned his affair, or how he had told her when she was pregnant with Zack that she was too fat to be attractive. Why were these amusing little anecdotes missing from his precious little book? And why was it that the world didn't notice that disgusting smirk on his face every time he talked about the nature of healing your soul?

Pam's mouth had gaped open when the Town Car pulled past the open gate and into John's driveway. She had never seen a private home this large before. The school where she taught was not as big as this building. The same man who had ten years ago insisted they keep the heat off during a snowstorm could not own this stunning mansion.

"Pam!" Cindy, the gorgeous, young Pilates instructor/whore, had said. She looked Pam right in the eye, but Pam knew that as she'd walked down the front steps toward the car the woman had taken in her wide hips, the wrinkles at her eyes, and the inappropriate braid.

"He's been waiting for you," Cindy told her. She had a bag of ice in her hand, the sort of thing you'd have if you sprained an ankle.

There was a man in a dark suit leaning against a white van that was parked in the shade of one of the many trees. *NuLife* was written across the door, the print small and unassuming. Pam imagined they didn't advertise much considering the morbid nature of their jobs. She had looked up the lab—if you could call it that—online when John had told her about it. Their secret facility in Arizona held dozens of heads and bodies in stasis, all awaiting reanimation. Fees were listed on the site as well. A neuroseperation (or decapitation, as it was known to the rest of the world) ran around two hundred thousand dollars. The whole body cost over half a million. For an additional fee, you could even store personal objects with the body so that when they were reanimated, they had some of their favorite things to remind them of their "first life."

"Let's just get this over with," Pam snapped, and Cindy seemed surprised. Yes, Cindy was young enough to be John's daughter, but she'd certainly read *Biological Healing*. Surely, she'd paid close attention to the chapter that talked about Pam's coldness after Zack's death, the way she had turned away from John, blocked him out and denied him the one thing that would bring them back together.

Sex played a large part in *Biological Healing*—not just sex, but lots of it. Sure, Pam and John had gone at it like bunnies until Zack was born, but then, as with most couples, their lives had changed when they had a child. Who knew that John was so interested in screwing? Certainly not his ex-wife. Apparently, it was the elixir of life, the succor through which both John and Pam would have reclaimed their marriage, if only she hadn't been such a frigid, uncaring bitch. The fact that John hadn't been able to perform the one time after Zack's death that they had tried to have sex, had also somehow been left out of the book.

"You've killed me," he had said after that failed attempt, rolling onto his back, more bereft about his flaccidity than he had ever seemed about Zack. "You have finally killed me."

If only she had.

Cindy led her into the house, which had the largest set of oak doors Pam had seen outside of a castle. The foyer was huge, their footsteps echoing up to an enormous chandelier as they walked into what must have been the living room.

"They're from NuLife," Cindy said, indicating a man and a woman sitting on a couch beside the fireplace. They had coolers stacked around them, the kind you would find at a family picnic, and they were each scooping ice into baggies similar to the one Cindy held in her hand.

Cindy said, "They're just waiting."

"Waiting for—" Pam started, but Cindy interrupted her.

"He's in his study," she said, leading the way down a long, art-lined hallway. The Pilates instructor's shoes were strappy little things, the kind that Pam had never been able to wear because they made her back hurt. The flip-flip of the sandals echoed in the hall as they made their way to the back of the house. Outside, there was a courtyard with a fountain. The windows and doors were open so that the splattering of the water mixed with the flopping of the shoes, some kind of mad cacophony that served nothing but to annoy.

John's study was slightly different from the converted garage space they had made for him back in Decatur. No flimsy pine paneling buckled off the walls, and the antique leather-lined desk was a far cry from the two sawhorses and the piece of plywood that had held his computer for all those years.

He was lying on a hospital bed in the back of the room, facing the large windows that overlooked the fountain in the courtyard. The glass doors were open here, too, and the water was more soothing, now that Cindy had stopped flipping her idiotic shoes. A ray of light beamed down from the heavens, showering the bed in warmth. Pam would not have been surprised if he had hired a chorus of angels to sing beside him, but no, there was just the usual apparatus of lingering death: an oxygen tank, a heart monitor, and the requisite plastic pitcher on the table beside his bed.

"Honey?" Cindy asked, her shrill voice cutting into the soft hiss of the oxygen tank. "Pam is here."

A frail voice echoed, "Pam?"

"I've got to go fill up more bags," Cindy said, then left, more like an overworked nurse announcing a visitor than a lover. The girl couldn't be older than nineteen, Pam thought. The fact that John was dying must be something she took as a personal affront rather than a fact of life.

And dying he was. As Pam walked toward the bed, she could smell death, the same odor that had clung to her mother as she rotted away from breast cancer several years ago. John's skin was yellow and his beard was completely white. He had always had a full head of hair, but most of it was gone now. Some of it had obviously been shaved by a doctor—she could see the healing scar where a surgeon had cut into his head—some probably chased away by whatever medications they were giving him to keep him alive for a few more days.

As if he could read her mind, he moved away the oxygen mask and said, "It won't be long."

She was facing him now, seeing an older version of John, the face of his father, his grandfather. Would Zack have looked like this if he had managed to survive that accident? Would her son have aged this badly if the first, second, third, millionth time Pam had told John that she thought Zack had a drinking problem, instead of saying, "He's just a boy," he had said, "Yes, you're right. Let's do something to help him."

Would Zack be alive if for just once in her life Pam had stood up to her husband and said, "No"?

There was a large cooler beside John's bed, and she

could not help but shudder at the sight of it. Were they going to chop him up and throw him in the van?

"Open it," he told her, and despite her better judgment, she did. What had she been expecting to find? A head-sized thermos? A steaming vat of liquid nitrogen? Certainly not the little baggies of ice she found.

"To preserve me while they . . ." his finger made a dragging motion across his neck.

"What?" But Pam understood. She could see where his finger had traced across his throat, a cut that would be real soon enough.

"Of course . . . the procedure is . . . illegal," he managed, his breath raspy so that he had to put the mask back over his face.

"What do you mean?" she demanded. When he did not answer, she found herself staring at the bags of cubed ice as if they were tea leaves and she a wise old gypsy.

"In California," he finally gasped. "It's illegal to cut off . . ." He took another breath of oxygen. "The law considers it mutilating . . . a dead body."

"Well, it *is* mutilation," she said, letting the cooler lid slam back into place. Of course it was illegal to cut the head off a dead body—even in this Godforsaken loony bin of a state. "What the hell is wrong with you?"

He laughed, the old John bringing a sparkle into his eyes.

"You're absolutely insane," she told him, but she laughed, too. My God, over twenty years with this man. A house, a home, a son, a life. Twenty years of her existence meshed in with his like the weave of a blanket.

"Don't cry," he said, reaching out for her hand. Before she could stop herself, she took his hand, felt the coldness of his skin. Had it been like this since Zack's death? The truth was that the reason she couldn't make love to

John was because his touch sent a deathly chill through her. Had John been a ghost all this time? Had he cried so many tears, wept for so many nights, that the life had seeped out of him?

He was wearing silk pajamas, a dark burgundy that only brought out the sallowness of his skin. There was a blanket folded at the end of the bed, his feet resting on top of it.

He said, "Gross," and she took a minute to realize he meant his toenails. They were long and yellow, disgusting to look at. "John Hughes."

"Howard Hughes," she corrected before she could stop herself.

There was a flash in his eyes, but he didn't pursue it. The John she knew would have never let her get away with correcting him. For the first time since she had heard from him, Pam realized that he really was dying, that this was it. No matter what she did with her life, where she went, she would do so with the knowledge that John no longer walked the face of the earth.

Granted, he would be in stasis in a vat of liquid nitrogen somewhere, but still.

"Remember," he began. "With Zack . . . you bit . . . his toenails."

She felt herself smile at the memory. Once, very early on, she had accidentally trimmed one of Zack's nails to the quick. Her heart had broken at the sight of blood, and Zack's screaming still reverberated in her ears if she thought about it long enough. After that, she had used her teeth to clip his nails, terrified she would hurt him with the sharp metal clippers. Standing beside John's deathbed, she could almost feel Zack's thin nails between her teeth, taste the sour, baby-soft skin of his feet.

"I . . ." John moved the mask back over his mouth and

nose, and she could see his chest rising and falling. "I need to . . ."

She shushed him. "It's okay."

"I want to . . ."

"Don't worry," she said, thinking that if he apologized now, she wouldn't know what to do with herself.

He took a few deep breaths, his eyes slitting almost closed. Suddenly, he opened them wide as if he remembered that he could die if he closed them too long. "I . . . I left you something."

Years had passed, but she could still remember the shame she had felt when she'd had to ask him for lunch money because she'd run through her allowance before the week was out.

He had refused her request and told her to be more careful the next time.

"I left . . . you . . . something."

She tried to keep her anger down, saying, "I told you I don't want your money."

"Not money," he said, his lips twisting in a half smile. "Better."

"Don't give me anything, John. I don't want anything from you." Why had she come here? Why had she agreed to get on a plane and fly all the way out here?

To watch him die. Somewhere in the back of her mind, she had known it all along that she wanted to watch him die, watch John succumb to something over which he had no control. She had wanted to see death wipe that knowing smirk off his face, and she wanted to be standing over him while this happened, watch him realize that there was one thing out there that he could not get the better of. Let the world think of him as their loving healer, but let Pam watch him die with them both knowing what a lying, conniving piece of shit he was.

The heart monitor gave an irregular beep and the oxygen mask cleared of fog from his breath. She waited, counting . . . one . . . two . . . three . . . until he took a gulp of air into his lungs, the machinery of life moving forward.

Pam felt ashamed. What kind of person was she that she could take such pleasure in his pain? How could think these things about the father of her child?

John's chest rose with effort. "Need to tell you . . ." he tried again.

"No," she said. She couldn't hear his apology, not now, not after hating him for so long. "Please don't." She could not bear more shame.

He waved his hand out, saying, "Sit."

She went to his desk to get the chair, but stopped when she saw the stack of old notebooks piled on top. She recognized the journals, remembered them from their married days when he would sit in his chair, scribbling down his private thoughts. Pam had been tempted, especially after the affair, but she had never read them, never violated his privacy.

Pam started to roll the chair over to his bed, but he waved her away. "No," he said. "Read."

"I'm not going to read your journals." She didn't add that it was hard enough reading his damn book.

"Read," he insisted, then, "Please."

Pam relented, or at least appeared to. She rolled the chair back, her hands gripping the soft leather. God, he had probably paid more for this chair than she had for her car.

She sat at the desk and opened the first book she put her hand on. She did not want to read the journal, could not handle the further blow to her self-esteem of reading his early diatribes on her failures. Her fingers found a letter opener, and she winced, jerking back her hand as she felt the sharp edge slice her skin. The letter opener was actually a stiletto. The small knife looked to be made of brass. Jewels decorated the handle, and the blade was finely sharpened as if John needed to defend himself from strangers entering his office.

The only person he would ever need to defend himself from was Pam.

"Read . . ." John admonished, his voice weaker than ever. "Please . . ."

Pam sighed, giving into curiosity as she picked up one of the journals. She thumbed to the first page. It was dated three years into their marriage, and she skimmed the parts about whiny students and a blister he'd gotten from grading papers.

Her eyes stopped on one word: Beth.

Pam finished the journal in under an hour—a year of John's life encapsulated in the blink of an eye.

Another year, another name: Celia.

Year six brought two names: Eileen and Ellen.

The door opened and Cindy asked, "Everything all right?"

Pam could not open her mouth to speak. She nodded.

"He just needs to check," she said, letting in the man Pam had seen in the living room. He went to John, pressed a stethoscope against his chest for a few minutes, nodded, then left.

Cindy told Pam, "We could use some help out here with the ice if you're—"

"No," Pam said. Her tone of voice was alarming, the kind she used to stop students in their tracks and elicit confessions of chicanery and cheating.

The door clicked shut and Pam returned to the journal.

Mindy. Sheila. Rina. Yokimito.

Blowjobs, finger fucking, ass fucking, sixty-nine, and a position that, even with her doctorate in human biology, Pam would have needed a diagram to understand.

She turned the page.

He had drawn a diagram.

From the bed, John wheezed. Pam thumbed through the journals, looking for the year of Zack's death. She found the day before, February sixteenth. John's cramped scrawl revealed that he had finally found love. He had been with a woman named Judy the day before their son died.

Judy Kendridge, the math teacher down the hall. Pam had tutored kids with the woman after school. They had both complained about their corns, their aching backs, their husbands.

The date on the next page was May third, three months after Zack's funeral. Pam recognized it as the first line of *Biological Healing*. "The biggest obstacle to overcoming the death of my son was finally admitting to myself that I could not be the perfect father, the perfect husband."

"No shit," Pam hissed, slamming shut the notebook.

She pushed herself away from the desk and walked over to John's bed.

"Wake up, you bastard." He didn't comply, so she poked him, then violently shook him. "Wake up!"

Slowly, his eyes opened. He glanced at the journals, then back to her.

"What does this accomplish?" she demanded, anger and humiliation bringing tears to her eyes. "This is the 'healing' you needed, dragging me all the way out here so I can read your deathbed confession?"

An eyebrow went up. She could have sworn he was enjoying this. He pushed the mask from his mouth and she saw it then: the smug smile on his lips, the twinkle in his eye. All of his self-help bullshit and his healing from within and his millions of dollars slapped her in the face like a wet rag.

"You . . ." he said, his breath coming harder from the effort. "You . . ."

"I what, John? I what?"

"Came," he said. "You . . . came . . ." he panted with exertion. "You . . . stupid bitch."

Pam's mouth opened—she felt the jaw pop, the breeze drying the back of her throat. The first class ticket, the warm towel, the nuts. She had even sipped from the bottle of cold water in the car. She had fallen for it all without even thinking.

"You . . ." he began again, smiling, showing his teeth.

Pam stood there. It was five years ago. Fifteen years. Twenty. She just stood there the same way she had from the beginning and waited for the ax to fall on her head.

"You . . ." The smile would not go away, even as he struggled to breathe. "You've . . . gained . . . weight."

The mask popped back on and he inhaled, his breath fogging up the plastic.

"I should kill you," she hissed. "I should kill you with my bare hands."

His left shoulder went up in a shrug, then he froze in place, his eyes opening in shock. The monitor went off, a piercing, metallic beep that signaled a flatline. The doors flew open and instead of doctors rushing in, the well-dressed man and woman entered, each carrying a cooler between them.

"Please step out of the way," the woman snapped, elbowing Pam aside. They opened the coolers and started to pack the bags of ice around John's body. Oddly, Pam wondered if the man she had seen out by the van was the person who actually chopped off the head.

"Mrs. Fuller?" the NuLife woman asked. Pam was about to answer when Cindy stepped forward.

"Yes?"

So, he had married her. He had married her in the end so that she would have all of his money. Pam wondered if he had put her on an allowance.

"We need you to pronounce him," the woman said.

"I . . . I don't think . . ." Cindy faltered. She burst into tears, her hands around her face, shoulders shaking. "Oh, John! I can't do it!" she sobbed, crumbling to the ground. "He can't be gone!"

"Oh, for fucksakes," Pam snapped, turning off the whining heart monitor with a snap of her wrist. "He's dead," she told them. "Look at him. He's dead."

And he was. Even without the heart monitor bleating its signal, any fool could see that John was gone. His eyes were still open, but there was no light there. His skin was slack—everything about him was slack, that is, except for that trace of a smirk on his lips.

He had gotten her. Even in death he had gotten the last word.

The NuLife woman opened the cooler and started handing bags to her partner. Pam watched as they packed the ice around John like a bowl of potato salad.

"Leave us alone," Pam said. She had used her teacher voice, the voice that shook hallways and sent students running for their homerooms.

"You can't order me around!" Cindy shrieked, but she wasn't very persuasive sitting on the floor.

"Get out right this minute," Pam commanded, and perhaps because she wasn't much removed from her high school days, Cindy obeyed.

John's beautiful library cleared quickly, but Pam took her time. She found herself staring out the window at the fountain, water burbling over into a copper bowl. There was a rock garden in the corner that she hadn't noticed before, and chairs were scattered around for guests. He'd had parties here. She knew he'd had parties here. They had never had parties at home. John had said they were too expensive and that they couldn't afford it.

Pam walked to the desk and picked up the knife. She couldn't kill him—John had robbed her of that pleasure, but there was one thing she could do, one thing she could take, that he would sorely miss after his reanimation.

Until she died, Pam would always remember those last moments with John, the smirk on his face, his last words to her about her weight, the way he felt in her hand when she had walked out of the room and into the beautiful courtyard. She had crossed to the living room and taken a small lime-green cooler before leaving through the front door. The driver hadn't asked questions when she got in. People who worked for millionaires had seen stranger things. The man had simply driven her to the airport where she easily changed her ticket and flew back home. First-class wasn't full, so the cooler had even gotten its own seat.

She certainly drank enough for two.

A week later, Pam had gotten a certified letter informing her that John had left her something in his will. Two weeks after that, a cargo truck had pulled up in front of the house, blocking most of the road. Pam had been too shocked to say much of anything when the shiny BMW had rolled off the truck, and without thinking, she had signed the papers the driver handed her.

Every morning, she got into her six-year-old Honda

and drove to school, her heart racing at the sight of the X3 parked in the street, exactly where the truck driver had left it. She was bound to let it sit out there until it either rotted or got stolen.

Then, one morning, her Honda would not start.

She would have gotten into a car with a convicted rapist with less trepidation than she felt when she first climbed into John's BMW. When the seat wrapped around her body like a well-worn glove, she suppressed a shudder. At school, the window snicked down with the press of a button, and the security guard gave her a wink.

"Well," the old fool had said. "Somebody's moving up in the world."

Pam was determined to get her old car fixed. The last time she had taken in the Honda, the mechanic had said the transmission was on its last leg. Pam had saved accordingly. Two thousand dollars and it would be fixed and the X3 would be back in its spot, waiting to be stolen. Maybe she would even leave the keys in the ignition.

Days went by, then weeks, then months. A year passed and she was still driving the BMW. The car had been John's way of rubbing his success in her face. He knew that her old beater was on its last legs. He knew she would eventually end up having to drive the damn thing. What he could not have anticipated was that Pam would enjoy driving it, that she would look forward to getting behind the wheel at the end of school every day with the same eagerness that she had looked forward to seeing John in the early part of their marriage. The soft leather reminded her of his soft touch. The wood grain called to mind his masculinity. Even the air bag behind the steering wheel reminded her of the way he had made her feel safe, protected. Until . . . well, she didn't let herself think of the "until," did not dwell on what had happened at the end, the way he had betrayed her, the way he had exploited her after Zack's death.

For almost two years, she had kept the cooler in the freezer alongside a much-contested slice of their wedding cake that her mother had insisted Pam keep until their tenth anniversary. When the anniversary rolled around they had found that freezer burn had claimed the cake and no one wanted to eat it. "Jesus, just throw the damn thing out," John had said on those rare occasions when he had opened the freezer. "It's just a fucking piece of cake."

She couldn't, though. They were having problems by then and she wanted to keep the cake, wanted to hold on to those early years of their marriage like a talisman. Throwing out the cake was the one thing she had resisted him on and in the end, it stood as a testament to her ability to stand up to him. Even after the divorce, Pam had kept the cake, moving it from their old house to her new one, tucking it into the top shelf of the freezer, where it stayed until five days ago, when she had bought a map and planned her trip during the summer school break.

Pam's third and final trip out west had lasted several days, and now, as she drove the BMW into the parking lot of NuLife Laboratories (not such a secret location, considering the large sign out front), she was almost sad to reach John's final destination. She smiled at the thought of the green cooler beside her, the piece of John she had taken sitting beside the piece of cake that represented their failed marriage. Pam imagined that in ten- or fifty- or a hundred-million years from now, if they ever figured out how to jump-start John's body, it would be a small thing to sew his penis back on, and the slice of cake would let him know who had done him the favor. Her one act of disobedience would allow her the luxury of having the last and final word. John could visit her at the cemetery, could urinate on her grave, but he was a scientist at heart and did not believe in souls or angels looking down from on high. He would know that Pam was gone, that Pam had finally gotten the best of him. There would be nothing he could say or do to hurt her, and he would live the rest of his second life—perhaps all of eternity—knowing this. The anger would be like a new cancer, and it would eat him from the inside out.

She could still hear the deep tenor of his voice, the tone he took when he was teaching someone.

"Pam," he'd cautioned her, his tone low as he tried to teach her an important lesson. "Don't let anger ruin your life."

She took out the cooler and shut the car door, smiling as the sunlight bounced off the X3's windows. The paint was an electric silver that went from gray to blue to green, depending on how the light moved. She ran her hand along the curve of the door the way she would stroke a lover.

It took everything she had not to skip across the parking lot, let the braid beat against her back. John's body would be rolling in its stasis tank right now, if he could see her. He would be doubly annoyed to know that the reason for Pam's happiness was a product of his own devising.

She was happy. She was finally happy.

God knows it helped when you drove a nice car.

*

KARIN SLAUGHTER has written nine books that have sold seventeen million copies in twenty-nine languages.

A *New York Times* bestselling author, Karin's books have debuted at number one in the United Kingdom, Germany, and the Netherlands. She lives in Atlanta, where she is working on her next novel.

Calling the Shots

KAREN DIONNE

He shouldn't be working in the woods alone. Jason knew better, running pole for his dad summers and weekends since he was ten; managing his own firewood business since he was thirteen. Jenny'd asked him not to come. Begged him, really. Claimed he'd promised to take her to the movies, though Jason couldn't remember any such thing. He suspected he was being played—it wouldn't be the first time Jenny manipulated him into doing what she wanted. Still, a movie about a woman who hooks the man of her dreams by cooking all of his favorite recipes wasn't such a bad idea when you thought about it. He'd been about to give in, but then Jenny'd poked out her bottom lip like her mom always did when she didn't get her way and started blinking real fast, faking like she was going to cry, and he lost it. Told her he couldn't go through with it—not the movie, but the whole getting-married-before-the-baby-was-born thing—and bailed. Got in his truck, and she started crying for real.

Driving out, he felt bad at first. But then he got one of those out-of-body flash-forwards and saw Jenny twenty years from now, a clone of her mother: overweight, domineering, an unhappy woman whose only pleasure seemed to be making sure everyone else felt the same, and knew he'd done the right thing. Yeah, he shouldn't have gotten her pregnant in the first place; he could admit his share of the blame. But adding to that mistake by making another was beyond stupid.

He stripped off his jacket and hung it over a bush. Reveled in the warmth and solitude of a sunny November Sunday, then started up the saw. Took out his frustrations on a skinny jack pine and smiled as the tree went down easily, branches snapping like toothpicks, the top landing exactly where Jason wanted it in the middle of the brush pile. He eyed the stand of mixed beech and maple that bordered his strip. The serious money was in hardwoods, but he wasn't about to cut a single stick. Jenny's father marked out the strips the way a dog marked its territory, making sure Jason always got the worst wood, as if Jason needed reminding who was boss. Man couldn't wear the pants in his own family, so naturally, he took it out on him. Jason would've rather hired on with any other jobber, but woods work was suffering along with the rest of the country, and Olaf Anderson would do anything for his daughter, so here he was. Lucky him.

Until an hour ago, all Jason wanted was to earn enough to set him and Jenny up in an apartment before they broke the news about the baby, or maybe someone's empty cabin. No way could they live in his parents' basement. The Finns and the Swedes in Michigan's Upper

Peninsula had hated each other for generations. Jason's parents hadn't even met Jenny. Said they didn't need to; all they needed to know was her last name. A saw that cut both ways, judging by the way Jenny's parents treated Jason. Anyone who thought Romeo and Juliet would've had an easier time in the twenty-first century had never met the Andersons and Niemis.

He bent to make another notch. A breeze kicked up, an early winter wind that swirled wood chips and sawdust in his face. He blinked—

—and came to with an elephant on his chest.

Not an elephant, a log—a big one. Nothing like the puny scrub he'd been cutting—a massive, long-dead maple—a widow-maker hung up for God knew how long in a nearby tree, just waiting for someone like him to come along.

He lay still and waited for his brain to come back to full power. The saw was running, so he couldn't have been out long. His hard hat was gone. No doubt it was the hard hat that saved him. They didn't call them widow-makers for nothing.

He pushed against the trunk with both hands, then twisted sideways and shoved with his shoulder, feeling like the beetles he used to pin inside a shoe box when he was little. The tree shifted. He shoved again, letting the trunk rock and settle. Each time it rolled back, it knocked the wind out of him like a sucker punch, but at last he built up enough momentum to carry it past the tipping point. The log rolled down his shins and over his ankles.

Breathing heavily, he sat up.

Bright, arterial blood spurted from his right leg like a fountain.

Holy— The saw must've caught him on the way down. He pressed down hard with both hands. Blood gushed between his fingers. Fumbling one-handed with his belt buckle, he stripped off the belt and cinched it around his leg up high near his groin. The bleeding slowed.

He sat back. Wiped his hands on his jeans. Tried not to panic. His cell was in his truck. The truck was a quarter, maybe half a mile away. Reception was always spotty, but if there was a God in heaven, the call would get through.

He grabbed one of the maple's broken-off limbs and used it as a cane to get to his feet. Blood ran down his leg. He shuddered. Wolves lived in the woods. Not many, but still. Bears and coyotes, too. Normally, they didn't come around people, but this was about as far from normal as you could get.

He tried a step. It turned out more like a hop. He step-hopped, step-hopped, using the branch as a prop. *Hop on Pop.* Dr. Seuss played in his head as he got a feel for the cane and his feet found their rhythm. *We like to hop on top of Pop.* Better than the Brothers Grimm.

Finally, the truck. He hobbled around to the passenger side and took his cell out of the glove box. No service. Okay then, he'd drive himself out. It wouldn't be easy without the use of his right leg, but he could do it. Eyeing the height of the 4 by 4's seat, he tried to figure out the best way to climb in.

The keys. The keys were in his jacket pocket. His jacket was out where he'd been cutting, hanging on a bush.

He sagged against the doorjamb. He couldn't walk all the way to his strip and back, he just couldn't. Even if he found the strength, it'd be full dark before he made it half way.

But he couldn't hunker down in the truck and wait for the crew to come along in the morning either. He could bleed out, freeze to death—Jenny *might* send someone looking for him when he didn't text her to say good-night. Or not.

All he could do was suck it up. Be a man.

The kind of man a father wanted for his daughter.

He straightened. Jenny was going to have *a baby*. He was going to be a father, whether they married or not. Maybe they were off to a bad start. Maybe Jenny *would* end up as shrewish as her mother. But there was no way he'd ever be as weak and indecisive as her father.

Hours (*Minutes? Days?*) later, he sprawled at the bottom of a hill he hadn't known was there until he'd stumbled in the dark and rolled down it. He'd flailed wildly as he fell, grabbing at branches, grabbing at vegetation, grabbing at nothing, but nothing had stopped him from landing in a heap with his bad leg bent beneath him. The tourniquet was gone. Jason's hands were locked in its place, squeezing at what he hoped was the right pressure point with fingers that had long ago lost feeling.

So cold. He shivered. How much blood could you lose before you were done for? He pushed away the thought and focused on the shush of the wind as he fought to stay conscious, letting the sound carry him back to when he used to work with his dad in the woods when he was little; laying the measuring pole alongside the downed trees so his dad could cut the logs to length, stepping in and around the brush struggling to keep up, listening to the trees crack from the cold and the chickadees whistle.

A chickadee called. A single high, shrill note.

No. Not a chickadee. What?

Another whistle. A voice calling his name. Then crunching leaves. Footsteps. A light in his face.

"You found me," he whispered.

"Wasn't me. Jenny asked me to come. Told me you were out here." A pause. "She told me."

Emphasis on the "told me." Not much. Enough.

"I thought—I was afraid—" Jason swallowed. "I was afraid you'd be too late."

Jenny's mother stuck the flashlight under her arm, took a pack of cigarettes from her purse, and sat down heavily on a stump.

"Not too late." She lit a cigarette and took a long, slow puff. "I'm too early."

*

KAREN DIONNE is the author of *Freezing Point* (October 2008, Berkley Books), a thriller Douglas Preston called "a ripper of a story!" Her second novel, *Boiling Point,* was published in December 2010. Karen's short fiction has appeared in *Bathtub Gin, The Adirondack Review, Futures Mysterious Anthology Magazine,* and *Thought Magazine.* Visit her on the Web at www.karendionne.net.

Afterword

Wasn't that a great ride? Lee Child promised in the introduction that this book contained a stellar lineup of high-octane writers—a purposeful mixture of seasoned veterans and remarkable rookies.

International Thriller Writers, Inc. (ITW), cofounder, David Morrell, once said, "If a story doesn't thrill, it's not a thriller." As this collection has proven, thrills come in all shapes and sizes, tongue-in-cheek and serious, domestic and international. There were stories that explored those fascinating moments where ordinary people face difficult choices between right and wrong; there were journeys to the dark territory of noir, where hope is a precious commodity; and there were some good old-fashioned, tried-and-true adrenaline-rush rides of danger and amusement.

Many of the names who contributed to this book are well known. The fresh faces are all members of ITW's Debut Author Program, a unique experience created to mentor thriller writers through their first year and beyond. Since the program began in July 2007, 103 ITW members have participated. So far, eight of those have garnered starred reviews in *Publishers Weekly*, *Kirkus*

Reviews, and *Library Journal.* Four became *New York Times* bestsellers. Eleven found themselves on bestseller lists that include Independent Mystery Booksellers, BookScan, Barnes & Noble, *The Sunday Times* (U.K.), the *San Francisco Chronicle,* Audible.com, and a variety of lists overseas. Seventeen sold rights to their books to foreign publishers. Four negotiated film and/or television options. And nearly thirty have already been published again, or are under contract for more books.

That's an amazing set of statistics.

No other writers organization can boast such dedication and success in its debut authors.

Which speaks volumes for International Thriller Writers.

Currently, over twelve hundred working writers, editors, agents, and enthusiasts worldwide are members. Born in 2004, ITW has grown by leaps and bounds. The Debut Author Program joins a host of other ITW successes that range from exceptional marketing and promotional programs to awards and recognition, to literacy efforts, to publishing projects, to the phenomenally successful ThrillerFest, the yearly gathering of ITW each July in New York. Those four days are, literally, summer camp for thriller writers and thriller enthusiasts. To learn more about ITW and Thrillerfest, I invite you to visit www.thrillerwriters.com.

Thrillers have been around a long time. Their magic, their allure, and their compelling nature come not just from providing readers an escape or rush. Rather they stem from an ability to transport the reader into another world that he or she, through his or her active participation, helps the writer create.

It's a shared experience.

Facing danger, searching for truth, avoiding despair,

finding hope, these are the essences of a thriller. My hope is that you've enjoyed this journey as much as all of us at International Thriller Writers have enjoyed creating these worlds for you to explore.

First Thrills is just one of many ITW publishing endeavors. We invite you to check out our other ITW products: *Thriller, Thriller 2, The Chopin Manuscript, The Copper Bracelet, Watchlist,* and *The 100 Greatest Reads.*

Just look for the ITW logo.

As Lee Child said in the beginning:

You won't regret it.

STEVE BERRY
ITW Co-President
August 2009